CW00725658

SEARCHING

CALLE J BROOKES

SEARCHING

Copyright © 2021 by Calle J. Brookes

PAVAD: FBI Copyright © 2011

978-1-940937-31-1

05112021PAV18PB

All rights reserved. Printed in the United States of America. No part of this book may be used or reproduced in any manner whatsoever without written permission except in the case of brief quotations embodied in critical articles or reviews.

This book is a work of fiction. Names, characters, businesses, organizations, places, events and incidents either are the product of the author's imagination or are used fictitiously. Any resemblance to actual persons, living or dead, events, or locales is entirely coincidental.

For information contact:

www.callejbrookes.com

Book and Cover design by C.J. Brookes

First Edition: MAY2021

10 9 8 7 6 5 4 3 2 1

1

ANDY HADN'T DESERVED THIS.

Max Jones stood over the body of a man he had worked with for more than six years, fighting the grief—and rage. The damage to Andy's skull was something he would never be able to erase from his head.

Andy Anderson would never smile at a stupid dad joke ever again. Andy and Max had traded dad jokes like their daughters traded cartoon playing cards.

Rain slipped down the back of Max's neck, soaking his neck beneath his Brynlock Blackbirds sweatshirt. He had been called out from his daughter's first basketball game of the season for this.

Andy's daughter might be at the school now, too. Andy's kids didn't attend the same academy as Max's daughter, but they competed in the same sports leagues. It was a small private school association with only four schools in the network. They interacted together all the time, from elementary school through high school.

Max knew Andy's family very well. "Do we know what happened?"

"Not yet. We're calling in forensics in an hour," said Ed Dennis, the director of PAVAD—the Prevention & Analysis of Violent Acts Division of the FBI. They were in the backyard of the reasonably sized, 1960s ranch house just over the river from St. Louis. "There are...things...we need to do first."

Max's attention focused on the men surrounding him. Ed Dennis, Michael Hellbrook, two of the three Lorcan brothers, and both Brockman brothers. They *were* PAVAD now. Legends. Each and every one of them. "Why am I here?"

Max held his own, but these men were upper level. He was the lowest man on the ladder here, and he was well aware of that. There was a reason Max was there. It wasn't because of his friendship with Andy Anderson.

"I need you to be the official face of this case," Ed said. He alone didn't seem bothered by the icy rain. The man was five inches shorter than Max, fifty pounds lighter, and a good twenty years older. He was also one of the few men Max would trust at his own back without hesitation.

He'd trust Ed Dennis with his own daughter. That mattered.

When the director called, PAVAD agents responded.

The director was wearing a damned near identical Brynlock sweatshirt, and they'd followed each other to the scene—from the school where their children waited.

A brief moment of concern went through him—he'd had to basically leave his daughter at the school by herself. She'd been with the school officials, but someone there specifically for *her* had taken him a while to arrange. Worry was always in his mind where his kid was concerned.

It was the curse of the single parent.

"He has an ex-wife," Max said softly, looking down at the body of his friend again. Agent Andrew Mark Anderson, eight years older than Max's own thirty-six, two inches shorter than Max's six four, and forty pounds heavier. His hair was thinning, and graying, his glasses were six feet away, on the concrete pavers Max had helped him haul from the home repair store. Andy had been a member of the third Lorcan brother's team of forensic accountants. "Three children, living. The oldest is about Emery's age, the youngest is three. His daughter plays basketball; she may be at Brynlock right now."

Ed nodded. "I'll handle the notification; I have to go pick up my sons after…this."

"This is a part of the search for the leak," Sin Lorcan said flatly. "I knew we had someone on Seth's team involved, but I didn't suspect Anderson. Still don't; not fully. But I can't explain this."

"None of us suspected Anderson," Mick Brockman practically growled, his anger almost touchable. The head of IA was unofficially in charge of the investigation into who was targeting PAVAD—and had been for years now. He and Sin. Very few PAVAD agents had been dialed in on what was truly going on behind the scenes. "We need to go somewhere secure—where we can talk."

"First, I'm going to call in Mari and her team. She's with the kids at the school now. Only those we're certain we can trust will work this," the director said. His wife was the head of the forensics department. If they couldn't trust her, there was probably no one in the division they could.

Thunder rumbled overhead, despite the chilly rain pelting them all. Max waited for one of the other men to say something. Anything to get this case going.

He looked down at his friend again. Every memory and image he had of Andy through the years would be forever overshadowed by *this*.

There was a bullet in Andy's head. It hadn't gotten there by accident.

Max was good at what he did. That he wouldn't deny. And he worked hard to ensure that. But this…this spoke of dark secrets Max feared the answers to. The body of a friend was pretty damned proof positive of that.

"Who called it in?" he asked. There weren't any lights on in the houses nearby. Andy had mentioned there were vacant places in his neighborhood and had suggested Max might want to check a few out for his rental business. Max hadn't had the time to yet.

"We don't know yet," Ed said. "There was an anonymous phone call—to Sin. Gloating. Threats that they were getting closer. That a PAVAD family would hurt again tonight."

Max looked at Sin, the man who had the reputation of being the absolute best at ferreting out internal corruption that the bureau had ever seen. They called him The Bloodhound.

Someone taunting Sin Lorcan like that was a damned foolish bastard. One who had opened the doors to hell tonight—and let a three-headed dog out.

You didn't make it to PAVAD by accident, or by being mediocre. No. PAVAD pulled *only* the very best.

Whatever was going on in PAVAD—it was far bigger than him.

Max wanted a part of it. He wanted in on bringing down the bastards who had threatened what he and the others had worked for over the last four years.

PAVAD meant something to the people who worked there.

None of them took threats to it lightly. Max certainly didn't.

Neither did the men surrounding him.

He didn't take the murder of a friend sitting down, either.

He'd held Andy's children in his own arms before, at their own brother's funeral. He owed them answers.

Max would get them, too.

"We need to find this sonofabitch," the third Lorcan brother said, coming from inside the house. There was grief for a lost teammate in his tone. "Andy has a family. He adored his kids. Was still in love with the ex-wife, too. Things just got tough after the baby died."

Max had always thought so, too. He'd hoped the Andersons would have been able to work out their differences; they'd broken up after the death of their fourth child from a heart defect two years ago. They'd never get the chance to work things out now.

Damn it, Andy. What had he gotten in to? The guy had been goofy, playful, intelligent, and...dependable. A bit of a conspiracy nut, which was odd for an FBI agent, but half the time, Max thought Andy had just been goofing around.

Like he read the conspiracies for fun. Was saying things to get a rise out of the people around him.

"We'll find the answers," Ed promised.

"Well, we'll need to find them fast. Because this is spiraling," Sin said, putting one hand on the shoulders of each of his brothers. Three identical men with fire and anger in their matching green eyes, just like the three-headed dog of hell. Max wanted to see the Lorcans tear into the man who'd done this. Wanted that with every fiber of his being now. "That damned sniper nearly killed *my* wife, with my children and my brothers' children inside one hundred feet away. I'm not going to wait much longer to have some names."

"Neither will we," his brothers said together in near unison. At any other time, it would have been humorous. Not tonight.

There was nothing humorous about tonight.

It was a sentiment they all agreed with.

Someone had a real ax to grind against PAVAD. They were making it known.

With one piece of collateral damage at a time. They'd had half a dozen agents targeted since Sin's wife had been shot knocking him out of the way of a paid assassin. An inch higher and it would have struck her femoral artery. Cody Lorcan would have died with her two children watching from the babysitter's front window. No wonder the Lorcan brothers were practically foaming at the mouth on this one.

Max would be too, if it had been Jac hurt.

Max looked at Sin. "I'll do whatever it takes to catch this guy. You just tell me what to do, and I'll do it. Even if it just means signing my name to the damned paperwork."

Max took another look at the dead man sprawled in front of them, a man he'd known well enough to sit with at their daughters' sporting events and academic tournaments—a man he'd eaten lunch with at the cafeteria at PAVAD dozens of times. They'd shared a table not even two days ago, talking about their kids. About the best place to buy the girls shoes. Max hated shopping for shoes. Andy, too. But they had little girls who needed new shoes, and Andy had promised his ex-wife he'd take the girls that weekend to get them while she worked a double shift at the hospital.

It had been so damned normal.

He'd considered Andy Anderson a *friend.*

Andy's three little girls deserved more than this.

Max made himself a vow—answers. He'd not stop until he could someday give those little girls answers about who and why this had happened.

He looked at Ed. "Let's find this sonofabitch."

2

JAC HAD MISSED *THIS*. SHE'D MISSED THE SIGHT OF CHILDREN ENJOYING themselves, missed the sight of families brimming with pride and love for their children. Missed the *normalcy* of it all. Missed being a part of it. She hadn't realized how much it mattered, until it had suddenly stopped weeks ago.

Agent Jaclyn Jones climbed the bleachers near the free throw line and watched a gaggle of little girls that she knew as they learned the game—she actually felt like she belonged there.

Jac waved at the assistant coach. Rachel was a friend. One of the few Jac had outside her work with the bureau. They'd met right there at Brynlock over a year ago.

Someone else called her name, and she turned. Angie Anderson sat holding her toddler. Angie looked a little frazzled. Jac took the seat next to her and smiled at the little girl.

She was such a homely little thing with her father's round cheeks and overly large lips. But her eyes...she was a sweet little girl who was very friendly. "Hi, Angie, how are you?"

"Being pulled in a million directions, and loving it," Angie said with a tired smile. "You look gorgeous, by the way. I can't remember the last time I looked gorgeous. Probably four kids, a nursing degree, and one divorce ago."

"Don't be silly. You are definitely gorgeous right now. Far more than I am. I feel like the FBI's leftover bin right now." Angie was a very pretty woman, but it was the love and joy in her eyes when she looked at her daughters that made her truly beautiful. "I could never get away with wearing that color. I'd look like a clown, but on you—gorgeous."

They laughed together. Jac took Angie's youngest daughter onto her own lap, while the middle girl sat with her nose buried in a book that looked to be about fairies. The middle Anderson girl was as beautiful as her mother—and not interested in sports at all. Jac had a bag of books in her hall closet, books that she'd found at a flea market in Wyoming for the little girl. She'd been meaning to give them to Angie's ex-husband to pass on.

"I hate to ask, but…I need to call Andy. Find out where he is. Abbie is going to be asking where her dad is. He always makes her games. I…I'm a bit worried. Andy's obsessive about not being late. He always texts me if he's going to be late. Even now."

"Sure. I'll keep these two under control."

Angie stepped outside to make her call. Jac kept up a running conversation as much as possible with the Andersons' three-year-old, while the six-year-old just kept reading.

Some of the tension filling Jac eased. Friends, families, the smell of the concession stand being ran by older siblings and parents—it was beautiful. Normal.

Free of the darkness that normally surrounded her workdays.

Sometimes, life at PAVAD could get pretty dark. Her last case had been dark—that was for sure.

She'd just finished a case where an eleven-year-old would never see the sun again. He'd been blinded by his own cousin and nearly killed. Jac's team had arrived just in time to save his life.

Not something she would ever forget.

When the little girls' basketball game at Brynlock Academy ended, Jac excused herself from the Andersons and headed down to where the green team was congregating.

She had an eight-year-old to catch.

The high school teams would be playing soon—and the crowd would double. She wanted to find Emery and get a spot closer to the action. Emery loved watching the teenagers play. She had a well-known crush on Simon Brockman, one of the star players.

She'd buy Emery dinner at the concession stand, say hello to a few friends from work who also had kids at the school, and get Emery distracted by getting to stay at the high school basketball game—which would end well after her normal bedtime.

Before Emery got worried that her father wasn't there to take her home.

Max very rarely missed Emery's games. It was a promise he'd made to his daughter years ago. One Jac had done her best to help him keep. It had been weeks since she'd been to one of Emery's sports events, since she'd been with the little girl.

Tonight's phone call had come completely out of the blue. He almost hadn't caught her at all. Emery's father had been desperate. *Jac* had been his last resort. That had come through loud and clear.

Max Jones, her former partner, had been avoiding her. In every way he possibly could.

That big stinking coward. She'd like to take his size thirteens and shove one right up his chickeny rear end for this.

But here she was now. Watching over his daughter, like she had so many times before.

Emery needed her; that was all it had taken to have Jac dropping her plans and rushing to the school. She came up behind a familiar strawberry-blond kid wearing the number 17 on her jersey. She tapped the little girl on the shoulder. "Hey, kid Jones."

Emery turned. Her eyes, a clear blue, widened. "Jac! Jac! You're here!"

Jac found her arms full of wiggling, sweaty little girl. She tightened the hug just a bit. She'd missed this kid so much.

Jac looked over Emery's hair at the crowd surrounding her. The coach was eyeing her with suspicion. Jac couldn't recall meeting her before. Jac pulled her badge free. "I'm Agent Jaclyn Jones. I'm here to pick up Emery. Her father got called in to work."

"I...no one called me about it. Are you her mother?" The woman eyed her appraisingly.

Jac shook her head. Jac knew the protocol for the school's events, and she understood how important it was. "I have permissions on file with the school. Her father is waiting for a phone call if there is a problem."

"There won't be," a voice said from behind the coach. Jac recognized the school principal, a woman around her own age she'd met many times before. "Emery's father called me a few minutes ago to ensure we knew Jaclyn had permission to pick Emery up this evening. Hello, Jaclyn. How have you been?"

Jac made small talk with the principal and a few of the other mothers while she waited for Emery to get changed out of her basketball shoes and grab her bag. Before she knew it, she found herself agreeing to volunteer at the next field trip, after the winter holiday break.

She'd have to make certain to put in for comp time, but she had plenty accumulated. She was an old hat at field trips now that Emery was in the third grade.

The principal, Jayda, was an extremely persuasive woman when she wanted to be. Jac made plans to call Rachel or Julie and finalize those plans. She'd volunteered with both of them before, and they usually split responsibilities for the group. They worked well together, playing off one another's strengths. She enjoyed it, the whole pseudo-PTA-mother thing.

It was so normal, so *opposite* of what she did on a day-to-day basis.

Emery had asked Jac to help with her school activities before. Jac understood why; most of the parents that volunteered at Brynlock were female. There were a few involved fathers, of course, but most of the volunteers were mothers.

Emery was very much about fitting in exactly as her friends did right now. She had some insecurities she was battling. There weren't many single fathers at Brynlock. Emery thought that made her too *different.*

That meant, if they had a mom or stepmom at the school, Emery wanted someone who looked like them, too. She was all about conforming now.

It drove Max nuts.

He was so insecure about his ability to parent a little girl. Jac understood it, though; she'd been that little girl before.

The father Jac had had was a monster.

Emery's father was the exact opposite. Emery was just going through a natural phase of noticing her contemporaries and obsessing over every possible difference between them. Jac hadn't minded; she loved working with kids. If her life had followed a different path, she would most likely have been a teacher, or pediatrician or child psychiatrist.

Now, she spent most of her time split between the Child Exploitation Protection Division and the Complex Crimes Unit Team Three of PAVAD. Team three ended up with the cases involving children more often than the other teams. It was starting to become their specialty. That was a natural evolution of law enforcement teams—some became better at certain cases than others.

Jac had worked with Emery's father for more than five years. She'd known and loved the little girl almost as long. She was going to enjoy this rare night hanging out with her favorite kid in the world.

It would help them all—Emery would be safe, Max would be free to focus on whatever he was doing, and Jac would be able to forget for a while a little boy whose entire world had changed over stolen video games.

Jac needed to forget right now.

She'd just try not to worry about the tension and the secrets in Max's voice tonight.

Because something had happened at PAVAD.

Max was right out there in the middle of it.

That...that could be very, very dangerous right now.

3

FBI AGENT TODD BARNES CLUTCHED THE ENVELOPE OF CASH CLOSE
and hoped no one saw him. He'd seen several people entering the
school gymnasium that he recognized. He'd only been a few yards
behind one of those people, but fortunately for him Jaclyn Jones
hadn't turned around long enough to identify him.

He slouched and pulled the ball cap down and tightened his
Carhart coat over his clothes. The jeans and sweatshirt beneath were
a far cry from what he usually wore. He'd bought the whole outfit
off the rack at a dollar store just for this.

He wanted to blend in with all the good little sports daddies at
Brynlock academy.

He had a *special* project tonight. One he wasn't about to screw up.

Todd knew he was being tested. Seeing just what he was willing
to do.

If it meant bringing down PAVAD, he would do anything asked
of them. It couldn't keep going on unchecked like it was. That was
going to get someone killed. Todd had the scar to prove it.

The man he was supposed to meet was late.

Todd pulled his hood over his head and waited under the streetlight like he was supposed to. He'd always hated the damned rain. Rain in November was ten times as bad. It was fucking cold out here tonight.

Someone walked by him. Todd swore and backed out of the light.

It was one of those damned Lorcan brothers' wives. The redhead with the weird hazel eyes and the chest that made men drool.

Well, Todd would drool, too. If she was his. He tried to heat himself up by imagining her naked for a few moments.

Hard to do with the two kids she was carrying into the building right there. They certainly ruined his image of her.

Maybe it was time he started doing the work to find another girlfriend. One he could be serious about this time. Could count on; the last woman he'd been seriously involved with had left him for one of his former teammates. He'd never forgive Agent Strette for that betrayal.

Once this thing with PAVAD was over, he'd have a hell of a lot more money in his pocket. He'd find a woman of *quality*.

He could buy a house. Find a lady to share it with. It would be nice to have regular sex again with a woman who cared about what he had to say. One he could train to do what he liked in the bed.

Who knew? Maybe he'd actually like her, and they'd tie the knot and have a few kids. Send them to a fancy place like Brynlock. Then he wouldn't be going back to a plain, empty apartment.

A school basketball game, he thought. What a shit-in-the-hole.

All TV-sitcom perfect.

There was the damned director of PAVAD's wife right there, a toddler on her hip and at least half a dozen kids trailing after her like ducks, with half of them wearing team sweatshirts under their coats.

She looked all prissy and rich and sexy in that older woman kind of way.

Even that billionaire asshole married to the blonde from PAVAD forensics was there, strutting around like he owned the place. Mr. Moneybags jogged up to the redhead and took the youngest baby out of her arms.

Hell, for all Todd knew, the guy probably did own the place now. News was always going on about him buying up stuff. Him and that Barratt-Handley guy from down in Texas. Like it was a competition or something.

After fifteen minutes, the man Todd was supposed to meet finally came out.

Todd was seriously unimpressed.

The guy was completely unremarkable. If he hadn't said the code word, Todd never would have realized it was him. What a wiener.

Todd handed over the envelope, turned, and strolled away.

He'd driven all the way from Dallas just to do this.

It would be worth it to see PAVAD destroyed.

4

Max and the rest of the men combed over Andy's office. It felt wrong to violate a friend's personal space like this, but the determination burning in his gut wasn't going to be stopped. Not until he had the answers. There were cartoons on the walls, signed with Andy's distinctive scrawl. Mixed with photos of Abbie, Alexis and little Audra. And Audra's twin Ashton, who hadn't made it to his first birthday.

Andy's *world*.

Max took one three-by-five candid off the wall. Andy and his girls—at the last PAVAD picnic. Max's daughter and his partner Jac were visible in the background, smiles on their beautiful faces.

Max had snapped the photo. It was shortly after Andy and his wife had separated.

Andy's ex had called twice to see why he wasn't at the basketball game right now, her voice ringing out on the old-fashioned answering machine. Andy always had been resistant to technology. Andy would only use his bureau phone when on the clock, and had complained about that many times.

Jac had set it up for Andy once or twice while Max watched. Not that Max was all that into technology, either. But he had had Andy beat by a mile.

Grief threatened again, but he shoved it away. He wasn't going to do Andy a damned bit of good if he turned into a blustering idiot.

Max slipped the photo out of the frame and turned it over.

In an obsessively neat hand were the date the photo was taken and the ages of all the girls, including Emery. Andy had been extremely detail oriented and mathematically inclined. He'd calculated the girls' ages right down to the number of days. Jac's, too.

Andy had fit in well with the forensic accounting team he'd been on. He'd been happy on that team, and passionate about his work. He'd enjoyed it. He valued it. And Max would have bet his left arm that Andy wouldn't have betrayed it.

Not without damned good reason.

Max was going to find that reason.

Ed came up behind where Max was videoing the office and the paperwork he'd seen there. "Sebastian has already grabbed all the computer equipment. He's going to take it directly to his wife. She'll process it...*outside* the PAVAD server, using her brother-in-law's, instead. They're both at Brynlock now. She's going to ride out to Lucas's place with his security team. Evidence won't leave his place until we're damned well ready for it to happen."

Not exactly strictly by the books, but no one was going to say a word about it.

Not tonight. Not after...this. They all knew the consequences of what they were facing now.

Andy was one of their own.

Sebastian Lorcan's wife was the head of the computer forensics team, and was also associated through family connections to two of the most advanced law enforcement tech companies in the world. That meant access to the best equipment out there—some that wasn't even released to the market yet.

She was the best with a computer Max had ever seen. He just

nodded. Of course, the director would be calling out the best for this.

It was PAVAD.

Andy had been one of *them*.

He switched over to still photo mode and kept snapping photos. He wasn't forensics, but he was going to document everything he could. Everything. Without even thinking about it, he slipped the snapshot into the pocket of his hooded sweatshirt.

He'd find the answers for those girls.

Then he'd return the photo to their mother.

This was going to tear Angie apart.

He was going to go through the rest of the house before the evidence techs got there as well.

There might be things that the general teams at PAVAD had no business seeing. He had already gotten clearance from the director and Mick to do just that.

Everyone knew this case was going to be outside the lines.

Andy would always cross those boundaries.

There were three memory cards taped to the back of a drawer in the small office that connected to Andy's bedroom. Max photographed them, then removed the cards, in gloved hands. He handed them to the director.

Anything. Anything at all could turn a case in an instant. They all knew that.

The cards wouldn't have been hidden if there wasn't something important on them.

"We sure he was the one selling secrets?" one of the Lorcan brothers asked. They sounded very similar; Max looked over his shoulder to see just which one it was. It was Seth. The earring was a dead giveaway. The other two triplets were more severe in appearance, and often confused for one another even more. "I really can't believe it of him. And I've seen where one teammate was framing another before."

"I don't know yet. I...he was a good guy. At least, he appeared to be. Hell, my daughter has spent the night with his a few times before." Max had seen things on the job that he still didn't understand, even with his experience as a profiler. Andy being a traitor to PAVAD—he wouldn't believe until he had irrefutable evidence of it. He just couldn't.

Seth nodded. "I thought so, too."

"If that changes, if I find anything that says he was framed... whatever happened here...someone shot him. Took him away from his family. I will find them." If nothing else, Max owed those children answers.

His phone beeped with a text, interrupting his next round of photos.

I have Emery at my new place. We have pizza. She can spend the night, no problem. Call me when you want me to bring her home. —Jac.

Some of his tension lessened. His daughter was safe and protected and with someone who loved her.

Now, Max could fully focus on what he needed to do.

5

ANDY'S HOUSE APPEARED EXACTLY AS IT ALWAYS HAD. MAX HAD PICKED him up there a few times. It had once belonged to Andy's parents, before they'd died. Andy had moved in after the divorce.

It was close to where Andy's ex-wife and girls lived. He wanted to be near if they needed him.

Max had hauled boxes from the moving truck Andy had rented—while Jac had set up Andy's computer and internet system.

Emery had played with the girls in the backyard. It had been a normal, if rare, off day for them all that had ended with a backyard barbecue—and Andy's neighbor coming by to check out the pretty redheaded lady wandering around the place.

The man had wanted Jac's attention. He'd been persistent.

Max and Andy had enjoyed chasing him off and teasing her about it the next day.

Beautifully normal. It had ended with three little girls and a baby eating hot dogs and marshmallows.

Andy would never have that again. Nothing Max could do would give that to him again.

He documented the basement, then stepped further inside. Andy was meticulous, everything was in its place.

The wires were out of place.

Max moved closer.

There was a timer. And it was armed. It clicked down another eight seconds before his mind processed what he was seeing. Seventy-two seconds remained.

Only seventy-two damned seconds.

Max ran, yelling for the other men to get the hell out of the house.

He grabbed the director of PAVAD from where the man was studying photos in the hallway. They were the furthest from the exits. "Out! Bomb in the basement! Everyone out *now! Get outside!*"

Both men ran.

They hit the backyard together. Forty feet from where Andy's body lay.

Next to the same damned grill they'd used to make the girls' dinner that day.

Fire slammed into Max's back. He went down.

Max knocked into the director, the force of the blast sending both men to the ground.

He stayed where he was, the ringing in his ears mixing with the roar of the explosion behind him.

Men were yelling. Moving.

But not the man next to him.

Max coughed, opened his eyes, and looked, afraid of what he'd see.

Ed sprawled unconscious next to him, blood at his damned temple. A roar sounded behind them again.

Max didn't stop to think. They were too damned close.

He grabbed the director, pulled the smaller man over his shoulder, and ran.

Just ran.

To the field behind the now burning house, fifty yards away. The house on the left of Andy's, unoccupied, was engulfed now. People were yelling from somewhere. Neighbors, coming running.

They'd have to keep them back somehow.

Max lowered his boss to the ground as the rest of the men that had been there crowded around them. He checked quickly: Hellbrook, Mick Brockman, three Lorcan brothers. Max and the director.

They were missing one. There had been *eight* of them.

Max counted again. "Where's Mal?"

Mick bellowed his older brother's name, then swore when he saw the other man lying a few feet from the back porch. Mick and Sebastian ran back and lifted Malachi, almost dragging him away from the flames.

Malachi was mostly walking on his own, but it looked like he'd taken a hit to the shoulder.

Max turned back to the director. Ed was still out.

Hell, it had probably only been a minute or two since the blast.

Seth held a hand to his own bleeding forehead. "We're all out. But every last shred of evidence was blown to the damned moon now. All we got is what was on our phones."

"Even the computers were in my car," Sebastian said, lowering Malachi to the grass next to the director. "It's burning now; I'd parked it nearest the drive. I don't know if Carrie will be able to do anything with what is left of the hard drives after the fire's out."

They had nothing. Son of a bitch.

Except for the memory cards in the pocket of Max's Brynlock sweatshirt. And that might be absolutely nothing.

"We need to get him to the hospital," Hellbrook said, leaning over his father-in-law. The director was starting to come around. "I think he was struck in the head. Malachi needs checked out, too."

"Who all has injuries?" Max took stock of their people. He had some burns on his back and his arms, but nothing a cold shower and some burn gel wouldn't fix. Seth was bleeding from a wound near his hairline. Sin Lorcan stood there with a damned piece of shrapnel lodged in his right shoulder, looking like the coldly invincible hunter that he was.

Nothing appeared to phase that guy.

Malachi was propped up against the damned side of Andy's garden shed. Hellbrook was covered in ash. They all were. But they were all there. Alive.

They'd gotten damned lucky.

Had Malachi or the director been any closer to the house when it blew, Max probably wouldn't have been able to say that at all.

"Let's get the director the hospital. We'll regroup when we can."

He looked back, to where Andy's body had been.

It was gone. He'd been right outside his back door.

There would be nothing left of his friend but ashes.

And three little girls who deserved to know what had happened to the father who had loved them so much.

6

JAC ROLLED OVER, GRABBED HER GUN INSTINCTIVELY, AND CHECKED the clock next to the bed. Someone was pounding on her door, at two a.m. That could never be good.

Jac checked on the little girl sleeping in her guest room—Emery was an extremely deep sleeper—then crept to the front door. She peeked out the window carefully. Jac never used the peephole. She'd seen people get shot that way.

Jac flipped on the porchlight when she saw who was standing there. She'd recognized the tall, muscled man illuminated in the nearby streetlight immediately. Jac threw open the door.

Her former partner stood there, covered in soot, eyes burning with a pain she couldn't identify. She immediately tensed even more. "Max, what—?"

Before he could answer, or she could say anything else, he grabbed her. Just grabbed her.

Max's hands went around her waist and he jerked. He scooped her right off her feet and into his arms. His strong, perfect, smoke-saturated arms.

Jac found her face pressed into his rock-hard chest.

At any other time, she would have enjoyed it.

He reeked. She coughed.

He just wrapped his arms around her even tighter and held her. Rocked. Right there on her front porch. Shaking and holding her as tightly as he could.

This was a far cry from the man who had run from her over a little kiss between friends weeks ago.

Jac didn't say a word about that. He was hurting. Broken.

She hated not knowing why. "Max? Talk to me. Tell me what happened."

"Inside." He pulled back and stared at her. Right there on her porch, as thunder boomed overhead, and rain pelted down around them. "I...can I come inside?"

"Yes. But lose the shoes. I just had new carpet laid. And you are filthy. What happened to you tonight?" They were whispering. It somehow just called for whispers, even though they both knew Emery slept like the dead. "Is everyone all right?"

He shook his head. "Andy Anderson, from Seth's team. He's dead. Executed tonight. In his home, Jac. Place blew up while we were first on the scene. Andy's body was burned beyond recognition."

Terror for her friends and colleagues had her practically choking. "Your team? Are they ok? Anyone else? Was anyone else targeted?"

She'd held Andy's daughter in her own arms tonight. Thank God the kids had been with their mother instead of their father. Andy and Angie had full shared custody. The girls were with Andy just as much as they were with their mother.

If those girls had been there tonight...Jac couldn't think of it.

They'd had agents targeted before. She and Max had discussed that before. Had discussed what they had to do to watch their own backs, since a friend had been abducted in back in August. Jac never forgot that.

She knew Max hadn't either.

No one at PAVAD was forgetting that right now.

The ones responsible for hiring an assassin to go after members of PAVAD hadn't been caught yet. Jac's friends Shannon and Cody had almost died by that assassin's hands.

Everyone had been living on edge, since.

"Not my team. I was with the director. Working on...a special project. Me, him, a few others."

"Is everyone you were with on scene ok?"

He shook his head slightly. Ash and debris fell from his shaggy brown hair to his broad shoulders. The man seriously needed a shower. "The director is going to be kept overnight at the hospital. He took a hard knock to the head. I'm...not supposed to be telling you this. But...it was so damned close. And I need to see Emery. Before I can sleep tonight. I just need to see her. Make certain she's ok. Then I'll head home and get out of your hair."

"Don't be crazy. You have a bag here. I found it when I moved last month, at the back of my guest room closet. I've been meaning to bring it to PAVAD. I just keep forgetting," Jac said quietly. That bag had taunted and tormented her for weeks. Now she was just glad she still had it. "I have another spare room. There's a bed in there. Take a shower. We can talk. You can go home in the morning. I'm off the entire weekend. I can keep her with me."

He just looked at her.

There was so much pain in the man's eyes. Jac just said to hell with it. She wrapped her arms around him and held him until the shaking stopped.

There would be time to deal with the kiss that should have never been later. Right now all that mattered was that Max was in pain. And he had come to her.

Jac wasn't going anywhere.

7

Eugene Lytel had worked for the FBI for fifteen years. He'd seen a lot of dead bodies since then. That he'd seen one all nice and toasty tonight didn't drag him down.

Far from it.

He was riding a high better than the time he'd done LSD during his undergrad years.

That he'd known the man as a colleague and a friend for over eight years didn't matter to him. The exact opposite.

That juiced him up even more. He'd walked right in and then watched the life fade right out of a *friend's* eyes.

Just like he'd done before.

Eugene didn't kill for any ideological reasons. Nor was he doing it for strictly cash reasons. Or revenge.

He wasn't stupid; he'd done his time learning everything he could about what motivated people to do what they did.

Lytel wasn't doing it just because he couldn't fucking stand Ed Dennis and his team of perfect boys and girls.

No. He was doing this because he'd learned the first time he'd taken a life while on duty that he *enjoyed* it.

Oh, he'd wanted PAVAD when he'd first learned of it. Everyone had been talking about the specialized unit. It had started off with eighty-two people. People handpicked by the director for whatever reasons known only to that sanctimonious prick.

He'd gotten that appointment. Two years later. When they needed some cannon fodder and someone to lead those no-name agents to fill in wherever good old Ed wanted them. None of those auxiliary agents were ever going to move up. They hadn't yet, even though PAVAD kept expanding.

Good old Ed was on a real power trip now.

Lytel had always hated assholes like that.

He'd been digging up whatever dirt he could find on all the key players of PAVAD. Especially the director. The director knew exactly what had happened twenty-three years ago.

Lytel would never forgive Ed Dennis for that.

Lytel knew his way around computers, and thanks to Ed himself, he had access to whatever he wanted to poke around in.

All in the name of *duty*.

Someone had caught on to him, though.

Maybe he'd sold information to the wrong person—but Lytel didn't care. They'd offered him far too much cash to refuse.

All he had to do was take care of a few *people* whenever he was asked to.

Then, he'd get a cool million deposited into his grandmother's account each time. She was so senile she'd never know any damned thing about it. He had the power of attorney and had been using her accounts to play the stock market for years.

Lytel knew exactly how to make it all work. How to make the numbers all add up.

He'd been outsmarting Ed Dennis and PAVAD for years, after all.

Lytel waited. The call came just as he expected.

His team was needed.

A fellow agent's home had been bombed. Someone needed to

guard the perimeter and all those cute little scientist pets of the director's.

Duty called.

Lytel was laughing the entire drive.

He pulled up in front of Anderson's engulfed home and studied his handiwork.

Damn, he loved his job.

8

THE NEXT MORNING WHEN HE WOKE, MAX HEARD THE SOUND OF HIS daughter's laughter. There was no better alarm clock than that, and it had him smiling before he was fully awake—and cognizant of where he actually was.

Jac.

He followed the sound of laughter to the small kitchen of the house Jac had bought a month ago. He hadn't seen the place before.

She'd been searching for the house she wanted for a good eighteen months. Max had promised that when she found it, he would help her move. She'd told him she wanted it to be absolutely perfect as it was where she planned to spend the rest of her life. Or until they transferred her out of St. Louis.

She had never said it, but he understood. He'd profiled her thousands of times over the years they'd known each other. Max had spent a lot of time trying to figure out how Jaclyn Elise Jones *thought*.

He had once thought he understood her almost as well as he understood himself. Jac wanted a life outside of PAVAD, but she was too afraid to go for it, yet.

Jac wanted to put down roots more than anything. Her stepfather's diplomatic position had meant their family traveled frequently. When they were stateside, they had stayed at the colonel's home in Virginia.

He suspected those times had been extremely dark for Jac.

She had never said. But she had nightmares; and not just when she was sleeping. There were parts of that woman she kept so close to her chest, he doubted she'd shared them with anyone other than her younger sister Natalie.

He had wanted to be there to help her celebrate the milestone of buying her own home.

Max was sorry he'd missed it. A quick look around him told him the place reflected the beautiful, feminine woman that she rarely showed at the office. The softer side.

The side Max adored.

There were floral accents everywhere. Jac could take a broken twig and turn it into a beautiful flower with just a touch, it seemed.

That was something else she kept hidden from the world. That and her love of the piano. She'd started teaching Emery to play years ago.

He found Jac at the stove, cooking breakfast. She had on thin little pink shorts that revealed tanned legs. He'd never really been into *legs*, but Jac... Jac was beautiful. Every inch of her.

The tank top she'd slept in was soft yellow and dotted with tiny pink flowers. Perfect.

She was summer bright in the midst of November gray. His hands actually trembled. There was a thin pink bra strap just visible on one shoulder. Out of place. He wanted to touch, right there. To slide his fingers along the satin, along the silky skin beneath. His gut tightened at the thought.

There was no woman on the planet he'd rather touch more than this one.

Max kept his damned hands to himself before he screwed things up between them even worse than he had weeks ago.

He hadn't meant to kiss her and run.

She hadn't had to help him out with Emery last night. Jac was well within her rights to have told him to take a leap for the way he'd acted after that kiss. But she hadn't.

He should have known she wouldn't. Not when it came to Emery. "Hey, Jones ladies."

They both looked over at him.

He liked calling them that. It made it sound like Jac was a *Jones* because of him, instead of random coincidence. He had never analyzed why he liked those simple words—until the weeks after he'd ruined everything between them.

Now, he knew why that coincidental connection between them mattered to him so much.

His inner Neanderthal was rearing his head again. Saying, "Claim your mate. Now!"

Her being a Jones made the subconscious part of him think she was *his*. That she was meant to be his in some odd way he hadn't yet defined.

Primitive, but true.

He knew exactly how he felt about the quietly beautiful redhead currently teaching his little girl how to flip pancakes at just the right moment.

They were the ones who mattered to him more than anyone else in the world.

"Hi, Daddy!" Emery finished her task carefully, then bounced over to him for morning hugs. "Jac said you spent the night here, too. I made three baskets last night, including my free throw. Abbie fouled me. We'll have to update my chart at home from last season. Livy made two baskets. Tabby puked, though, so they had to stop the game for like twenty minutes to clean it up. She had to go home. That's why the coach let Livy play most of the game this time."

"It was close to the half-time mark." Jac said, amusement in her tone. "I think her friend had too many hot dogs before the game."

"She only had two hot dogs, but bunches of cotton candy." Emery hugged him again. Jac gave him a tentative smile over his daughter's head. Emery was extremely tall for her age—both Max and his ex-wife were over six feet—and only about eight inches separated Emery's height from Jac's five six.

They looked perfect together. Like they belonged together, right down to the red in their hair.

He'd always thought so.

Jac was more of a mother to his daughter than his ex-wife had ever been. Even Pamela had said that on the occasions she breezed through town and had seen Jac and Emery together.

Part of the reason he'd flipped so badly after the kiss had changed their relationship had been because of that very thing. The last thing he had ever wanted to do was screw up the relationship his daughter had with Jac. But he'd done just that, to the point that Jac and Emery hadn't seen each other in several weeks. His fault.

His stupid, cowardly asshole fault. The last thing he ever wanted to do was hurt the two of them.

Well, he was ready to change that now. He'd had some damned time to think while lying in her purple guest room last night. It had been either think about Andy and what had happened, what Andy would miss with his daughters now—or think of the woman Max had long admitted he wanted. Knowing she was just down the hall had made his choice clear.

The look Jac was giving him was beyond wary. It told him one thing: Jac didn't trust him any longer. Not at all.

Max had to find a way to fix that.

He'd had a lot to think about on the twenty-minute drive to Jac's home after leaving the hospital where he, Seth, and Hellbrook had taken the director and Malachi. The shrapnel that had been lodged in Sin Lorcan's left shoulder had been removed on scene.

Sin had refused to go to the hospital; his wife was the supervisor who had been called in to deal with the remains of Sebastian's car. Sin hadn't been about to leave her there with the potential for more explosives. Not after what had happened.

Max hadn't blamed him.

Max had seen the look in Sin's eyes when Cody had first stepped out of the bureau SUV. Max had understood. He'd known he'd have felt the same if it had been *Jac* walking over the broken sidewalk toward the inferno.

All he had been able to think about was Jac and Emery.

Since the moment he'd hit the ground in Andy's backyard, he'd thought about Jac and Emery.

About how he had come close to dying. His first thoughts had been for Jac and his daughter. Because they were the ones who mattered most.

Jac didn't know how he felt about her. He'd been too much of an idiot to realize, to tell her.

Max wasn't certain how he was supposed to make his feelings known. Without making a complete and utter ass out of himself. He couldn't just say, "Hey, it took me five years to figure out how I feel about you."

That would go over well. It was more of an insult than anything else.

His only answer was that after Pamela, *any* woman had terrified him.

He pulled in a deep breath. He had waited long enough. He opened his mouth to send Emery into the living room to watch cartoons. He and Jac had some things to say to one another. To finally repair their relationship somehow.

Before he could, the cell phone he'd plugged in on her kitchen island buzzed.

The ringtone of PAVAD.

He swore. He knew what it meant. He had hoped he'd have an extra hour to spend with his family before he had to go in and face what had happened to Andy. The first of the forensics from the explosion were going to start rolling in soon.

Max needed to be there for that.

"Go. I'll keep her today. I'm off until Tuesday, built up comp time.

We'll go shopping at the mall. Have a girls' day. Looks like she's about to outgrow her shoes. Again."

He almost flinched. Shoes. Little girls' shoes. Andy had bought his little girls shoes just a few days ago. He'd told Max all about the sale at the mall.

He pushed that aside and tuned back in to Jac.

She'd shopped with Emery before, saving him from that torture, just giving him receipts when she was finished. He'd give her cash in return—and his eternal gratitude. "All of them, heaven help me. Why she needs more than a few pairs of shoes is beyond me."

Then, just because he wanted to, he wrapped his arms around her and just breathed her in. Her hair was silky against his cheek. He ignored how she stiffened briefly. "We're going to talk, Jac. And very, very soon. There is a lot I want to say to you. *Need* to say to you. I've put it off long enough."

Wary green eyes looked into his.

"Go. PAVAD is waiting."

He went, leaving his daughter behind with the woman he loved more than any other woman he ever had before.

9

LYTEL HEARD THE RUMORS THE INSTANT HE STEPPED INTO THE PAVAD building. So they were finally letting it leak that Anderson had been ambushed and the bomb hadn't been the result of a gas leak like the news was reporting.

No doubt, the director's little media liaison teams had been hard at work since it had happened over a week ago.

The director was back after his little "health scare," too. Rumor had it Dennis had needed some medical tests done; but Lytel had known the truth. There wasn't much in PAVAD that he didn't know about.

Hell, he even knew a secret about good old Ed he doubted Ed himself knew about.

There were a handful of men who had been there that night and had been injured. He'd seen them for himself.

Sin Lorcan, for one. He'd seen that icy sonofabitch getting shrapnel removed in the ambulance at the Anderson scene himself. Lytel doubted they'd even numbed the bastard first.

His wife had been hovering around behind him. She hadn't been allowed to touch the evidence because of her connection to one of the injured, but she'd watched everything her people had done.

Not that Lytel gave a fuck. If he'd left any evidence behind, he'd blown that evidence to the moon.

PAVAD had taught him a lot of neat little tricks, after all.

No one had given any explanation for why Sin Lorcan or his brother Sebastian had been there. Nothing more than the idea that Anderson was a *friend.*

No one questioned Sin Lorcan. No one.

He'd seen what the bastard had done to Saul Hernandez. As far as Lytel knew, Hernandez was still in prison, awaiting trial.

Hernandez had been a good guy. He and Eric Brady both.

Sin Lorcan had nearly ripped Brady to shreds for getting too close to that wife of his.

Lytel had seen that for himself that day. He'd seen the director and Lorcan running through the halls and had followed.

Just to see what was happening. He'd ended up escorting Brady to an interrogation room himself.

Always a part of the action, never a part of the limelight.

PAVAD was all about not taking the glory for any one agent or team. It was the whole organization who deserved the credit, as the great *team* that it was.

Well, Lytel called bullshit on that. Ed Dennis was getting his glory somehow; he had no doubt about that.

Men like that always did.

No matter who they had to bury to do it.

He waited until the end of the day. Then he did some more digging. He needed to see what was going on.

And he had a payoff to make.

He wasn't the only one on a secondary payroll around here, after all.

Even the subcontractors wandering around the building—not all of them were on the up-and-up, either.

Lytel had a five-forty meeting with one of them right there in his office.

Wonder what the director would do if he ever found out some of the shit designed to bring him down was happening right there under his damned fucking nose?

Lytel didn't intend to be around to see that.

He was almost fifty-six now. He was going to take his cash from this and retire.

He wanted to find an island somewhere and just relax. He'd divorce the wife, keep in touch with the kids by email if he chose to, and then he'd live his life for himself for a change.

After all these years, he deserved it.

But first, he had a few meetings lined up for the day. Todd Barnes would be there in fifteen minutes, and he still had that damned IT contractor to talk to about the latest security updates for his department. He personally couldn't stand the two sonsofbitches, but they all played for the same side now, after all.

He had to remember that. At least for the time being. PAVAD meant being a part of the *team*, after all. Lytel always had been a team player.

10

Todd left Director Dennis's office a week after he'd visited St. Louis to make the delivery, forcing himself to keep a smirk off his face. The guy was such a stupid prick. Todd couldn't wait until Edward Perfect Dennis got what was coming to him. He'd get exactly what he deserved. It was just a matter of time until that happened.

In the meantime, Todd was going to do what he was told. At least on the surface. He was ready to move up the ladder. It was about time.

There were people in the waiting area of Dennis's office. Todd forced himself to nod politely. Agent Len-Royal, the director's prissy little assistant, was watching him. It was obvious she didn't like him, even though her face was blank when she looked at him.

Her and that beefcake husband of hers who was running around in the CHILDS department one floor down from the Complex Crimes floor.

They didn't just have areas for each division of PAVAD now. They had entire *floors*.

Fucking ridiculous. No division of the bureau, or of any federal agency that he knew of, had grown so quickly. Everyone was saying there had to be some sort of corruption within it somewhere.

The bureau just didn't work the way PAVAD did.

It was bound to destroy itself from within. Soon.

Very, very soon.

One of the men waiting in the outer office was the envelope guy. That had Todd flinching a bit.

Sturvin wasn't an agent. The prick was an independent contractor hired to service the human resources and benefits and accounting departments of PAVAD. Their servers.

Sturvin wasn't PAVAD. He was an outsider.

From what Todd's contact had told him, that was something Dennis had been shot down about too. He'd wanted to keep everything IT within PAVAD itself. Dennis had wanted actual agents from the computer departments to handle everything within the sanctified walls of PAVAD. Barring that, he'd wanted Lucas Tech involved.

The moneymen had told Dennis differently. Lucas Tech was too damned expensive, apparently.

And Dennis was pissed.

Todd had to admit, he would have felt the same thing.

Although he understood why Sturvin was there now.

Outside eyes and ears for the ones who wanted Todd in St. Louis, too.

The destruction of PAVAD was a massive scheme.

It wasn't something just one man could do. Nor was it something that was going to be easy. Sturvin was a plant.

A plant they thought Ed Dennis would eventually trust. Sturvin's kids went to the same school as the director's. Just like every damned big name in PAVAD who had a kid now. Keep them all safe and sound at Brynlock Academy with its five figure a semester tuition and its armed guards—paid for by Lucas Technologies.

Whoever was orchestrating this shit was very, very good.

This infiltration of PAVAD had taken years to build. Years to plan. Someone had been planning this from before PAVAD was realized fully.

It wasn't likely to fail.

Todd's eyes met Sturvin's, and he nodded. Just once.

Just an acknowledgment of their common purpose.

Although...Todd doubted the other man had a philosophical or moral reason for doing this, not like Todd. Money drove that man.

Todd had done his own digging into Sturvin, after all.

As cash-strapped as that man was, Sturvin's motivation was cold, hard cash. Had to keep that pretty wife of his in the lifestyle, after all.

Todd finally made it into the hallway and let his smirk go free.

Fuck PAVAD. It was finally going to happen.

Todd was going to be a part of it. He checked his watch.

He had fifteen minutes to go before he had to meet with his check-in point here in St. Louis.

Plenty of time to take a few digs at Paul Sturvin.

Just to see what the guy was made of.

A team was only as good as the weakest link, after all.

11

"SO IT'S BEEN A FULL WEEK SINCE HE SPENT THE NIGHT AT YOUR place?" Miranda asked from the passenger seat as Jac drove. Miranda wouldn't stop talking about the last subject Jac wanted to think about: Max. Miranda was always asking Jac about Max. Questions Jac didn't have the answers to. "And you *still* haven't spoken to that man?"

"Two. Closer to two weeks." Jac shook her head, after checking the gas tank. They had a while to go, and there was a gas station up ahead. "I've barely passed Max in the halls since then. He's been busy with the director and a special project."

Andy Anderson. Max was quietly working that case with the director and Sin Lorcan, but no one was supposed to know that. Jac hadn't said a word. Even to her best friend.

She'd worried about Max the entire time she was in Masterson with Miranda. He and Andy had been good friends. Not as close as she was with the woman next to her, but enough that Andy's death hurt him. Haunted him.

She knew how Max's mind worked, after all. She had seen his face at Andy's funeral, too.

That day wasn't one she was easily going to forget.

Miranda said something. Jac focused back in on her friend.

Jac was still frozen through to her undies, after leaving the small Wyoming town where she'd driven up to fetch her best friend. Masterson had been under more than two feet of snow.

Miranda had been up in Wyoming visiting with her family for the past three weeks, following the final surgery she'd had in Masterson to repair the nasty break in her arm from a case gone bad back in September.

Had Jac not delayed her travel plans that particular day, having decided to stay and visit with Miranda's family, Miranda would have been killed, right there in the Talley Inn's kitchen.

Miranda had been very lucky. Just how fleeting a friend could be lost had sunk in for Jac that day, too. It wasn't a lesson she wanted to forget—or repeat.

Jac truly hadn't minded the drive to Masterson last week. It had given her time to think about the CPED's last case. It had been a tough one, too.

One that had her seriously considering switching to the CCU full-time instead of floating between the two divisions.

She didn't know how much longer she could handle cases involving child victims. It was getting too hard.

Just as she'd arrived in Masterson, a nasty snowstorm had hit, trapping her and Miranda in the county for a few more days than planned.

They'd spent that time with Miranda's grandmother Flo and Miranda's two sisters and her cousins, who all lived at the family inn right in the midst of downtown Masterson. Miranda had one cousin who lived down in Texas, near Wichita Falls, who had also been visiting. It had been a wild family reunion—or as wild as the Talleys got. Jac had loved it.

The Talleys acted as if *Jac* was one of them, as if she'd always been a part of their family. They'd even given her a suite in the family wing of their inn.

That mattered more than anything Jac had ever experienced.

They were as close to a real family as Jac was ever going to get, except for her own little sister Nat. Worry flooded her mind when she thought of the hell her sister had gone through, losing the man she loved in a nasty explosion a year or so ago.

It seemed like all Jac did was worry lately.

Nat was struggling, but she would make it through. Her sister was one of the strongest woman Jac knew.

Jac had seen photos of another bomb scene. One that had happened a lot more recently. Max and the rest of the men out there that day could have been killed.

It had been three weeks since Andy Anderson's death.

Company rumors said that it was the director, Max, Malachi Brockman, and at least two of the Lorcan brothers who had been there that night. But no one was supposed to know *who*.

Jac had seen the files by accident, then put it together quickly.

Max had reeked of smoke, after all. It had been the night Andy died.

She wasn't an idiot.

They had all been lucky to survive. Family men, all of them.

PAVAD really wasn't all that great for families, in her opinion. There were far too many risks.

Those involved in this case were of so high a security clearance they got nosebleeds when they were all together on company time.

Worry for Max hit her again. She was seriously worried about that man.

From what she had been able to see of him, and what other friends had told her, he was working himself practically ragged to find out who had killed Andy Anderson.

That was another reason she was heading home today. She had four hours left to get home, shower, change, and get over to Brynlock Academy. Emery was counting on her to be there. Jac wanted to check on Max herself. Just to make certain he was ok.

He was obstinate enough to be a real dog with a bone when he felt it was important enough.

Andy was important enough.

Jac had attended the funeral, staying near Max, surrounded by the rest of Andy's team. Angie had been devastated. The girls had been little ghosts. It was obvious they didn't understand what had happened.

They'd buried Andy next to his son. That had stuck out to Jac for hours after. Life…was so fleeting.

How could Andy's kids understand this?

Jac barely understood it herself.

Jac had made a vow a long time ago to never let down the people she cared about. Not the ones she considered her family. Afraid-of-a-little-kiss Max was definitely on that list. She was going to find him, check on him, and read him the riot act if needed.

"I can drive for a while," Miranda said next to her after a few hours on the road. "If you need a break. Or want to sit over here and send sexy texts to the hot Dr. Jones—just no pics. I don't need to see you take them."

"I'm good. Maybe in half an hour. We need to find food." Miranda terrified her when she drove. The woman had no fear whatsoever—it would be even worse if Miranda was driving one-handed. "And that's a no on the texts. He'd probably freak, and move himself and Emery to the northernmost corners of Maine or something. Especially if the pics were of actual naked-Jac skin. A kiss was enough to send the man running for the hills, after all. I can only imagine what he'd do if I was naked in front of him." She resisted the urge to shiver.

Jac *may* have had a few moments of imagining what had happened if the kiss had gone deeper than it had.

Until he'd skedaddled, anyway. Hard to miss that part.

"I think he'd figure it out fast. Dear Max ran because you were too much woman for him. My grandmother did pack us sandwiches and brownies. And oatmeal-cranberry cookies." Miranda shot her a grin. "Want me to crack open the tin?"

Those cookies were Jac's favorite in existence. "You've been holding out. Hand over the goods."

They shared the best cookies Jac had ever tasted on the drive, talking and laughing the whole way. Nat was her sister by birth, but Miranda was her sister by choice. She loved them both more than words could ever express.

She dropped Miranda off at Miranda's condo and booked it back across town to her own place.

When she finally pulled into the Brynlock Academy parking lot at fifteen minutes past seven, she was relaxed but tired from the drive. Miranda had a way of breaking tension. It was one of her best friend's strongest gifts. People relaxed with Miranda. That was a gift more prized than gold.

She stepped inside the multipurpose room of the school as the sounds and sights rushed her. The private school was one of the more expensive private schools in the city, but it had a warmth about it that belied that fact. Not super-prestigious. Or pretentious. The focus was on the children as whole beings, not just students competing for test scores. They also had generous scholarship and financial-hardship packages funded by local business organizations.

Jac had donated a thousand dollars last year to the financial-hardship fund.

Emery did well here. She had friends among her classmates, she loved playing sports and Brynlock had plenty for her to try, and she did great academically. She struggled with math, but the school provided one-on-one sessions with her for that, when needed. Brynlock wanted their students to succeed.

Max was a very proud daddy, who had often shared his daughter's accomplishments with Jac. And begged her help with tutoring for that math two years in a row. Once a week, until recently, she'd have dinner with Max and Emery, and then she and Emery would hit the math book. They were making progress; it was just taking time. A mathematician Emery most certainly would never be, but she tried hard.

Max had freely shared his daughter with Jac.

Until the Kiss-That-Shouldn't-Have Happened. She'd lost more than Max's friendship after that moment. She'd lost Emery. Even if it had just been for a few months.

That had been long enough for her.

Well, she was going to fix that.

Max had delivered the invitation to the Brynlock Fall Festival—made by Emery out of construction paper and ribbon and glitter, lots and lots of glitter—to her desk personally, three days after he'd slept in her guest room.

He'd looked at her and asked quietly if she would attend. For Emery.

There hadn't been any hesitation when she'd made her promise.

There never would be.

Emery Jones was the child of her heart.

No doubt, Emery's father knew that.

Things had changed between them again the night he'd crashed in her guest room. She just hadn't had time to figure out how yet.

Mostly, it was in the way he looked at her.

She looked around for people she knew. Jac was never fully comfortable in a crowd of strangers.

There were actually quite a few people she knew very well already in the multipurpose room. The first man she saw was her CCU team leader Sebastian Lorcan and his two brothers. They were identical, and very hard to overlook—even if they weren't all around six-five and absolutely gorgeous. Sebastian's niece and nephew attended Brynlock, though they were younger than Emery. There was an older nephew in the high school, too.

Simon Brockman, the absolute love of Emery's life. Max flipped the first time Emery had said how hot Simon was. Jac had laughed for fifteen minutes after that.

There were several children whose parents worked for PAVAD

that attended Brynlock. Brynlock had excellent security. That was one of the important points for Max, too. His ex's parents hadn't been too happy when Pamela had given full custody to Max and had made threats when Emery was around five or so.

Thankfully, the attorney Max had hired—that his ex-wife had helped him pay for—put Pamela's parents straight. Emery hadn't seen them since.

Then she saw the man she was looking for. Max looked good. She'd always thought he looked good in jeans. He wore a Wildcats jersey. It was the same team their friend Ken had played for in his younger days.

Max was stressed, though he had on what she had privately always thought of his don't-worry-Emery face. He was speaking to the director.

Neither man looked very happy at the moment. Jac headed across the floor.

Speaking of...Ken and Leina Chalmers were right there behind the director and Max, with their four children. Ken held their toddler. Leina had their newborn in a carrier on her chest. Their two girls were bouncing around in front of them, ready to rush around the carnival at any moment. Jac smiled seeing the bright faces of kids she'd met many times before.

Except for the newest.

The baby boy had been born while Jac had been in Masterson. Jac wanted to hold him, if Leina was willing to share for a few minutes. Leina should be sitting down and resting—she'd just had the baby last week.

Ken was hovering. Shannon, another agent on Jac's computer forensic analysis team, was there, too. She made goofy faces at the Chalmers kids, then took the toddler from Ken, while her fiancé scooped up the younger girl. They didn't have children yet, but she knew they were close to Leina and Ken's. Invited by the girls to the carnival, probably.

Families. There were *families* everywhere.

She loved PAVAD. Loved how the people she worked with had formed bonds that went beyond biology.

A smile escaped, not that she was trying to keep it back. PAVAD was a family all on its own.

Emery saw her before she made it halfway there. The little girl started running—her philosophy was why walk when she could run —calling Jac's name.

Then Jac had her arms full of her favorite kid in the world.

This was where she belonged, right here.

12

Paul Sturvin carried his daughter Ava in his arms as he and his wife, Rachel, and their elder daughter, Olivia, made their way through the crowd at Brynlock Academy's Annual Fall Festival. He had been looking forward to this networking event for weeks. Rachel was getting more obstinate each and every day. He was going to have to find a way to deal with that. Before she ruined every opportunity he was creating for their family.

There were men here he needed to see.

He needed to build their trust.

Brynlock was his creative ticket to getting that.

He suspected his association with Brynlock was the main reason he'd been chosen for this little *special assignment* of his.

Paul smiled at how easily his plans were coming together.

He'd been the IT consultant for the PAVAD division of the FBI for two and a half months now. That was just his first step. He was busting his ass to make sure he did that job very, very well.

He was giving PAVAD no excuse to dissolve his contract.

He wouldn't be slogging as a consultant for too much longer. If he made this work, he would be paid enough to never *need* to work again.

The money that would bring...that was his ultimate goal. Paul wasn't afraid to do what he had to do to make what he wanted happen. He would take that money and make even more for his family.

So that his children would have a future.

It would be nice to not have to worry about scraping by every month when the bills came due again. To not have to worry about the neighbors getting their mail with the past due notices by mistake. To have them looking at him and Rachel and their children and mocking them for their financial circumstances. That mere idea infuriated him.

His children would have the best.

Paul was adamant about that.

Then Rachel wouldn't look at him with that expression that told him *he'd* failed her.

The fall festival was the biggest event at the small, exclusive private school he had chosen with deliberate care.

He had been planning this day for weeks, right down to the clothing his daughters and his wife wore now. They looked like exactly what he wanted them to: an upwardly mobile, typical all-American family. Successful, well-groomed, attractive, and engaging.

He had very exacting standards.

Paul bit back a curse, seeing the throng of imbeciles blocking their way. Brynlock was supposed to be the best the city of St. Louis had to offer. Paul wasn't exactly impressed with what he was seeing right now.

It wasn't living up to his standards. Educationally, it was spot-on, but...it wasn't the educational tools he had chosen for his children that Paul was ultimately after.

It was far more than that. It was the connections his daughters would make at Brynlock that mattered the most.

He fully intended that both Olivia and Ava would marry into the wealthiest families at Brynlock as soon as they were of age to do so. Anyone who was anyone in the city competed for placement at the small private school. At one point, it had catered to upper-middle-class families, with heavy scholarship opportunities.

Now...competition was so fierce to get in, the price of tuition was rising. Drastically. The middle class were being squeezed out—unless they were already grandfathered in at the previous price. It all had to do with that damned Davis Lucas and his family.

Everyone wanted to send their kids where the billionaire's family went. For the connection and the prestige.

Paul understood that very, very well.

He and Rachel had fortunately been locked in on the previous tuition rates. Or they wouldn't be here right now.

This was where his daughters would do what he wished of them.

They would not dare defy him. He would ensure they understood the importance of what he wanted from them.

For them.

He had expected to see those of high class walking around this place. Sophistication. The coolly wealthy as they deigned to condescend to something as quaint as a fall festival for their equally sophisticated children.

He had had to miss last year's festival when Olivia and Ava were ill with a virus that had increased Ava's asthma complications, but this year...

He had had such plans. This was disappointing. He'd spent all year thinking about this event, and the several other events Brynlock hosted each year.

Connections were worth more than gold right now.

Paul did his best to ensure that disappointment didn't show as they walked further into the multipurpose room.

He hadn't expected this.

Not this...upper-middle-class-family fun. That could be found anywhere. What separated Brynlock from the other dozens of private schools catering to white-collar families? He wasn't seeing that now.

Here, he and his family were just a part of the crowd. They didn't stand out at all.

That was not acceptable.

Paul wanted the absolute best for his daughters. He'd scraped together enough for Olivia's tuition to the elementary school, and Ava's to the three times a week preschool on the same campus for damned good reason.

They were his tickets to the life he had been working toward for years. The life Paul deserved.

Every sacrifice he had ever made had been to ensure his current family had the very best. He would do better for them.

Paul would not fail again.

Their names would be ones that were remembered. They wouldn't be shuttled off to strangers to be raised without a name.

Both were bright girls, and if their mother followed his instructions for how they were to be raised, they would have brilliant futures ahead of them. Excellent educations, all the right friends and connections, remarkable marriages, outstanding careers. They would have it all.

He would ensure that. It was what a father was supposed to do, after all.

Paul would not fail as a father again.

"There are her friends Lucy, Emery, and Ruthie," Rachel said, motioning to a small crowd nearby. "With their families."

Paul studied the people closely. He'd made a point of knowing exactly who was in his daughter's class at Brynlock, and who she chose to associate with.

Lucy Lorcan was associated with the head of Lucas Technologies in some way, the wealthiest man in St. Louis. In the state; probably the region. Paul believed she was the man's goddaughter or niece or something.

Paul had been trying for years to get contracts with Lucas Tech, the leading developer of law enforcement technology around the world. A connection to Lucas Tech would had made him a very wealthy man. He didn't need that now. At least not right away.

He was being paid very well for his work with the FBI.

The Brockman girl's parents weren't as wealthy, by any means, but they were both very prestigious names within the federal law enforcement community. Between the two of them, they had a list of impressive connections. And, he suspected, investments. The neighborhood where they lived wasn't exactly *cheap*.

Paul's family attended the same church as the Brockmans. Their daughter was near in age to his own. He'd chosen it deliberately. He found the couple to be a bit reserved—the wife far more than the husband—but intelligent, cultured. Very well-connected.

There were several business associates who attended services at the same church as well. Paul had planned his family's life very, very carefully. Down to the smallest detail.

He had needed those connections with Lucas Tech. He had needed the in with the director of PAVAD. His IT contract with the FBI was currently only temporary. He had wanted to make that a permanent part of his business plan.

Soon. His contract expired at the end of January. That was fast approaching. His contract would be renewed when the time came. Paul had been reassured he had nothing to worry about.

Everything he needed would be taken care of for him. All he had to do was funnel some information from PAVAD to a nifty little email on the dark net, a few times a week.

He'd already received two payments from the men involved.

Payments that had kept Ava and Olivia in Brynlock.

In exchange, Paul would do a few little favors when he could. The money was just too good not to want more. It was going to turn everything around for his family. Erase the mistakes he'd made with his investments over the last several years. Fix *everything*. Make right everything he had ruined.

They would have far more than Paul ever had.

He was going to see to that. All he had to do was uphold his part of the bargain, without completely screwing things up for them all.

But Rachel...she was more willful and intractable than he ever would have expected when he had met her years ago. He had yet to determine how to address that. He needed to. Before *she* screwed everything up, too.

One reason he'd been singled out for this new project had been because of the connections *Rachel* had made at Brynlock. Paul hadn't forgotten that.

All he had to do was find a way to get the information they wanted without Rachel realizing what he was doing. Paul always had enjoyed challenges.

"There's Emery!" Olivia said excitedly. She pointed to a little strawberry-blond girl in the distance. Paul studied the child quickly. *She* was not someone he recognized.

He looked at Rachel for clarification. His wife knew he had to give approval. She just rolled her pretty blue eyes at him. He hated when she looked at him like that, like he was being ridiculous. She knew that. "She's a classroom helper in Olivia's class once a week and is on the same basketball team. Star player, two or three years older than Li—Olivia. Emery Jones. Her father works for the FBI. Rather high up on the food chain, too. Max Jones."

Paul thought for a moment. He'd heard the name before. He vaguely recalled meeting a man by that name. A tall, brown-haired man a good eighty pounds heavier than Paul, and six inches taller, stood near the girl. He looked familiar.

From the Complex Crimes Unit, Paul thought. "Dr. *Maddox* Jones?"

"He goes by Max. He's been at the school a few times."

The CCU. One of the departments his consulting company couldn't go near at the PAVAD building. Paul was going to change that.

"And her mother?" The little girl stood next to a classically beautiful woman with auburn hair and a perfect, slim feminine figure.

She blew Rachel's sleek blond soccer-mom presentation out of the water.

She looked exactly like the type of woman he would expect to find at Brynlock Academy. Sleek, expensive, sophisticated. Graceful and beautiful.

He was certain he knew the girl's father. He looked like an ex-jock—big, muscled, shaggy, and brainless. Like half the men he'd seen in the FBI building.

But the woman…if he had seen her before, he would remember.

He would most certainly remember *her.*

"That's not her mom," Olivia said. "That's her aunt, I think. She calls her Jack, not Mommy."

"Jack? Odd name for a woman." There was nothing masculine about the woman he was looking at. Far from it.

"Her name is Jaclyn Jones. She's a friend of mine," Rachel said quietly. He shot her a look. She knew he wanted to know everyone she considered a *friend.* Who Rachel interacted with was just as important as those who the children did. He wouldn't have her associating with just anyone. "A new one. We've met at the school a few times. She's a connection of the family."

"Please, Daddy? Can I go play now?" Olivia begged, shooting him the smile that was identical to her mother's.

Paul studied his daughters quickly. Olivia was presentable. Her clothing was still neat, her face was washed, and her blond hair had been groomed into two braids perfectly. She looked very pretty. Ava, however, needed her face cleaned once again, and her dark braid straightened. And there was a stain on her shirt.

His younger daughter was a bit less meticulous than his older. Hopefully, that would correct itself as she aged. She was his star, after all. Far more than her sister could ever be. Ava was far more *gifted* than Olivia.

Both of their children were physically beautiful, appealing children. He and Rachel ensured that was enhanced with meticulous grooming and the proper clothing. Even if Rachel had to spend hours hunting for that clothing second hand. She knew all the best places now. He considered it her duty as his children's mother.

"Can I go hang out with Emery, Daddy? She's my best friend."

As the woman with the child turned, he nodded.

He wanted to learn more about this aunt as well.

And exactly what Rachel had told her. If she'd said anything that would cause trouble for Paul, if it got back to the other Jones from the CCU—that could jeopardize things significantly.

That would have to be dealt with.

Swiftly.

13

MAX THOUGHT ABOUT THE MAN'S WORDS FOR A MOMENT AS THE crowd swirled around him. The director of PAVAD had pulled him aside, telling him they needed to speak as soon as possible.

This was not what Max had expected.

He'd thought Ed had something to tell him about the Anderson case. They'd stalled on Andy's murder two days into the investigation. All they had was encrypted data—that had been in an additional code—on the memory cards Max had found.

Sixty-three pages of gibberish that no one had been able to make sense of yet. PAVAD was working on it now. It was going to take time.

As the crowd swirled around them, he thought about what the man was saying. What it would mean for Emery. Everything he did had to be filtered through the window of what was best for his daughter. "It will still mean travel. I was hoping to eliminate a good portion of my time away from home. Having me gone has been a struggle for Emery lately."

Max had finally put it together *why* last week.

Jac.

It came down to Jac. The days she'd spent with Jac while he'd combed over the evidence in Andy's case had triggered this separation anxiety now. His daughter feared she'd not see Jac again for weeks.

That and Emery had heard somewhere what had happened to Annie Anderson's father. She knew Andy had been with the FBI.

Just like Max. Just like Jac.

Every adult Emery loved and was significantly bonded with was *FBI*. His daughter was at the age when she was figuring out that people didn't live forever. It terrified her—she was afraid she was going to lose her father or Jac.

Emery missed Jac. His daughter was subconsciously afraid that Jac was going to leave her, just like her own mother had.

Or that Max was going to suddenly be even less available, like she felt Jac was.

That was entirely Max's fault.

Today would hopefully go a long way to helping his daughter heal from that blow he had unintentionally dealt her. Max would find a chance to speak with Jac, see if she would be willing to keep being the most important woman in Emery's life.

Like she had been since his daughter was three years old.

Ed nodded as one of his younger sons tugged on his hand. "I can understand that. I've been in your position, myself. If my sister hadn't been able to help with Georgia, I would have had a more difficult time than I did. This is a promotion for you, and the travel will be the same as now."

"She's having a tough time. Our former housekeeper retired six months ago. We've had trouble finding a replacement that Emery is bonding with." Max nodded. He understood all of that. He wanted to stay with PAVAD, but his career had to come second to the needs of his daughter. She needed a more on-site parent right now. He had meant to talk to Ed and Hellbrook about that after they found Andy's killer. Found the traitor in PAVAD.

The director and Hellbrook were both fathers themselves, with their children running around them now. They would at least understand where he was coming from—even if they couldn't help him work it out.

PAVAD was a large organization now, with over four hundred employees. Even if it meant a lateral move into some type of administrative position, Max was open to that.

He didn't know how much longer he could handle the traveling and being away from Emery for two or three, sometimes as many as five nights a week. That was a lot to ask of a nearly nine-year-old with a single father.

Emery worried. About everything lately. Mostly, she worried about him disappearing and leaving her all alone.

He would never let her be all alone. *Ever.* He had a will with very clear instructions for her care, if anything should ever happen to him. He'd updated it three years ago to make sure that very thing didn't happen.

If anything happened to him, his daughter would be provided for. Loved.

"I'm honored you think I can handle running a team, Director. But my first priority will always have to be Emery." Max looked for his daughter as he spoke. And then he found her.

Talking animatedly to a familiar redhead.

One he had been waiting to see. He hadn't known if she'd make it when he'd given her the brightly colored construction paper invitation Emery had made for Jac specifically.

Jac had made it to the school on time, even though he'd heard she'd driven to Wyoming to get Miranda a week ago. He'd kept one eye on the Wyoming weather report for the last week. He'd asked her teammates if they'd heard from her. Probably been a bit obvious about it, too.

Jac had made it. For his daughter.

Relief filled him. It was important to Emery that it wasn't just him there today. She was so hungry for family; his own mother and sisters were in central Illinois. Emery didn't get to visit with them as often as he would like, and she didn't *know* them.

As the holidays approached, it just made it tough on all of them. PAVAD came with sacrifices.

They'd spent the last two Thanksgivings and Christmases and New Years with Jac. Just the three of them. He and Jac had always ended up on call for the CCU, and they'd spent the holidays together. They'd been determined to give Emery as wonderful a holiday as they could.

It had taken Max a few days after their argument to put it together—he'd been building a family with Jac all along.

Stupid of him not to see that.

He didn't know what he and Emery would do *this* year. Thanksgiving was next week. "I'm away from her enough as it is, if I add extra paperwork and more time on call, I don't know if that will be the healthiest option for her. I need time to think about it."

"Take a few days to think about it. But you should know Washington has transferred another agent in. They are pushing for him to have his own team within the CCU, starting after the new year. At least for six months. He's nowhere near qualified. But I don't know how much I can push back." And there was fury in the man's brown eyes at that thought. "It's a dangerous line I walk sometimes."

Someone pissing off Ed Dennis was pretty damned stupid. A smart man thought twice before willingly stepping in the middle of that.

Max wasn't stupid.

"May I ask who?" Max respected Ed, probably more than he did many other people—especially within the bureau itself. Through the last five years of working for the man, first for the St. Louis field office, and then at PAVAD once it was officially up and running, Max liked to think the man respected him in return.

Max trusted Ed to be a straight shooter.

"Todd Barnes." Ed practically snarled. Max winced. He recognized the name. The man had shown up occasionally in St. Louis before PAVAD had been created. He'd cropped up in a few other cases over the last five years. Never in good ways. "With…what else we are working on, I don't want him anywhere near PAVAD. But I've been overruled. I don't take that lightly."

No one had liked Todd Barnes much back then, having him running a team in the CCU would guarantee problems. Of the extreme sort.

Max thought of his friends and teammates and what having Barnes for a team leader would mean for all of them. At best, the man was incompetent.

In PAVAD, that could be dangerous. Lives could literally be at stake. "He's had no PAVAD experience."

"Certain people seem to think he'll be successful as a leader in the Complex Crimes Unit. As if the CCU was just any other unit, in any other division." Ed lowered his voice as the crowd shifted closer. "They think he's seasoned enough now."

"Ignorance can be highly dangerous," Max said.

The director nodded, his expression smoothing as he handed two of his children some money. When they hurried off to join their friends, he turned back to Max. "So can politics. And this has the stink of that. Manipulation. I don't play those games very well. I never have."

Max checked on Emery again. She had Jac by the hand, leading her to the nearest game booth, chattering away. His eyes met Jac's. She nodded, wordlessly letting him know she'd watch over his daughter while he spoke with Ed. He turned back to the director.

"To be honest, if you agree to take the position, even for six months, it will help me out a great deal."

"Why me?" There were other agents within the CCU who could do exactly what Ed was asking. They both knew that.

Hell, Jac could do it—probably much better than Max.

That would free Max up to work with Sin Lorcan, who ran an unofficial internal corruption unit within PAVAD now. Sin had called Max in to his own office once a day since Andy's death.

Sin was determined. Max's respect for the man and what he did for the bureau was growing. He wouldn't mind switching to that department full-time. Sin's team didn't just keep an eye on corruption within the bureau, they were branching out to other governmental organizations—both on the state levels and federal.

But no one was to know that. Sin's unit wasn't even going to exist *officially,* anywhere. Max wanted to be a part of that.

It would mean far less travel, for one thing. For another, it would mean keeping the people he worked with and cared about from ending up like Andy. Keep them from getting shot in the damned babysitter's driveway like had happened to Sin's wife.

Cody was laughing with Jac right now, her son tugging on her shirt for attention. He looked just like his father, and his uncles.

Everywhere he turned were families that he knew. People he worked with and their children. They deserved to be kept *safe* while they did the jobs they had sworn to do.

"Because you have experience, education, and a proven PAVAD track record. There is nothing anyone can object to in your personnel jacket. Your dependable, too. I need you, Jones. If I am going to keep Barnes out. They've sent him here already. He'll be shadowing PAVAD for the next three weeks to see if *he* wants the position. Team Three."

Team Three—the team Jac most often worked with, when she wasn't assigned to the CPED. His skin crawled just thinking about it.

"He does." The sanctimonious asshole Barnes wanted nothing but a PAVAD position. Everyone who had ever encountered him since PAVAD began knew that. PAVAD appointments were golden in the bureau now since the fourth year had passed, and it had proven itself time and time again. "He's wanted PAVAD for years."

"I'm hoping we can find something on him in that time to put an end to this. Barnes will not be in my division. Not even as a file clerk. Not if I can help it."

Todd Barnes wasn't just sloppy and ingratiating. He thought his every breath should be gilded with gold. He was so arrogant and sure that he was a god amongst agents that he was going to prove dangerous one day. He was going to get someone hurt.

As a familiar redhead passed in his field of vision again, Max made a decision. Todd Barnes wasn't getting close to *her*.

Jac had his daughter in her arms, celebrating. A big blue stuffed dolphin was clutched in Emery's hands. She'd most likely wheedled a few extra tickets out of Jac.

Or Jac had won the toy for her. It was a shooting game, even if the weapon of choice was a water banana gun. Jac was the best markswoman he had ever seen. Carnival games were barely a challenge for that woman. The last thing anyone expected when they looked at her was her skill.

Jac was often assigned to team three, as the computer liaison, when needed. He'd be damned if he was going to leave her to work for Todd Barnes.

No way in hell. If he could do something to protect Jac then Max would do it. Max made a decision, one he hoped he wouldn't regret. "Six months?"

"Six months. Then we'll talk about something more grounded in the St. Louis area. Dan is talking about retiring soon to take care of his twins before they get school aged. He wants time with them. His position as coordinator will be open then. It'll be yours if you want it. No questions asked. Or we can work something else out somewhere."

"I want on Sin Lorcan's team. I…don't want what happened to Andy to happen to anyone else."

"Noted. And I'll see what I can do. In the meantime, I think there are a few beautiful redheads waiting for you." Ed nodded in Emery and Jac's direction.

Six months. He could juggle this for six months. He'd make a point of doubling the time he spent with Emery when he wasn't on the road for those six months. And he'd talk to Jac, see if she would mind keeping Emery sometimes.

He'd talk to Emery. Explain to her that if they did this for half a year, he'd be able to take a position where he would be home every night by six. She'd been wanting him home every night since she first realized that was how other families lived.

It would thrill her.

Six months was a small trade-off for that. It sounded like a pretty fair deal to Max. "I'll do it. Six months. Then I want in with Lorcan."

Ed's face relaxed, as he scooped his youngest into an affectionate hug. The little boy grinned at Max, a dead ringer for Ed's wife. He was in the same class as Emery. "You sure about this?"

"I am. But after that six months, I'm looking at moving into admin of some type, Ed. I have to do what's best for my daughter. And she needs me here now."

14

"Em's glad you're here." Max stepped closer to Jac as the crowd pressed into him. He put a hand on her shoulder, wanting to protect her from the press of bodies. Jac was perfectly capable of taking care of herself, and he knew that. He'd seen evidence of it time and time again. But he liked doing it. Liked how it made him feel. He just liked touching the woman. Every chance he could.

"I'm glad I'm here."

The sweater set she wore made her look soft and feminine. Deceptively so. He wanted to touch, see if the sweater, and the woman beneath it, were as soft as they looked.

Jac sure as hell made him forget everything but her sometimes—just by breathing. "I wasn't certain you'd be back from Masterson in time. I saw the weather report—and Miranda's post about you two being polar bears in Masterson."

"We borrowed those coats from her sisters. I told Emery I'd be here today. And I meant it. I will always keep my promises to her. I know what that means to her."

"I know." Max wanted to say more, but refrained. They were still on shaky ground between them. He didn't want to screw things up.

But he appreciated it; Emery was starting to struggle with the inevitable broken promises associated with his job. And the fact that her mother constantly broke every promise Pamela made to Emery. That hurt their daughter, each and every time.

But Jac—Jac had never broken a promise to Emery.

Or to Max. "I saw Miranda is back on the roster. How is she handling this latest?"

"She's ok. More frustrated and impatient with being on modified duty than anything. This broken arm is the first thing that's ever slowed that woman down. She's had two surgeries on it now. And I'm not sure she's fully dealt with what happened in Masterson."

Emery demanded their attention. They both turned to her. Max slipped his fingers around Jac's. Just for a moment.

He just wanted to touch her.

15

He was scheming. That man was definitely plotting against her.

Maddox James Jones was up to something, right up to his six-foot-four height.

She enjoyed the carnival, but Max...that man was most certainly up to something where she was concerned. Half the night, Jac had to evade his hand.

For some reason, he wanted to hold hands when they walked around.

Hers, specifically.

She wasn't even certain the man was aware of what he was doing. Jac certainly was—and she was far too old to be holding a guy's hand in a school gymnasium.

Most of the times when he touched her, he wasn't even *focused* on her. He was just there.

It seemed to be instinctive.

Seemed to be.

Jac wasn't putting anything past him. He was a master manipulator, after all. And there was something in those eyes of his that made her feel a little…hunted.

That was a little disconcerting.

At one point, she'd found herself between him and Emery, her hands trapped in theirs. They'd been laughing at her the whole time as they pretended to tug her in different directions. He'd teased his fingers up her inner wrist in a way that definitely wasn't platonic.

She'd looked up and seen Leina and Shannon smirking knowingly at her. But what did they know?

They'd just fallen for men they worked with; that was all.

He'd introduced her to other parents as Jac. That was it. Nothing about them not being related or anything, or them working together. Nothing. Just Jac.

Half the people had assumed she was Emery's mother. Max's wife.

When she'd looked at Max after the fourteenth time she'd been told she and Emery looked just alike—they didn't—he'd just grinned wickedly.

But she'd seen the shadows in his eyes. The director had said something that had upset Max. In a way that had him going quieter than normal. More pensive.

Max was a talker. He always had been. Talkative, outgoing, but reserved with personal information. He had friends, but he kept a bit of a wall between him and them, sometimes.

Except with her. Max had once been so different with her.

He bought her a funnel cake. Jac studied him as the powdered sugar got all over her mouth.

Max reached out, brushed his thumb over her bottom lip.

His eyes burned as he looked at her.

For a moment, the world narrowed to just her and Max, even though they were in a sea of people. Her mouth instantly went dry. Her skin tingled.

There was hunger in those eyes.

And not for funnel cake.

Jac just knew that.

Emery pulled them out of it, demanding Jac's attention.

But his touch felt different. Far less casual and a whole lot less platonic.

The next time he touched her, she *knew* the man was doing it deliberately.

Jac spent the rest of the evening trying to figure out exactly what that man was up to now.

16

Paul had watched Jaclyn Jones, comparing her to Rachel all evening long. He would admit it: his wife hadn't measured favorably. The redheaded woman was very attractive—and she knew her way around the elite.

Those parents had finally arrived an hour after the carnival had begun. Even the mayor had been there. Jaclyn had spoken with him for several moments, perfectly comfortable with someone of the mayor's stature.

When he'd been given the name of the computer analyst for the Complex Crimes Unit that he was supposed to dig up dirt on for the corporation's future use, two days after the carnival, he had just *known*.

It was a sign. A given. Meant to be.

He'd made love to Rachel that night while imagining *Jaclyn* in Rachel's place. It had been the best sex he'd had in a long, long time. Paul always had enjoyed fantasizing.

But now…he had to do what was needed to secure that money. Tuition for the winter term was due in two weeks. And he wanted to move Ava into kindergarten early. She was certainly clever enough, but it might take a sizeable donation to achieve. The school could be resistant because of her age, though there had been grade advancements made before.

He'd managed it with Olivia.

It took little to get himself inside the reasonably sized ranch-style home that Jaclyn owned. For an experienced FBI agent, Paul would have expected Jaclyn to have better security on her home.

Of course, Rachel had stated that it was a new place. Still, the system she had wasn't sophisticated. He was in within moments.

Perhaps she felt that she had nothing to worry about. That she was safe where she was. It was a nice neighborhood. Not as affluent as Paul's, of course. But he had worked hard to build his IT consultant business over the last five years, narrowing his market focus to only the more lucrative government contracts.

He was also thirteen years older than Jaclyn. Paul had had time to build on the company he had inherited from his brother.

Time Jaclyn hadn't had yet. At a year younger than Rachel, Jaclyn was young enough to still be building her profession. And her investment portfolio. She had a very healthy investment portfolio.

The woman didn't have to be working at all. That she did was just another contradiction that fascinated him.

Paul was routinely fascinated by the women he watched.

He had dug deeply into her human resources file. Learned all about her that he could. Even her psych evals had been in those files. It had started off with him looking for information to be used against her.

But that had changed within a few hours. He'd found himself becoming intrigued by her. She was a fascinating, brilliant woman. One that pulled him on every level. Her background as a diplomat's daughter was absolutely impeccable.

She had connections he once would have cut off his own arm to make.

Perhaps, he *should* encourage Rachel to cultivate a relationship with Jaclyn. It could be advantageous.

He stepped inside the midsized, midcentury ranch-style home confidently, just south of the city. If anyone was watching, it would look as if he belonged. A guest, perhaps.

The house smelled feminine. There had been flowers on the porch. Mums, he believed they were called. Rachel loved flowers as well. It was something feminine that she and Jaclyn shared.

Paul had to admit flowers were a nice touch to making a home.

Rachel...she didn't compare to Jaclyn now.

Rachel was questioning him too often about where the extra funds were coming from. She'd found files; files she knew he wasn't supposed to have.

Files on people *she* knew from Brynlock.

That could prove very dangerous. If she opened her mouth to the wrong people, it could ruin everything Paul was working toward. Or it could get them the wrong sort of attention.

He couldn't afford for her to blow this opportunity for him. For them, for the children. He would have to discuss that with her again —once he found out what he could about this new friend of hers.

The hallway had hardwood. It looked like someone had recently repaired it. He wondered if it had been Jaclyn or if she had paid to let strangers into her house to do it. Her hands were delicate; he couldn't see her holding power tools and doing manual labor. That was not something *her* type of woman engaged in.

His lips thinned.

He didn't like the idea of strange men anywhere near her. That could just be dangerous. The men who had paid him to dig into her were dangerous. Very, very dangerous.

The last agent he'd investigated had been killed. A bullet right between the eyes. Paul had sweated about that for a week until he'd realized no one had connected him to that man.

It was a deadly game Paul was playing now.

He'd seen Jaclyn again in the St. Louis field office two days after the carnival. He'd had a consult with the head of the new PAVAD: Cold Case department on what type of system they would be using. The man hadn't moved offices to the PAVAD building yet.

Paul was supposed to feel him out somehow. He was to find out how the other man felt about PAVAD—and what had happened to him the night he had been shot in his own apartment.

Paul hadn't gathered the courage to ask the man *that*.

Dr. Knight was one terrifying bastard. The people who were paying Paul probably didn't realize that.

But the men who had hired him wanted Dr. Knight, too.

Paul wasn't certain why Jaclyn had been there that day. She'd had a stack of files in her hands. Jaclyn had been laughing with another, taller redheaded young woman who had an equally large stack of files.

He had had a hard time not staring that day. Not leaving Dr. Knight standing and just going after Jaclyn.

Just to talk to her.

He wanted to get close enough to talk to her. To have her attention on him. At least for a few moments. He was only human. A man, after all. Jaclyn Jones was a beautiful, cultured, sophisticated woman.

He had always wished for a woman like that. Rachel was as close as he had ever gotten. But even she…had faults.

Paul was faithful to Rachel, and he would remain so. He had little respect for men who cheated on the wives dependent on them. That wasn't the type of man Paul was, but Paul could fantasize about other women as often as he wanted.

When he was thinking about her, the stress he felt from trying to make all of *this* work just somehow melted away. Paul didn't have much time, though he had checked the PAVAD database to find her exact location.

Jaclyn and her team would be in Vermont at least through the next day. The killer they were chasing hadn't yet been identified, as far as Paul knew. He would take his time. Learn everything he could about her. What she liked, what she didn't.

Who she loved.

He started with the half-dozen photos she had spread around the room. Six photos.

There was a young, dark-haired woman who greatly resembled Jaclyn. Her sister, most likely. Beautiful, in the same classic way. Jaclyn's personnel file had referenced another woman in the division as being a relative.

The woman he vaguely recalled seeing at the FBI building was in another photo with Jaclyn. Tall, statuesque, redheaded. A good friend, possibly. That same woman was in a group photo with Jaclyn and a bunch of other attractive young women, surrounding an older lady.

The older woman was patting Jaclyn's hand where it rested on her shoulder. They were in front of a building that had a sign: *The Talley Inn*. He took a photo of it with his own phone. He would find out exactly who they were—and what connection they had to Jaclyn.

He was being paid for information, after all.

The next photograph was of the Jones child from at least a few years ago. Emery, he believed her name was.

A beautiful girl. She had her arms wrapped around Jaclyn's neck from behind. They were both smiling fully at the camera. The sun shone through their red hair, though their hair was of differing shades.

He wondered who had taken that photograph. What relationship the photographer had with Jaclyn.

It had most likely been Emery's father. Max Jones. That made the most sense, and they were close. That man could prove a problem. Paul had dug through his file, too.

The next two photographs were older. Jaclyn's mother, he suspected. She held a small girl in her arms whom he knew was Jaclyn. The hair and smile were very distinctive. She had been a classically beautiful child who had grown into a perfectly beautiful woman. Her mother had been a senator's daughter, he believed. Her class and sophistication shown through the faded print.

He scanned each photograph with his phone. Information was golden, after all.

The last photograph was of Jaclyn, her sister, and a few women he recognized from PAVAD. Her friends. The PAVAD building was visible in the distance.

Interesting.

He saw no indication she had many connections outside of the FBI. Just those women at the inn.

Perhaps on his next trip, he would check out the Talley Inn. Once he figured out where it was, and her connection.

He'd slipped his shoes off at the door. He buried his toes in the rose carpet that was obviously new in the living room. She should have gone with the more luxurious hardwood like she had in the hallway. Rose was a ridiculously feminine color for carpeting. Very impractical.

But then again, Jaclyn Jones was an exceptionally feminine woman.

Paul wasn't too thrilled that she had been targeted, though.

Perhaps he could misdirect them somehow. They trusted him somewhat. He had proven his worth to them several weeks ago. For a very hefty sum.

He could make it clear there was nothing on Jaclyn that they would ever be able to use. He had a very specific list of things they were looking for, after all. He could play the gallant, even if she never knew. Rescue her, much like he had Rachel.

He could do that—but if that pissed them off, he could lose this contract. His most lucrative contract.

Paul wasn't ready to do that. Not with Olivia and Ava's upbringing to consider. Jaclyn would be but a small price to pay for that.

He reclined on her bed. Smelled the light floral scent on her pillow. Paul uncapped her shampoo and just breathed it in for a long while. Fantasizing.

He would stop at the store on his way home, buy the same brand for Rachel. That would have to do for now. He'd just close his eyes and imagine…

Rachel was a poor warm-up for being with a woman like Jaclyn.

Before he left, he made certain every sign of his presence was erased. She was an excellent agent, with more than a dozen notes of recognition in her file.

It wouldn't pay to be stupid about things.

He never had been stupid before. Rash, careless, impulsive—once or twice.

Paul had learned from past mistakes.

Paul had a plan to create. Part of success was taking time to always plan properly. It would just be a matter of time until he had her right where he wanted her.

But first…he had other things he had to take care of now.

17

JAC WAS GREETED WITH THE NEWS THAT MAX WAS TAKING THE CCU2 position when she stepped into the PAVAD building a week after Emery's school carnival, a day after she made it back from Vermont.

Miranda delighted in telling her. She always had been the one to go to for finding out internal gossip, although Miranda was never malicious about it. And it was just between her and Jac. "Apparently, our hot and handsome Dr. Jones will be bouncing from Team Five to Team Two in three days."

"What about Malachi? Where is he going?" Jac asked, placing her bag on the desk that was pushed up next to Miranda's with just a partition to separate them. They had desks in the CCU bullpen, but were routinely still assigned to working on the CEPD team when needed. They had their own desks there, too.

Miranda liked to joke that they were the vagabonds of PAVAD.

PAVAD had a habit of shuffling agents around when needed. Jac and Miranda more than most. They were adaptable.

Jac had been nervous of that at first, but now that she was more seasoned, she understood the reasoning behind it. And fully agreed with it. She and Miranda were the floaters—going between the Child Exploitation Prevention Division and the CCU.

At any one time, the director of the CCU could grab an agent or two from each team and create a fast, mobile, and *effective* extra team to send out where needed. Officially, there were five full six-member teams in the CCU. But PAVAD teams operated efficiently with as little as four agents working together at a time. The units were designed that way.

Two additional teams could form in an instant, teams that had agents who had worked together before time and time again. Sometimes, the expertise of the CEPD was needed as part of the CCU.

It was a rather clever setup that she had rarely seen in the FBI before. But it worked. Fortunately for Jac, she liked most of the people in the CCU and CPED and didn't mind working with any of them.

"Mal's moving into heading up the entire psychological analysis department. That new department they are talking about expanding. Once they get enough profilers to fill it. More of Director Ed shuffling the cards, I think." Miranda shot Jac a significant look. One that said Miranda was going to meddle again. The woman had a problem—a real problem—when it came to trying to direct her friends' lives. Probably from being the oldest of her siblings and cousins. Since they were all up in Wyoming, she had somehow transferred that habit to her closest friends. Top of that list was Jac. "I think you should take the exam with me. We can both go around head-shrinking people. Official profilers. It'll be fun. And we won't have to hop all around the country nearly as much—we'd have time to shoe shop and get actual manicures done. We could go to the border collie rescue. Get us some puppies. Have puppy playdates and use the same puppy day care. Find a gorgeous set of brothers *outside* of PAVAD to take us on walks and to the park."

"Are you talking about men? Or puppies?"

"Either. Both, for that matter. Two gorgeous brothers with

puppies? We use our puppies to meet hot, handsome, single veterinarians who don't have to worry about catching bad guys?"

"You really need to get out more, Randi."

Miranda had mentioned taking the profilers' exam before, and Jac had given it serious consideration. But her educational background was in computer software design. Maybe someday, after she'd spent a few more years on the job. She could do profiling if she had to—and she had, with Max as a supervisor—but she wasn't certain she could pass the rigorous exam involved. Not yet. "I'm not sure I'd pass."

"I have no doubt that you would. You're one of the best I know at understanding how people think. And predicting how they will behave. You have half the profilers in this building beat. We both know that. So do Malachi, Hellbrook, and Sebastian, for that matter. Your problem is a lack of confidence. And the fact that you think you're invisible and that no one sees you. Or that you'll never live up to expectations. Yours...or anyone else's."

Jac couldn't refute that. Not really. Miranda knew her strengths and weaknesses just like Jac knew Miranda's. Sometimes, Miranda got so convinced she was right about something that she missed what was staring her directly in the face.

That was going to cause Miranda trouble someday—Jac just knew it.

Jac didn't feel quite as confident in her profiling skills as Miranda was in her own. Put a computer in Jac's hand and she could do what needed to be done. Put a rifle in her hand—and the same thing.

Competitive shooting in college in Virginia had gained her notice by Ed Dennis himself.

She'd done what she had to do not even four months ago when her friend Shannon had been endangered by a hired killer. Jac still relived that moment in her sleep. She could still see that man's eyes as he'd died. She'd go to her grave knowing she'd put him in his.

But predicting how people would behave in extreme emotional circumstances? She just didn't trust herself in that regard. She didn't think she'd ever be able to predict that. "I'm not so sure about that. But I'm happy for Max. He'll be a good leader."

"No doubt about that." Miranda leaned forward. "And the best part? The other agent up for the position was none other than Todd Barnes. I heard he's not too happy Max got it and not him."

Jac just stared. She'd seen the man walking around PAVAD earlier, but she'd assumed the ones stuck with him in Texas had just been using him as a courier again. From what she'd heard before, Todd Barnes was sent just about everywhere he could be—so no one truly had to deal with him full-time. "Barnes? Seriously? He's not PAVAD material. And definitely not CCU."

PAVAD had a very definite structure. Each division worked efficiently together. They were all parts of the cog.

Except the CCU. The CCU was the most unique division in bureau history. The people who worked PAVAD, who worked the CCU specifically, they were the FBI's best. Everyone knew that, and the last four years had just proven that. A jerk like Todd Barnes had no business being there. *Ever.*

"That's what everyone else is saying, too. I guess we're just going to have to watch what happens. Anyway, Barnes is going to be our Max's problem for now."

No kidding.

The last thing Max needed was Todd Barnes screwing everything up just as he was taking the helm of his team. If he was a team leader, she'd inevitably end up working for him at some point. That was the nature of PAVAD. "I'm glad for Max. He deserves this."

Max worked hard and took promotions and success as they came his way, but she didn't think he had burning passions that urged him on. Max wasn't the type to claw himself to the top, pushing others out of his way. No.

He was far better suited to being part of a team than a man with ultimate power. He could lead. And he could lead well. He was quick, intelligent, fair…

A CCU team-leader position was perfect for him.

He'd worked hard, and had earned it. The pride she felt in that didn't surprise her at all.

Pre-superkiss, Jac would have willingly volunteered to work on any team he ran. She'd trust Max with her life—in a heartbeat. More importantly, she'd trust Max with Miranda and Nat's. Unconditionally.

Unfortunately, she no longer trusted the man with her virtue. Not after the carnival.

She hadn't even told Miranda that yet, though. Maybe she was imagining it. It had just been a few casual touches. A few hot looks. Maybe. She could be reading more into it than was there. Maybe because of the Kiss-That-Never-Should-Have-Been.

Jac didn't know anymore. She never had been very good at the whole male/female kind of thing. Max had thrown everything into a tailspin with those lips of his. By the time she'd recovered enough to think, the man had hightailed it out of there.

"Yes, he does. And you can congratulate him at Emery's birthday party tomorrow, too. Better yet, send Emery home with a little buddy, get Max naked, and cover that impressive chest of his with birthday cake and icing. Then enjoy the snack."

Miranda leveled a smirk in her direction. Jac wanted to throw something at the other woman. She and Miranda had met at Quantico, during their training days and had taken the appointments to St. Louis together. They'd ended up on the same team within months, often rooming together on cases, until Miranda had become the one person—other than Max—that she absolutely trusted.

She'd been Jac's best friend for more than five years now. "You going?"

Miranda shook her head. "I can't. I'm flying up to Masterson for Meyra's birthday. I've not missed one yet. I'll only be up there for a day, then back here the next. She and Emery share a birthdate. She makes a bigger deal out of birthdays than Max's kid. I dropped off my present for Emery yesterday."

"Then I guess I'll go by myself." She already had gifts picked out and wrapped. She hadn't missed Emery's birthday since she'd met Max's daughter. She was going to have to talk to Max first.

It was time to clear the air, make everything as right as it was going to get. So they could both move on. This had gone on long enough. She couldn't keep wondering what that man was up to.

She'd go nuts, just waiting for him to do something else. Or worse—get the shivers every time his skin brushed hers.

There was just enough time before the Monday morning briefing to confront that man in his brand-new office.

She stood.

Miranda looked at her. "Going somewhere?"

"Yes. I'm going to go talk to Max." Get some answers. Figure out what that man had going on in that complicated head of his.

"Good. I figured you be the one to make the first move."

"Why me?"

Miranda shot her wicked smile. "Simple. You terrify that man far more than he does you. Right down to his toes. Go get him. I'll let Seb know you'll join us in the conference room as soon as you can."

18

Jac had never been the type of woman to let unpleasant tasks build up. She'd learned the hard way years ago to face problems head on.

Maddox James Jones was a big problem.

Six foot four and a half, two hundred eighty-five pounds of strong, muscled, beautiful male...problem.

She wasn't even certain what had happened to turn things between them sideways that day. They'd been in a small country motel in Arkansas after they'd spent hours searching for Shannon. They'd been arguing—something that had happened more than a few times in five years—then his hands had been on her.

Max had lifted her off her feet, and somehow, they'd been kissing.

Really kissing. Hotter than she'd ever kissed anyone before.

She'd analyzed that moment a thousand times in her head since then—she still wasn't certain who had moved first. His arms had felt so strong around her. Perfect. Familiar yet exciting at the same time. Trustworthy. At the heart of everything, she had trusted Max to never hurt her.

She'd buried her fingers in his hair and kissed that man right back.

And then he'd practically dropped her. To compound the insult, he'd done a complete skitter to the hills, like his boxer shorts were on fire. Leaving her staring at the smoke he'd left in his wake.

Well, she'd corner him in his office now. He couldn't get away from her there. Enough was enough.

What had happened had apparently given that man ideas—Max could be slow to act on something when he was unsure of the results. Or nervous. At least in his personal life. She'd seen it before.

But once he made up his mind, the man was like a hurricane.

It was time to deal with him so she'd stop feeling like the man's prey.

At heart, Max was a hunter, after all.

Mostly, he hunted the bad guys. Now, she was afraid he was hunting her.

Miranda was irritatingly right most of the time. It drove Jac nuts nine times out of ten. But she wouldn't have her friend any other way.

Jac knocked on the door to the office that now bore the name *Dr. Maddox Jones, CCU2* on the doorplate. A rush of pride in what he'd accomplished hit her and had her smiling as she knocked on the window to the office next. The man had worked hard—he deserved every bit of recognition he got.

He'd seen her.

He wasn't escaping her now.

19

MAX LOOKED UP AND WAVED HER IN BEFORE HE STOPPED TO THINK about what she could possibly want from him. "Hey."

"Nice place you've got yourself here. Love how you've decorated."

He snorted. He had a desk and a chair and a small loveseat crammed across from the desk, for the rare instances he'd have consults or interviews in his office. And a lamp. There was a lamp behind the desk. That was it. The walls were a utilitarian light gray. The window was eighteen inches in height and six feet long. That was it. Austere didn't even begin to describe it. "It's the decorator's year off."

"And you've only been in here for what? Two days?"

"One. I took yesterday off to spend with Em. Let her know there may be a few changes over the next six months."

"Why six?"

He hesitated. The director had made it clear he wasn't to breathe a word about the temporary nature of his position. Even to those he trusted. To the people in Washington trying to yank Ed's strings, Max had to appear fully entrenched and not going anywhere.

But he had never lied to Jac before. "That's about how long I think it'll take for the adjustment to happen. What can I do for you today?"

There was once a time when he wouldn't have even asked. She would have come in and sunk to the sofa, and he would have immediately *known* what she wanted because they were that attuned to each other.

He missed that. Max was still trying to find a way to get that back.

As well as get her where he ultimately wanted her.

Strategy was half the battle, but as well as he knew this woman, Max had no clue what the best tactics would be to convince her to take that leap with him.

Not as hesitant as Jac was when it came to men.

But that was something for *off* the clock. Not when she was right there in his office, looking all prissy and buttoned up and proper.

He'd always loved it when she looked like that. He loved flustering her to put red in her cheeks, and get her eyes to snap green fire at him.

"Emery's party." She crossed her arms over her chest, a sure sign she was feeling nervous. Then her green eyes locked on his. "I've not missed one of Em's birthday parties since we met. And I made her a promise I'd be there. I don't want it to be awkward between us. So I need to know what's going on in that head of yours. What are you planning?"

"What do you mean? It's a kid's party, with thirty other kids invited." He tried to look as innocent as possible. But Jac always had seen through him.

Jac uncrossed her arms then hopped up to sit on his desk, as she pulled in a deep breath. She stared at him. "Shut the door."

"Yes, ma'am." He did what she instructed, mostly out of curiosity. Jac was in confrontation mode—something that was a rare occurrence. She was about to read him the riot act. He bit back a smile. He loved this woman, every bit of her. "So...talk."

"Let me boil it down for you. We argued. We kissed. We took a big break from each other, one that got us noticed around here, by the way. Everyone's speculating it's a lovers' spat. Which is embarrassing. Now, we have to fix all of that. Both for professional reasons and because...I miss your kid, Jones. She's a big part of my life; we both know that. I demand visitation rights. I think you've avoided me long enough. We'll just have to put that kiss behind us—and you can keep your man paws to yourself, if that's what you're plotting. So whatever you are planning—stop."

"Man paws? That one of Miranda's phrases?"

She looked so...feminine...sitting on his desk like that. If he stepped closer, he could wrap his hands around her knees and pull her closer. Lean her back on the desk and just kiss the hell out of that sweet mouth again. Maybe pop open a few buttons, see what kind of silk there was beneath.

He considered it; Max actually considered it.

There were blinds on the door.

If he was the kind of man to kiss a woman while on the clock, he would do just that. Tangle his hands in that red hair, disturb the prissy little braid she had it in. Get his hands on her like he really wanted. Looking at her, he knew the truth.

Jac had no clue how he actually felt about her. Not a clue.

"Visitation rights? I'm not sure it works that way. Besides, you keep her too many times and she might just want to stay. She loves you."

Jac smirked at him and nodded. "Yes, visitation rights. For slumber parties and trips to the mall, and movie theaters and cooking classes and shoe shopping. Those sorts of things."

All things Emery loved. Things that terrified Max to his own size thirteens. Maybe he'd give Jac these visitation rights—provided he was included with her and his daughter. The two females he loved the most. "And how do you suggest we do that?"

"We stop avoiding one another? Stop letting it feel so awkward when we're together. So that we're not so aware of each other when we are together? That would be a good place to start. It was just one kiss, you know. Nothing earth shattering. Not even the least bit memorable." She shot him a snarky look from green eyes. Max snorted. "Not even the last kiss I've had this year, by the way."

It had sure shattered *his* earth. Changed everything about his world in an instant.

"We haven't exactly been avoiding each other. Our schedules just haven't overlapped much. Except for Masterson. Who have you kissed?" Now, he had images of her wrapped up in another man's arms. Jealousy and fury warred until he got himself in control.

She was free to kiss whoever she wanted.

For now.

They'd probably been in the same room two dozen times since the original argument. And that night. Most of those two dozen had been on their case in Masterson.

When they had been in the same room it was all about work. It had been driving him crazy—seeing her, not being able to touch her the way he wanted.

Wanting Jac, but not having her.

He never would have imagined feeling this way about her even a year ago.

Or maybe he'd just been a stupid idiot with blinders on. Maybe he'd wanted her for a good long while.

Hellbrook had pointed that out to him when he'd first applied for the transfer the day after the kiss. Hellbrook had claimed he was speaking from experience. He'd suggested that Max hadn't let his attraction for Jac surface before now because he had been hurting over Pamela and what had happened with her when he'd first met Jac.

Hellbrook thought Max had most likely suppressed how he felt for Jac as a form of self-preservation. They'd built a comfortable relationship between them after that. Until that comfort became the status quo.

Hellbrook and his wife, Georgia, had hated each other on sight. That was the exact opposite of Max and Jac.

Or maybe Hellbrook had been right. Max had used friendship to hide what he was really feeling because he hadn't been emotionally ready to let those feelings *in*.

Not where a woman was concerned. Any woman.

"You have been avoiding me even when I am standing right next to you." There went the arms again. Right under her small breasts.

He found that...distracting.

He'd spent the last eleven weeks and six days dreaming about what her breasts would look like, late at night when he'd wake in a strange hotel room and *wish* she was in the room right next door.

To be honest with himself, he'd wished she was in his bed every time he woke. Every single time. The things he'd imagined the two of them doing...

That was driving him crazy. "I...hell, Jac...what was I supposed to say?"

"Come on. What happened wasn't that big of a deal. Or at least, it shouldn't be." She shot him a smirk. One that had his gut heating. Jac knew she had him on the hook, and she was feeling confident. She liked having him twisting right now. "You're not the first guy I've kissed. First one I've sent running for the hills, though."

"It wasn't about the kiss." The words slipped out before Max could stop them.

"Then what was it about?"

"*Change.*" He was never going to lie to her about it. He owed them both that honesty. He'd rehearsed this speech a thousand times since then. "In that moment, I saw my whole world change. And I panicked."

"No kidding. You ran like your pants were on fire."

"And I hurt you in the middle of it. That was the last thing I wanted to do. I just...Pamela had asked me to consider reconciling that weekend. And I was trying to figure out how to tell her no without jamming a wedge between her and Emery. You know how rocky it's been between them lately. I had to let her down easy, without her going off the rails and hurting Emery somehow. You...

you have always been my constant and to have that changing, too…I panicked. Flat out panicked. And ran. I'm not proud of it. Hell, it's one of the few times in my life I've ever run from anything like that."

She nodded. She'd witnessed firsthand some of the problems between him and Pamela.

"When you came at me over your sister…arguing with you, I just sort of flashed back to arguing with Pamela. I lost control. And I'm sorry for that. I've regretted it a million times since that night."

"You can't control everything. We both know that. That lesson is one we both have in common—that's for sure." Jac leveled a look at him, still perched on the edge of his desk. "Why didn't you just talk to me? Instead, you were gone the next day. Off the team. Even though we've argued before."

"Hell, I panicked. Made a split-second decision when Hellbrook asked me to consider switching teams when he needed someone to fill an available spot. Temporarily. It was supposed to be temporary reassignment. I thought some distance between us would somehow fix what I felt was happening. Stupid, and I've regretted it. To some extent. I never intended this to be a permanent change, but that's the way it's happening. I just needed some distance—before I screwed everything up between us. Instead, I nearly did all that anyway by running."

"And you probably wouldn't be in here if you hadn't run like a rabbit. At least not as quickly. With Al going on maternity leave again and everything. So it's worked out well…for you."

She was going to keep sticking that knife in, wasn't she? Needling him because she knew she had him.

Jac only did that with him. He'd long thought it was because she trusted him. Felt safe enough with him to make him squirm when she could. Or she had. Once. He wanted her to tease him again—just not at this particular moment. "I did. It took me a few weeks to get Pamela straightened out. And I…"

"Put what happened between us on the back burner." She hopped off his desk and just stood there in the middle of *his* office.

He didn't want walls between them. There wasn't any other way to put it. "I hurt you. I am so damned sorry for that. By the time I resurfaced, it was too late. You were in Tallahassee, I think."

"That was a few weeks before Masterson. You could have sent an email. Even a carrier pigeon."

"And said what? Sorry I acted like an asshole after the best damned kiss of my life?"

Heat hit her cheeks. She glanced away.

Max studied her face as he realized the truth. She was unsure because of the *kiss*.

Of course, she was; Jac wasn't extremely experienced. She'd never told him that, but Max knew.

"That would have been a good place to start. Instead, you just dropped me like a rock and left me hanging. I would have understood. If you had bothered to trust me." She came close enough he could smell the shampoo she favored. "We've worked together over five years, been good friends for at least three of those years. You should have trusted me to know that I would never do anything to hurt *you*."

Max wanted to close his eyes and just breathe her in. That's when her words registered. She was right; he hadn't trusted her at all. "Jac..."

"Just...tell Emery I'll be there. I wouldn't miss it for the world. And there is no way that I will ever break a promise to her. I know what it means to her for someone to keep their word. Trust...it's the most important thing there is."

She darted out of his office as quickly as she had come in. Leaving him staring at her like an idiot. Damn it. He had hurt her through his careless actions all those weeks ago.

Deeper than he had realized.

Making things right between them was going to be harder than he'd thought. Convincing her to give him a chance for something more with her was going to be even more difficult than that.

It was a definite uphill battle.

Especially with PAVAD in between them, demanding so much of their souls.

He needed a plan. A stronger strategy. Something.

Max sank into his chair and sat there for a long time, just trying to think. He'd broken her trust. Now, he had to find a way to earn it back.

20

JAC TOOK THE LONG WAY TO THE MULTIPURPOSE ROOM WHERE THE
Monday morning briefings were held. Max's words were replaying
in her head now. No wonder he'd overreacted to one simple kiss.

Pamela had nearly destroyed Max, just before Jac had met him.
Pamela had left him for her career and because she'd hated being a
mother. Pamela had told Jac once that she had flat out despised the
whole process of dealing with an infant on daily basis.

They'd even had a live-in nanny at that point. It hadn't been
enough. Pamela loved Emery in her own way, but there was some
significant abuse in Pamela's past that made her not want to be a
full-time parent. Or even a part-time one.

It was probably for the best.

Because she did love her daughter, she'd chosen not to be an
active part of Emery's life. Pamela paid child support and for
Emery's tuition to the best school in the city, and that was about it.

Pamela visited from Chicago a few times a year. Sometimes.
Following through on her promises to Emery was not something
Pamela considered important. At all. Jac had always known that,

from the moment she had first met the statuesque blonde who worked in corporate law in Chicago.

Pamela and Max had been divorced for two years by the time Jac had transferred to St. Louis. That the other woman had wanted to reconcile with Max shocked Jac to her toes. Pamela had barely seemed interested in him at all.

She'd mostly treated him like a slightly dimwitted younger brother.

It had infuriated Jac every time.

It had most likely been a spur-of-the-moment thing for Pamela. She was rather mercurial. Most likely, she'd seen what she'd given up and was feeling broken that day.

Max's second post after coming out of the academy was St. Louis. He'd been stationed in Illinois before. He'd gotten a later start at the academy than Jac had. He'd finished a PhD degree in sociology before entering law school, where he'd met Pamela.

Max was as brilliant as they came, and a phenomenal profiler—but when it came to interactions with women, he was completely clueless. Jac had observed that a time or million herself.

He'd dated other women since Jac had met him, quite a few. There had been one woman named LeeAnn who had taken a particular dislike to Jac and had tried to poison Emery against her repeatedly.

Who they were sleeping with—if anyone—was very high on that do-not-discuss list for both of them.

She hadn't given much thought to Max's love life before. Those were just details they hadn't ever shared. She hadn't exactly lived chastely over the past five years. There had been two men that she'd felt comfortable enough to have slept with since coming to St. Louis.

She hadn't known he'd been having trouble with Pamela again. Usually, he talked to her about his ex. They tried to figure out what was motivating Pamela together. It wasn't easy. Pamela was one of the most complicated women Jac had ever met, and profiling her had never been easy.

It was going to take time for her to think her way through that. Time she just didn't have now.

21

SOMETHING HAD DEFINITELY HAPPENED BETWEEN THE WARRING JONES and Jones. Miranda had been waiting for that since about the moment Jac and Max had met. Miranda had been there that day—she'd practically been singed by the sparks.

She wasn't certain she believed in the idea of soul mates. Miranda liked to think she was more a woman of study and science, but there were some people who just seemed to *fit* together.

Max and Jac were two of those people. Something about the way they looked at each other, and the way they almost seemed to breathe for each other. The way they had unconsciously just made each other more whole.

The way they just seemed to fit together. They had acted like an old married couple almost from the first week they'd met. It wasn't the common last name that made strangers assume Jac and Max were together—though the two both misunderstood that. It was far more than that. It was the way they were attuned to each other. She doubted anyone had missed it.

Except Max and Jac, that was.

It was obvious when someone saw them together.

Miranda had been trying to think of a way to get the two of *them* to stop being so stubborn and admit it to themselves.

Before they kept hurting each other.

The two of them belonged together. She just had no idea how to make them see that.

The briefing started. The director did a rundown of everything that had happened over the last week, including introducing Max as the head of team two.

As everyone clapped, some just politely, she looked up.

Her eyes met washed out blue ones from almost clear across the conference room.

Todd Barnes sat at a table all by himself, a scowl on his face. He wasn't even making an attempt to hide how he felt. Several people were shooting glances his way.

None of them happy. She certainly wasn't; she knew a few things about him from friends who'd unfortunately run up against him before. Todd Barnes was trouble. For everyone who got anywhere near him. He had no business anywhere near PAVAD. None at all.

This wasn't going to be good. She just knew it.

22

Paul had screwed up. Again.

Ruined everything.

Paul had screwed up. He never should have confronted Rachel after the carnival that night. Never should have let it slip what he was doing. She had never looked at him with quite that look of disappointment in her eyes. He still remembered that look even now, weeks later.

To his surprise, it still mattered what Rachel thought of him. He hadn't realized that was still true.

Perhaps he had gotten too caught up in trying to build his empire that he had overlooked how his choices would appear to her.

It had stung, seeing her disappointment.

Knowing he had failed her. She had looked up to him for what he had accomplished for her and the girls.

Paul shouldn't have failed. He was too good for that.

She was to see him as the perfect man, the provider, the protector. Everything that a good husband was supposed to be.

Instead, she'd looked at him like *that*.

He had reassured her that what he was doing wasn't illegal. Paul knew she hadn't believed him, though.

That had been reaffirmed when he'd asked if she'd told anyone, any of her friends from Brynlock, what he had been doing. He hadn't mentioned anyone from the bureau specifically, but Rachel had *known* who Paul had meant.

Suspicion had been written all over her. Suspicion and mistrust.

There had to be a way to fix that, because there was no way in hell she was going to ruin this for him. For *them.*

The girls' futures depended on what he could do for them now.

He hoped he'd gotten through to her; she knew finances were sometimes tight. Especially with tuition and her needing a new car.

He'd been paid for his special services again just yesterday. He and Rachel were going to look at SUVs tomorrow; he'd driven through the Brynlock carpool lane yesterday to see what makes and models Brynlock parents seemed to prefer.

Paul was doing his *best.*

He was trying his best. Rachel needed to understand that.

He was doing what he had to in order to succeed.

She had no right to question him on those types of decisions. Providing was *his* job. However he chose to make that happen.

23

Ed Dennis stared at the files spread out in front of him. Andy Anderson's face stared back. He had nothing. They'd found nothing, in weeks. Thanksgiving had come and gone. Christmas was right around the corner.

Ed was starting to lose hope.

Even the best he had hadn't come up with anything. Nothing more than a code no one had broken yet.

The hit on Andy was just too well organized. Professional. And with the destruction of evidence, almost impossible to trace. Ed was terrified Andy had been just the beginning.

Even the memory cards they had had revealed nothing more than gibberish.

Someone out there could damned well be hunting Ed's people.

"You're worrying," a soft, feminine voice said from behind him. Ed turned. There she was. The most beautiful woman in his world. "What is it?"

"Rumors. Gossip. A few things I've heard from friends in Washington."

Marianna put her skinny arms around him. She was a tall

woman, but thin. He ran a hand down her back absently as he pulled her into his lap for a moment. Sometimes, a touch from his wife was all it took to remind him of what he was doing.

Why he hadn't retired yet.

Retirement sounded damned good now. He could do what his friend Dan intended after his own upcoming retirement—be a stay-at-home dad. Enjoy the time with the boys, and his granddaughter. "What are you doing today?"

"Taking the younger three and Matthew and Evalyn to Dr. Jones's. Emery has invited them all to her party. I think Jamie wants to go. I'm not so sure about the other three. Except for the cake and ice cream."

James, one of their younger twins, was extremely sports oriented. He and Emery Jones had become good friends playing soccer recently. "Be careful."

"I will."

He had doubled the number of guards on his family since Andy's murder.

His children, those beautiful, wonderful boys he had been blessed to love after marrying their mother, would go to a birthday party guarded by four armed men.

To the boys, that had become normal. To Ed, it would never be.

To lose her or one of the boys or Georgia and her two children, even his pain-in-the-ass son-in-law, to lose one of them would devastate him. Completely.

"Ed?" Marianna said, grabbing the four younger boys' coats— they had Matthew and Evalyn for the weekend again. "Try to relax for the day. The rest of the boys are around. Try to forget that you have the entire PAVAD on your shoulders. At least for a few hours, ok?"

Ed nodded. "I'll try."

"Do more than try. You're starting to worry me." Marianna had the most intense blue eyes he had ever seen. Blue all seven of her boys had inherited. Blue that was now worried—for him.

That worry hadn't left her eyes since the explosion.

"Once we have the people responsible for threatening the division, I will." Ed kissed her one more time. When he pulled back, he looked into her eyes again. "You and me, we'll take the boys and go away for a while. During school break. While we still have the older boys here. We'll see about getting Georgia and the rest of them to go with us. We'll just pretend PAVAD doesn't exist for a while."

She touched the scar at his temple that was still fresh. The hair was just now starting to grow around it a fraction. Neither had missed how close he had come to serious injury.

He hated the worry in those blue, blue eyes. The fear.

Marianna had lived with enough fear to last a lifetime.

Ed waited until his family was on their way and grabbed his phone. He had the printouts from those memory cards here. He needed someone else to take a look at them. From what he knew of his agents, the list of those who could crack such a code was slim. There was one name at the top of his list now.

24

JAC PULLED INTO MAX'S DRIVEWAY TEN MINUTES AFTER THE PARTY HAD started. She'd just finished up a phone consult with Ed Dennis.

The call had delayed her, and had her consumed with confusion.

She'd been told to report to Max that the director wanted *her* on something Max had found. A code.

No one but she and Max were to know she was working on it— and Sin Lorcan.

She pulled into the spot closest to the road. Most of the vehicles far eclipsed her little SUV. No surprise. The properties Max owned and rented out provided a steady amount of passive income for him and his daughter.

Max and Emery were perfectly at home in this neighborhood.

It was an infinitely more comfortable home than the wealthy show palace where she and Nat had been forced to grow up.

She had enough money in her bank account; she could have bought a house here, too. She'd considered it—until the kiss.

The trust she'd inherited from her mother when she'd turned twenty-five ensured that she wouldn't have to worry about living expenses. She made a good yearly salary from PAVAD. Her house had been a cash purchase, as had the upgrades she'd made.

She probably could afford to have bought Max's house, too. Outright. The kind of people her stepfather had forced her to interact with were far different from the upper-middle-class ones she would most likely find inside Max's home.

They were real people. Jac sometimes struggled to find ways to connect with *real* people.

Awkward. That was the word.

She could fake her way through a state function in Washington, DC, but a kid's birthday party made her feel like a fish out of water sometimes. Like she was on the outside just looking in.

Even Emery's.

Jac clutched the big box in her arms tightly, as she pushed open the door.

In a child's scrawl in dark-purple crayon on pink construction paper was a welcome sign bidding people to enter without the need to knock.

Emery. That child had gone a bit overboard with glitter and what looked to be scratch-n-sniff stickers.

Jac placed the gifts on the foyer table with all the others.

Then she turned as someone yelled her name. Emery had spotted her. "Jac!"

The little girl left her friends and came running. Jac laughed, all nerves instantly forgotten.

It was about this kid. Always.

Her arms wrapped around Emery. "You've gotten taller. I think you'll be as tall as your dad by next month."

"Silly. Daddy says I can sign up for spring soccer this week!"

"That's great, sweetheart. I want a copy of your game schedule, ok?" She'd watched as many of Emery's softball and soccer and swim meets and basketball games as she possibly could. No matter what happened between her and Max, Jac had no intention of not continuing that. Unless he flat out told her to stay away.

But she didn't see him doing that. Not to Emery.

Or to her, for that matter.

"Ok. I've missed you. You stayed away too long."

Jac went down to eye level with Emery. She didn't have to go far. Emery *had* gotten taller. "I would have been here if I could. But your dad and I aren't on the same team any longer. They sent me to Vermont for six days, kiddo. There was snow taller than me. I thought I was going to turn into a snow-woman before it was done."

A pout hit the pretty little face. "That's what Daddy said, too. But maybe you can come over even when Daddy isn't here? We can do things. Or you can be on Daddy's team again."

"I'll talk to your dad. See what he thinks about that. And if he says it's ok, I have that purple room in my house ready for you anytime. You can help me decorate it. Give me another hug. I've missed you bunches this week. Then…I think your guests from school need you now."

"Promise you won't leave?" There was uncertainty in the big blue eyes. Jac hugged her again.

"I won't leave until the last party guest is gone. I promise." She had taken a vacation day for this, to ensure she didn't get called in. One of Emery's biggest struggles was people breaking promises to her.

Pamela, unfortunately, had a horrible habit of doing that. She breezed in to visit Emery two or three times a year from neighboring Illinois. Always spouting off promises that she inevitably never kept.

Jac had her theories why, but she had never discussed that with Max.

Not yet. But Emery was getting older now—and Jac suspected she had somehow convinced herself her mother rejected her time and time again because of something Emery had done. Things the little girl had let slip the last time Jac had seen her had finally started to make sense.

Jac was going to bring that up to Max as soon as she could.

Speaking of Max...she pulled in a deep breath. Time to face her particular lion in his own den.

She walked through to the large kitchen at the rear of the home. There was an enclosed garage that was easily big enough for three cars. A few years earlier, Max and Jac had turned it into a large recreation room, complete with pads on the floor. Emery was getting deeply involved in martial arts. She had plenty of room to practice now.

Plus, with the mats rolled back, it made a great space for birthday parties, complete with a small half bath off to the left.

She suspected that was where most of the guests were now.

But first...

The kitchen.

And the man she could hear in there speaking.

He looked up when she entered. "Jac, I'm glad you're here. She was getting worried you wouldn't make it. Pamela cancelled twenty minutes ago. She's on her way to London with a client. Should be landing any minute. She promised to call—if she gets a chance."

Jac winced. This was the second year in a row that had Pamela had missed Emery's birthday party. Most likely, an overly expensive present would arrive from London next week. Cold, pricey, and impersonal. Just like every time before. "I'm sorry. The director called. He wants me to take a look at that...code...for you. And he had questions about the Jason Evanton case from two years ago. I was almost out the door when he called, then I had to look up the case number on my laptop."

"Everything ok with Dennis?"

Jac shook her head. "I need to go in tomorrow and show him my reports. What I did to try to find Jason. He said it ties into the new cold-case division Agent Knight will be heading up."

"Let me know if I can help with anything."

"I got it covered. You just need to get me a copy of the code before I leave. But that's PAVAD. Today is for Em. It looks like you are having difficulties of your own. Anything I can do in here?" Jac was used to *doing*. Especially in Max's home. And the poor man…he really was in over his head.

He looked adorably flustered at the moment. The hair had gotten longer—usually, she scheduled reminders for him to get his and Emery's hair cut on a regular basis.

Before.

The man was not good at scheduling details at all; she'd always handled that when they worked together. She took a quick look around the kitchen; at least, he was using the whiteboard calendar she'd installed when Emery had entered first grade.

"Yes. Help me. There are just too many of them. There are little girls and a few boys everywhere. When you turn your back, they clone themselves. I'm pretty certain I saw doubles earlier—but the director's wife was in there. That might be part of it."

"Marianna brought the twins?" Rumor had it that the director was keeping his family under wraps lately.

Since Andy.

"Maybe. Or maybe they just cloned themselves when my back was turned. At this point I just do not know."

She didn't have much time with him after that—thank goodness. Jac ended up acting as the unofficial hostess, keeping things moving smoothly while Max prepped the food and drinks. She never even made it to the rec room in the first hour she was there.

Jac was just kept too busy for that. She didn't have a chance to talk to him about what was going on with Emery, either.

Jac was as comfortable in Max's home as her own. She'd missed him and Emery. Missed the social connections being so involved in Emery's life had brought her. She had spent two or three nights a week with Max and his daughter, outside of PAVAD.

To have that suddenly change had hurt. There had been a real void. She'd thought to fill it by finally buying her own home and focusing on that, but it hadn't been the same.

She had never expected that it would be.

It occurred to her as she was helping carry gifts to the rec room that they had become her world for those years. Almost her entire world. Only Nat—who she'd seen maybe three or four times a year before her sister transferred to St. Louis—and Miranda, who was in and out of St. Louis sometimes on opposite cases from Jac, had also had a place.

That had just made the rift between her and Max all that much more painful. Probably more so than it should have been.

She'd meant what she'd said to Emery, though.

If Max would allow it, she'd do her best to spend time with Emery whenever she could. That was one promise she intended to keep.

"Let me help you with that," a female voice said as Jac was juggling the last of the heaping pile of presents.

Jac recognized the voice. She smiled at the blond woman who'd just come in. "Hi, Rachel, I'm glad you and the girls could make it."

"We had a bit of car trouble, but Paul brought us in his sedan. We're a little late. I'll make my apologies to Max in a moment. You look like you need help." Rachel Sturvin took half the stack, giving Jac her characteristic shy smile. "The girls have already run off in search of Emery. They hero-worship her."

Jac looked past Rachel, a woman she'd volunteered with at Brynlock several times over the past two years, to the man she vaguely recalled seeing before.

Rachel's husband was a bit on the ordinary-looking side. He had a slight paunch, and she thought he was a good ten years or so older than Rachel. At least three or four years older than Max, she thought, but he looked far older and far less put together.

He wore a suit, but it was wrinkled, and his tie hung slightly crooked. He was sweating, profusely.

She was immensely glad her hands were full, and she couldn't shake his. Jac didn't like touching strange men at all—even handshakes. She doubly felt that right now. "Hello, Mr. Sturvin, we're glad you and your family could make it today. Max is currently in the rec room, supervising the party games. There are a few other fathers back there, too. They were making noises about moving into the media room and watching the game in there."

"It's nice to meet you, Mrs. Jones. You have a lovely home," he said in a slightly nasal voice. He looked around, obvious curiosity in his eyes. He was cataloging everything in Max's home; she just *knew* it. When he looked back at her, she knew he was cataloging her as well.

He was the exact opposite of Rachel.

"Please, it's Jaclyn. Most call me Jac. And I'm not *Mrs.* Jones. Max and I aren't married. I am an Agent Jones, though. We work together at the FBI."

"So you and Dr. Jones are siblings, cousins?"

"No. Just colleagues and friends—with a very common last name. Please feel free to grab a soda or something. All the refreshments are on the table along the far wall."

"Thanks, Jac. Anything I can do to help after this?" Rachel asked.

"Max may need a break. He's great at crowd control, but when the crowd is a bunch of little girls, I think he gets overwhelmed. They terrify him from his shaggy head down to his overly large toes."

Rachel laughed, quietly. She was usually a more subdued woman. But she had a wicked sense of humor and a great knack for gardening. She had already volunteered to help Jac figure out something to do with the area around the walkway of her new place. "I can understand. We still on for Saturday next?"

"Of course," Jac said. "I put in for a few comp days, just to make certain. My friend Miranda will be joining us. Her sister runs a nursery in Wyoming. Miranda has promised me starts off of anything we want, as long as her sister has them. If we get the planning done in time. You'll like her. Miranda can be very entertaining. Especially when she misbehaves."

"Great. I'm looking forward to it." Rachel beamed at her. Jac understood; Rachel's closest friend had moved recently. Jac suspected the other woman was feeling a little lonely and adrift right now. Looking for connections with other women—connections outside of her children.

Jac could understand that. She was looking for connections outside of *PAVAD*.

Jac finally got a good look at the guests as she stepped into the rec room. There were around thirty kids, mostly little girls around Emery's age, with a few boys thrown into the mix. And a good twenty adults. She recognized some from the school.

And some from PAVAD.

Including the director of the forensics lab. Jac's friend Cody, head of the automotive-forensics department, was there with her daughter nearby, too. Lucy was a few years younger than Emery, but they all attended the same school. Brynlock was small; the different grades often grouped together for events and specialty classes. And PAVAD kids saw each other often, it seemed.

"It's appreciated," Max said, bringing her attention back to him. The man looked good with the oversized red apron wrapped around his jean-clad hips. Very…mouth-watering, when she thought about it. "I don't suppose you want to volunteer to help with the cooking?"

"Not in a heartbeat. I'm just here as a guest this year since you decided I have girl cooties. You're on your own, now."

"You are heartless, Jaclyn Jones. Utterly heartless. Gorgeous. But heartless."

"You'd better believe it." She looked around once, ignoring the masculine appreciation in his eyes. She wouldn't think about the last time he'd looked at her like *that*. "I'm going to go say hello to Cody. I haven't seen her at PAVAD for a few weeks."

"She's taking some time off to spend with the kids over Christmas, I believe Sin said." Max moved closer. He leaned down. "Thanks for coming. I…I know it means a lot to Emery. She's missed you. And Pamela hurt her this morning. I want to wring that woman's neck for that. She could have delayed her trip for a few hours. We can talk later. I have a few things to say to you, too."

Jac just nodded. This was not a conversation she wanted to have now. As far as she was concerned, they'd discussed it in his office. It wasn't getting any more of her attention than that. "I...we'll just put it behind us. Ok? Life moves on. *We* move on. For Emery."

25

LIFE MOVED ON. MAX THOUGHT THAT WAS A GOOD WAY TO PUT WHAT had happened between him and Jac.

Today was the first step in making things right.

Even if they didn't get back what they had once had, he wanted them to be back on a balanced front. For his daughter's sake, if nothing else. This morning's phone call from his ex-wife had just cemented that.

Like Emery had told him when she'd disconnected from the call with her mother, at least *Jac* had promised to be there.

Jac would be there. Emery had just known it. Because Jac had promised.

Max had been sweating, worrying the weather would keep Jac from delivering on that promise.

As he watched, Emery and a few of her friends ran up to Jac. Emery hugged her quickly, beaming. His daughter adored Jac.

And it was mutual. He'd been an idiot to jeopardize that because his hormones rose up and shocked him at how strong they had been. Hell, if he hadn't run from her, maybe he would already have her right where he wanted her.

Maybe she *wouldn't* be going home after the party, then. Max had plenty of regrets for how he had handled things.

"Pretty lady," a male voice said behind him. "Your sister? I believe I heard she was Emery's aunt from Olivia."

"No, Jac and I aren't related. She's a colleague and friend. We just happen to have the same last name." Paul Sturvin had accompanied his wife and two daughters to the party. This was only the second time Max had met the man. He had met Rachel several times before and found her quiet and kind.

Jac knew her better. Jac had filled in as room parent for him at Brynlock many times when cases had sent him and the rest of the team out of state and Jac had remained behind to work the computer-tech side of things. She'd bailed him out more times than he could count.

Just how much help she'd been in raising Emery over the last three or four years finally wasn't lost on him. At all. He couldn't have done it without her. And he could not repay her for what she had helped him do. Ever.

"My mistake. My daughter had mentioned Emery's aunt, and I just assumed..."

"Easy mistake." And one he understood. It was the red in their hair. Jac had told him that hers was identical to her mother's. Hers was a richer brownish red than his daughter's strawberry blond, but from a distance, it was easy to assume there was a biological tie between the two. Especially when one watched them together.

Jac was so easy with Emery, relaxed. Natural.

Then again, she looked relaxed with all of the kids surrounding her. Children had a way of getting Jac to open up quickly. He'd noticed that before.

Probably because they weren't threats.

"Emery and Jac are very close. She's been a great friend to both of us the years we've known her. We were team partners for several years."

"She's with the bureau?" Sturvin asked, almost incredulously. "She doesn't look the type."

From what he recalled, Sturvin was a consultant with the FBI located in St. Louis. Something to do with the IT divisions, of both PAVAD and the regular field office. But he didn't think their paths had crossed often.

Max was almost certain he'd seen Sturvin in the building recently. Maybe. Paul Sturvin was the type to blend in.

"Jac and I are both with PAVAD."

Sturvin let out a whistle between his teeth. "Nice."

PAVAD's Complex Crimes Unit did have a reputation that was growing within the law enforcement industry. "We've been with PAVAD since the beginning. Before."

"She's an agent?"

"Yes. Joint specialties. She is one of the best." Looks could be deceiving; Jac looked like she should be sitting on the board of fifteen different charities, using her wealthy family's money for good, in between manicures and dinner parties. She had that understated sheen of sophistication that a wealthy background gave some women.

She'd grown up in just that environment. Like Pamela had. They both came from very affluent backgrounds. With abuse in their history. It was a coincidence he had contemplated before.

Pamela had gone toward corporate law and her money-making ambitions; Jac had chosen law school after getting her undergraduate degree in computer science as well.

The bureau had recruited Jac straight out of law school, weeks before she'd even passed the bar.

She didn't look like a federal agent at all.

She looked like a wealthy soccer mom. Especially with a little girl of around four held on her hip while she talked with the blond woman next to her.

Paul Sturvin's wife, Max thought. The young girl Jac held was his daughter. No wonder Jac had captured his attention.

"Proves point that you can't judge someone by how they appear," Paul said. "Thank you for inviting us. Olivia has been struggling to make connections with the other children, since we moved her up a grade midsemester."

Max just nodded. He suspected he knew why the man had latched on to him. There weren't a great number of men in attendance—no surprise, considering it was a little girl's birthday party. "We're glad she could make it. Emery is very fond of her."

He listened to Paul drone on, his attention more on the women chatting and laughing than on the man next to him.

Jac liked Rachel a great deal. It was in how she was laughing. How relaxed she was. She reached out and wiped the little girl's face with a paper towel. Natural. He smiled.

He liked seeing Jac like that. Most of all, he loved seeing Jac happy again. She looked over at him. Their eyes met.

Max made himself a vow. He wasn't letting her leave without telling her exactly how he felt. He'd waited long enough.

26

JACLYN. PAUL STOOD BACK AS THE PARTY GUESTS DELVED INTO THE traditional cake and punch and ice cream. And presents. He did his best to hide his excitement.

She was a mark; he wasn't supposed to be fascinated by her. It just didn't work that way. His one and only job right now was to find out all the dirt on her that he possibly could.

Pure coincidence she was there in front of him now.

The woman, Jaclyn, was at the forefront of the party. It was obvious Dr. Jones's daughter was close to Jaclyn. As was Dr. Jones. The child looked for her often, much the way Olivia and Ava looked for Rachel.

Maybe Jaclyn and Max Jones were having an affair? It was possible, though he hadn't confirmed it yet. He'd make note to check into it. That could be potentially useful information.

Jaclyn would make an excellent mother; it was evident in how she interacted with the children around her. So graceful.

He pursed his lips and forced himself not to scowl at his wife. This birthday party was not an event he had originally approved. She had insisted the girls be free to attend and had argued with him for an hour before he'd given in and driven them himself, though she knew he had some very important work to do.

Rachel had said it would make it easier on Olivia at school.

Dr. Jones's daughter was a year-and-a-half older, but they were in the same portion of the building. And in some of the same combined classes.

Looking around, he wasn't too put out by the ones Rachel now chose to associate with. Perhaps she had learned her lesson last time.

It had taken him six months to chase off Claudetta, the last woman she'd become friends with without Paul's permission.

Paul studied each guest quickly. That was the director of PAVAD's wife there. The one who was the ex-wife of a state senator from Indiana, he believed. Another woman was the daughter of a local politician. Her daughter was running around with his somewhere nearby.

Even the Jones girl was a connection of the Chicago Holstelds. That was an important connection to foster. Rachel had informed him of the little girl's lineage on the drive over.

Paul winced; Rachel had known exactly how to play him today. That concerned him. Yes; those kinds of connections met his approval. What didn't was how Rachel had behaved.

Once things fell into place, and Paul received payment for his work with the FBI databases, those connections could be extremely important.

He needed to earn the trust of the people at this very party. Just in case that side gig didn't quite work out the way he needed it to.

Paul probably needed to find Rachel or the children and show how much of a good husband and father he was. Set things up for later.

This party was more fortuitous than he had assumed during the drive over when he'd been arguing with Rachel.

Paul still hadn't forgiven or forgotten her blatant disregard for the rules. Rachel knew better than that. She should have run this party by him *first.*

She'd demanded to know why. He wasn't certain his answer had satisfied her at all.

He was going to have to make it known exactly how he felt tonight. When he had her alone.

Rachel needed to be reminded of who was in charge.

It wasn't her, and it never would be.

27

Max's beautiful house looked like a crime scene.

Jac had seen far too many of those. But nothing like this.

Jac took another look around, then revised her initial evaluation. There was a definite resemblance to the worst disaster scene she'd ever seen.

It looked like a…well, there was no real word for it. It looked like the aftermath of chaos that only thirty-eight children under the age of twelve could create.

The PAVAD parents of the Brynlock kids had helped with some of the cleanup, but she doubted Max's rec room would ever be fully the same again. Red punch stained the concrete floor everywhere she looked. He'd probably have to put some paint on it at some point.

Jac really hoped that was chocolate icing smeared on the wall—and not something else. The Hellbrooks' two-year-old had been over in that corner while her grandmother was busy with Evalyn's older brother Matthew. That…anything could have happened.

There was no way Jac was going over there. Max would have to handle *that* corner by himself.

There were balloons floating halfway to the floor, obscuring visibility as the helium leaked free.

Emery was curled up in her new gaming chair, an American Girl book in her hands, and the new 1980s-style eighteen-inch doll Jac had bought her sitting on her lap. She'd been asking for that particular doll for months.

The 1980s accessories were cool now—because they were *vintage.* That cracked Jac up when she thought about it.

Emery had cat ear headphones on her ears and an iPod plugged in. The doll wore headphones and had a cassette player in bright colors. Jac had picked it out herself.

Jac was doing her best to get the ghosting balloons down and into a trash bag. Max was grabbing trash bags out of the kitchen.

Jac looked up when he entered the rec room again. He'd lost the apron. His deep-brown hair was sticking out everywhere on his head—it was definitely time for a haircut. There was a shell-shocked, exhausted expression in his gorgeous blue eyes. Even his broad shoulders drooped from exhaustion, making her want to cuddle the man.

Jac watched him for a moment. Max liked order.

A kids' birthday party was as disorderly as it could get.

Emery had had a wonderful day. That was what mattered.

She moved a chair off to the side. A stuffed animal fell to the floor.

Jac scooped it up.

It was Rachel's daughter's. "Do you want to send this to the school with Emery on Monday? It's the little Sturvin girl's. His name is Mr. Bird, and he's very special."

Max nodded. "I found a few other things. I'm sure that's Bobby Dennis's coat. Under all that icing. Or Matthew Hellbrook's. I'll probably have a box to carry in when I drop her off for those kids who don't have PAVAD parents."

"You survived another year. I'm proud of you."

"It was horrendous. When do they outgrow birthday parties like this?" he asked in a whisper.

Jac looked at the little girl rocking out to her new iPod, with the doll cuddled close. Such a mix of growing up and little child all rolled into one. "Too soon?"

His gaze followed hers. The love he had for his daughter was written right there for her to see. She loved Max the Dad. He was just so good at it.

"Yeah. Too soon. I remember my mother baking her a little cake for her first birthday. Now…"

Max stepped closer as Jac stretched up to grab a taunting pink balloon just over her own head.

His hands went around her waist, and he lifted.

Right where her shirt had risen.

His hands scorched her skin. She grabbed the balloon—and an undignified squeak escaped.

He lowered her to the ground.

Jac's front pressed to his. "Maddox James, what do you think you're doing?"

It came out in a breathless whisper.

"We're not at PAVAD right now. I…like the new shirt." His fingers tightened. Max had perfect hands. Big, strong, hot. "It looks…soft. Beautiful. You should always wear this color."

Jac looked up at him. Ten inches separated them in height. One hundred and fifty pounds. He made her feel feminine and breathless right then. *Sexy, desirable, feminine.* In that moment.

Like he hadn't before.

Even during the Kiss-That-Shouldn't-Have-Been.

They weren't arguing now. They weren't in the heat of the moment.

"Max? I thought we said we weren't going to do this?" There was a look in his eyes now. One that told her Max liked knowing he had her so confused. The jerk—he liked disconcerting her.

Playing with her. Hunting her like the prey she most certainly felt like. Jac shivered.

It had been a while since a man had made her feel like *this*.

She fought the urge to close her eyes and just breathe the scent of man and birthday cake in.

He was enjoying himself. Her front tingled where it was pressed against his absolutely perfect chest. Max felt hard and strong against her. He had a six-pack under that sweatshirt—she'd seen that before.

Jac didn't know what to do with her hands. Somehow, her arms slipped around his waist. Then they were pressed almost as close as they could be with clothes on—and a nine-year-old in the room with them.

She sent a look across the room. Emery had her eyes closed and was doing a kid version of head banging to the music. "I think...we'd probably better back away here. Before we do something else we'll regret. Something I don't think you're ready to talk to your daughter about just yet."

"I'll never regret this." Max's mouth covered hers. It was enough to tilt her entire world sideways.

Heaven help her, Jac kissed him back instinctively. Before she could stop herself. Or think about the possible repercussions.

She kissed him back right there with Emery fifteen feet away. Until someone knocked on the door that led to the driveway from the garage.

She pulled away.

Her eyes met his.

"You...you and I...we're going to talk. One way or the other, Jaclyn. You can count on that."

Someone knocked again. The shadow at the window shifted.

Jac stepped back.

Paul Sturvin was peering into the window.

No doubt, he'd come to retrieve his daughter's stuffed animal.

Jac didn't care. She scurried to the bathroom, leaving Max to deal with the man at the door.

Leave it to Max—just when Jac thought she'd figured things out, the man did what he could to shake things up completely.

Jac brushed one finger over her lips. She could still taste him. Could still feel him pressed against her. The man just kept changing everything, just when she least expected it.

28

ANGER. PAUL HAD ALWAYS KNOWN HE HAD A PROBLEM WITH ANGER. Most of the time, he was able to control that. Even for years. But it built. Inside him, so strongly that he sometimes couldn't keep it in.

That's when impulsive, stupid things happened. Things he'd always regret.

He hadn't meant for this to happen. He had meant to wait until he had the money, they were established in their new lifestyle, and the girls were doing well, and then he was going to quietly discuss his plans for their separation.

Meeting Jaclyn Jones and feeling the passion that she brought in him had made it clear that he was only harming himself by being tied down to Rachel.

There was another, *better* woman for him out there. A better mother for the girls. One who wasn't so weak all the time.

He hadn't wanted to repeat past mistakes. Not like he had before.

He had intended to make Rachel understand that he would be the best choice to raise the girls, with generous visitation rights, of course. And then they were going to separate, go their own ways.

Leaving him free to build a relationship with someone else.

He had even considered Jaclyn as a perfect replacement for Rachel. She was cultured, wealthy, beautiful, and the girls already thought well of her. It had made the most sense. He had discounted Max Jones, at first.

He had revised that idea after the party, after what he had seen.

Liars. Jones had lied to Paul, making him think that Jaclyn was free. All the while she had been with Emery's father.

Most likely, it was to protect their reputations at the bureau. He wasn't clear on PAVAD regulations, but fraternization was generally frowned upon, or so he assumed.

Unless one was the director of PAVAD and the head of forensics, that was. Or that director's daughter and the head of the CCU. Or a CCU team leader and the top medical examiner in the country. Paul had a list he'd created somewhere in a spreadsheet.

Being special people evoked special privileges.

Nothing he had found on Jaclyn told him that she had broken the rules. If anything, she was extremely adherent.

Red was everywhere.

Paul couldn't stay there. He had to make this look like an accident.

Then he would find his daughters. They would move on.

Build the life he wanted.

With Jaclyn, perhaps. She was rather perfect.

Except for her relationship with Max Jones.

Rachel was out of the way now. He had to figure this out.

Nothing else he could do. He had to move forward. Otherwise, everything he had worked for would be destroyed.

Again.

He had their savings, he had the money he had been given for his information. He would be ok. He would find the girls and start over.

They would all be ok.

He would figure out what to do about Jaclyn later.

Right now, he had to focus on his daughters.

And the woman who had taken them away from him.

29

ED ANSWERED THE CELL PHONE ON HIS SIDE OF THE BED BEFORE IT could wake his wife or the child snuggled in the bed between them. From the size, he suspected it was one of four little boys. They had nine-year-old twins, then another boy a year younger. Ed's grandson Matthew was the same age as his youngest son and was in his own bed down the hall.

The hair was too dark to be Matthew, though. So either James, Timothy, or Bobby.

One benefit of having a large house was plenty of bedrooms for his children and grandchildren. That didn't help when it was storming and the kids got frightened. Usually, that was when Ed ended up on the couch, leaving Marianna with the little kickers.

For a while there, it had just been Ed, his daughter, and his grandson. Over the last few years, their family had grown.

Ed had one daughter in her early thirties—Matthew's mother— and his wife had brought with her to their marriage seven wonderful boys whom Ed had adopted over eighteen months earlier.

In that time, Georgia had given him one beautiful granddaughter, who was now two years old, and was midway through another pregnancy.

His family.

He loved them fiercely.

He'd kill to protect them, each and every one of them—even his son-in-law, massive irritant though Hellbrook was.

When the director of the FBI received a phone call at six a.m. on his day off, it was never going to be a good thing.

It meant someone he knew was in serious trouble.

He took responsibility for the four hundred and eighty-seven members of PAVAD—from the newest intern and mail clerk, all the way through his assistant director, Fin McLaughlin.

His instincts were flaring. Telling him that something was going on. He listened quickly to the voice on the other line.

When he heard the name, he flinched.

He'd met the family before. What was going to happen now would never be easy. But it had to be done. "I'll be there as soon as I can."

By the time he disconnected, Marianna was waking, snuggling their son close. The kid in their bed was his youngest. Bobby was plagued by nightmares and still looked for his parents at night, especially when it stormed.

His thoughts landed on another child, a year or so younger than his son. Fear for that child, one he had met on a few occasions, had him making a quick decision. If it was Bobby or one of the other kids he loved, Ed would want the *best* there to help find him.

It was his day off, but there would be time to relax when this was over.

The little girl's face flashed into his mind. She was just a baby. This…she didn't deserve *this*.

"Mari…" He leaned over and kissed her quickly. No matter what Ed had going on with the bureau, he would always stop and show her how much he loved her. Show her how blessed he was to have her in his life.

Because he knew just how blessed he was.

"What is it?"

"There's been a murder." He explained the details quickly, quietly, mindful of the still-sleeping boy in the bed behind them. Marianna would have to get the kids up and moving in the next half hour, to get them to school on time. Then... "I'm going in. I'll text you the address when I get there."

"I'll call in my team. As soon as I drop the boys off, I'll join you there." She slipped skinny arms around him. "We'll manage this, Ed. I promise."

He just buried his hands in her rich, dark hair and held her for as long as he possibly could. And he wondered.

Just what had happened out there last night to cause *this*.

30

It was the photographs that caught Jac's attention first. Always.

No matter what crime scene she worked, it was the photographs of the victims that she studied first.

Photographs were windows into the victims' souls, after all.

Her eyes focused on the victim's face first, in the wedding photo that took center stage on the wall, as grief threatened to freeze her where she stood.

She had seemed content in her marriage, thrilled with her children. She didn't work outside the home, but she'd mentioned volunteer work through a church and at the school to Jac a few times before. And flowers.

Rachel had loved flowers. She spoke so animatedly about mums and tulips and gladiolas. Her passion. A passion Rachel and Jac had shared.

It was *Rachel*.

Jac shouldn't have been called to this scene.

The local police officer who had let her in had checked her creds and told her to step inside after she put on the familiar paper booties and gloves.

He'd told her the director of PAVAD was waiting for her.

Inside.

She'd already found Ed Dennis and spoken with him.

Jac's name and address had been stuck to a post note prominently displayed on the refrigerator.

Director Dennis had wanted to know *why*.

He wanted to know what she knew about the family. Wanted to know how she was connected to Paul and Rachel Sturvin. If she knew anything of them outside of Brynlock.

She would.

Before the next day was over, she would know everything about them that she could.

Her first stop was the hallway.

Rachel had fallen in the hallway.

Rachel's hand was stretched out in front of her. Like she was reaching.

Toward her daughters' rooms.

Or for help. Jac's throat threatened to close as she imagined the last thoughts Rachel might have had.

For her *daughters*. It would have been for her daughters. Just as Jac's would have been for Emery, Max, Nat, and Miranda.

The ones she loved.

Jac crossed her arms over her chest to make herself as small as possible as she walked carefully around the area the forensics teams had sectioned off. Hugged the walls. There was a twelve-inch-wide path around the woman's body.

Around...Rachel.

Rachel Sturvin lay dead in her recently recarpeted hallway floor.

Jac had seen more bodies than she wanted to count, but this...

This was different.

This was her *friend* right there.

She stepped into the first bedroom just to get away from the sight of Rachel's body as the ME's assistant Jayne covered Rachel's face respectfully.

Jayne and Tony would be moving Rachel soon.

To the morgue. To Jules Brockman and Mia Stephenson and Gia and the rest.

There was only one place Rachel was going now.

Jac pulled in a deep breath. She ignored the copper scent of blood surrounding her.

She had to focus. Had other things to think about.

Jac heard the sounds of a gurney being carried up the stairs of Rachel's home.

She closed her eyes and pushed her personal feelings away.

She opened her eyes. Jac had work to do now.

Ava. Ava had just turned four. It was her room Jac suspected she was in now. The toys were all dog themed. Stuffed animals littered the place, but they were neat. Arranged on shelves and above the bed. There were no toys out of place, not like Emery's room where everything was always strewn everywhere. Emery was always in too much of a hurry to put her toys away.

The first thing Ava had asked Jac had been if Jac had a dog. Ava wanted her own dog more than anything else in the world, but her father said no. She loved the neighbor's little dog. Ava had told her all about Sadie, the mutt.

Perhaps Rachel had straightened the room as she'd tucked Ava in the night before. Jac stepped closer. Tried to look objectively.

The bed didn't look slept in.

Rachel had been dead since about midnight.

Where had Ava slept?

Jac stepped back out into the hall as they were lifting Rachel onto the gurney. Blond hair was just visible at the top of the body bag. Tony finished zipping her in, as Jayne started fastening the straps.

Jac had seen similar sights before. None...none had hurt like this. Jac struggled to breathe for a moment as she watched the body of her friend being wheeled away. She had to control herself, or she'd be off this case before she could blink.

She hadn't known Rachel that well. She'd have to keep reminding herself of that if necessary. The only thing she could do for Rachel now was find the person who had killed her.

Olivia, the seven-year-old, had the room across the hall from her sister.

The parents' bedroom was at the opposite end of the hall.

It wasn't out of the realm of possibility that the girls had slept in Olivia's room—or their parents'.

Little ones of that age bracket often had nightmares. They went looking for the people that loved them, to reassure themselves that they were safe.

Emery did. The times she'd spent the night with Jac, there had been a nightmare or two.

Olivia and Ava probably had nightmares, too.

Olivia's room reminded her of Emery's. The walls were painted a similar shade of pink.

Jac had helped Emery and Max pick it out and paint Emery's room two years ago, erasing the sweet baby yellow that Max's mother and sister had painted it six years before when Max and Emery had first moved to St. Louis.

Emery had been thrilled with her big-girl room. Now, there were USA softball team players on Emery's walls and American Girl posters. And paintings Emery had done that Jac thought were good for her age.

There were no such decorations on Olivia's walls. The artwork was tasteful and sedate.

It didn't shout little girl to Jac at all.

There was a familiar character printed all over Olivia's pillow. The bedspread was of the highest quality. Very feminine.

Emery would sneer at something that girly in *her* room.

Olivia's room was as immaculate as her younger sister's. Just as showroom decorated.

That stood out.

The entire house was in perfect condition. *Nothing* seemed out of place, which was odd in a house with children.

The only thing out of place had been Rachel.

And the blood.

Nausea threatened; Jac pushed it away.

Olivia's math book was spread out over the small white desk in the corner. Jac looked at it for a moment. She'd helped Emery with problems out of that same math book a year ago. Jac used a pencil to open the book to the front cover, to the names of the previous students. Just to see. Just to *not* see Emery's name written there.

She flinched at the line before Olivia's.

Timothy Dennis's name was listed above Olivia's in super neat block printing. One of Ed Dennis's twins had used the textbook before.

Olivia's handwriting was far neater and more precise than Emery's left-handed scrawl would probably ever be.

But there were horses doodled into the margin of the open notebook.

There were horse paintings on Olivia's wall, too. Tasteful reproductions of popular prints. The lamp base was an elegantly carved horse.

Olivia's bed hadn't been slept in, either.

Jac had one more stop to make.

The Sturvins' bedroom.

Rachel had apparently been alone in the house. The girls hadn't been in their beds. Most likely, they hadn't even been home.

Jac prayed they hadn't been home to see their mother like this.

Their father was on a business trip, setting up an IT consult two states away. That had been confirmed with some of the neighbors before Jac had even gotten to the scene.

Someone had those girls.

Or knew exactly where they were. It was possible Rachel had been killed and her daughters taken.

Or Ava and Olivia had been killed elsewhere. Or the girls had been the targets and had been whisked away to be trafficked hundreds or thousands of miles away.

Jac had seen that very thing time and time again with the CEPD.

"I'm going to find them, Rachel. I promise."

Rachel and Paul's bedroom was just as neat as the girls'.

It had a cold feeling to it that Jac couldn't put her finger on.

Everything was lined up exactly. It was orderly. Perfect. As if it was on a home-decor website. A showpiece. Absolutely nothing was out of place. An elegantly staged home ready to be shown by only the most successful real estate agents.

Jac liked her own home neat, but this…this was almost extreme. The couch in the living room barely looked like it had been sat on.

It had been white leather. White leather—in a house with two small girls. That was an odd choice. You'd have to be rigidly set on cleaning to have a house look like this.

Unlike Max's house, which was of a similar size, there had been no toys out of place, no signs of children in the house, other than a playroom on the first floor and the two bedrooms on the second.

Rachel hadn't seemed all that rigid to Jac. She'd been very laid-back. Quiet, but laid-back and calm. Warm.

The colors weren't exactly feminine; they leaned far more in a masculine direction. As if Rachel was a footnote?

Jac checked the nightstand. In most cases, the more dominant spouse would sleep closest to any potential threat. Or entry point.

Most likely, Paul's side of the bed was the one closest to the large French doors leading to a third-floor balcony that overlooked the backyard of the Sturvin property. The backyard was surrounded by wooded acreage. Potential threats. Paul would have slept between his wife and those threats.

She confirmed that with one look into the nightstand drawers.

Rachel's side of the bed was mussed. Paul's nightstand drawer was precisely organized. Rigidly so.

Jac made note of that.

Rachel's side of the bed was the only sign in the house anywhere that someone had been in the house at all.

That the house was *lived in* at all. That was what it was—the house seemed empty.

Rachel's bed wouldn't have been slept in if her children's hadn't. Unless she had known exactly where her daughters were and hadn't been the least bit concerned.

Maybe Rachel had been having a rare mom's night to herself. Maybe Paul had taken the girls with him on his trip.

No. That didn't make sense. Olivia had school today. She wouldn't have been too far from Brynlock on a school day.

A middle of the week sleepover with a friend or relative was a possibility. She'd kept Emery on weeknights before. There had even been a few times when Miranda had kept Emery, when both Jac and Max were out on cases.

Jac sent up a quick prayer that the girls were somewhere safe now. A relative or family friend. Or their father.

Someone who had protected them by taking them away from all of this.

31

ED STOPPED SPEAKING TO THE LOCAL LAW ENFORCEMENT OFFICER when Max Jones pulled in.

Ed had been on scene for a good twenty minutes, but suspected that Max had had to drop his own child off at Brynlock. He remembered the days when juggling Georgia's needs and the bureau had damned near torn him apart.

The bureau hadn't exactly been all that friendly to single parents when Georgia had been young. He'd argued himself blue in the face to get some much needed policy changes made through the years.

Marianna was in the bureau-issue vehicle directly behind Max. Marianna had probably followed Max to the Old Jamestown area, eighteen miles north of the PAVAD building. Marianna had only been in the city of St. Louis for a little over three years now. She didn't always know the quickest routes to the various crime scenes.

Of course, she rarely ventured out into the field any longer. As the wife of the director of PAVAD, she should be behind guarded doors right now, too.

If anyone were to go after Marianna again, it would devastate him. It had happened before. That had been one of the darkest days of his life.

Ed had made enough enemies in his years with the FBI that that was a distinct possibility. One they had discussed numerous times.

She didn't care. She loved him, she said. And wanted to be with him.

But this case...it was one that would have the very best PAVAD had to offer. And that meant Marianna. And him.

The CCU.

The PAVAD: FBI security guard that was their compromise was visible next to the forensic van. His sole purpose was to guard Marianna while on scene. Ed nodded at him quickly.

Ed crossed the end of the drive and met Max before he went inside, just as Eugene Lytel and an auxiliary team of agents Ed had requested pulled up behind Marianna's forensics van. "Jones."

Ed had spent the last twenty minutes with the police chief, making deals to get this case moved to the CCU. All he'd known was that he had a team coming.

"Director, what do we have here?" Max asked. His team was pulling in behind him.

"We're not sure yet. But we have two dead. It was brutal. And...Todd Barnes will be assisting."

Ed didn't miss the scowl. No one wanted Barnes anywhere near PAVAD at all. Ed was no exception to that.

But someone somewhere was pulling strings.

Ed couldn't find the marionette to cut the cords.

That didn't matter now—they had more important things to worry about right now.

Like who had killed Rachel Sturvin in the second-floor hallway.

32

Jac had to get off scene somehow. She pulled in a breath and fought a panic attack. She looked around. There were people gathering. She assumed they were some of the Sturvins' neighbors. She pulled off her gloves and bagged them quickly in the bag Cody Lorcan held out for her.

Ed had called out all the forensics supervisors. Even automotive, apparently.

The same pain was in Cody's eyes that was in Jac's heart. Her daughter Lucy was a Brynlock student, too. Cody had met Rachel before. "Did you know her well, Cody?"

"A little. Parents' organization meetings mostly. Rachel...she always volunteered to help with snacks. We worked concessions a few times. Sin jumped her car once when it wouldn't start. And... Lucy...same grade as the older girl. Same class."

Jac just nodded. Periphery. People didn't realize who was on the periphery of their lives sometimes. "Let me know as soon as forensics finds something. I... Rachel was a friend, too."

"I'll do that. And Jac? We're not going to stop until we have the answers."

Of course, they wouldn't. Jac thought about all she had seen PAVAD accomplish since it began. The four-year anniversary had been four months ago. There had been a huge picnic—right before they'd rescued her friend Shannon from another case gone bad—at a local park.

It was the last time she'd done anything with Emery and Max before the argument. They'd attended together, with Miranda. She shoved thoughts of Emery ruthlessly away.

Now was definitely not the time to think about Max's daughter. About the fact that Olivia showed natural aptitude at basketball, just like Emery. Or that little Ava had wanted Jac to give her extra birthday cake when her parents weren't looking.

Jac turned her face up to the rain, hoping the chill would wash the terror for the girls away. Enough for her to somehow forget her last sight of Rachel and focus on doing her *job* so Jac could find those sweet little girls.

Before anything else could happen to them. She had to focus on the girls first, then finding Rachel's killer.

Rachel would want her daughters safe and protected. She would want that more than anything else, and that was something Jac could make happen.

She zipped up her FBI-issue jacket and started toward the closest cluster of people determinedly.

Answers. They needed answers.

And that meant the people who had a front-row seat to the Sturvins' lives.

Neighbors were always watching.

Always.

It was time for Jac to go digging. She scanned the crowd for a moment. Until she found someone she suspected would talk the most readily. The one Rachel, a stay-at-home mother, would have connected with the most.

There was a woman a few years or so older than Jac near the

edge of the crowd, white-faced and nervous. She had one hand on the preteen next to her, clutching his shoulder. Clutching him close.

Jac walked straight to her. "Hello, I'm Agent Jaclyn Jones. With PAVAD: FBI. May I ask you a few questions? About the Sturvins?"

"Are the kids ok? I saw...them...a body bag..." The woman's lips trembled. "Someone said it was Edith, from down the street. Is it?"

Jac nodded. They wouldn't be able to keep the IDs quiet. Not with so many people watching, including the news stations. "What can you tell me about Edith and the Sturvins?"

The woman blanched. Her hand tightened on the boy. "I..."

"Can we go inside?" Jac asked softly, as her teammate Whitman came up next to her. She looked at him. He was a few years older than she was and had started off with PAVAD around the same time. He was a good agent, in an understated way. He touched her shoulder and nodded. He'd accompany them, per PAVAD protocol. Whit had a calming, dependable air about him that victims and witnesses tended to respond well to.

He looked like everyone's favorite older brother. He made people feel safe. "Out of this cold rain?"

The woman pulled in a deep breath, then looked at her son. She turned back to Jac. "The girls, Ava and Livy?"

Jac shook her head. "We don't know the location of the Sturvin girls at this time. But I'm going to find them. I know the Sturvins personally. How well did you know them?"

Jac and Whitman followed the woman into her home. It was very similar to the Sturvins, down to the same paint color on the exterior trim.

No doubt because of homeowners' association regulations. A neighborhood like this one would have some. "Is there a homeowner's association here?"

The woman shook her head. She quickly took off her quilted coat and hung it on a peg by her kitchen door. The home was immaculate—and cost a good ten times what Jac made in a year.

But it felt *warm*. Lived in. Not like the designer showpiece the Sturvins' home was.

There wasn't an inch of white leather anywhere. There were... toys. Photos of children. An elderly beagle wearing a pink harness and two hair ribbons clipped by her ears watching them from behind a baby gate to the hallway.

Jac far preferred this place to the one across the street. The Sturvins' home felt sterile.

That was one thing that had stood out.

The neighbor sent her son to his room with a soft order to get his backpack for school. There were two other children inside the house. The woman hugged them quickly.

Jac tried to ignore how the little girl reminded her of Emery. She was just as tall as Max's daughter, with blond hair in two braids. Emery had the same sweatshirt, but in purple.

Jac had bought it for her the last time they'd gone shopping together.

"The school bus will arrive in a few moments. If...if it can get through the police cars."

Her husband came in. He studied Jac and Whitman closely. "You're with the FBI. Or do you work with Paul?"

"FBI. PAVAD, actually. Paul Sturvin was a contractor with the local field office, but I never worked with him. I did know his wife through the girls' school, somewhat."

The husband nodded. He had a pinched look on his handsome face. "Bethy, I'll drive the kids in. I don't think they need to be here for this. I'll have my mother pick them up at three and take them home with her for the night. You...call me if you need me."

He brushed a hand over her hair. The gesture shouted love to Jac. The woman looked at her husband for reassurance. Just for a moment. He touched her—like he didn't want to leave her. He loved her. How she felt was written on her own face.

They were lucky to be loved like that.

"I'll be ok," she said shakily. Once the husband and children were gone, she turned back to Jac and Whitman. "I'm sorry. I'm Beth Ann Watson. That's my husband Henry. Edith...I check on her every morning. Rachel would check on her of the evening. How could someone do this to Edith? And Rachel...is she ok? She's a nice woman. Always volunteering at her children's school."

"Your children don't go to Brynlock?" She hadn't thought they had. Brynlock students wore distinctive uniforms; her children had been dressed in street clothes.

"No. Too expensive. They go to Worthingstone Christian. It's not nearly as expensive as Brynlock. Still a great school. We considered a public school, but our daughter has some special needs. Worthingstone has a great special education program, and tuition discounts for multiple children. It's just much more affordable than Brynlock."

"I've heard that. How well did you know the family?" Jac asked. They settled into the woman's living room. "We're trying to find out what we can about them, see if we can find out who would want to focus on them. Or Rachel, specifically."

"They stuck to themselves. Rachel would occasionally let the girls play with my youngest, but not often. Only when her husband was out of town." Beth Ann looked around, as if she was ashamed of what she'd said.

"I met Paul a few times. He was a bit abrupt," Jac said.

Whit was taking notes. He was very organized in his notes. One of his skills was looking at patterns, too.

"Social climbing. That's what Edith had to say about him. Nobody in this neighborhood is good enough for him to associate with. Not enough disposable income. Edith had definite opinions about Paul. Several people in the neighborhood did. We wondered what Rachel saw in him. She is a very kind, compassionate woman. He...is not well liked."

"Were the Sturvins more economically sound than the rest of the neighborhood?" All of the houses were in excellent repair and the neighborhood shouted upper-middle class. If not the wealthy upper class.

Jac could have afforded a place here, but it would have required her using interest payments from her mother's legacy to do it.

To her, it hadn't seemed worth it. That money was for later. For her future. After she retired from the bureau when she was in her fifties.

Beth shook her head. "No. That's why we all thought Paul was so strange. They bought their house as a foreclosure. The lowest purchase price on the block. I've seen Rachel shopping for the girls' clothing at secondhand stores and clearance sales. I got the impression money was a bit tight and they were hiding it. If we were living in the 1950s, people would say the Sturvins—at least Paul, anyway—were putting on airs. Paul, especially, thinks he's better than everyone else."

33

MAX SWORE THE INSTANT HE SAW THE NAME PRINTED NEATLY ON THE mailbox of the three-story brownstone home in the Old Jamestown area of Florissant.

"They connected to Brynlock?" he asked, looking at his bosses as they stood quietly talking at the end of the drive. Away from the blood. "Is this those same Sturvins?"

Crime scene techs worked quickly to set up tents over the larger bloodstains and surrounding areas before the encroaching rain could wash away the evidence. There were four tech auxiliaries now setting up a fifty-by-twenty tent over the Sturvins' drive. Lytel's people were going door-to-door, getting as many witness statements as possible.

Lytel was visible near the command post van.

PAVAD teams were damned efficient at what they did.

Michael Hellbrook nodded. "Yes. We called your team in because of the Brynlock connection. You'll see why, inside."

Max looked the man next to him.

There was grief in Ed's dark eyes. And anger. A great deal of boiling anger that had Max just knowing...this case...it was going to be a bad one.

And he knew the people inside. That was every agent's nightmare. He prayed to God he wasn't about to see the bodies of Emery's friends inside.

Please God, not those girls.

The memory of Jac holding the little Sturvin girl at the party passed through his head. He doubled that prayer. And added another —he hoped Jac was nowhere near this scene today.

Max still saw Andy in his dreams at night.

He didn't want similar nightmares for her. "What do we know so far?"

Max studied the Sturvins' home.

There was a child's playset in the immaculately manicured backyard. The swing blew in the wind, as if a ghost child rode it now. Max resisted the urge to flinch at that thought.

He had never believed in ghosts before—he wasn't going to start now.

A pink bicycle almost identical to the one he'd bought Emery for her birthday rested on its side next to the slide. It looked shiny and brand new. Pink streamers blew in the freezing late November wind.

"No sign of the children," Ed said. "The mother—they're bringing her out now. It wasn't easy. Rachel Sturvin, thirty-one. She's in the hallway."

Max flinched inwardly. He knew exactly what the woman looked like. Warmly pretty, friendly, blond and blue-eyed with a classic appeal. She had had a clever sense of humor that came out when she felt comfortable, but she was a very reserved woman.

She had felt comfortable in his kitchen with Jac. Rachel had practically stuck to Jac's side for the entire party. Just helping where she could; she and Jac had laughed together and teased him, so comfortable with one another.

Friends. She and Jac had been friends. *Damn it.*

Rachel and Max had served on the damned PTA together.

The last time he had seen her, she had been laughing with Jac over something her youngest daughter had said. While Jac held that four-year-old close. The little girl had hugged Jac before she'd left the party. Jac didn't connect very often with people outside of PAVAD. He swore as he thought about what this would mean to Jac, once she learned what happened.

This case was going to turn personal fast.

Hell, it had been personal before it had even started.

This shouldn't have been a PAVAD case. Murder was a state crime, not federal. PAVAD shouldn't be there right now.

Ed knew the family, too. Several agents at PAVAD most likely did. No doubt, Ed had called in favors to get it.

Neighbors stood in clusters in front of half the houses. Watching.

There were always people watching. Max was used to it.

PAVAD agents were the best of the best, too. Max wasn't arrogant. He knew his own skills. He would use every one of those skills if it meant finding the answers to this. "You know much about the Sturvins? I spoke with them both at Emery's birthday party. I know...knew her better than him. I'd just met him once or twice."

Ed shook his head. "Not much. Of course, I have all boys, and they're a bit older than the Sturvins. My view might be a bit skewed, considering that."

"The Sturvins have two girls." Emery was around two years or so older than the eldest Sturvin daughter. "Seven and four. Olivia and Ava. I probably have recent photos of them from the party on my personal phone. If I don't, Jac Jones does. She...knew the mother better than I."

Ed nodded.

Brynlock Academy was small, exclusive, and pricey. He and Emery's mother agreed fully on one thing—Emery deserved the best education they could provide. Pamela had enough income to make that happen. Max would handle everything else, but Pamela paid for Emery's education.

Brynlock had some seriously tight security, thanks to a few extremely wealthy families—including Ed Dennis's children and grandchild as well as the teenage brother of one of the wealthiest men in the world.

The school would be in turmoil over what had happened to the Sturvins.

Emery was there now; he'd dropped her off on his way to the scene. Max wished he'd kept her home with the housekeeper today.

Worry for what was happening at Brynlock now snuck in.

Personnel at the school might have heard about this by now. The news vans would have ensured that. Even some of the older kids would have heard. Brynlock was a small school. Rumors would spread fast.

Max forced himself to focus on what he had to do. Brynlock had two licensed psychiatrists on staff. Personnel at the school were excellent. He knew that. Emery would be fine until he could get to her tonight. She was safe.

"Anyone call the school to see if the children were there?" Max asked. "It's a wild shot, but…"

Ed nodded. "I did so myself. No signs of them. The school is going to play it by ear. They are already getting phone calls from worried parents. They don't want older kids spreading rumors and scaring the lower grades. That's inevitable. I'm sure my own boys will be talking about it."

Max shoved his own worry for his daughter aside. He had a duty here—to catch the bastard who'd done this. And find the Sturvins' daughters. Those girls had been in Max's house. They'd played with his daughter, laughed with her, and eaten food Max had prepared himself. He was going to find those little girls. So that he could look at his daughter and tell her honestly that he had done his best to do just that.

"I met the father at Emery's party," Max said. He hadn't been impressed. Paul Sturvin was the type of man who grated on other men's nerves. The man was older than Max's own thirty-six and had come across as believing he was superior to most of the other guests that day. Except for Max—and Ken Chalmers, former-pro NFLer turned PAVAD: CCU team leader.

Paul had obviously wanted Ken's attention.

Max hadn't forgotten that initial impression. Attention-seeking. External validation.

But Paul had been involved with his daughters, and he and his wife had seemed happy together. That Max hadn't cared for him personally didn't mean the man had done *this*.

No. He couldn't jump to conclusions here.

Paul Sturvin could be out there somewhere, hurt. Or somewhere completely innocent with his daughters. Or Paul and the girls could be out there, all of them injured. Dying. At this point, he couldn't make any definitive predictions.

Max tried to force those images out of his head now. He had to follow the evidence. Not speculation. "I know the mother better."

"Rachel Mills Sturvin. Her thirty-first birthday was last month. I gave her a card," someone said quietly behind him. "I…just saw what happened to her."

Max turned at the familiar voice. He winced. He'd hoped he would be able to break the news to her himself, back at PAVAD. He'd wanted to protect her from seeing…this. "I didn't realize you were here."

"They just called me in. My…address and phone number are on a note stuck to the fridge. We had made plans to meet Saturday. She was going to help me plan my landscaping for the new house. Rachel offered to help me get my yard in order. She worked as a landscaper before she met her husband. She was planning to get back into it once Ava was in school all day. I was going to help her out, be her first client. She wanted to turn my whole yard into a sample brochure this summer. She was planning it in great detail." Jac was shaken. He could tell that with one look at her green eyes, though her outward appearance showed nothing but cool professionalism.

And wouldn't until the case was over and they'd found their

answers. Everything was bottled up now. Compartmentalized. Zipped up inside so she could face what she had to do.

It was how she dealt with things. Work first; fall apart later. He'd seen it dozens of times before. Max had always been there to help her put herself back together again. He made a vow that he would do just that this time, too.

"You were friends?" Ed asked quietly. "Close?"

"No, not close. More casual than anything. I spent a good deal of time with her at Emery's party, at sporting events, Brynlock field trips, that sort of thing. We worked snacks at Brynlock together several times, supervised field trips, she helped with sports events that I attended. She seemed lonely, and very shy with the crowd. Intimidated by people. She'd mentioned her closest friend moved away about six months ago. I think she was looking for connections. Outside of the girls. We've run into each other before, at Brynlock. Helped in the group A events." Brynlock grouped different grades and classes into larger groups for assemblies and celebrations so the children could mingle outside of their classes and grades. Emery was group A. She'd asked Jac to help so many times before because it was usually mothers that helped with the classes.

Max had many times before, but his daughter was all about fitting in with the other girls now. Apparently, Max tended to stand out like a sore thumb among eight- and nine-year-old kids.

Jac hadn't. *Jac* had stepped up that first time three years ago, when Pamela had cancelled last minute. Jac probably knew some of the Brynlock parents better than he did.

"Are you going to be able to handle this case on a personal level, Jaclyn?" Ed asked quietly. "I had them call you when I saw your name in the kitchen. If you can't...can you give Team Two what you know about the family, and formally recuse yourself? I'm not going to push you to do this case, if you don't feel you can be objective. If it is too painful. I'll be telling the others connected to Brynlock the same. There's no shame in not being able to handle this. Seeing a...friend...

like this, it is not something I ever want my people to have to go through."

Jac pulled in a deep breath. "*Yes*. I can do this. More, I want to do this. For her. I think she deserves my help. She wasn't a good friend, Director, but she could have been eventually. I have the skills to find her killer. More than that, I want to. She didn't deserve this."

"No. That she most certainly didn't."

Max followed the director's gaze. To the bloodstains so garishly red on the white concrete drive that were washing away with the rain. The forensics teams were moving as fast as they could, but they were only human.

There was only so much any of them could do.

There was nothing to be done for Rachel now—other than to find her family, and the answers. "No one does."

Jac looked at him, finally. He could see the pain in her eyes she thought she was hiding. "Max? Where are the girls? Where are Rachel's daughters?"

Max couldn't answer.

Because he just didn't know.

34

PAUL HAD SPENT FIVE AND A HALF YEARS GETTING TO THIS POINT. BUT Rachel...Rachel had destroyed it, destroyed him.

Paul felt devastated.

There was a lot of work involved in what would come next.

Paul pulled in a deep breath and tried to reassure himself.

He'd done it before. He had done it before and healed.

He hadn't meant for this to happen to Rachel. He had loved her for the years they'd been together. Had protected and provided to the best that he could.

Sadness threatened; Paul pushed it aside.

He opened his phone. He needed to see, to remind himself of what he was supposed to be doing now.

Jaclyn Jones was in the first photo he opened. He'd meant to open one of the girls. He lived for his daughters now.

But it was Jaclyn Jones he stared at now.

She was beautiful. Paul touched the screen lightly.

He had taken the first photo at the Brynlock carnival. The lighting had been perfect. He had captured this first image while she had been half turned, next to that ex-jock buddy of hers. Max Jones hadn't been that far from her the entire night.

Her lips were parted in a half smile. The red of her hair shown beautifully in the light of the gym.

At the angle the photo was taken, she was looking right at him. At Paul.

Which made sense; she most likely was looking right at Paul. That had been confirmed when she had first noticed him at the birthday party.

Their eyes had met, right there in that damned Max Jones's foyer. He had been so angry that day, angry that Rachel had defied him. Watching Jaclyn that day had soothed him so that he was not nearly as angry with Rachel as he could have been.

He needed that right now, needed it after what Rachel had made him do. Rachel just hadn't understood what he had been working for all this time.

Nothing he had done or said had made her understand. Had erased that look of disappointment from her eyes.

He'd failed her. Paul had had no choice but to finally make it right. He had. Now, he had to make it right for their daughters. If nothing else, he owed Rachel that one thing.

Paul was going to find his daughters. Find his girls, tell them about their mother, put St. Louis behind them, and move on.

He couldn't do that if he was fantasizing about a woman he barely knew at all.

The girls. He had to focus on them. He couldn't fail his children again.

35

Today was going to be *his* day. Todd just knew it. He'd heard the reports on the radio as he'd driven in to PAVAD. Something horrific had happened somewhere in Old Jamestown. Something that was drawing the news vans there like vultures. The radio had reported that PAVAD was already on scene.

The PAVAD: FBI teams were already being called in.

He was going to be on one of those teams.

It didn't matter where he was in PAVAD. He just wanted PAVAD. For the time being anyway.

He was here now. Time to do his thing. Earn his spot, move on, and then watch as the damned division completely imploded. When he entered conference room 6B, there were three women inside. Sweat slicked his palms when they looked at him.

Hot. The three of them were hot. He straightened his shoulders and smirked at them. He recognized two of them.

He'd had a thing for Jaclyn Jones long before he'd known who her father was. But now that he knew who her father *was*, that was just icing on the cake.

He'd hook up with her eventually. Todd tended to get every

woman he wanted. He was in no hurry. He had too much to do right now to worry about chasing a woman.

The hunt was part of the fun. Especially since rumors said she'd just recently ended things with her longtime lover, that other Agent Jones.

There were two other women on each side of her. He couldn't remember the one's name, a computer tech who he thought had once worked in the same Texas field office he had. A bit young for Todd's taste. He'd worked a few places over the last five years.

He hadn't paid much attention to any of the techs back then.

He still didn't. But he remembered this one, mostly. Because of the wheelchair.

She was usually in a wheelchair when he saw her. Today, she was on crutches.

The other woman was long, tall, and hot. Arrogant bitch, though. She always had been. She had reddish-brown hair that curled down her back wildly. Untamed.

That was a good word for her. Wild and uncontrollable when a guy got too close. She'd probably even bite, if given half a chance.

And not in a good way.

She always looked at him like he was a slug.

Yeah, he remembered Dr. Miranda Talley well, too.

"Dr. Talley, Agent Jones," Todd said, then looked at the third woman, expectantly.

He didn't remember her name—and she knew that. She just smirked back at him, not saying a word.

Dr. Talley stood. She was around five eleven or so. Only three inches or so separated them in height. That had always irritated him. No doubt, the bitch knew that. She liked being able to look men straight in the eye. Got off on it, he thought. Probably wished she was a dude or something, but was too chicken to make that happen.

"Look who's here. Shouldn't you be down in Texas harassing people in the Dallas office?"

"I'm here now. Trying out PAVAD for a case or two to decide if I like it, if it's a good enough appointment for me. Got the paperwork last week. Dennis told me to find Agent Jones. She's supposed to fill me in on what we know on this case so far." Todd turned his attention to Jaclyn and sent her his winningest smile.

The one that had always worked with women before.

Well, *most* women, anyway.

He waited, puzzled by her lack of reaction.

Jaclyn didn't say a thing. She barely looked at him.

"Jaclyn? Can you tell me what we're doing here today?"

36

Barnes was invading Jac's space when Max made it in from the scene and into the conference room. She didn't even seem aware of it.

He took a quick look around the conference room at the people quietly speaking to one another. He had a team now. Miranda occupied the chair next to the whiteboard.

Miranda wanted to feel useful. She hated the cast. That was clear to see. His eyes met hers, and she nodded. She was back and would do what she could in spite of the cast on her arm.

Whitman waited quietly for instructions. He'd started off as a young, enthusiastic agent around eight or nine years ago. He'd grown more solemn as he'd gained more experience in the bureau.

He was good at what he did, but tended to blend into the background at times. Max had worked with him many times before. Jac always said he had the absent-minded professor thing going on. He was dependable. Steady and detail-oriented.

On a case like this, it was going to be necessary. Jac stood, started walking around the room.

Max watched her for a moment.

Barnes was watching her, too.

"What do we know so far?" Jac asked suddenly, looking straight at Max.

"This is it? The *team?*" Barnes asked. "Shouldn't there be like an entire squad? Go in with a major task force."

"We have more agents on standby with Agent Lytel, ready to do whatever we need. First, we need to figure out what we're dealing with here," Jac said.

"Let's go over what we've got," Max said. He turned to the woman seated next to Miranda. "Dani, show us what you've got so far."

37

JAC TRIED NOT TO FLINCH WHEN THE CRIME SCENE PHOTOS SHARPENED on the screen. Rachel's face dominated the first image. Followed by one of an innocent older woman who looked so much like Miranda's grandmother Jac had to fight back nausea.

What had been done to Edith Lindsay was the worst kind of crime imaginable, next to those against children. If someone had done that to Flo Talley...

Edith wouldn't have been able to fight back.

Any more than Rachel had been able to.

The next photos on the screen were of the Sturvin family. Individual snapshots taken from Jac's own phone. Paul, unsmiling near the pile of presents. Olivia in Max's kitchen, holding a red cup of punch and smiling. Ava in the garage of Max's home.

The photos had been taken at Emery's birthday party.

Jac herself was just visible in the background behind the youngest Sturvin daughter. Jac had the girl's favorite stuffed animal in her hand.

She stared at that photo for a long time. There was cake on Ava's T-shirt. Jac had cleaned the little girl up herself while Rachel was busy, then played with the little girl's stuffed purple emu. Apparently, Jac had missed that spot of cake in the cleanup.

Personal. This case already went well beyond *personal*.

She trembled before she looked at Miranda on her left. Miranda hadn't looked away from Edith. She'd paled, and looked sick.

"Have any of the forensics reports started coming in yet?" she asked. Max was the agent in charge. That was a good thing.

She knew how he worked, he knew how she worked, and together…together they would find those little girls. And the killer.

Dani nodded. "Starting to. Preliminaries."

"I'll head down to forensics in a moment. Any word from the field?" Jac asked as thunder shook the building. Storms were on the forecast off and on for the next few days. That could slow them down.

Whitman shook his head. "Still canvassing. Still looking for Paul Sturvin. Neighbors confirm he travels a lot setting up consulting gigs for his IT company. On the surface, he and his wife are exactly what they appear to be. We're waiting on warrants to get deeper into their financials and online activity. It might take an hour or two; I do have the legal department trying to escalate on exigent circumstances."

"The search for Paul coordinates through you, here? You'll take point on coordinating information?" Max said.

"I can handle that." Miranda put her hand on Jac's shoulder. "We'll find those kids, Jac. We have to stay positive."

"Every minute we are here, putting this together, is another minute we get farther from doing just that. But I don't know what else we can do," Jac said, knowing her friend would understand what she meant. Jac looked at the rest of the people at the table. "You should know—Max and I both know the Sturvin family. I took these photos—in Max's house ten days ago. This…is very personal for me."

"For us," Max added. "Both."

"Then we follow our training. We're good at what we do. We have to trust that. We have protocols for a reason," Miranda said quietly. Barnes was there, just watching them. Jac had already almost forgotten him. "Because they've been proven to work as much as anything else can in this business. We have no reason to believe anything has happened to Olivia and Ava."

"Livy, she likes to go by Livy. All her friends' names end in -y or -ie, she told me. And she wanted to be different than her sister, and like her friends instead. Rachel...Rachel was humoring her. But it angered Paul, so she would only do it when he wasn't around."

"You met him. Tell me about him," Miranda said softly. "Initial impressions."

Jac thought back to Emery's party.

It had been such a beautiful day. A good memory.

Now, it would forever be tainted by *this*.

"He is just your ordinary man in his early forties. He's not particularly fit—nor unfit, not overly handsome, not even particularly well-groomed. He's around your height, I think. About thirty pounds overweight. I remember him sweating. Which was crazy; Max's place wasn't hot that day. He seemed anxious about everything. He watched every move the children made. He was a nervous guy. He was the man that stuck out as just not fitting well with the rest of the group."

"How did he act with his wife and children?" someone asked from behind her. Whit, she thought, though she didn't turn.

"I just saw him with the girls in passing. I spent more time with Rachel. Even more time with the girls. The little one...she was competing with her older sister for attention amongst all the older kids in the room. She was one of the few not elementary-school aged. She recognized me from her sister's sporting events; so I gave her some extra attention while her mother was busy helping with drinks. I held her, played with her, for about ten minutes. Paul was around, watching. Until he joined the other fathers in the media room that day. Rachel made a joke about him wanting to hobnob with the really important people in the room—especially Ken Chalmers. He was following Ken around. It stood out. She was embarrassed by it. She'd just asked him to take the younger girl to the restroom, and he cut her down. Refused to do it. I ended up taking her myself."

"Signs of abuse?" Miranda asked.

Jac shook her head. "I don't know. I didn't see any overt signs. And I never have. No bruises on either girl. Both are bright, happy, outgoing, and extremely confident. Rachel was a quiet, timid woman, but I got the impression that was more personality than anything. Maybe there was abuse, and I missed it, but my instinct says not of the girls. Maybe if I had seen something—"

"Maybe you could have done something to stop this?" Max's voice came from somewhere behind her. Then a strong hand landed on her free shoulder. Miranda on her left, Max on her right. Jac pulled in a deep breath. "Maybe we both could have. I interacted with the Sturvins just as much as you did, Jac. This could have been random. Maybe someone thought the house was empty. Broke in and surprised her."

Random would make it so much more difficult to find the answers. Jac hoped it wasn't random, hoped there was an explanation stronger than just simple bad luck. But if it had been random, there was a greater chance the girls had been nowhere near that house last night.

"It doesn't feel random."

"The neighbors say Edith Lindsay took her dog out every night at 12:05 on the dot. After her favorite show ended. They said they tried to talk her into going out a little earlier, maybe getting a DVR or something, but she insisted that the dog had a set routine. She loved that dog," Max said. "She...she's as good as a liver temp for time of death."

"Who could bludgeon an eighty-two-year-old woman to death for any reason?" Miranda asked. Jac silently echoed that question.

"After attacking a stay-at-home mother inside her home." Jac thought for a moment. "Rachel was targeted, most likely. Mrs.

Lindsay was simply to cover the crime. Or buy the killer time to escape, I mean. There is no way to cover this."

Max's hand squeezed her shoulder in comfort, then fell away. "I have Rachel's contacts from her phone. I'm getting auxiliary agents to start calling around. See if someone can find out where Rachel and Paul might have sent the girls for the evening. But we shouldn't just jump to zebras from horses. It's possible Paul took his daughters somewhere. Or maybe they have separated, and he had the girls for the night. There could easily be a simple explanation for their location. Has anyone contacted Brynlock for more specifics? I know the director spoke with them earlier. They might have an insight to the girls and their home life. Other than her husband, we're still trying to run down the closest next of kin."

Jac looked at Max and pulled in a steadying breath. "I called the school. Spoke with the principal, Jayda Hewitt, actually. No signs of Livy. Ava only attends preschool three times a week. She would most likely have been with her mother today. Does Paul have employees?"

"No call on the attendance line?" Max asked. "It's automated."

Jac shook her head. "Nothing. Jayda said Livy hasn't missed a single day of school since original enrollment in preschool four years ago. She's had no issues with the family in that entire time, other than somewhat routine late-tuition notices. But she said many of the Brynlock families were in the same situation since the tuition hike two years ago."

It was possible it could be coincidental, but the odds were stacking up: something had happened to those little girls, too.

She prayed they'd be alive when PAVAD found them.

38

Todd knew exactly who his contact at PAVAD was going to be. As soon as he could, he shook that prick Whitman and headed down to the first floor where Lytel was assigned. He'd had to tell Whitman he needed to take a piss and call his own mother while they waited for the warrants the guy was all about getting.

He had worked with Eugene Lytel before. Then Lytel had gotten PAVAD in the auxiliary resource agents department. Todd had wondered why many times before.

Lytel certainly wasn't anything special.

Then again, he'd heard Lytel was a connection of the director's going back almost twenty-five years. Lytel was connected to both the director and Colonel Boyd Jones. Two very powerful men, when it came down to it.

He was part of the fifty-agent auxiliary unit. Used to do grunt work and canvassing. And guard details. Nothing special.

Lytel's team was PAVAD cannon fodder. Everyone knew that.

As far as Todd knew, Lytel spent most of his time researching and doing door-to-door canvases when needed or babysitting the director's snooty wife when she deigned to come off her throne in forensics.

He was nothing special. Lytel never would be.

Lytel was his tie to the real people pulling Todd's strings now, if Todd ever wanted to move up in the bureau.

Todd wanted to be the director of the whole shebang someday.

He wasn't thinking PAVAD any longer.

He'd been promised *Washington*. Todd was going to make that happen.

Sometimes, you had to play the game.

Todd knew how the game was supposed to be played. *Quid pro quo*. Todd gave them what they wanted.

In return, Todd got what he wanted.

Todd almost whistled as he hustled down the hall, just imagining the fall of Edward Dennis and his puppets.

Max Jones walked by, on his way to his office now. Todd's lip curled. He had always hated that guy. Everything Jones touched was golden. Max Jones hadn't ever messed up, apparently.

He had the position now that should have been Todd's. Everyone knew that. But Jones had friends at PAVAD. Jones had been in St. Louis for years; the other man had had ample opportunity to make those kinds of friends.

Friends Todd most certainly did not have. Yet.

But Todd had friends outside PAVAD. Friends who were going to start delivering on the favors they owed Todd. Finally.

Todd had been banking up those IOUs for years. It was time to cash them in. Todd stayed where he was and watched some of the PAVAD agents now as they were in the preliminary stages of the hunt for who had killed that woman and possibly taken those girls.

He hadn't realized Jaclyn knew the family involved.

That stunk for her. Todd had never lost anyone he'd been friends with before. He'd been lucky that way. It was no wonder she felt so distracted.

It was obvious Jaclyn Jones was pulling lead for this one.

She shouldn't be anywhere near this case. That was information he'd use if he had to. He didn't want to cause trouble for her; for the most part, he liked her. She'd never been a bitch to him, for one thing.

Not like the great Dr. Talley.

If Jaclyn's father wasn't as important as *he* was, she probably wouldn't be in St. Louis. He didn't blame her for taking advantage of that. They all had to do what they had to do. To be honest, Todd doubted she would be at PAVAD at all if it hadn't been for her father's contacts at the justice department. Everyone knew how important Colonel Boyd Jones was in Washington.

Those types of connections could come in handy.

Hell, maybe he should push to get Jaclyn to go out with him sooner rather than later. Her father's connections could do wonders for Todd's career. He wasn't going to be at PAVAD for long, after all. Maybe he'd be stationed in New York after this. Or California. One of the California posts would be great.

Honolulu would be the best, though. Maybe he'd ask for that.

He'd need to work a few years to build his reputation before he could ever hope to get Washington. Todd would get there —eventually.

First, he'd mark some time with Jaclyn. Help her take her mind off this friend of hers.

It wouldn't be a hardship to screw around with Jaclyn at all. He'd imagined doing just that before.

Of course, he'd imagined doing that with her good buddy Talley, too.

All that fire in *her*…yeah…taming Miranda Talley would be one hell of a ride. If a man was stupid enough to climb on.

Todd looked around the bullpen as he finally gave up looking for Lytel and returned to the CCU's floor. He'd find the guy when he could. Right now, he needed to make himself useful. Put his eyes on the CCU where they belonged.

He had been told to get information after all. He'd trade it—for the connections he needed.

He'd been assigned the worst desk in the place—right next to the elevators. Not so bad, in his opinion. He could see every person who stepped foot on the CCU's floor. That could prove handy.

But it was a knock against him—and he knew that. Someone in PAVAD was already screwing with him.

Stupid fucking pricks.

He didn't get ahold of Lytel for another two hours. He'd kept himself busy digging up everything he could find about that stupid prick Sturvin's business contacts.

What had made Sturvin snap and kill his wife *now*? That was pretty stupid of the guy.

If they caught that guy, Todd would have to make sure Sturvin didn't get a good look at him. It had been dark that night at Brynlock, but he wasn't going to take any chances.

All Todd had done, after all, was deliver an envelope as a favor to someone from his own field office. Wasn't anything wrong with that.

Jaclyn was at the end of the bullpen where team two tended to congregate when he finished his little meeting with Lytel and made it back up to the team.

The computer analyst—Danielle something or other—was at her side. He wondered at that. Jaclyn was more than capable of doing that particular job herself.

At first, he had been certain Jaclyn was one of those socially awkward screwup computer nerds. But she was actually pretty decent in the field.

Miranda Talley was hovering at Jaclyn's side.

The digital screens behind the three women flashed, changed. Bloody crime scene photos spread out on the screen. Todd tried not to flinch.

He'd admit it: he'd always hated the sight of blood. Of victims.

Those dead women hadn't deserved to be treated like that. To be left like that. Whoever had done that needed to be found and stopped soon.

Even if it had been Sturvin.

Someone bumped him from behind. Todd turned.

He sneered. He recognized the tall, dark-haired man who'd stopped in the bullpen. No doubt looking for that fluff-brained blond bitch of a wife of his. She ran team five now, he thought.

Probably because of who her older brothers were. They'd certainly greased the wheels for *her*.

He'd always thought Seth Lorcan was a stupid prick. He should have been tossed out of the bureau long ago. Todd had thought he would have been after that screwup with Riaz two or three years back. But no…he'd ended up getting rewarded and assigned to PAVAD. And a hot bitch in Lorcan's bed whenever he wanted her.

Of course.

She'd fallen right into Lorcan's lap. Now, she walked around with her stomach jutting out in front of her, getting attention wherever she went. Todd wanted her team. Her going on maternity leave soon would be his ticket. *After* this case. Once it was over, he'd confront Dennis about what he was due. But first, he wanted that asshole Sturvin to pay for what he did last night. "What do you want, Lorcan?"

"How long are you sticking around, Barnesy?"

"As long as it takes. I'm joining the CCU soon."

Lorcan snorted. "Like hell you are. I predict you'll be gone within a week."

"Don't you have some blond piece of ass around here to screw or something?" Of course, he did. Lorcan's wife was none other than the precious little sister of two important players in PAVAD. Lorcan's own two identical brothers were just as important around the place.

No other division in the bureau had ever had as many biological connections as PAVAD.

It was almost unbelievable.

Until one took into account *nepotism.* The Nepotism Game at its finest.

Starting with Ed Dennis and his wife and daughter.

That shit shouldn't be allowed.

The scar at his temple twitched. If PAVAD had been as good as it was, Todd wouldn't have gotten knocked in the head with a damned lead pipe. Hard to forget that.

Ed Dennis owed him something for that.

"Watch it, Barnesy. Or I'll feed you to the giant in IA. You know how he feels about you—and I'm his favorite brother-in-law now, don't you know? Better yet, I heard Cam Lake's team just made it back. Bet Cam is going to be thrilled to find you hanging around this place. Maybe he and Mick will draw straws to see who gets to deal with you first?" Lorcan shot him a grin, and then the middle finger. Low enough no one could see. "Don't get too comfortable around here. We all know it's just a temporary gig. No one wants you here."

"Yet here I am." Todd smirked, though he didn't feel confident at all. He wasn't stupid. He hadn't exactly made a whole lot of *friends* around the place. Nothing he could do would change that.

If they hadn't treated him like shit, then what happened next— each time—wouldn't have happened. It was their own damned faults.

But they were part of the popular clique around this place. He hadn't had a chance of getting back into PAVAD, thanks to them.

Todd had had no choice but to make a deal.

Maybe he'd sold his soul to the devil, but it was well worth it. Washington would be *his* someday.

And he was going to uphold his part of that deal. It wasn't too hard of a gig. A bit of information here and there, a few deliveries.

He was good enough at what he did to keep it in check.

Todd was keeping notes of every contact they made with him, anyway. He could always say he was investigating—going cowboy because he didn't know who he could trust.

Hell, he could say he had taken his cue from Seth Lorcan. Wouldn't that be the shit?

First thing he had to do was get Eugene Lytel the information he needed to proceed.

Todd didn't know what would happen with that information after that. And he didn't give a damn. As long as his interests were met, he didn't give a damn about anybody in PAVAD at all.

To meet those interests, he had to keep himself from pissing off the ones who had put him there in the first place.

Knocking that cocky smirk of Seth Lorcan's face would piss them off now.

They had plans for PAVAD.

Plans Todd aimed to see happen.

First, he had to deal with Max Jones.

Easier said than done, though.

Max was a mean son-of-a-bitch beneath that jock-nerd exterior. Todd didn't know exactly how he was going to get around the guy.

He'd seen the man in a fistfight during a case four years ago when Jones had been sent to Texas. The man had decimated four stoned-out meth heads. Without breaking a sweat.

Jones hadn't even been pissed when he'd done it. He'd just used those oversized fists of his to do it. While Jaclyn stood back and watched quietly. Holding her boyfriend's coat.

No. Todd hadn't been stupid enough to hit on Max's lady after that.

But Jaclyn wasn't Max's lady now. There were perks to being in St. Louis. Todd was going to enjoy them.

39

THE ME WAS FINISHED WITH THE PRELIMINARIES ON RACHEL. Someone from team two would have to go down there.

Talk to the ME personally.

Jac stood. It was going to be *her*. She had to find a way to do something. Instead of just sitting around worrying while combing the Sturvins' social media and email accounts. Anyone on the teams could do that.

She needed to be out there, hunting the information that would them find Livy and Ava.

"That's what Knight was doing in Masterson, though," Miranda said, picking up a previous conversation. Miranda brought up Agent Allan Knight often—probably more than the other woman realized. "Trying to determine if he wanted to be a part of the cold-case team. So it's happened before. I can't see anyone choosing Barnes as a PAVAD agent—not after what happened with Kyra. Definitely not as a CCU team leader."

"That's different. Knight's a thousand times the agent Barnes is. That's the last way I would describe Todd Barnes." He was the proto-typical screwup, the definition of sloppy. It was a miracle he'd lasted this long in the bureau at all. That he was even periphery involved with this case gave her knots in her stomach.

Jac had also heard he had connections in Washington. Strong ones. With people she didn't want to remember at all.

"You're telling me. Watch yourself on this one. It doesn't quite ring true. And I've heard rumblings from friends back at Quantico and in California that PAVAD has angered a few people lately. Within the bureau. And in Washington," Miranda said as she walked alongside Jac. She hadn't asked where they were going; she'd just followed.

Rather like Jac had known she would.

She suspected Miranda was keeping an eye on *her* for this one. Miranda could be a bit overprotective of her friends at times. All it would have taken was one word that Jac might struggle on this case to have Miranda going into high alert. Probably from the years she'd spent taking care of her younger sisters and cousins. It was almost a part of Miranda's DNA.

"Not all that surprising. Kyra said that conference in Texas eight months ago made it clear there is a lot of internal jealousy going on inside the bureau. Which means backstabbing and machinations. I'm glad I'm not Ed Dennis right now." She opened the glass doors to the rear entrance to the forensic lab. Then scanned her badge to get through the security door. They had doubled security on the entire PAVAD building, especially the evidence department, after someone had attacked PAVAD a few years ago.

The PAVAD building, while secure, was not infallible. That was a hard lesson they'd had to learn. A few times, now.

Every move someone made in the building was tracked now, it seemed.

She took in a deep breath as familiar sounds and scents assailed her.

This was the best way to find the Sturvin girls. Logically, she knew that.

"Still with four hundred positions to keep filled in this building, we'll occasionally end up with a lemon," Miranda said. "Or someone nobody wants around. I can't think of anyone who fits that description more than Todd Barnes."

"No kidding," Jac said as they started down the hall toward the blood-and-biologicals lab. "He asked me out. I'd rather not relive that experience."

She resisted the urge to shudder. The guy was a total creep. The way he had looked at her had made her stomach turn. Then...and now.

"Oh, how romantic. Why didn't you ever tell me?"

"You'd been sent out with Mal's team. I don't think we saw each other after that for over a month. I tried to scrub the incident from my mind."

"So Barnesy has a crush on Jac. How did that go over well with your guard dog?"

"I never told Max. I knew...that he'd go all stupid protective. He's not too fond of Barnes either."

Understatement.

"We'll just ignore Barnes while we find those little girls," Miranda said. "Max is not fond of any man who gets too close to you. Told you so before."

"Let's just find the girls and the killer, and then we'll get rid of Barnes somehow."

"Sounds like a plan to me."

She'd printed a photo off her own phone of Rachel and her daughters taken at Emery's party. That photo rested in her back pocket.

It would stay there, until the moment she had them safe.

Livy liked Disney princesses. Ava loved dogs. They loved each other, too.

Jac's arms almost ached when she thought about them. She'd held Ava until the little girl had fallen asleep on her shoulder. While Rachel had helped arrange snacks in Max's kitchen.

It had been normal. Beautiful. Jac had freely admitted to Rachel that holding little ones was a joy she rarely got to experience in her job. Not in happy moments, anyway. Rachel…had somehow understood what Jac hadn't been able to say that day.

Those little girls deserved to be safe. She was praying with all her might that they were, that for whatever reason, they'd been with someone else—far, far from the home they shared with their parents.

She just had to keep herself focused. No matter what.

"How well does Max know the Sturvins?"

"He…I think he considered Rachel a friend, too. She was helping with Emery's party. They've handled field trips together. Casual, not really friends, but not *not* friendly, either. Secondary social group. That sort of thing. He…Livy, the older girl, is one of Emery's friends from school, from basketball, too."

"Ouch."

"Yes. Rachel…she was nice. Sweet. She reminded me a bit of your cousin Dusty. She was the one who was going to meet us at my house Saturday to help us plan the landscaping around the walkway."

"I…hell, Jacs," Miranda said, pausing just outside the door to blood-and-biologicals. "I'm sorry. I didn't realize you knew her that well."

"I think…I didn't know her well. But I would have liked to. I liked her when we did things together at the school. And it was nice to have someone to talk about things other than crime scenes and profiles with. I'm trying not to think about that. I need to find her daughters first. Make certain they are ok. That's what she would have wanted more than anything. She was a wonderful mother. Her every thought was for those girls, it seemed. She'd want me to find them. Protect them."

"And you will. *We* will. We stick together, remember that?" Miranda hugged her one-armed quickly. "It's one of the things we're good at."

40

THE FORENSICS LAB HAD A FEEL, AN AURA, ALL ITS OWN.

Jac had once considered going into forensics. She had, in a way. Computer forensics.

Thanks to her stepfather forcing her to learn how to handle a weapon before she'd been out of grade school, she had excellent marksmanship skills.

Not to mention her experience in computer forensic analysis. That had been another lifelong passion of hers. Cyber law had drawn her toward law school. That had led her to the bureau. Everything combined had drawn the attention of Ed Dennis one day at Quantico when he'd been head-hunting for St. Louis. They hadn't known it at the time, but he'd been recruiting for PAVAD years ahead of its inception.

He'd snagged Miranda that day, too.

She loved fieldwork. Except when it came to dealing with victims. That was one area where Max outshone her by a mile.

Max.

She was worried about him, too.

Little girls in jeopardy would always be hot-button cases for him.

At one time, that would have been the exact type of cases on which *she* would take the lead. So that he didn't have to.

She would take the lead on this one, or share it with him, for Rachel.

It was something she just knew they both needed to do.

She wanted to be in the field searching, but with Max out there, it was time they divided and conquered. He'd handle the legwork. She'd handle the organization.

That had been their strategy too many times for her to think about. It was second nature now. Even if every instinct was urging her to get out there and find Livy and Ava herself, that it was her job to do just that. "It'll be personal for him. It's kids. Little girls who have been in his home, been with his daughter. It won't get more personal than that for him."

"Being a single parent, it's understandable. I know seeing what was done to Edith Lindsay burned me, hurt me, intrinsically. Because of my grandmother. Just like two little girls, sisters in trouble, is no doubt haunting you. It is what it is. We don't end up in this kind of a job without a good reason. We all have triggers. But we've been trained to know our own triggers—and how to work through them. Max will be ok, Jac. We'll both make sure of it."

She, Max, and Miranda had been together since the very early days. Before PAVAD they'd been a part of the St. Louis field office. Then they'd worked briefly for Ana McLaughlin in the CHILDS division of PAVAD, then they'd transferred to the Child Exploitation Prevention Division.

They'd found they worked very, very well together.

She pulled in a deep breath. Pathology was waiting.

The pathology lab was down the hall and down a flight of stairs in the annex. Jac led the way, not saying another word.

The morgue was filled with ghosts of previous cases. It always would be.

She'd always hated going down to the medical examiner's office.

But today...she was going to oversee every aspect of Rachel's case that she could.

For Rachel.

The dead always passed through the morgue presided over by Jules Brockman.

Jac had always liked Jules. Jules had a snarky sense of humor and a brain that went a million miles a minute. They'd worked together in PAVAD's early years, when there were far fewer members of the Complex Crimes Unit.

It had been four years and four months ago when PAVAD had taken its first official case.

Jac had worked the periphery of that first case. Jules came around a year later or so. The older woman had always struck Jac as being no-nonsense, practical, and down-to-earth. And she knew what she was doing.

Rachel would have the very best.

"How are you feeling?" Jac asked. She'd heard through the grapevine that Jules was pregnant again. Her husband, Malachi, had been one of Jac's early team leaders. Jules had struggled with her last pregnancy, too, from what Jac remembered. Malachi had been a nervous wreck.

There was a mother on Jules's table now. One who had two children who would never see her again. Jac could never take that lightly. "I'm here about Rachel Sturvin."

"We suspected that someone would be down soon. I recognize her, of course. I just spoke with her about supervising Ruthie's field trip three days ago. She was organizing the chaperones," Jules said in a tight voice that spoke volumes. "I had to decline, but promised to take the next one, if I can."

"I know. She...hit me up, too. I couldn't say no. Is there anything you can tell us?"

"There's not much to tell, Jac. It was a simple bludgeon job. Blunt force trauma. Here, here, and here. Any of those three blows would have been fatal. We estimate there was another twenty-six strikes.

But she didn't feel them. She was already gone. She…there wasn't a lot of time for her to feel pain, to know what was going on. Let's do this so you can get out there."

Jac tried not to flinch when Jules pulled back the sheet.

Jac was never fully prepared for this part. The cold stare of dead was seared into her soul. This was far worse.

This…this was the first time Jac had ever seen anyone she *knew* on the autopsy table.

She would never forget this moment. Rachel was right there.

Jac fought back a panic attack. This…she was going to find who had done this. For Rachel. For those little girls. No matter what. She had to. She had to—so they couldn't do this again to someone else.

She pulled her professionalism around her shoulders like a cloak. Like body armor. She could do this. She had to.

"How many blows were before death?" Miranda asked.

"The majority were after. I'd say he killed her rather early on. Or *she* killed her. Can't rule anything out at this point. The majority of the blows were postmortem." Jules pointed out several more of significance. Her words were grim, and there was pain in her eyes.

Pain Jac understood.

Jules's daughter and Rachel's sat next to each other every single day at Brynlock. Ruthie, Jules's daughter, had told Jac that herself so proudly at the party.

"It seems like overkill," Jac said. "Unnecessary. Rage."

"That's for you guys and girls figure out," Jules said. "But it does seem quite a bit excessive."

"Personal," Jac said, looking up. "It was most likely personal."

Jules nodded, replacing the sheet over the victim respectfully. "Now, I'm not a psychologist, of course. But I live with one. It seems to me she most likely knew her killer. There were no defensive wounds. None. So I'm suspecting that the first blow was probably the fatal one. Or incapacitated her enough so that she couldn't fight back. Dear heaven, I hope so. So she had to let someone close enough to her to do that. Rachel didn't have a clue what was about to happen to her. She never would have imagined. She…has there been any word on the girls yet?"

Jac shook her head. "Max is overseeing the search now."

"Let me know when they are found. The school called a few minutes ago. They've dismissed early. Some of the older children have learned what has happened."

"Someone she knew was in the house that late at night. Someone she trusted," Jac looked at the other women. "Who could she have angered so much that they would do this to her?"

Jules just shook her head, obvious tears in her eyes. "I don't know. But find them, Jaclyn. Please. Just find those little girls before something happens to them next. I…can't stand the thought of those children on my table. Livy has been to my house; I've held her in my arms when a bee stung her."

"I'm going to find them, Jules. I promise."

There were too many people counting on her for her to fail now.

41

It took a moment for Jac to pull herself back together. Miranda stood with her in the hall outside the morgue, her good hand on Jac's shoulder. Miranda didn't force her to talk.

Jac appreciated that. She didn't know if she could.

Jules's fear and grief had been too much of an echo of her own.

Finally, Jac pulled in a breath, promising herself that would be the last time she fell apart. She wasn't doing those girls any good by wasting time like this. She and Miranda had one more stop to make before they would be able to head back out to the crime scene.

Forensics.

The blood-and-bios supervisor, Kelly, caught them just inside the door.

"I have preliminary results for you. I know this case is high priority. The director called me in from comp time himself. When I heard who it was…and the connection to Brynlock, I…"

Jac followed Kelly to the larger blood-and-pathogens lab near the back. Kelly's office was off to the side behind a reinforced door. An explosive-resistant material created by Lucas Tech surrounded the entire lab. PAVAD learned from past mistakes.

"The blood samples matched Mrs. Lindsay and Mrs. Sturvin. But we have a third sample that is also female." Kelly pulled the reports up on a large monitor, then motioned to files she'd already prepared. "I've circled the location on the house schematics."

Miranda took the file report. "You're sure it's a woman?"

"DNA shows female. I'm running more in-depth tests on the sample now, to see if we can get something to match. But, yes, definitely a woman. Well, a female. No way to tell how old. But the sample does not show familial to Rachel Sturvin. So it's not one of her daughters. These samples were taken near Mrs. Lindsay. Whatever happened, happened in that general location. Rain had the samples mixing, but we've isolated two separate samples now. The only blood samples we found in the hall belong to Mrs. Sturvin, so far. But we're only a quarter of the way through them. Of course, we're eliminating reference samples from the husband and the children now. Toothbrushes were collected at the scene."

Jac stared at the diagrams of the scene, where each sample had been taken. An additional victim explained the sheer amount of blood.

Everyone had thought it seemed like a lot of blood, but with it being a drizzly, rainy morning, Jac had just thought it had been slightly diluted.

A third woman changed everything.

Jac looked at Miranda. "Is it possible that we have a female killer? That the blood was the UNSUB's?"

Miranda nodded. "It is possible. We all know women can be just as deadly as men." Miranda waved the plaster cast on her arm significantly.

Jac winced. Yes, Miranda had experience with that.

"Hell, yes," Kelly added. She'd faced her own nightmares thanks to her association with PAVAD.

"How likely is that, though? Bludgeoning isn't exactly a common method of murder for a woman," Miranda pointed out.

Kelly had a different opinion. "Of course, it's possible, but the location is problematic. The unknown woman's blood samples were in the driveway, and there was a great deal of it. Almost as much as there was of Mrs. Sturvin's and Mrs. Lindsay's. And we're testing now."

"And you're certain it's not either one of the children's?" Miranda asked quietly.

Jac's breath seized as she waited for the answer to the question she was glad she hadn't had to ask.

Kelly shook her head. "Preliminary DNA doesn't match either of the girls. I'm not an ME, but if I had to give a good guess based on the amount of blood evidence—it's highly probable you have a third victim out there."

"And we still have two missing little girls." Jac's stomach tightened at what that meant. "We don't know who's out there now."

"You'll find them. *We'll* find them. No one is doing this alone." Kelly touched her own stomach briefly. If Jac recalled correctly, she was due with her first somewhere around the end of April, six months away. "Shayna has something from you as well."

"Thanks, Kel," Miranda said. "And...take it easy. You look green. It doesn't go well with the purple and orange hair."

"I have a feeling it's going to be my main color for a few more months. Good luck, you two. We're here on standby the instant you need us. Just find those kids. Livy was at the sleepover my dad and stepmother hosted last month for Aislyn's birthday. I...just find those little girls."

Jac thought about Kelly's words as she and Miranda stepped into the hall.

Too many at PAVAD were connected to Brynlock Academy.

To those little girls.

This...this felt like a blow to the very family Jac loved so much.

42

Jac was silent as the crossed the hall to the next lab. The tech inside looked up when they entered.

"About time someone from the CCU showed up," the assistant blood-and-bios supervisor said. Jac nodded to her.

"We just left Kelly. She said you may have more."

"They called me in to deal with...this." Shayna Hawkes was a recent transplant to PAVAD from one of the west coast field offices. About Jac's height, she was brown-haired, brown-eyed, and snarky. "Welcome. I was just about to get started with...*her.*"

The evidence she was referring to give a small yip and growl.

Jac stepped closer, to take a better look.

Harnessed to the exam table was a small dog of indeterminate breed, wearing a fluorescent-green cloth muzzle. She suspected the dog had some Yorkie and Chihuahua. Maybe a little bit of beagle or hound. She was so completely ugly. Jac's heart melted just seeing her.

Most definitely a mutt, of less than ten pounds or so. Shayna, wearing nitrile gloves, was attempting to run a small fine-tooth comb through the dog's two-inch fur. "Who's this?" Jac asked. She murmured to the dog, then grabbed a pair of gloves for herself.

This looked like a three-person job. Well, two and a half, considering the cast on Miranda's arm.

It took them a few minutes, but eventually the little dog calmed. She almost seemed to enjoy the grooming—and the attention from the three women.

"Agents Jac and Miranda, meet Sadie Gayle Lindsay. This is your elderly victim's dog. Vet records show she's not quite eighteen months. Very well-loved, according to the vet tech I spoke with twenty minutes ago. St. Louis police found her on Mrs. Lindsay's porch about an hour ago. Had a bit of trouble catching her from what I understand. She's little, but she's quick."

Jac wanted to pet the dog. To help calm her. But she refrained. The dog was evidence. She knew better. The dog had to be processed, meticulously. Cases had hinged on tiny details many times before.

"She kept outsmarting them," Shayna said. "Something I would have paid to see."

"She was at the crime scene, I take it?" Miranda asked.

"We believe so," Shayna said. "There were small dog prints found near Mrs. Lindsay's body. They led up toward her house. We believe that Mrs. Lindsay heard what was going on and came to investigate. Mrs. Lindsay probably witnessed what had happened. And the killer turned on her. At least, that's what the evidence is showing so far."

"Edith was most likely collateral damage," Miranda said, her tone grim. No wonder. Jac adored Miranda's grandmother. Every time she looked at a photo of Mrs. Lindsay she saw Flo Talley in that woman's place.

Shayna nodded. "Now, I know that I'm supposed to stick to the science, but that's what most of us believe. There's blood on Sadie's muzzle; most likely, it's that of Mrs. Lindsay. As if maybe the dog licked her to try to wake her. But..."

"We have to confirm." Jac said.

"Poor little thing," Miranda said. "I think she's traumatized. No wonder. I fully believe dogs grieve. Especially when they are well-loved. They just *know*."

Jac agreed wholeheartedly. She hadn't had a dog since she'd been a child. Miranda had an elderly dog back in Masterson. A border collie who stayed with Miranda's cousin, a vet tech in the county.

Jac knew Miranda missed her a great deal, but she'd decided that moving the dog to St. Louis would be too stressful for the dog at this stage in her life. In Masterson she could go outside, and be with the rest of the family that loved her so much.

Jac carefully gripped the little dog's hips and her chest. And held her still. The poor little thing was shaking. Terrified. Shayna took the swab samples she needed efficiently.

Jac just watched. "She has been traumatized. Tonight, she danced with the devil. She's not going to forget that anytime soon. It's not an easy thing to ever forget."

Jac had danced with the devil enough to know that. Memories of her stepfather threatened to break back in. No wonder; they always did when she felt vulnerable and unsettled. Unsafe. Hurting.

Shayna shot her a look, as if she could see in Jac's soul to the hurt beneath. "From what we can tell, Mrs. Lindsay has no family. Once the dog is processed, we'll be turning her over to the humane society. Hopefully, she'll find a good home soon."

The dog would be forgotten about. Just passed around like old luggage. Unless she got lucky and someone took her home. Even as homely as she was.

The dog's whole world had changed, too.

The dog whined and licked Jac's hand through the muzzle. Jac knew procedure.

The dog would remain muzzled while being processed, for everyone's safety. Her sister, who worked extensively with dogs, made certain her animals were always muzzle trained. Nat had said many times that you didn't know how or when an emergency can occur, where a dog needed to be muzzled for everyone's safety—including the dog's.

Nat hadn't wanted her dogs to have to face being muzzled for the first time when they were already terrified for their lives. But that was a viewpoint most people didn't have. They thought muzzles were inhumane—or a sign that the dog was dangerous.

Dogs were one of the few topics Jac's little sister was fiercely vocal about.

There was the same age difference between Jac and Nat as there was between Olivia and Ava. Olivia was probably watching over Ava right now.

Just as Jac had once watched over Nat.

This was probably the first time little Sadie had ever been muzzled.

She was terrified, she'd lost the owner who adored her, and she was all alone in a scary place. Jac felt for the little thing, so much. It sucked to be facing the world alone and terrified.

"Can we hold off on that? I...just until we know what the dog witnessed? It would make it easier in case we need her again."

Shayna nodded. "There's quite a lot of blood on her face. I'll get her processed. Then, I'll give her a bath. I'll sign her out to one of the agents on your team. Just have someone pick her up in a few hours."

"Let us know if you find anything?" Miranda asked.

"I'll do that."

Jac pulled off the gloves carefully. They would be labeled and kept, in case something had transferred from the dog to her in the processing. "Make certain to get a bite impression as well. Just in case."

"Will do. Good luck out there, Jones. I know you'll catch this guy soon."

"I hope so." She thought of the victims, and the two missing little girls. Even the dog. Innocents who hadn't deserved their worlds destroyed. "I really hope so."

43

JAC HADN'T BEEN ABLE TO SIT IN THE BULLPEN, WAITING, AFTER leaving forensics. Miranda had been called into the director's office to update him on their progress. Everyone in the CCU was using Miranda as auxiliary admin due to her broken arm.

Jac dragged Whitman back to the Sturvins' home. Old Jamestown. The least they could do was canvas neighbors. First, though, they'd stopped by the small office where Paul Sturvin worked out of.

He was a contractor, hired solely to service all the IT equipment located within the St. Louis and PAVAD offices. Eventually, the plan was for PAVAD to absorb the regular field office, but that was going to take some time and careful planning.

From what the director had told her, Sturvin was in the process of setting up the office equipment that the newly forming cold-case unit would need. It was run-of-the-mill IT work. He had had to pass all security checks in order to be awarded the contract.

Nothing in his background was throwing up red flags. As far as she could tell, Paul Sturvin was exactly who he seemed to be.

An ordinary guy, not overly well liked or well-connected, who went to work, came home, and lived his life. Nothing indicated that he would brutally bludgeon his wife to death in their upstairs hallway. From what Dani had found, there were no criminal complaint, domestic complaints, traffic tickets, or any other indication that the Sturvins had ever been on the police's radar.

This was a nice, middle class family, in a nice neighborhood. So ordinary they wouldn't be recognized by half the neighbors.

Sometimes, people just snapped, though.

Jac tried to imagine what it could have been—*if* Paul was their UNSUB, in the first place. There was nothing yet to say that he was.

She and Whit discussed that as they drove from Paul Sturvin's office to the crime scene.

Whit parked, and she hopped out, pulling her PAVAD: FBI jacket tighter around her. The steady rain of that morning had switched to intermittent showers. But it was cold.

Colder than November usually was, even with the sun threatening to come out from behind the clouds.

She could see Max in the distance, talking to Marianna Dennis as she oversaw the rest of the forensics collection. He had spent the last few hours interviewing neighbors of the Sturvins and some of Paul's work colleagues, with that toad Todd Barnes supposedly *assisting* him. She wasn't certain what Max was looking for, but she kept him in sight.

Paul Sturvin had a home office. It was covered by the warrant, but she couldn't get into the man's computer systems. Yet. She would eventually, if the warrant went through.

But there might be paper files. Or at least contact information for where the man was right now.

She'd do one more perimeter search, then work her way inward.

There had to be something they'd missed.

That was just inevitable.

44

JAC HAD WANDERED AWAY. MAX KEPT AN EYE ON HER, WONDERING what was going on in her head. This was pure Jac. She usually walked the crime scene a couple times, alone. He'd long thought it was his job to keep an eye on their surroundings for her, while she did it.

To protect.

She'd go deep into her head. Then she would come back with some piece of insightful information. Many times the case would hinge on it.

She'd make a damned fine profiler when she was ready. He knew of the self-doubt she wouldn't admit to anyone.

She walked over to the sidewalk, where the first victim had been found.

Max ran over what he knew about Mrs. Edith Lindsay.

Eighty-two years old. A widow. No children or grandchildren living. All alone. Neighbors had described her as a shut-in who only got out long enough to walk her small dog around the block twice daily. The belief was that Mrs. Lindsay had heard the attack and came over to help.

That had been her fatal mistake.

Barnes followed Jac into the large forensic tent over where Edith had been found. Max shifted direction. She didn't need interrupted.

"What are you looking for?" Barnes asked.

Jac looked up, appearing startled for only a millisecond. Her cheeks were so pale that concern went through Max. "The blood, Barnes. Take a look. What does it tell us?"

Max watched as the man did what she said, looking where Mrs. Lindsay's body had been found. The tents had preserved a good portion of the scenes, thankfully. Barnes immediately turned green and stumbled back. Carelessly.

"That someone died here. But we know that. It was the old lady."

Jac's cheeks turned red, and anger flashed through the green eyes Max loved so much.

"Way to put it, Barnes. Her name was *Edith*. Remember that." Jac said. "Don't make assumptions, Barnes. That's not just one person's blood there."

Max waited, knowing she'd tell him what she meant. She'd texted him that information hours ago.

"So who else was out here?" Barnes demanded.

"There was another woman injured here last night. Rachel, Edith…and a third. Forensics are trying to get us more to go on. We have to figure out how that changed the dynamics last night. Who was she, and why she was here. Victim or perpetrator. We don't know yet."

She looked at Max. "What if Edith interrupted the attack on the mystery woman, rather than Rachel? It was out here at some point. I don't know if it started inside and ended up out here, or if it was outside and ended up inside. Has anyone said anything about directionality of the blood drops?"

"We have a few photos. The teams are working on it, but the rain that fell before the crews could get here did a number on blood trail outside," Max said as they stepped outside the tents to give the remaining forensics techs room to work. "Inside…there were a great deal of samples taken. It'll take time to tell us who was where officially. I'll see if Mari can give us anything about directionality."

The shape of a blood drop told what direction the movement would be—but not who had been doing the bleeding. Or it could have dripped from the murder weapon itself.

Forensics weren't Max's strength; he was more a social scientist at heart. Jac understood the science aspect much better than he ever could.

If directionality could tell them anything at all—forensics weren't always a given.

He didn't bother cursing that fact—it just was. Sometimes, the forensic evidence was less valuable than he would want. He had long ago learned to run with that.

The rain had finally stopped, but it still glistened on the yard. On the black canvas tents the forensic teams had worked quickly to erect over the bloodstains.

The tents stood out like the eyesores that they were.

There were neighbors and gawkers everywhere still, watching. Always watching.

"She wouldn't have heard what happened to Rachel. Not out here. Rachel died too quickly. She didn't even have a chance to scream, most likely. According to what the ME said it was someone she trusted, someone who could get close enough to bludgeon her. We need to find the murder weapon." Jac said, shading her eyes as the sun peeked out behind the clouds. She slowly panned, studying the scene, much as Max was.

"Still waiting on that. Teams are looking." Max had agents searching the Sturvin house, the yard, the woods behind the subdivision and throughout the neighborhood. They had another team of PAVAD: SEARCH coming this afternoon as soon as they could get there, to expand that search. "I have Lytel's C team out searching dumpsters and trash cans now."

That weapon was somewhere. Unless the killer had taken it with them. Finding it could mean a turning point. But he wasn't about to get his hopes up.

"So you think that Mrs. Sturvin was killed first? The second woman heard or saw and tried to escape outside? Where she was attacked, and then Mrs. Lindsay? What about the children?" Whit asked, coming up behind Jac. "Where were they? They weren't in their beds."

"They weren't out here, then," Jac said.

"How do you know?" Max asked. Jac had an uncanny gift of getting into the mind of the killers *and* of the victims. She could also see things that others couldn't see so quickly. She was one hell of a profiler, even if the division hadn't made that official yet.

"Rachel was killed first. I have no doubt about that. She was the main target. The mystery woman ran outside, screamed, needing help. Mrs. Lindsay saw. Heard. Or the dog started barking. Instead of running and calling the police, Mrs. Lindsay ran toward whatever happened next. She wanted to help. Or maybe it was too late, and the killer saw her before she saw him. The killer panicked, and Edith just couldn't get away. Maybe the killer stopped the mystery woman here. The children weren't here, but the dog was. The dog left paw prints. There's no sign that the children were out here at all. The girls...they would have left prints in the blood."

"So say the killer attacks Mrs. Lindsay then. Where did the mystery woman go?" Max asked quietly. He looked around and tried to imagine the scene as it had been. Tried to think of what could have happened.

Jac stood still. Max watched. She looked all around. "It was raining this morning. Wouldn't there have been an umbrella? Edith was eighty-two, she'd have had an umbrella to keep herself and the dog dry. It's November. Cold. She'd do whatever she could to keep herself dry. Or Sadie. The dog was all she had, except for her neighbors, from what the neighbors said. She loved the Sturvin girls. She loved her dog. She'd have kept Sadie dry as much as she was able. You can tell how much she adored the dog just by looking in her home. One entire room was devoted to dog toys and dog furniture. She had an actual tiny couch for the dog. Clothes. There was a shelf with tiny dog clothes everywhere. She'd have protected that dog."

Max nodded. It was best to focus on horses, not zebras. Until the zebras presented themselves as absolutes.

"I think Mrs. Lindsay's attack interrupted the second attack. And then she became the target to prevent her from identifying the killer. During that time, the mystery woman ran, climbed into her car, and sped away. Possibly taking both girls with her, though that would have slowed her down significantly," Jac said.

Max shook his head. "At this point, we have no proof the girls were with her."

"The mystery woman could have already had the kids in her car," Jac said quietly. "Maybe she'd already had them and was bringing them home when she stumbled on what was happening? Maybe the girls never got out of her car?"

Max nodded. It was certainly a possible scenario, could move into a working theory. Although midnight on a school night was extremely late for two little girls that age to have been with someone other than their mother or father.

They could have been asleep in the car. It would have been easy enough to carry them inside to their beds, even in the rain. He'd done it countless times, himself.

"So where were they?" Barnes asked, shifting close enough to Jac to touch.

"We don't know, Barnesy. That's kind of what we're doing here, too," Miranda said, coming up behind them. He'd thought she was at the bullpen. She deliberately stepped between Barnes and Jac. Protectively.

She always had been overprotective of Jac in some ways. He'd likened it to her being the eldest of so many cousins and sisters that she'd felt responsible for. Having now met those sisters and cousins —and seeing a superficial resemblance between some of them and Jac—he understood why she tended to watch over Jac.

Miranda missed home, and Jac was her best friend. They were as close as sisters. Miranda was used to being the leader, a protector, and *she'd* needed people to protect in St. Louis to feel subconsciously validated.

They might be PAVAD profilers and agents—but they were human, too. And this case was going to hurt them all on that human level.

There was no way that it wouldn't.

"I don't think forensics is going to tell us much more than it already has. Now, we need to build a profile. Two—one of someone who could do this, but didn't know the family, and one where someone knows the family and took the girls."

Jac took one more look around. Her attention stayed on the bank of windows above the front door. The girls' rooms. They looked right out on the drive.

Had the girls been there? Had they seen what had happened? Max felt sick at the very idea.

Because he knew the truth—if those girls had been abducted by their mother's killer, time was running out.

45

THEY SPENT A FEW MORE HOURS POKING AROUND THE STURVIN HOME, trying to get a picture of who they were. Max spent half that time speaking with Marianna. When the head of forensics left to meet with her team, he went in search of Jac.

"Dani find anything out on that car?" Max asked, coming up behind Jac in Paul Sturvin's home office after checking in with forensics about the search for the murder weapon.

Miranda was keeping Barnes distracted outside.

Miranda could handle that task just fine on her own. She'd probably enjoy it, as perverse as she could be.

"Not yet." Jac shook her head. She had her phone out, snapping photos of Paul Sturvin's desk calendar. "Dani's checking traffic cams, but at the distance they are from here, there's no guarantee that it even had anything to do with the Sturvins' case. All she has so far is one Pontiac driving at an erratic rate of speed at approximately 12:15. That's it. Nothing probative."

"Do they think it's the killer?" Barnes asked, almost too enthusiastically, as he came up behind Max.

Apparently, Miranda hadn't been as good at distracting Barnes as Max had thought.

"Dani's going to keep looking. Seeing what she can find. She's trying to track the Pontiac now. Last I spoke with her, she was trying to isolate a still of the license plate."

"We need to go on the assumption that this mystery woman is the third victim. And boys, there was enough blood that she's bound to turn up sooner or later. It didn't look good. Shayna called; a third of the blood samples inside the hall came back to the mystery woman," Miranda said.

"Dani's calling around to the hospitals and the local law enforcement posts to see what we can find," Jac added. "She's pulled four from Lytel's department to help."

"If that woman has the children with her...well, she'd be in no condition to care for two children," Max said as images of the girls popped into his head. "If she is in need of medical help, that leaves the girls with her alone. Call Dani again. See if there's been anything new, anything at all, that we can possibly roll on. We can't just stand around here doing nothing."

46

TODD HAD ALWAYS LOVED THE SMELL OF WOMEN. HE PROBABLY ALWAYS would. Miranda Talley smelled like warm vanilla. Just his luck, he'd gotten sent back to the PAVAD building with her. She'd insisted on driving, even though he'd offered, since she was in that cast. He'd been trying to be helpful.

The woman had just smirked at him and said she could handle it.

Talley had serious control issues, that was for sure. He studied her, making no bones about what he was doing.

She smirked at him again. Taunting him.

Damn, she was a looker. No wonder she strolled around the place like she was hot shit.

She was. As far as he knew, she'd been in St. Louis for years. She wasn't all that old—a good seven or eight years younger than he was, but she'd gone far.

With PAVAD.

He wondered who she'd screwed around with at the academy to get to where she was. There were a few names he could think of, including old Dennis himself—even if she was younger than the director's daughter. There was no other explanation why she would have gotten into PAVAD so quickly.

No reason she'd have gotten in and not him. He'd probably been on the job five years before she'd even started at the academy.

One look at her made it clear just how a woman like her had gotten so far in the bureau. The women who'd been in his cohort at the Academy had all been dog ugly. Or married. Three of them had been married—two of *them* had been married *and* dog ugly.

He didn't mess around with married women. Ever. Good way to get his ass kicked. There were a lot of men in the world who thought with their dicks. Hell, Todd was one of them, at times.

A lot of smart women used that fact to their own gain. He might not like her, but she was an intelligent woman. Very wise to the ways of the world...no doubt *very* wise.

"You're staring, Barnesy. That's annoying. Do I have spinach in my teeth? My hair out of place—that tends to happen a lot with this hair."

"Guys probably stare at you all the time." What the hell? They had a twenty-minute drive. He'd have a little fun taunting her. See if he could shake her. He was just as good an agent as she was, after all. Better. He had earned his way to where he was—and not on his back. He'd like to have her on her back, though. Just for one night, anyway. He bet she'd be a wild ride. "It's the way you look. And the three miles of legs."

"I do have long legs, don't I? You jealous?" She sent him a mild look. "Yours are a bit stumpy, Todd."

"Do you wear colored contacts? The green can't be real. Not like Agent Jones's." Both she and her little friend had reddish-brown hair, and green eyes. Though this woman's hair was a few shades lighter. And long, wild curls, whereas Jaclyn's hair was straight and midlength silk. But the color was a weird coincidence. "You two competing with each other? Same guy maybe? Good old Max move on from Jaclyn and to you? You two seem pretty chummy."

To his surprise, she laughed. A full, gorgeous laugh that sent those green eyes sparkling. She just looked at him as they waited at a stoplight. Her lips were curved. Her eyes sparkled.

Todd's gut tightened with swift, unexpected lust. He had a thing for beautiful women. Well, his dick did, anyway. He might not like her much, but he liked how she looked.

"Once this case is over, why don't we go out somewhere?" The words came out before he could stop them. Oh well.

Todd had always lived by the idea of giving it a good shot. Especially where women were concerned. Maybe she got under his skin and irritated the hell out of him, but she would be damned fun in bed. He didn't have to like her to screw her. There had been plenty women he'd gotten dirty with that he hadn't liked in the last twenty years.

She laughed again, then sent him another look. One that said she was mocking him. "That's never going to happen, Barnesy. I don't date guys like you."

"What? Successful ones? Thought that was all the rage around PAVAD?"

"Naw, I'd date half the men I know at PAVAD. They are good guys. I don't think you fit that description, pal. You just aren't my type. No hard feelings, right?"

He would have said more, but his cell vibrated.

Not the one he'd been issued by the bureau. But the prepaid in his pocket. It was enough to remind him exactly why he was there in St. Louis in the first place. It wasn't to screw around with women like her.

The phone vibrated close enough to his balls to act as a warning.

It wouldn't be smart to let someone get his pants off, in any way, right now. Too many ways he could screw things up.

That didn't mean he couldn't needle her right now, though. Push her buttons.

"So…who got you into PAVAD in the first place?"

"What? Don't you think I earned it?" This time the amusement was written all over her. Did the woman laugh at every man who asked her out? Bitch. How he would love to tame her. "Tell me exactly what you think, babe. I can't wait to hear it."

47

Jac was combing over the Sturvin financial records a super-helpful judge had signed the warrant for when Shayna came into the bullpen. The younger woman stopped at Jac's desk.

"I got something for you. Dani found the owner of that Pontiac."

Jac stood, reaching for the paperwork. Shayna obliged. "Who?"

"Deborah Miller, age fifty-six. Get this: she's Rachel Sturvin's only relative. Deborah was married to Rachel's paternal uncle for fifteen years. According to records, after Rachel's parents died in a car wreck when she was eight, Deborah assumed custody. She raised Rachel. I'd say we've most likely found your mystery woman."

Jac stood, grabbing for her phone. "She might have the girls."

"Possibly. Who doesn't want to spend the night at their grandmother's house when they can? I have forwarded the info to Dr. Jones. Dani is calling the Missouri State police as well as that of the neighboring states. Focus on Iowa. Deborah owns a small cabin up there, too. If I was afraid for my life and had two little girls I loved more than the world itself to protect, I'd head up there. Well, I'd most likely head to the police, but…"

Jac was already grabbing her coat.

She'd find Max, and they'd go.

If Deborah Miller had the girls, Jac wanted to know why. And if Deborah was hurt, she needed help.

"Call every hospital between here and that cabin. See if any woman matching Deborah's description has come in. With or without two little girls. Have agents from auxiliary contacting police and fire precincts and every ambulance service possible. I saw Lytel around a few minutes ago."

"That's going to take hours," Shayna warned. "If it's a dead end…"

If it was a dead end, they would have wasted all those hours and manpower, but that was a risk they had to take. "It's the only real lead we have."

48

Max knew when he saw Jac's face that something had happened.

"Where are we going?"

"Rachel had an aunt who raised her," Jac said. "Dani is sending me the address now. Rachel's only living relative, other than the girls and Paul."

"What about Paul's family?"

"Adopted when he was four or so. Both adoptive parents are now deceased. No other relatives, except possibly a biological cousin. I have Barnes tracking down the cousin now."

"Good." He wrapped his fingers around her elbow and stopped her in her tracks. "Slow down. We have to find her first."

"We find the car, we'll find her," Jac said. "If nothing else, we're doing something. Instead of just sitting here, coming up with theories."

She always had been impatient when she felt passionately about something. Max tightened his hold on her elbow. "What do we know about her?"

Jac pulled in a breath. She was close enough Max could almost feel her exhale. "Dani is forwarding that information. The aunt drives a red Pontiac. They've confirmed the license plate number. It was her there. The mystery woman. We can say definitively that she was at least in the vicinity shortly after Rachel was killed."

Max nodded. "I'll drive."

They discussed the specifics as Max drove toward the address Dani sent them.

"Maybe she had the girls? Was bringing them home, running late? Maybe she pulled in and saw what was happening with Edith? Maybe she got out of the car first? Went to get Rachel to help her carry the girls in, leaving the girls alone in the drive for a minute? When she saw what happened, the killer turned on her and she just ran—back to her car?"

Max nodded. It made sense. "She stumbled right into it. Was attacked herself, but managed to get away. We don't know yet how much of the blood was hers, or Edith's or Rachel's. That's going to take time. She could have jumped into the car and driven away."

"With Ava and Livy still in the backseat. I hope that's it. I hope she got them far away from this place. Most of all, I just hope they are all safe."

"Me, too."

They pulled into a small bungalow and killed the engine.

The house was deserted. Max knew it with one glance. A cat, yellow and white, jumped into the window at his knock. It mewed at him plaintively.

Jac peered into the garage window.

"Nothing. The car's not here."

Max almost said something in reply when a woman from the house next door called out. "Can I help you with something?"

Jac came around on his left side. "We're with the FBI. We're looking for Deborah Miller."

"Is she ok? I can't imagine Debbie being in legal trouble." The woman was around Deborah's age. She eyed them with suspicion. Jac held out her credentials for her, trying to look unthreatening. With hesitant witnesses, she often led—Max, at six four and solid male muscle, was just too intimidating at times. He tried, but that wasn't something he could always control.

"She's not in trouble. We are here regarding her niece, Rachel."

"Oh my. Is Rachel ok? Debbie thinks the world of her. And the girls, of course."

"Can you tell us the last time you saw Rachel and Olivia and Ava?"

"Yesterday, of course. Debbie was keeping the girls. Rachel wasn't feeling well, and she'd driven the girls over here during the afternoon. I suspect that husband of hers is out of town again. He is always leaving the girls with their mother. Even though he has to know Rachel is a bit frail at times."

That was information they hadn't been given yet. Max made a note to check with Rachel's primary physician. "How so?"

"Always pale. Always sickly. Migraines, I think I've heard. Or fibromyalgia. Would send her to bed for hours, even days, I think. Saw a migraine come on myself just a few months ago. Fine one minute, pale as death the next. Anyway, Debbie gets the girls whenever she can to help out. She had them all yesterday and last night. I saw her leave around eleven thirty, last night, though. Both girls were still awake, which I thought was a little odd. The younger one was crying. I asked Debbie what was going on. She said something about the little one not feeling well, and Debbie was going to drive them both home. They wanted their mother, of course, as little as they are."

"Thanks," Max said.

They'd just confirmed *who* had Paul and Rachel's daughters. Now, they had to find where they were now. He wasn't going to relax until he had those girls safe. Not yet. "So you didn't hear her return last night?"

She shook her head. "No. I just assumed she spent the night with her niece. She's done that before. To help out with the girls. Is Rachel ok?"

"We're not releasing that sort of information right now. We just have some questions for Debbie regarding Paul Sturvin. Have you ever met him?"

"I've seen him at a distance. But the likes of him won't have anything to do with the type of people that live around here in this neighborhood. He despises Debbie—and the feeling is mutual. You have any more questions, you should ask the preacher where she works. He'll know. He and Debbie are pretty close."

49

MAX CALLED PAVAD FROM THE CAR WHILE JAC ASKED THE NEIGHBOR a few more questions. When she finally joined him in the SUV, he had good news to tell her. Comparatively.

"He's her emergency contact, other than Rachel. The pastor of her church. Dani mentioned it to Whit. Whit's calling the pastor and letting him know we're on the way."

She shook her head. "I was so focused on just evading Barnes, I wasn't really paying attention to Whit."

"The last thing we needed on this case is Todd Barnes."

"Tell me about it. Hopefully, when this is over, he'll slink back under whatever rock he came from. And keep his hands to himself this time."

Max shot a quick look at her before returning his gaze to the road. "What do you mean by that?"

"Nothing. It's not that important."

"Jac...don't shut me out. Not on this one." Not ever again. Max knew what he wanted, but if he just told her—especially now—she'd build the wall around herself so fast he couldn't stop it.

He'd watched her do it time and time again before.

"I…" She turned toward him. She was pale, worry was clear in her green eyes. "I don't know that I can let *anyone* in right now. I feel this close, Max, this close to the edge. And I'm holding on by a thread. Cliché, maybe, but truth. My head keeps running with the what-ifs. What if something was *wrong* and Rachel knew it? What if this wasn't just a crime of passion? What if there was something so broken in the Sturvins that it's going to take all of them eventually? Maybe Rachel was going to ask for my help when she came over to work on the yard. I've held those girls. Ava calls me 'Mith Jac.' And Livy…she tried so hard to be just like Emery at the basketball game. She's too young to be on Emery's team, but she's so good they moved her up to a more challenging level. You could just see the pride and awe in her eyes that night. These girls…they aren't just victims or witnesses…"

"They're people we care about. I know. For every moment, I *know*. And it hurts." Max reached out and wrapped one hand around hers. "We'll make sure they are ok. Not forgotten. No matter what we find before this is finished."

"We'll take care of them—for Rachel. And for everyone out there that loves them."

Max just hoped they could keep that promise.

50

"So what do we know about Deborah Miller, Debbie?" Jac asked as Max drove through the small town an hour northwest of St. Louis where Rachel had grown up.

It was just a small town with around five hundred people. Most commuted into the city. It was surrounded by fields and forest. Most of the houses had probably been built somewhere between the 1920s and the 1960s. They probably cost a fourth of what those in the Sturvins' neighborhood had. But there was a warmth that was hard to miss.

There were flyers for a community Thanksgiving hung up where they could read them.

They found the church. The Hope Life Church near the western boundary of the small town stood out, a metal building with a bright gold steeple standing almost garish on top. It was the largest building in the town. The newest.

It stood out of place like a turtle in the midst of a pack of puppies.

"Hope Life?" Jac looked at Max as something jogged her memory. "Wasn't that the name of the church—"

"The case we worked with the Chalmerses in Evalyn, Nebraska. Yeah, same denomination. They range from Canada all the way down to Brownsville, Texas. And are starting to expand west toward Utah and Nevada. It's a growing movement."

"Great. Hopefully, this branch will be different than the last." Jac hadn't forgotten that case either. Some of her friends had had a personal involvement in what had happened. That case had left an indelible mark on quite a few members of PAVAD.

"It's a growing denomination in the country. Most are above board. I think it was just the one in Evalyn that was corrupt."

"I'll take your word for it. But just in case, if it comes down to it, you and I, Dr. Jones, we've been married for ten years and have six kids, with another on the way in about seven months, ok? And you are really, really mean and possessive. Just flex the muscles and growl for me. You know how to do it."

She startled a laugh out of him. She used to always love to make him laugh. To tease. He was the only man she had ever teased with. Jac had seriously missed that.

"I'll remember that."

"Thanks."

"I always have your back."

Jac just stared at him as everything that had happened between them threatened to rise up and choke her again.

She loved him. And probably always would.

But nothing would ever come of that.

She had gotten used to that idea weeks ago.

MAX SHOULDN'T HAVE SAID THAT. THEY BOTH KNEW THAT HE *HADN'T* had her back two months ago. He'd panicked, and he'd overreacted. Publicly.

He'd gone over every second of what had happened, looking for hints of why the kiss had impacted him that strongly.

He still hadn't figured that out. Other than it had signaled a massive change in their relationship that he had been unprepared to deal with right then.

She'd been arguing with him.

Jac avoided arguments whenever possible. Jac rarely raised her voice. She rarely disagreed with people. If it was something she didn't believe in, she just quietly did her own thing anyway. It once drove him mad until he figured out why she was that way. Until she'd revealed more about her childhood.

She did what she wanted for one simple reason—she'd always had only herself to guide her way through life from a very early age. And she'd dragged her younger sister along right behind her.

Child abuse had a lifelong impact. He'd learned that with his ex, and what it had done to her.

He had always wanted Jac to talk to him. That wasn't her way; she had always internalized everything.

They'd been arguing in Arkansas that day in her hotel room. Her cheeks had been flushed, her eyes shooting green fire at him.

Before he had realized he had moved, Max had cupped her cheeks. Brushed his thumb over those soft, pink lips. Just trying to stop her angry words.

He'd had enough of angry words that day.

Max had just wanted the arguments to stop. He'd wanted to celebrate finding their friends safe when he'd been completely convinced that they would only find bodies. The last thing he'd wanted to do was argue with Jac.

Not Jac.

And then his lips had been on hers.

That was all it had taken for his world to shift sideways.

Kissing Jac.

Kissing Jac had changed everything.

He wanted to do it again.

He wanted to do it again and again and again. And had since that night. That was part of his problem.

He wanted Jac in his bed, in his arms, and in his life. Period.

It was his inner caveman wanting to claim the woman he wanted. As his mate.

Max wanted to spend forever with Jac. He wanted to watch Emery grow older, wanted to maybe have another kid or two, and he wanted to be with Jac every day for the rest of his life.

That realization had absolutely terrified him.

He'd studied sexual attraction. It was one of his specialties.

He was in touch with his more primitive side. He knew one thing without a doubt—it wasn't just sex between them. It wasn't just sexual attraction. It was far more than that.

There had been a deep trust between them, a trust he had never felt for another woman in the twenty or so years since he'd first noticed girls.

He had thought time apart from her would change things. That had been behind his transfer request.

That had been the dumbest impulse of his adult life.

He'd shown up at PAVAD earlier than usual and run into Malachi Brockman and Michael Hellbrook.

The other men had asked him what was wrong. Max had ended up spilling his guts. Spilling exactly how he felt to men he trusted—who had been involved with women they worked with and married.

Malachi had asked him what he wanted to do about it.

Like a fool, Max had asked to be transferred to one of the other complex crime teams.

Just like that, he had been, courtesy of Hellbrook.

He thought he had loved Pamela, but that had changed.

His ex-wife breezed into town once every six months, they had a half hour to hour visit every so often. And that was enough for her.

Emery hadn't seemed to miss her.

Until lately.

She missed Jac far, far more. It had taken Max a month or so to figure that out. He'd been stupid, in that regard.

It was after a particularly bad tantrum—Emery still hadn't quite outgrown tantrums, though she was getting there—that she'd told him how she was feeling. She had wanted her Jac back.

She had thought Jac didn't love her or want her any longer. Just like her mother. He hadn't realized Emery had felt that strongly about Pamela's actions. He should have. He'd failed his daughter in that regard. He knew better now.

That one tantrum had given him new insight into himself. Into his entire *life*. Max had spent weeks thinking about every aspect of his life and what it meant to him, and what he needed. Wanted.

Emery, Jaclyn, his mother and sisters, his friends, and PAVAD. They were what he valued the most. *They* were his world.

Jac had been fulfilling the role of substitute mother for his daughter for years. Max hadn't even realized it. His theoretical run for the hills had impacted not just his life, but his daughter's as well. And not in a good way.

He'd damned himself a hundred times for that. Now, he was going to do his best to fix what he'd screwed up for all of them.

"We'll talk more. Once we find the girls and…" He parked the car in the church parking lot and they got out, almost silent. He looked at her. "You and me, and what's there between us."

The killer. He hadn't forgotten what they were doing right now. Not even for a moment.

Jac turned and approached the small church. Before he knew it, she was in the foyer. The pastor, a man around forty to forty-five, greeted them inside. He was pale, thin, and balding, with a solemn look on his face.

"I understand you're looking for Debbie? Debbie Miller?"

Max nodded. Usually in interviews, especially with men over the age of forty, he handled it. That's the way they'd always done it.

But she surprised him. She stepped closer to the pastor and shook his hand, immediately taking charge. Max studied her for a quick moment. "Pastor Bartlett? I'm Agent Jaclyn Jones. Of PAVAD; out of St. Louis. We do have some questions about Debbie Miller. If you have time to meet with us?"

Max just stood back, until the pastor looked at him, questioningly. "Dr. Max Jones, also PAVAD. No relation."

That was how they had always introduced themselves. *Jones*, but no connection between them.

It felt awkward on his tongue. He damned well *did* feel connected to her now. The pastor nodded. Then turned his attention back to Jac. "Debbie works part-time as the church secretary. Mornings usually, about ten to two, Monday through Friday. When she didn't show up this morning, I drove by her place. She wasn't home. I was about ready to make some calls. See if anyone knew what was going on. It's not like her not to call me."

He led them to a small celebration hall next to the sanctuary. Max estimated the church probably only held about one hundred people at full capacity. If the church had enough draw to fill it to full capacity.

Objectively, it felt comfortable, welcoming. Far different than the one in Evalyn, Nebraska, had. That Hope Life Church was enough to give anyone nightmares. At least…any man with a daughter.

"Her car was seen near the location of a crime scene," Jac said gently.

Max was surprised at how she sounded. He had always been the one to handle interviews, in general. He'd just immediately stepped up and handled them.

Maybe he had been a bit too willing to handle it for her. It was entirely possible he had overshadowed her without even knowing it. Protecting her automatically, especially on the job, against any threat.

But now, Jac didn't need him to do that for her. She didn't need him at all.

He just hoped he could make her *want* him when this case was over.

51

"Is Debbie ok?" the pastor asked. Jac studied him for a moment. He seemed sincere, genuinely worried. She didn't find him threatening, or overwhelming. He wasn't forceful or overpowering. He was rather just average, the kind of man you could pass on the street a thousand times and never know it. But he had kind eyes. His eyes would make him stand out anywhere. "She's a good friend of my mother's. They've played cards together for years. To be honest we're worried. Debbie doesn't go many places. I wouldn't call her a shut-in exactly or reclusive. But she goes to work part-time, pulls a pension from the school where she once worked as a cafeteria worker, and spends most of her time with her niece and her niece's children. She often babysits the girls. She values her family more than anything."

What she was going to tell him was going to hurt. Jac knew that. There were no easy answers in this job. "Pastor Bartlett, Debbie's niece Rachel was murdered this morning around midnight last night. Rachel and an elderly neighbor. We believe Debbie may have been a victim as well."

"You believe? Where is she? Is she in the hospital?" The man had paled right in front of her eyes.

Jac studied his reactions carefully. "We don't know where she's at yet. We believe she was able to make it to her car and drive away from the scene. We also don't know the location of her great-nieces. Anything you can tell us about Debbie may help us find them quickly. Our first objective is to find Livy and Ava, then the killer. We're hoping Debbie can help us do that."

"Those girls are sweet little girls. Debbie adores them and they adore her." Tears fell unabashedly from his gray eyes. His hurt was almost tangible.

The man broke down. It took almost a half an hour to calm him down enough for him to be able to speak articulately about Debbie. "She's as close to me as my own aunt. I've known her since I was fifteen."

"What can you tell us about her relationship with her niece?" Jac asked. Max just sat quietly taking notes. "Rachel's relationship with her husband? The girls?"

His face tightened. "Rachel and Debbie are extremely close. Debbie raised her. I've known Rachel her whole life. I knew her mother, before her mother passed away. After that, Rachel went to live with Debbie. She was seven or eight at the time, if I recall correctly. I was probably around twenty. We lived next door for years. I eventually married, and then when Rachel was a teenager, she babysat my daughter and my son. I officiated her marriage to Paul."

His mouth twisted at the last.

Pastor Bartlett didn't like Paul Sturvin.

His was another name to add to the list of those who didn't like Rachel's husband. That list kept growing.

"What can you tell us about him?" Jac asked. "We have yet to be able to locate him to tell him about his wife. To see if he has the girls with him. We understand he is on a business trip in Indianapolis."

"He was always traveling somewhere. He kept to himself. He

didn't attend services, but Rachel did every few months or so. Occasionally, she'd bring the girls. We're a small church, still growing. Not many offerings for young families. Not the type that they were looking for anyway."

His face tightened at the end. Jac seized the hint.

"What do you mean by that? What were they looking for?"

"Paul Sturvin considers himself up-and-coming. I believe he is around thirty-eight or so. He wants to move up financially and socially. He wants his girls to go to the best schools; he is always speaking about his investments. Trying to make himself appear wealthier than what I suspect he is. Business contacts that he has. That sort of thing. I'm not exactly certain what business he is in, but he travels frequently. Leaving Rachel alone with the girls most nights."

"Was that a problem?" Max asked.

He shook his head. "Not with the older daughter, Olivia. But with the baby, Rachel became violently ill. I believe she almost died during the pregnancy; I know Debbie was extremely worried. Debbie kept Olivia for a month or so midway through the pregnancy. To give Rachel time to rest. I don't think Paul was very supportive at that time. I think they were having some difficulties then. Debbie let it slip that Paul seemed very angry at Rachel, as if he was blaming her for the troubles. Six months or so after Ava was born, Debbie said Rachel tried for another pregnancy, but wasn't ever successful. That...Debbie thinks that made Paul angry. That they weren't successful. She...Debbie didn't have many people she confided in. I acted as a sounding board when I could."

Jac was trying to keep up with what he was saying.

They had to find Paul Sturvin. That man out there somewhere.

Possibly with all of the answers they were looking for.

The pastor continued. "After the baby was born, Rachel was bedridden for about a month. I remember Debbie being upset that Paul hadn't taken any time off to help his wife with the baby or

Olivia. None at all. Debbie moved in with them for that time. And she helped. She seemed to dislike Paul even more after that."

"In the four years since the baby was born, had they had noticeable marital problems?" Jac asked.

He shook his head. "I don't believe so. After about a year, he convinced her that they needed to attend a larger church inside city limits. There were quite a few people there that he wanted to make connections with, Debbie had said. And there were more social activities for the girls. Which I can understand that. We're building our programs here. But I got the sense that they were attending church with Paul simply to appease him. Rachel was comfortable here, loved living in this town. She did not want to move to the city. She told me once it is so impersonal there. But Paul...he sees church just as a way to hobnob with those of the social crowd he wants to connect with. Debbie said once that he's always going on and on about being upwardly mobile, moving up into the lifestyle they deserve. This town wasn't big enough for him, even though this was where Rachel and he met, where they lived for the first year or so they were together. He seemed content then—it is almost like he was an entirely different person back then. It's sad, the damage greed can do to someone. It was always about going up, up, up with Paul. He never seems content."

"With Rachel?" Max asked quietly. "The girls?"

"Both. Rachel, she doesn't dress correctly. Isn't poised enough. The girls don't behave correctly. Olivia was having some struggles in kindergarten, and Debbie said that wasn't good enough for Paul. Their home wasn't enough, either. They'd paid off a small home in a neighborhood near the elementary school that Olivia would attend here. But it wasn't good enough. Somehow, he managed to scrape together the money to buy a foreclosure near Old Jamestown. And instead of the public school, he enrolled Olivia in Brynlock Academy. Rachel knew nothing about that. He just told her to pack one day, that they were moving. He'd spent all of their savings—and the money she had from her parents' life insurance policies—on a house she'd never even seen. Debbie had kept most of that money for her when she was an adult. Then it was just gone. If they had stayed where they were, money wouldn't have been a problem, but the new house put a strain on their budget. Debbie said Paul threw a fit when Rachel suggested taking on a part-time job. He wanted no part of that, I think. They argued about it."

"It's a good school," Max said. "A great reputation, my own daughter goes there."

The pastor nodded. "I've heard it's a wonderful school. Olivia seems to like it, according to Debbie. But they have to borrow money in order to pay her tuition each year. They argue about that a great deal. Rachel wanted her to go to a smaller school, far less expensive. Closer to the house and where the neighbors send their kids. But Paul would have no part of it. The director of the FBI's children go to PAVAD, he told her this past school term. The mayor's grandchildren. If it was good enough for them, it was good enough for Paul Sturvin's daughters."

"So they argued a great deal about money?" Jac asked.

One of the prime motives for murder was money. She'd have to get Dani on running life insurance policy checks as well. If the woman hadn't already started.

After they were back in the car, she looked Max. "I'm getting more and more interested in speaking with Paul Sturvin."

"You and me both. Studies show that wives are most often the victims in murders within families. Money is often a major motive."

"We need to go over Rachel's cell phone; it might show us the most recent contact between her and her aunt. It might give us a clearer picture why the aunt was there. Although I believe the neighbor this morning. It makes sense. The girls wanted their mother, or maybe Debbie was ill herself and couldn't handle two little girls. So she took them home, and into a nightmare."

Max nodded toward his phone. "Check my notes. We need to check Rachel's phone. See if there are calls from Debbie or texts."

Jac nodded, and checked the list of items found by the original forensic team. The phone was listed. "I'll text Kelly, see if the forensics team has started on it yet."

After a minute or two, the evidence supervisor texted her back. "That was quick. Kelly says that have the phone, and it's with a tech, but they haven't gotten fully into it yet."

No surprise. It took time to process every bit of evidence. Jac had seen some cases with tens of thousands of pieces of evidence collected that would have to be waded through. Hopefully, Rachel's wouldn't be anywhere near that scale.

"Then that's where we're going. Back to PAVAD. Have you eaten anything today?"

She shook her head. She hadn't even had time to grab breakfast. She'd gotten the call from the coordinator Dan around six that morning. She'd showered and dressed quickly. After she realized what she was seeing, food had been the last thing on her mind.

It was so common, normal, something they had done a thousand times together. Yet everything felt different now.

Two months should've been long enough for her to forget, but apparently, it wasn't. It was hard to forget those years of friendship in just two months.

"What do you think happened?"

He just shook his head slightly. "Until we find the location of Paul Sturvin and Debbie Miller, I'm not making any theories. But I know you have one."

"What if they were having financial trouble? It seems likely. I mean, the house they lived in didn't come cheap. And if they were scrimping for tuition to Brynlock for Livy, paying for Ava's preschool wouldn't be any easier—the exact opposite. I'd be interested in talking to someone who knew more about Paul and Rachel's relationship—and their finances. But that would most likely be Debbie. Until we can get a warrant for bank records. But...who is Paul close to? We need to find any friends he might have."

"Why do you think it was the husband? For all we know he is on a business trip to Indianapolis, about to be greeted by his worst nightmare."

Of course, Max would point that out. He always had been the devil's advocate.

"Possibly. But we should have found him by now. We both know that." And the fact that they hadn't deepened her suspicions. Jac knew the statistics. "Someone with nothing to hide isn't all that hard to find."

"That doesn't mean he was involved."

"But it doesn't mean he wasn't."

"Don't make assumptions."

He must have told her that a thousand times over the last five years. Jac almost never listened. "I'm not. I'm theorizing. We need to find Debbie Miller."

"She has the answers. I just hope to hell that she has those kids someplace safe."

52

THEY GRABBED LUNCH IN THE CAFETERIA LOCATED AT THE BACK OF THE first floor of PAVAD. It was plain, utilitarian, but convenient. It reminded Jac of a run-down high school cafeteria, even though the paint was fresh and it was immaculately clean. The food wasn't too horrible, either, though the sandwich and fries Max had ordered for her tasted like sawdust.

She had her phone out; every texted result they'd received from forensics were available at the touch of a button. But Max wouldn't let her think about it for the fifteen minutes they spent eating.

He was a stickler about that; brain breaks, that was what he called them. He was almost rabid about taking care of *her*.

He, Nat, and Miranda were the only people in the world who had ever done that since she'd been six and her mother had died. She'd become the caregiver then, focusing on keeping three-year-old Nat as safe as she possibly could while in the care of a monster.

"Eat, Jac. You'll not do anyone any good if you don't take care of yourself."

"I can take care of myself, you know" But Jac dutifully picked up a French fry. "I'm pretty good at it."

"I know you are. But *I* need to take care of the people I love." He stared straight at her. "And that includes you."

With one look at his eyes, she knew the truth. He didn't mean platonically. No. He meant something far, far more than that.

That was not something she could deal with right now. "Yeah, sure."

She deliberately looked away.

"We'll talk soon. I promise."

"No doubt, we will." Jac stared right at him as something occurred to her. "Everything is changing, isn't it? In general, and in between us."

He didn't even hesitate before nodding. "Yes. But I think it needs to. I think it's about time, don't you? Five years is long enough for me to stop being so oblivious to what, who, has been right there with me from the very first moment. If this case shows us nothing, it's that time…is fleeting. We expect tomorrow to be there, when it just might not be. I'm tired of living off waiting for tomorrow. Especially with you."

Before she could even react, he had her hand trapped in his. No one could see, not where they were sitting. But that touch scorched her.

Made her feel a little less alone. Jac flipped her hand over and laced her fingers through Max's without even thinking about the consequences. She stared into his eyes. She could almost see what he was thinking in that moment.

He meant it. He truly meant it.

Now, she had to figure out what she was going to do about *him.*

As soon as they found Rachel's daughters.

"Making out on the clock? Thought better of the great Mr. and Mrs. Jones," a voice Jac recognized said from behind her shoulder. She couldn't help it—she flinched and yanked her hand from Max's. As if they had done something she should feel guilty about.

"Shove it, Barnes," Max said quietly. He pulled his hand back, but it was obvious he wasn't in a hurry about it.

Of course, he wasn't.

Max didn't care if everyone in the building saw him touch her. To him, *they* were a done deal. Period.

Now that Max had made his decision where she was concerned —whatever that decision was—he wasn't going to ever hide that.

Jac half feared she'd just be along for the ride. Max could be the most implacable, hardheaded man on the planet when his mind was made up about something.

Jac was now that something. He was going to turn that Max power on her full force.

It was just a matter of time.

"So do you want what Eugene Lytel found or not?" Barnes asked in his slightly nasal tone, bringing Jac back to the issue at hand. She and Max—they were a time for later. Not now.

"What?" Jac balled up the remainder of her lunch trash and turned to the man more fully.

"The highway patrol found that Pontiac just over the Iowa line, abandoned. I figured the two of you might want to know."

Jac jumped to her feet. This was the first solid lead they had gotten in hours. She definitely wanted to be a part of it. "How long ago?"

"Fifteen minutes ago. Lytel called me; he knows I'm working this one. We go way back."

Jac looked at Max. He was already on his feet, moving. Like she had known he would be. "Let's go."

Barnes was two steps behind her. "Wait, so you're just going to take off up there? Just like that?"

"Yes," Jac and Max replied together.

Of course, they were. If Debbie had those girls with her, they needed to find her. Get them all into protective custody while they searched for the answers.

Answers Debbie most likely possessed.

There was no hesitation in her at all.

53

TODD HATED HELICOPTERS WITH A PASSION. BUT THERE WAS NO WAY he was going to let himself look like a pussy. He'd forgotten PAVAD had helicopters at its disposal. Helicopters and jets; he wished that prick Jones had gotten a jet instead of *this*.

Now, he wished he hadn't been in such a hurry to tell Jones about what Lytel had found. When Lytel had called him with a reminder of what Todd's true purpose was, Todd hadn't been able to resist using the new information the man had given him as an excuse for the call for his own advantage.

He should have kept his stupid mouth shut and let someone else deliver the report that the car had been found.

He was not going to puke. Todd was better than that.

Airsickness had been one of his own secrets for years. But as he looked at Mr. and Mrs. Jones there across from him—they were so fucking obvious in how gone they were over each other—he refused to let that show.

Jaclyn was pale, but there was a determined look on her face. Todd got the impression she was lost in her head somewhere. Of course, she was, she had her big guard dog there next to her protecting her from everything possible. All she had to do was *think*. The prick beside her would do everything else. Especially the heavy lifting. She'd not have to even lift a finger for anything with Dr. Jones there.

Todd would just drop any idea of hooking up with Jaclyn permanently. That guy wasn't letting her get snagged by another man anytime soon.

Hell, Todd knew it—he envied the guy. Jaclyn was pressed up against Jones on the small bench seat across from Todd. The two of them looked good together.

Like the PAVAD: FBI poster couple. Surprising envy filled his chest.

Todd sat there and thought about his life and what he wanted next.

Came to a decision.

Once he made it to PAVAD long enough to do what he had to, he'd find a woman of his own there. Just for the hell of it.

There had to be one or two he could be bothered dating. Finding something *more* with.

There was Miranda Talley. *Miranda*. She'd made him laugh several times earlier. He found that very attractive.

Maybe she was bigger than the women he usually found attractive—Todd's taste ran to small, petite women that did what they were told, both in the bed and out—and had way more attitude than he was used to, but a change from his usual taste wouldn't be all that difficult. She'd keep him fired up—that was for sure.

And she would understand the job, that part of him that had brought him to the FBI in the first place.

No. If nothing else, he suspected Miranda knew what she was doing in the bedroom. A woman like that always did.

She'd probably be hot and fierce and demanding. He liked that idea.

Jaclyn was the exact opposite. Soft and alluring and easily guided into exactly what a man wanted her to do. No doubt, the great Dr. Jones got off on that—liked feeling like the man.

Todd used thoughts of the two women to distract him from what he was hurtling through the sky in.

When he made it back to St. Louis, he was going to get more serious about convincing Miranda to give him a chance.

She'd probably like him if she'd stop listening to the pricks in St. Louis who hated him. He was strong enough to handle a woman like that.

Far more than any of the other pricks in St. Louis.

The helicopter finally landed on a desolate stretch of Iowa Route J56. Todd breathed in, thankful his feet were back on firm ground.

He took a look around. There was a gravel road off to the right of where the helicopter had landed. A pond was nearby.

The sign for the Iowa/Missouri border was right there, too. There were a lot of fields, trees, and barren pavement.

The red Pontiac was the only real spot of color. Garish and out of place.

Todd's stomach clenched—he had a feeling in his gut, someone had probably died right there.

He hoped it wasn't kids. Todd hated it when it was kids. He'd studied those photos of the two little girls, too.

That and the state patrol cars with their lights blazing. Half a dozen local LEOs were waiting for them to take charge and do their job for them.

The car sat awkwardly off the side of the gravel road, nose deep in the ditch. Pointed straight at the old wire fence separating the ditch from the field and pond.

"So where did she go?" Todd asked. There wasn't anywhere in this pit of desolation for anyone to go.

54

JAC APPROACHED THE CAR CAREFULLY, AWARE THAT SHE WASN'T IN sterile coveralls. She did not want to contaminate the scene. Barnes apparently felt no such concern. He lumbered down toward the car.

"Be careful, Barnes. Don't touch anything. Do not contaminate the forensic evidence, or you'll be dealing with Marianna Dennis—the director's wife."

"I'm not an idiot, Jaclyn." But he stopped when she told him to.

The rear window on the Pontiac was down.

Jac used the flashlight Max handed her and ran the light across the rim of the window. There was a slightly purple film on the edge. "We have child-size fingerprints. Reasonably fresh."

Four handprints. Two different sizes. Right there on the glass. As if two children had put their hands on the glass and pulled themselves out of the car through the window.

It would've been difficult, but the kids could've managed. Especially if they were scared enough. Or their aunt was helping them. The car door was wedged at the bottom against the ditch. They couldn't have opened the door. And at the angle that the car sat, climbing out of that window would've been extremely difficult.

But they had. "There's blood on the car here. Outside." Jac looked around where she stood.

There were footprints. Child-sized, and some slightly bigger than her own. Debbie's, most likely.

And there was blood.

"Yes." Max said from behind her. She hadn't realized that she'd spoken aloud.

"What do a typical seven-year-old and four-year-old do when they're scared?" She asked the one agent who was also a parent out there with her now. Her eyes met Max's.

There were too many memories of when she and Nat were little like that. Jac had spent her entire childhood protecting her sister.

Olivia probably felt that same responsibility for Ava.

It was a heavy burden to put on such small shoulders. It had taken Jac a long time to realize that about herself.

Jac shined the light inside the car, looking for any clue to where Debbie could be headed.

It was possible she'd killed her niece and Edith Lindsay and taken the girls for some reason known only to her—revenge, psychotic break, a need for children of her own again. Jac wasn't making any assumptions.

Not until they had more answers. The forensics team would be there as soon as they could get the van there. It would just take time. The teams were at least three hours by car from St. Louis.

Time they couldn't afford to lose. Not if the girls were out there.

"There." She focused the light on the interior.

"What do you see?" Barnes demanded, practically stepping between her and Max.

"Ava's stuffed emu. Mr. Bird."

"How do you know? It could be any kid's toy."

"It's a specialty item that you can only get down at the mall. Max's daughter, Emery, and I made one together about six months ago. Emery's is purple and named Humphrey. That one in the car is the younger girl's. It's an emu with rainbow eyes named Mr. Bird.

Not exactly a typical stuffed animal. They were limited edition. Only a dozen of that color were made, the store clerk told me. I...made one in that exact color, but I gave mine green eyes. Because Emery insisted they were the same color as my eyes. Ava doesn't go anywhere without that stuffed bird, Max."

"But that means there are still ten out there. No reason to *assume* this is the Sturvin kid's," Barnes said.

"It's hers. I can confirm that," Max said.

"DNA will have to prove it, but for the time being, we'll act as if it is. They'll find my DNA on it, too. I've held it before. At Max's house, and at the girls' last basketball game. I know this kid, Barnes. It's Ava's. It's all we have to go on. She was here. Now, we have to find her and her sister." Jac turned to Max, afraid to let her hope show. "They were here. And from the handprints, they were alive."

It was far more than they'd had before.

55

MIRANDA SCRATCHED AT THE AREA ABOVE THE CAST WITH frustration. She hated being sidelined like this. She wanted to be out there doing something productive, something that was going to get them just that much closer to finding those little girls.

Every time they were mentioned, Jac got a look of intense pain in her eyes. Miranda doubted the other woman knew that it was there, but Miranda hadn't missed it. She didn't think Max had missed it, either.

On the outside, Jac was acting the professional, but on the inside, the other woman was barely holding herself together.

Her friend was hurting.

Miranda wanted to find a way to fix that.

She stood. There was the whiteboard, and it could use some updating. She might not be out there physically searching for those girls, but she could find something *here* that helped.

Whit came in the conference room, long, lanky, broad-shouldered, and adorable with his shaggy caramel-colored hair and big puppy-dog-brown eyes. He didn't look as much like a kid as he had when she had first met him five or six years ago. He'd grown into himself or something. He was a few years older than Miranda. And always seemed so alone now.

That was going to be her next project, once she fixed Jac and Max. Finding a woman for Whit. He deserved it. He was one of the best men—and agents—that she knew. And he had information for her.

"They found the car; signs of the girls were in it. They are calling the search teams out now."

Miranda prayed it would be enough. That they would find those girls and soon.

"Any word on Paul Sturvin?" The man had to be out there somewhere.

"Not yet."

She would have said more, but her phone buzzed. A quick check of the screen had her glancing at Whit in surprise. "It's the director. He wants me in his office ASAP."

"Go. I'll take over here."

"Keep me posted on anything from Jac or Max, ok?"

"Gotcha." He nodded, shooting her a rare smile. Whit used to smile a lot in the early days. PAVAD had changed him. Miranda made herself a vow. She was going to have to find a way to fix Whit, too.

Someone had to do it, after all. It might as well be her.

56

ED CLUTCHED THE ENVELOPE CLOSE. IT WAS A STANDARD ENVELOPE, manila and large. Old. The contents had haunted him for twelve years now. The envelope was starting to show its age. Perhaps he should put it in a clean envelope, but that almost felt disrespectful in a way. Sacrilegious.

This file...it was the last one Darrin Hull had ever touched. Darrin. Twenty-eight years old at the time someone had tracked him and his wife and two young children down and executed them, along with a relative of Darrin's wife.

In their own home.

Darrin had been the most junior agent on Ed's team before Ed had moved into more administrative roles within the bureau.

Ed had stood at the back of the crowd at Darrin's family's quin-tuple funeral and made the dead father a vow.

He was going to see this case solved. He owed it to Darrin. To Theresa, Darrin's wife. She'd been all of twenty-four when she'd been shot straight between the eyes. To Lois, Theresa's grandmother who'd lived with them.

Theresa and Lois had done nothing to deserve what had happened to them. Nor had Darrin.

The children certainly hadn't.

It was their children that he couldn't forget. The youngest had been two.

Ed's granddaughter Evalyn was a little over two now. The older Hull child had been four.

Four.

Defenseless.

He would have been sixteen now.

Ed had seven boys of his own; the adoption papers had been finalized eighteen months ago. The three older boys were around that age now, sixteen-year-old twins and seventeen-year-old Nate.

They had their whole lives ahead of them.

Darrin Hull's son should have his life ahead of him, too.

"Give it to Agent Gabriella Sloane, at the Indianapolis field office. I want her to take one more look at this before she retires." His old friend deserved to retire without shadows over her own head.

Darrin would always be a shadow—until they had the answers. Or a ghost that had haunted them both for far too long.

"Yes, sir. I'll put it in her hands personally."

"I'm going to hold you to that. This is the original case file. I have other copies, if Gabriella asks."

"Should I expect anything in return?"

Ed shook his head. "But watch your back. I...it's been twelve years, but I'm not sure the ones responsible aren't still...a part of the bureau. With eyes and ears everywhere."

Green eyes widened when she looked at him. There was a great deal of intelligence in those eyes. And in her file.

Miranda Talley was the same height as Ed. She had a direct, open manner about her. Trustworthiness. She was as honest as she was open. He liked that about her. She also had one of the sharpest minds in the bureau—and was very loyal. "No one knows I'm sending this with you. I'd like to keep it that way. Call me when you get there."

"Director?" She looked down at the file in her hand. "Is there anything I can do to help? I...recognize the name. I saw it in the cold-case database."

"You spend much time there?"

"Some. I'll occasionally study cold cases to see if there is anything I can do. I don't want them to be forgotten."

Ed filed that away for a later time. Cold cases were his own personal kryptonite as well. It took a certain kind of agent to go looking for answers in the past. "You can read it. But whatever you find...keep it to yourself. It...we've lost enough people because of this file, Miranda. I don't want to lose anyone else."

"Yes, sir."

He watched her walk away, spine straight with the confidence of youth and skill, and wondered.

Wondered if he was doing the right thing—Gabriella deserved to know he was still looking into Darrin's death. Sending Dr. Talley to hunt for Paul Sturvin in Indianapolis was just an excuse.

They all had ghosts that haunted them.

Ed didn't have much room for any others.

57

PAVAD WAS FAST; MAX HAD ALWAYS APPRECIATED THAT. WHEN HE'D called for the SEARCH team, there had been as quick a response as could be possible.

Max studied the two trackers quickly as they hopped out of the second helicopter. It had taken them a little over ninety minutes to mobilize and arrive. That was it.

He'd worked with both before.

It did surprise him to see Jac's younger sister, Natalie, walking next to Micah Hanan, her two dogs trotting alongside her obediently, though.

He'd heard through the grapevine that Nat had transferred from the ATF to the newly forming PAVAD: SEARCH team. He just hadn't crossed paths with her yet.

The other man was one he'd met before.

Micah Hanan was a transfer from an Oklahoma field office and the best tracker the FBI had. It wasn't exactly a shock to see he'd taken a PAVAD appointment. PAVAD was the top of the line for those who dominated in specialized skills like tracking. Nat probably gave Hanan a real run for his money.

The woman was the best he'd ever seen working with K9 search dogs.

The absolute best.

She had a sixth sense for where people—especially children—would hide. Or be hidden.

She was only twenty-six years old, and looked about fourteen from a distance. The last time he and Jac had taken her out, she'd been carded twice. He'd teased her about that both times.

Worry for Nat was real; she was thinner than she had been before. If Nat broke one hundred pounds now, Max would eat his own hat.

Nat was looking too damned thin. Beneath their fragile exteriors, the Jones sisters were forged from steel. Forged in hell. Neither one of the sisters had had it easy living with that bastard Colonel Boyd Jones.

Fathers were supposed to protect their children. That hadn't happened for Jac and Nat.

Jac hadn't turned yet from where she was talking to the local LEOs who'd secured the scene. They had four officers, all the locals could spare, out canvasing the fields for any initial signs of Deborah Miller or the girls. So far, nothing.

"Jac." Max put one hand on her shoulder and turned her slightly. "Nat."

She recognized her sister and started down the road to meet her.

They had auxiliary agents on their way now. They'd be there in less than two hours. It was standard from here. Max knew that.

If Ava and Olivia were out there in these woods, they'd find them.

It was just a matter of time. The real question was what condition they'd been in when they were found.

58

Nat Jones gripped the leads to her two Belgian Tervurens as she took her first good look around the small Iowan road just one hundred feet from the Missouri border.

This was not the first time she had been searching for missing children. It wouldn't be the last. Every single time, she imagined the nightmares that those children were feeling. In intense detail.

She'd been four the first time she and her sister had been left in the woods and told to fend for themselves. They had. For more than nine hours that first time.

Nat had enough nightmares of her own. Limited vision in her left eye thanks to the bomb that she had barely survived was a constant reminder of one of those nightmares.

She had barely passed the vision exam to get certified to work for the FBI now.

Had her sister not already worked for PAVAD, Nat wouldn't have passed PAVAD's entrance standards at all.

Nat snorted. That's what she had heard a so-called *friendly* colleague saying to another teammate just three days ago.

Never mind that she had a reputation for being one of the best K9 handlers in the country.

Edward Dennis had been the one to get her here, and she was well aware of that. She wasn't going to let that man down. But that was their secret. He'd cautioned her the day he'd interviewed her to keep that to herself.

She'd only gotten the job because of her sister, after all. Her sister and the father they both despised. Never mind the years she'd worked in the field to get to where she was.

Well, screw them. Nat knew what was important. Her sister, her dogs, and her job. In that very order.

She had nothing else now.

Nat ran a calming hand over her younger dog, Kudos. He always felt excitement when it was time to work. He fed off the energy of the searchers around him.

He wasn't a quiet dog. Those unfamiliar with Kudos's great amount of skill often questioned her training methods. Said he was too high strung and uncontrolled. A liability. Said that *she,* as small as she was, couldn't truly control him.

She controlled him just fine. Because he loved her.

Once he was on the job, Kudos was the most intense search and rescue dog she had ever worked with. He and his partner—and great love—Karma.

They'd lost the third of their trio, Candy, in the bombing. She had been almost eight. She had been the dog Nat had first trained and learned with.

The first dog she had loved.

Nat would always grieve for Candy. Candy had been her heart dog. And always would be. Candy had helped *her* heal from the trauma that had been her childhood.

But Kudos and Karma were her loves now.

A familiar redhead caught her attention. Jac. Nat pulled in a breath. She always had mixed emotions whenever she first saw her sister. Jac was the only human left on earth that Nat allowed herself to love.

That always reminded Nat of exactly how alone she was.

"You take the east quadrant," her new boss said. He stared at her out of eyes so dark they looked black—eyes that told her everything she needed to know about him. She'd learned early on to read a man by the look in his eyes. "If you think you can handle it."

The east—which looked to be the least strenuous terrain. Of course. Because he didn't think she was capable of anything more.

"I can handle it just fine."

There was skepticism in the man's eyes.

Micah Hanan, FBI tracker extraordinaire, didn't think Nat could cut it. Not him, the great and wonderful Micah Hanan who never messed up at all.

Very few on her team now actually thought that she could cut it.

She understood. Nat barely made it to five two. She weighed in at ninety-six pounds now. The FBI had no minimum weight or height requirements—a good thing, as she would never have made them. They hadn't had those requirements since the mid-1970s. Thankfully.

Nat had passed the sprint requirement three minutes faster than required. The sit-ups and pushups had been nothing for her.

She was just small.

People thought she was insignificant. Maybe she was.

The dogs were her great equalizer.

Kudos, a Tervuren cross, at ninety-eight pounds actually outweighed her.

Nat didn't care. People had been making assumptions her entire life. All she cared about was doing her job and making a difference. An impact on the world. Leaving her mark in helping others.

So that she wasn't insignificant after all.

Right now, her job meant finding those two little girls, as fast as possible.

"In a moment. I need to check in with my sister. See if there is anything to help us out."

"What is this? A family reunion? Is your sister here anywhere? If she's a civilian, Jones—"

"Stupid isn't on my resume, Hanan." Nat shook her head. Did he think she was that incompetent? Jerk. There was only one other woman on the scene in the first place. Jac was close enough for him to see the resemblance between them. Total ass. "Jac is the agent in charge of this investigation. She's with PAVAD: CCU. Over there," Nat said pointing. "I'd be checking in with the AIC, anyway. The AIC is my sister, by the way."

She didn't like Hanan. Something about him had her on edge. Scared her. There was an indefinable element about him that told her he was a threat to her well-being. She'd always trusted her instincts. That lesson had been beaten into her by the time she was ten and Jac thirteen.

"Agent Jaclyn Jones? We've met, worked together before. That's your sister?"

Nat just nodded once. Nat had a reputation with S&R. Jac had a reputation in the field. Nat was so proud of her sister. "She's almost as good as I am at S&R. She can work Karma, if needed. They're very well bonded."

"She's good at what she does. I've seen her work before." For him, that was a real compliment.

Nat just nodded. Of course, Jac was good at what she did. Being the best at anything they did had been a requirement for survival when they were children.

Failure had never been allowed. Failure was always instantly punished. Only being the best was good enough. Some lessons stuck for life.

Jac looked up. Nat studied her sister quickly. Jac looked thinner than she had before. There were dark circles beneath her sister's eyes.

That wasn't unusual, though. Considering that Jac most likely had been up all night. Nat shivered as the case details sank in.

This had been a bloodbath. Her sister dealt with these kinds of things every day. Concern for her sister hit her. Jac seemed so alone sometimes.

Not that Nat had room to talk. Jac at least had friends now. People she worked with. Nat didn't even have that.

If something were to happen to her out there, no one except Jac would even care.

She'd come to terms with that lying on her back in the hospital room, missing James with every breath she took. Losing him had devastated her.

It always would.

He had been the one man she had ever let close to her. Then he had died. That still stung every minute of every day.

A tall man approached behind her. Nat didn't have to turn around to know that it was Hanan.

PAVAD: SEARCH had twelve people in it. Teams of two were often sent out in various directions, with the ability to pull PAVAD auxiliaries to beef up numbers whenever needed.

She'd only been sent out twice with someone other than Hanan. Nat was the last one sent out at all. Only as a last resort.

Nat was well aware of that.

He didn't trust her. No one on her team trusted her.

Hanan definitely didn't trust her skills.

She'd only transferred to the FBI because the director of PAVAD had asked her to specifically. And promised she'd be closer to her sister.

That was invaluable to Nat.

Jac was all she had.

Kudos bumped her leg. Besides Kudos and Karma.

Nat didn't want to keep living alone. She wanted to have the kind of life that she saw other people leading. The kind with friends, families of their own. Just people who cared. She and Jac had never had that. Their father had seen to that. He wanted to be the only one that mattered to them at all.

Colonel Jones wanted Nat and Jac one hundred percent dependent on *him*. That she and Jac had escaped still infuriated him.

She bit back a shiver just thinking about him. About how her own escape had happened, after he'd run Jac off when Jac had been only sixteen.

It wasn't Jac that he wanted to idolize and worship him. It was Nat. Because Nat was his by blood. Jac wasn't, despite the legal claim. But Nat—he'd always thought he owned her.

He despised Jac, had almost washed his hands of his late wife's daughter from a previous relationship. *Jac* was flawed to him.

He wanted to control Nat. To have her one hundred percent broken to his will.

The colonel's harassment since the bombing was just getting worse.

She was eventually going to have to tell her sister. Just so Jac would *know* what was going on.

If anything ever happened to Nat, the colonel would be the first place Jac would need to look.

Nat wasn't certain their father hadn't killed their mother, either. She'd find out one day, though. One way or another.

Nat was still looking. One day, she would *know*.

Max was the one to fill them in on what they were doing out there today. Nat nodded at him, quietly thinking once again how good he was for her sister. He stood at Jac's side, strong and protective—not even realizing he was doing it. He was strong enough to protect her sister from the nightmares of the world. Nat almost envied her that.

Jac gave the orders. Nat knew what was expected of her.

Jac looked at Nat. "Watch yourself out here."

"Of course. Be careful out here, Jac. I'll talk to you later." Nat nodded and gave the signal for Kudos and Karma to flank her. They moved to obey immediately. "We'll be ready, if you need us."

"I know."

Nat nodded at Hanan one more time. She had a job to do.

It was time to do it.

Nat started toward the woods. The forest was where she felt most at home, after all.

Safest.

Despite the lessons her father had beaten into her when Jac wasn't around to protect her.

In the woods was the only place Nat had ever been able to escape him, after all. The very lessons he'd taught her—had been the only tools she'd had to escape all those years ago.

59

Todd's phone rang, right when he was watching the woman with the dogs as she started ordering the local guys around. Half of them had incredulous looks on their faces as they stared at her.

No wonder.

She was just a kid.

She didn't look like she belonged out there at all. She'd even rolled up the sleeves on the damned PAVAD jacket.

This woman had gotten a PAVAD appointment and not him? It didn't make any sense.

Jaclyn walked across the road to the woman. Side by side, he was struck by the resemblance. Jaclyn was taller by several inches, with more red in her hair. The other woman was a great deal thinner, shorter, and darker haired. That was about it.

He'd heard she had a sister somewhere in PAVAD. He wouldn't have guessed search and rescue.

Not for one of Colonel Jones's daughters.

They'd grown up with prep schools and trust funds and dinners with heads of states. Tramping around the woods with dogs bigger than she was didn't make any sense to him at all. An enigma—even more so than her older sister.

She wasn't as pretty as her sister. Not really. Jaclyn had a more classic appeal—this woman had a lost-waif look. Girl next door in trouble look.

Not his type at all.

Especially with the guard dogs watching every move everyone made. The bigger one looked like he belonged in a Stephen King novel or something.

He pulled his phone out quickly and checked the display.

Eugene Lytel.

Todd texted him back quickly. Now was definitely not the time.

Lytel was on his way with the auxiliaries. He wanted to meet with Todd as soon as possible. They had something to discuss.

Damn it. Sweat beaded on the back of his neck.

Something didn't *feel* right about Lytel. Not by a long shot. Not anymore. Todd wasn't so certain what he was doing now was that great of an idea. Not a good idea at all.

He was going to have to find a way to get out of this somehow. And not destroy everything he had worked for.

As thunder cracked overhead, with the storm getting closer, Todd wondered exactly how he was going to accomplish that.

60

IT PROBABLY WOULD BE FASTER TO GET OFF THE PLANE AND DRIVE. Miranda thought about the possibilities as the plane was delayed once again.

She's already been sitting for more than ninety minutes. It was a four-hour drive between St. Louis and Indianapolis. As the stewardess walked by, Miranda caught her attention. "Excuse me?"

"Yes? How may I help you today?"

"How long of a delay is this going to be?" Miranda discreetly flashed the credentials that she carried with her everywhere.

The flight attendant's eyes widened. "Is there some sort of trouble on the plane?"

Miranda shot her smile and shook her head. "No, but I'm expected in Indianapolis soon. I'm wondering if it might not be a good idea to trade my ticket in and drive."

The flight attendant nodded. "From what I saw on my phone, this storm is going be a big one and coming in fits and spurts. We'll be sitting here for a while. But it's moving through rather quickly. But being what it is, you may be better off driving."

"Thanks. I'm on time sensitive business." Miranda took it as the sign that it was. She stood and grabbed her single bag.

Twenty-five minutes later, Miranda maneuvered her small SUV onto the road. "Indianapolis or bust," she yelled at the top of her lungs.

Just for the hell of it.

Why not?

There was no one next to her to hear.

61

Todd felt absolutely useless as he stood back and watched what was going on around the red Pontiac. The forensics team had finally arrived, hopping out of their two vans and hustling around like they were a group of superheroes. They had the car loaded into a large box truck and removed from the scene before the rain broke free.

Cody Lorcan was good at what she did, at least.

Rain pelted his jacket, but Todd ignored it.

He'd seen Lytel wandering around, strutting like he ran the place.

Objective, Todd supposed the man did. When it came to his team of auxiliary agents, Lytel was most certainly the agent in charge. Todd knew the numbers; there were one hundred PAVAD: AUX agents. Lytel, five coordinators, six teams of ten each, and support staff. But he didn't want auxiliary. Everyone knew that was a place where an agent went to land in no-man's-land.

Auxiliary agents never left auxiliary. In four years, none had promoted out into other PAVAD areas.

That was telling to Todd.

He wanted more than that.

But he supposed that the *head* of the auxiliary unit was a position that meant something. He had no idea what Lytel's beef with PAVAD and Ed Dennis was.

He wasn't interested in finding out.

But he had to play the game now.

First opportunity he had, Todd left the initial crime scene and walked up the road. Crossed the state line right next to the Welcome to Missouri road sign.

Lytel was there, scanning the scene with binoculars, checking on the auxiliary teams he had out, plus the SEARCH agents.

Todd stepped up to the man's side. "What did you want?"

"An answer. Are you in? Completely?"

"I'm not sure."

"What's the hesitation?"

"A man like Paul Sturvin seems like a damned good hold up. What in the hell happened?"

"Your guess is as good as mine. Best thing I can figure—the guy got into it with his wife, and things got out of hand. Just shitty coincidence Sturvin was…on the payroll."

Todd nodded. That's what made the most sense to him, too.

"Make a choice, Barnes. You in, or are you out?"

"I'm in," Todd said. He'd come up with a working plan. It was the best he could do.

Hell, he knew the truth.

He had no other choice.

62

Hours passed. The waiting was the hard part. Jac was kept busy coordinating at the command post when what she truly wanted to do was take the dog Nat had left with her and get out there looking for the girls herself.

But she couldn't do that; she had a job to do—and that meant doing it right there at the command tent.

She had to trust the people she worked with to do *their* jobs.

Her sister was out there. If the girls were out there somewhere, Nat would find them.

She was the best Jac had ever seen after all.

Finally, her sister emerged, after five long hours. Nat came right to her, ignoring the agents and locals and the man she'd arrived with.

Jac stepped toward her sister. "Nat?"

"We found a body," Nat said quietly. "A woman matching the description of Deborah Miller. I'm sorry, Jac. Signs of the girls remain within fifteen feet of her body, but never branch out after that. There are fresh tire tracks. From the way Kudos kept losing the trail, the girls were taken away—either carried off or by car. Whatever it was, they didn't walk out of here. But they…are just gone."

Jac ran over the possibilities in her head as Max came up behind her. "Initial forensics are reporting that the car was run off the road."

Jac flinched. "She made it this far. And what? Was killed here, or was this just as far as she could make it?"

Nat shook her head. "She didn't just end up here, Jackie. She has a clear handprint over her face. She was suffocated. And as beaten up as she is, she couldn't fight back."

They'd have to confirm it with forensics, but Jac trusted her sister's words. She turned to Max.

"The killer tracked Debbie here, killed her, and took the girls away in another vehicle?"

"It's the most logical conclusion. Which tells me he or she may have wanted the girls in the first place. Or just to silence Debbie, and the girls are incidental. He took them for a reason. When he could have killed them and left them out here. We'll have search teams continue to comb over this area, but right now…we're almost back to where we began."

"And the girls are now definitely in the care of a killer."

63

DRIVING ONE-ARMED FOR FOUR HOURS WAS PROBABLY ENOUGH TO GIVE any woman a nasty case of tennis elbow in her good hand. Miranda tried to shake it off as best she could.

Dani had called her halfway through the drive to give her an update.

They hadn't been able to get a hold of Paul Sturvin by phone.

Nor had local officers been able to locate him.

She'd confirmed that with Jac not even five minutes ago.

He'd disappeared. At the time his wife was brutally murdered? Uh...no.

That didn't sit well with Miranda—or anyone else involved.

They had seen family annihilators before. She speculated that was exactly what she was facing. Miranda headed to the field office first. Anything could go wrong in a case like this. She wasn't about to go poking about looking for a potentially dangerous man one-handed without backup.

The last thing Miranda considered herself was stupid. If the contents of the file had gotten people killed before, she didn't want to be added to that list.

Ed Dennis said there would be an agent waiting for her at Indianapolis.

There was.

Miranda liked it when things went according to plan.

She took a look at the long, tall, dark, and handsome man in the suit and mirrored sunglasses and almost sighed. Her day had certainly gotten a lot brighter.

"Agent Walker Taggart?"

The man, a good six inches taller than Miranda's almost five eleven, nodded. She wished he'd take off the sunglasses. Miranda had always thought you could tell a man's character by that first look in his eyes.

It was something her grandmother had taught her early on.

He held out a hand, she shook as well as she was able to around the bag in her one good arm. "It's nice to meet you. I understand you used to work in St. Louis, with Agent Knight?"

He nodded. "I did. About four years back, but I've…known…him for a good twenty-five years. I heard what happened to him. Is he doing ok? Haven't heard much from him, not since it happened. I was up there in the hospital with him for a few days. Until he kicked me out."

He had a deep rumbly voice. Broad shoulders, warm dark-brown skin. A way of walking that shouted he was all-male. Miranda wasn't blind to the effect. Then again, she bet most heterosexual women wouldn't be.

"Knight... Knight does his own thing, and as far as I know, he's doing fine. We worked together a few months back. He showed up just as I…well…" Miranda waved the cast a little. That was a case she'd never forget. "Just as I really needed him to. Came in real handy in keeping me from getting offed. Of course, he's in and out all the time. Transferring to PAVAD soon, with an entire division to his name. At least, that's what the rumors are saying."

Miranda had had mixed emotions about Knight from the moment they'd worked together on her last case. That case had taken too much of a personal turn for her—and not just because it happened in her grandmother's home. In her hometown. With people Miranda knew, had grown up with.

No, Allan Knight had made it personal.

Miranda hadn't forgotten that.

One brief kiss. That's all it had taken. It was well beyond the bounds of professionalism. He'd had no business putting his hands on her that day.

She hadn't invited it. Of course, she hadn't exactly pushed him away either. Even today, she wouldn't. She had very complex emotions where Allan Knight was concerned.

Even if he was a curmudgeonly old ass. Well.

"You can set your stuff down in my office," Agent Taggart said. He finally removed the glasses, revealing hazel eyes that were absolutely gorgeous.

This man was a real heartbreaker. Even though he did have the mannerisms of the soberest undertaker.

Miranda bit back a smile. She had always enjoyed figuring out enigmas.

"I'm trying to locate a man from St. Louis who was supposed to be here on a business trip." She named the hotel quickly. "Unfortunately, we haven't been able to locate him. His wife was murdered in the early hours of the morning yesterday. An elderly neighbor heard the commotion; she was also killed. His two young daughters are missing. We need to find him."

"I'm sorry to hear that. We'll see what we can do."

64

THE GIRLS WERE FINALLY ASLEEP. IT HAD TAKEN PAUL FAR TOO LONG to calm them down after he'd finished with Debbie. Paul checked them both in the rearview mirror. He probably shouldn't have killed her with the girls watching. He could have just left her there. That would have been best for the girls, after all.

Debbie had been on her last legs as it was. Chances of her being found in time for it to do any good would most likely have not happened.

But what was done was done.

He was going to have to work on controlling his temper. His actions.

Paul couldn't afford mistakes like this.

Olivia had been watching him ever since, but now she was asleep.

She was becoming more defiant. Like her mother. He was going to have to address that when he could. She had to learn. Had to understand that everything he had done had been for her.

He would have to erase the sight of him dragging Debbie away into the woods, leaving her and Ava behind.

Paul looked down. He was going to have to change clothes soon. Debbie's blood was all over him.

Olivia had seen it. He just knew it.

She was old enough, smart enough to know something bad had happened in those woods.

To his shame, he had done nothing to protect her. He had made a vow the first time he held her in his arms all those years ago and she'd smiled at him.

He was supposed to protect her. To give her the life she deserved. He had failed.

Paul straightened in the driver's seat. He had failed her now. He would not fail her or Ava ever again.

What was done was done.

It was time to look to the future now.

65

Miranda searched the generic hotel room, looking for some signs of the man who'd occupied it last. Security footage had shown that it was Paul Sturvin. She'd gotten a full view of him on the camera. Enough to easily identify him.

Nothing in his manner had shouted unease, or that he knew what had happened in St. Louis. Paul had checked in at 5:03 p.m. two evenings before. Phone records showed that he had called home for approximately thirty-two seconds.

The exact time length of the message he had left on his wife's cell phone. A second phone call came fifteen seconds after that to the landline phone. To the voice machine. That call had lasted sixteen seconds.

He'd ordered room service two hours later. And seen opening the door wearing what appeared to be sweatpants and a T-shirt.

He'd been barefooted. Miranda had made note of that on the camera.

Just a regular, average, normal businessman away on a business trip.

While his whole world fell apart behind him.

She was revising her earlier opinion on what had happened to the Sturvins. She'd thought family annihilator, but things were looking the exact opposite direction.

"So where is he?" she asked Taggart. He told her to call him by his last name. Said that he abhorred the name Walker.

Miranda wondered why he didn't just change it. It wasn't that much of a hassle. He was just as cantankerous as Knight. She could see the two men being friends. They had the same surly attitude.

Miranda fought the urge to do things just to shake Taggart up a bit.

She always had been contrary like that.

"No one saw him leave. He's still checked in. At least according the supervisor at the front desk." Which wasn't all that unusual. People took off from hotels all the time. She'd seen it thousands of times before.

If there was someone checked in this room, well, Miranda would gnaw her cast off with her own teeth. There wasn't a sign of anyone even having stayed there. Unless Sturvin was beyond fastidious.

Although the bed showed obvious signs where someone had laid, that was no indication of how long someone had been in that bed. She knew that. She checked the drawers in the cabinet quickly. Nothing.

The bathroom looked undisturbed, except for a wet towel hanging over the bar. Miranda checked it carefully, not wanting to disturb any evidence if any existed.

The towel was damp. Damp enough to have been used just that morning.

Miranda knew hotel rooms, knew when something felt *off*.

She grabbed her own cell phone and texted Dani quickly. The computer analyst had gotten her the information in the first place. Within seconds Dani's face appeared through video chat. *"What's up, Doc?"*

Her friends had started calling her Doc in the last month. Since her return from Masterson County. Her degree was so new that the ink was barely dry on the certificate, but Miranda was proud of it. She'd worked hard for that degree. She'd earned it. While working for the FBI.

It hadn't been easy, and it hadn't been fast. But she'd done it.

She now held a doctorate in social psychology, with a specialization in small towns.

She'd work for the FBI for a handful more years, maybe five, possibly ten. Then she would retire, to work on the research projects that had been burning within her for a long while.

Miranda was fascinated with how small towns worked. That, more than the FBI, was her true passion. Her heart project. The culmination of years of hard work. She'd go home. Where she belonged. "It says his phone is here somewhere."

"I know. I'm the one who messaged that information, remember?" Dani had a snarky humor that Miranda had always enjoyed.

"Well, can you tell me where?" Miranda turned her phone, panned it around the room so that Dani could see. Dani and whoever else was there with her. "Because I have nothing. It's possible the man was here this morning. But it's also possible he left last night and drove home in time to commit the murder. I have pretty much…nothing. He could have easily left here last night." Which would put him well within range of the Sturvin home with plenty enough time to kill his wife and Mrs. Lindsay. "Going to say this is inconclusive."

"No, it's elementary, Doc. Look around. I bet you his phone is there somewhere."

"What makes you say that?"

"Because I'm far cleverer than you are? Look around. His phone is there. It's binging towers in your vicinity. Has been all night. By the way, Jac just texted—they found the body of Deborah Miller just over the Missouri border less than an hour ago. Murdered. Watch yourself out there."

Miranda disconnected and then looked at her new best buddy.

"Well, how do you feel about playing search? There's a phone in this room somewhere. Or, at least, Dani says so. I love proving her wrong, so let's get to it."

He looked at her and gave a quick smile. She shivered. The man was hot as hell. But his smile, cold. This was a very scary man.

"Well, let's get started. We have a phone to find."

66

Jac was holding herself together, but Max sensed that it was just barely. The sun had come and went. Search teams, led by Lytel and Hanan were out, combing the area around where Debbie Miller's body had been found. Max doubted they would find anything.

Nat was buzzing around, coordinating search teams consisting of local LEOs and Lytel's auxiliaries.

For such a small woman, she commanded respect—once she started giving orders.

Quiet, but more than capable of leading.

Much like her older sister.

They were taking the body back to PAVAD via helicopter within the next hour.

Max intended that he and Jac would be on the same flight.

They needed something to tie a suspect to Debbie, to get them *something* to say definitively that it was Paul Sturvin.

News from Indianapolis said the man possibly could have made it back to St. Louis in time to kill his wife. Which meant the odds were good that it was him.

Approximately twenty percent of female murder victims were killed by their intimate partners. The number of women killed by men they knew was fifteen times higher than that of women killed by strangers. Those weren't numbers Max could discount.

Especially considering the facts of the case.

"What are you thinking?"

Max turned. Jac was there, watching the searchers, just as he was.

"The facts as we know them. Rachel knew her killer. The girls were already with Debbie. She was alone in the house, but she knew her aunt was on her way. Maybe she unlocked the door."

"That fits. Dani said the only prints on the door locks were Rachel's."

"She had already unlocked the door. Paul came home and pushed it open."

"Wouldn't his fingerprints have been there?"

"Not if he wore gloves when he came in. He had a pair of black gloves on when he arrived at Emery's party. I remember him taking them off very carefully."

"So he comes in. She sees him, confronts him about something. Maybe...he was supposed to be working. And they needed the money. They argued. He killed her."

"We never found the murder weapon," Max said. "But let's assume he bludgeoned her to death right there. Crime of passion, right at that moment. Nothing premeditated."

"But Debbie was in the house. Either while it was happening or immediately after. Maybe Rachel had heard him come in and went to meet him, thinking it was Debbie and the girls."

"But she never made it down the stairs."

"Just like Debbie and Edith never made it away from him. But how do we tie what we know happened to it being Paul Sturvin who did it? And if it's not him, then who was it?"

"I don't know. But I bet our answers are already back in St. Louis."

"Then let's go."

67

IT TOOK THEM A WHILE, BUT THEY FOUND IT. THE PHONE WAS ALONG the back wall beneath the headboard. From the dust and cobwebs back there, hotel housekeeping hadn't done that great of a job at keeping the place clean.

Miranda's grandmother would have been incensed if any of the housekeeping staff—whether one of her granddaughters or the dozen or so they employed—were that slipshod in their duties.

"I guess hotels are going downhill these days," Taggart quipped.

"Not the one my family owns. You should check it out sometime." She sent him a wicked grin as she carefully grabbed the phone in a gloved hand. It would be bagged and tagged appropriately, of course. "Best hotel in Wyoming."

"You take me there, and I'll do just that."

She hadn't missed the appreciation in his eyes. Not at all.

Miranda would admit it—that boosted her confidence just a tiny bit.

He was a hot-looking man, after all. "Let's just find Sturvin and rescue those little girls. Then…I'll show you around St. Louis. Take you to Smokey's. Best onion rings on the planet."

He'd already volunteered to ride back to St. Louis with her after she'd delivered the special package to the director's friend. He said he wanted to see this case through to the end, before going on vacation in two days, himself.

He was hers to do with whatever she wanted.

Oh, if she was a different kind of woman...

They ended up driving. There was more rain and thunderstorms threatening. She checked the St. Louis weather report and shrugged. It was a four-hour drive. Better than waiting around on a plane that may or may not take off.

Her companion was entertaining. And he drove well.

Miranda liked the guy. She didn't know if there would be enough *spark* between them for something more to develop but she liked him.

Quite a bit.

"So...tell me," he said about three-quarters of their way back to the city. "What happened to Knight exactly? I tried to keep up with him after he was injured, but to be honest, he cut off most of his friends right after. Even me and my foster brother. It's been a year or so since I even tried."

"Oh boy. Good thing we have a four-hour drive. There's lots to tell you about our good pal Knight." Knight's face flashed into her mind.

Miranda shivered.

That was one man she'd probably never understand.

68

Max studied what was written on the whiteboard in a mix of Jac's precise scrawl and Dani's more flowery hand. Debbie's body was currently in autopsy. They were all hoping something would have been left on her to either confirm her killer's identity or tell them where the killer was most likely headed next. He knew the odds were against it, but the hope was there.

Miranda was on her way back from Indianapolis with Paul Sturvin's phone. Indianapolis Metro police were combing the city for signs of where he might be, as well. Dozens of people were looking for that man now.

In three states.

From what had happened to Debbie, Max was almost ninety-five percent certain they were looking for Paul Sturvin as their number one suspect now.

Max had been trained on different types of homicides. At heart, most could be boiled down to a few simple motivations. Power, greed, anger, jealousy, financial instability, control, hiding other crimes—he didn't quite know Sturvin's motive yet, but he knew enough to form a picture of what they were looking for.

Someone came into the conference room. He knew without turning that it was Jac. He would always almost feel her presence. He was well beyond the process of accepting that fact.

He was more attuned to her than a super-magnet. He probably always would be.

"Shayna called; she and Dani have been doing some digging while waiting on test results."

"And?" There was exhaustion on her face. Her skin was paler than usual. They had been getting closer to finding the girls. Only to be knocked back again. That would have sent her reeling, even if she wasn't outwardly showing it.

"Paul Sturvin was adopted by a maternal aunt when he was four."

"Is she still living?"

"She and her husband were killed fifteen years ago. Carbon monoxide poisoning one night while Paul was in college." Jac put copies of death certificates on a clip attached to the board. "But it gets more complicated."

"How so?"

"Paul's paternal aunt adopted his twin brother, Philip, at the same time."

"They split them up? Why?" Max asked.

"No clue yet. But his paternal aunt and uncle died—in a fire ten years ago."

"And the twin brother?" Whit asked, having come in behind Jac. "What about him? Would Paul go to him if he was in trouble? Would he know where Paul would go?"

"Not possible. He was killed in an auto accident almost six years ago." Jac put another photo on the wall next. One that looked identical to Paul Sturvin. She put the name Philip Sullivan beneath that photo.

"Tragic family," Whit said. "That sucks. So is there anyone left alive who knows Sturvin well now?"

That's when Max zeroed in on Jac's face. Her eyes were trained on the final report in her hands. "Jac?"

She shook her head. "Philip Sullivan, Paul's brother, lost his entire family a month before his own death. In a house fire. Suspected arson. Philip and his infant son, Bentley, were the only survivors. His wife and three other children were killed. Only the baby and Philip were found outside."

Max swore. "What happened to the baby?"

"He went to live with a relative of Philip's adoptive mother. But *she* died six months ago from cervical cancer."

"I wonder why the Sturvins didn't take him?" Whit asked. "He was Paul's nephew. They were financially able, and the closest living relatives."

"Where is the boy now?" Max asked.

"I'll have Dani check. See why the Sturvins didn't take custody." Jac pulled out her phone. "It's not much, but someone out there has to be able to help us narrow down where he's taking the girls. Or where he might be now."

"And we think his family's past has something to do with it?" Whit asked skeptically.

"There is a lot we don't know at this point," Max said. "We need to find out exactly what kind of man Paul Sturvin is. Because until we have him back here, he is our person of interest number one."

69

"You doing ok?" a male voice asked from behind Jac. One she recognized. Fortunately, Barnes wasn't with him.

Barnes had become an almost nonentity. She didn't know exactly what he was doing. It was almost like he'd wondered away hours ago —and no one had even noticed.

Not so with Whit. He was staring at her with his gorgeous brown eyes—eyes filled with concern.

Jac paused a moment to consider his question. "Yes. I'm focused on finding the girls. I'll...deal...with the emotional side of things later."

"See that you do." Whit squeezed her shoulder gently. "Take care of yourself, Jac. Promise me. I've...seen too many of us struggling lately."

There was a world of pain in his words. Pain that had her attention sharpening. "You ok?"

"Yes. Just...demands of the job. You know how it goes."

She almost asked about the woman from admin who he'd been dating so heavily the last she knew. But something made her hold off on that.

Now wasn't the time for that.

But she wouldn't forget. Something was going on with Whit. She just couldn't put her finger on what.

Dani came in, hurrying as quickly as she could. Most days, she preferred the crutches, but some, like today, she had to use the chair. Jac knew Dani's story, but it wasn't something the other woman broadcast. "Dani? What is it?"

"I have a list of every known address, every property, every camping *spot* Paul Sturvin and his brother ever visited. If we go on the theory that in times of stress—"

"People seek out the familiar," Jac finished. "We need to figure out which of these properties is the most likely."

"And one other thing…"

Jac turned toward the other woman.

"I'm not entirely certain, but…something feels off about the two men."

"What do you mean?" Everything felt *off* about Paul Sturvin to her.

"I'm looking into it now. But there's something about the photos of Paul Sturvin that don't look right to me. I'll dig deeper and get back to you as soon as I can."

"Can you be more specific?" Whit asked.

"I'm not certain, but if you look at the photos of Paul Sturvin from eight, ten years ago, he carries himself much differently from more recent photos. And…look here." She took the keyboard for the digital display board from Jac and brought up a file from the main server. "Here is the photos from Rachel and Paul's wedding. Here's the most recent photo."

The photos were both close-ups, with Rachel and Paul in a similar pose. There were lines around Rachel's eyes in the most recent. A sadness. Jac wished she had seen that earlier, wished she had made more of an effort to know Rachel before.

That was a guilt she would always have.

"There are nine years between them," Jac said.

"Well, look at his neck. At the birthmark. In the first photo, it's approximately an inch and a half in width and more oblong."

Jac moved closer to the screen. "It's in a slightly different place."

"And if we do a size comparison," Dani said, illustrating what she was saying. "It's also twenty-five percent smaller and more circular."

"Seriously?" Whit asked, clear skepticism in his tone. "What does that even matter?"

"Well, it's a café au lait macule. They usually show up on the buttocks. And unlike some other types of birthmarks that fade with age, this type doesn't. It's rather distinctive."

"So his birthmark changed over nine years?" Whit asked again. "I don't know what the significance is."

"The significance is *this*." Dani pulled up a photo of two young boys, around the age of eighteen months. "Check out the birthmarks on both boys."

Dani zoomed in on the photo.

Each boy had the birthmark. It took her a moment, but... "The birthmarks are different."

"The baby on the left is Paul Sturvin, according to the photo. I thought his birthmark looked a bit like the state of Georgia, there. His brother, Philip's looks a bit like Alabama, minus the Mobile area."

Jac saw it, too.

Then she looked at the birthmark in the Sturvin wedding photo. "That's definitely the same birthmark as the boy on the left."

"From photos I've found of the couple before they were married —Debbie had several photo albums; Kelly brought me one when I asked—we're talking the birthmark of Georgia. But more recent photos, those taken in the last five or six years, it's changed a bit."

Jac studied the most recent photo, the one taken in Max's rec room.

"Alabama!"

"Exactly. But I'm not entirely certain. I mean, the birthmarks are very similar. And Philip is dead, so we really can't compare. I'm waiting on someone to find me photos of Philip as an adult. But that's taking a while."

"When you find something definitive, besides just these photos, let me or Max know, ok?"

"Will do."

Jac looked at Whit. "Can you find me everything you can about Philip Sullivan?"

70

Eugene Lytel owed him money. Paul was going to need that cash, and soon. He hadn't intended to go to his old cabin near the Wabash River in Indiana.

He'd always hated this place. He'd inherited it from the aunt and uncle who had adopted him shortly after his fourth birthday and separated him from his brother forever. They had been a big part of destroying his only concept of family.

It had never meant as much to him, the family they had tried to create around him. Not when he'd see his identical twin six times a year at so-called family functions. They'd had no business splitting him and his twin up. He and Philip had been parts of the same *whole.* They never should have split them up like that. Take them away from each other like that.

It had destroyed his entire relationship with the one person who had mattered the most.

The whole idea of it sickened him.

He unlocked the cabin and carried Ava inside, first. It smelled musty, unaired, but it would do for the time being. He returned to the car and lifted Olivia into his arms.

She knew. His eldest daughter *knew* what he had done. He'd seen it in the eyes so like her mother's. Paul suspected she'd watched from the backseat of the car where he'd told her and Ava to wait for him. As he'd dealt with Debbie.

Debbie always had gotten under Paul's skin. She never had liked him. Always getting in the way between him and Rachel. Trying to separate him from the one woman who meant the world to him. Debbie had had no right to do that.

No one should separate *family* like that.

He hadn't intended to kill her, though. Had she not shown up with the girls in tow while he was arguing with Rachel, she would have been fine. Rachel's death would have been attributed to a random break-in. No one would have known he'd driven home to get the files from Lytel that he'd printed out and left behind.

Paul would have been notified in Indianapolis and would have been allowed to grieve properly.

Instead of chasing Debbie through the countryside to get his daughters back.

They were *his* children. And no one else's. No matter what anyone said.

The girls were *his*. He would not ever be separated from a child of his again.

Rachel...he ached for her. And he grieved, because of the memory of what he had done to her. He hadn't meant to.

She had found those files, and she had found the messages in his email, too. Messages that very clearly laid out instructions for finding out everything he could about the list of agents in question.

A list that had names on it that Rachel had recognized.

She had confronted him, demanded to know what he was doing. She'd been in the checking account. She'd see the deposits, too. Questioned where the money had come from.

Rachel had demanded to know what was happening, what he was doing.

It had just escalated from there. He could still see her blood on his hands. Debbie—Debbie and Edith were both incidental. Forgettable.

They hadn't truly mattered. No one cared if they lived or died.

He had regrets for what he had done. They were both old, lonely women, who were better off gone than taking up space.

But Rachel...she had had so much potential. She could have found someone else. Had another child or two of her own. Built herself a new family. That was never easy, but it was doable.

He would have given her generous visitation with Ava and Olivia, too. Or...he could have taken Ava with him and left Olivia with her mother.

They could have worked something out between them that was best for everyone.

Paul tossed a blanket over his sleeping daughters and stepped back. He had things he still had to do. He was only a few hours away from St. Louis.

He had plenty of time to do it before the girls woke.

He wrote a note for Olivia and sat it where she would see it, giving her very clear instructions of how she was to care for her younger sister, and then Paul got started.

Lytel owed him money. That was going to be his first step.

There were a few places left in the States where a smart man could go to disappear. Even with two young daughters in tow.

Paul just had to find them.

71

IT TOOK THEM HOURS TO DIG THROUGH EVERY POSSIBLE PROPERTY Paul Sturvin would be associated with. Max's team was dropping, but no one complained.

The setback of finding Debbie Miller had stung them all. A big part of Max was hoping to have found her alive, with the girls.

Finding Debbie the way they had...the biggest part of him was certain they were not going to get to the girls in time. He knew how family annihilators operated. Each type was different.

Each type was motivated in different ways.

If they were after Paul Sturvin, and he was ninety-nine percent that they were, he suspected Paul's motivation was financial.

He was an anomic family annihilator.

Perhaps he had returned to the house he shared with Rachel to kill them all, but Debbie interrupted. Debbie had the girls and ran.

Thwarting his plans.

Perhaps Paul had followed Debbie in order to get his daughters back to finish what he had started. Family annihilators had done so before.

John List had driven to the school to pick up his son at a soccer game after having already killed the rest of his family, back in 1971, before taking that boy home and killing him, too.

Paul most likely believed his family would be better off dead than without him to provide materially for them. It was what the evidence—even though it was circumstantial and hearsay at this point—was telling him.

Which meant that if things went even more south for Paul, there was a likelihood he'd kill his daughters before killing himself.

They needed to find the girls and get them away from Paul before that could happen.

To do that, he needed his people at the top of their game.

They needed to eat. It was almost midnight now, he and Jac had been on the case since seven thirty the previous morning.

Hopefully, wherever the Sturvin girls were, they were safe for the moment.

Sturvin had to sleep sometime.

He had to tell himself that.

He looked at Jac and Whit. "Break. Half an hour. Get some caffeine, something to eat. Take showers in the locker rooms. Whatever. We are going to keep pushing through on this. We need to find Paul."

Jac blinked at him for a moment. "You, too. You need to eat. Is Em ok?"

"She's staying with the Brockmans. I asked Malachi to pick her up after basketball practice. He was getting his nephew anyway."

Jac gave a tired smile. "Bet that thrilled her to be with Simon."

Max's daughter was deep in the midst of her first crush, on a much older "man" of about thirteen. Simon Brockman was kind enough to tolerate it whenever their paths crossed.

"No doubt. I called her a few hours ago. She's ok; it's you I'm worried about now." He put his hands on her shoulders. Just to touch. She looked so fragile now. "Go. Take a break. This...this will still be here in thirty minutes."

She drooped into his arms the instant Whit stepped out of the conference room. He doubted she was even aware she was doing it.

Max just pulled her close. He needed to touch her. Even though he fully meant to keep it platonic. For now.

"Two steps forward, fifty back."

He didn't say anything. Just tightened his hold on her. Her head rested against his chest and he could breathe her in. "But we'll eventually get there. We'll find them."

"Will we? When?" He felt her sigh against his chest. His hand slipped up and cupped the back of her head, beneath the now drooping French braid she'd woven it into that morning. She felt so fragile, whenever he got his hands on her.

"When we're meant to."

"I wish it was that easy." Her arms slipped around his waist. Max wondered for a brief moment if she even realized she was holding him just as tightly as he was holding her.

Max would have said more, but someone opened the door and stepped into the conference room. Max stepped back from Jac immediately.

There was a light of amusement in the director's brown eyes. Amusement, and understanding. Then the amusement faded and concern slipped in. Determination.

Max fought the urge to tense. Like it or not, the director's presence—especially this late—never brought *good*.

72

MIRANDA HAD MADE TAG TAKE HER OUT TO DINNER IN A SMALL TOWN along their route. Miranda wished she had a day or two to poke around. Maybe a week.

She had taken in all of it she could while Tag drove her around like a good chauffeur. He'd asked her if she'd never seen a small town before. Two stoplights, there were two stoplights.

She'd laughed and told him about exactly where she'd come from. And that small towns fascinated her. "I'm eventually going to write a book about all the towns I've visited in this job. I'll come back here, eventually. On my downtime. I'll probably drag Jac along with me."

"Boyfriend?"

"Bestie. Jac stands for Jaclyn. We were in a Rowland Bowles movie together last year when I dragged her to my hometown. It was fun. She's a bit on the serious, reserved side. It's my job to get her out there a bit more."

"I suspect you can make just about anything you *do* fun."

He reminded her of Clint, her former boyfriend. Same serious wall of hurt around him. And that core of honor that ran so deep.

She thought about that as they drove toward home, even though it was now close to midnight.

The call came just as they were an hour and a half away from St. Louis. Miranda put Max on speaker. "Hey, hot boss number three. I'm on the road with Agent Walker Taggart. Speak to me."

"Where exactly are you? Or rather, how close are you to Daviess County, Indiana?" Poor man sounded beyond exhausted.

"Let me check. What's shaking? How's Jac holding up?"

"She's doing ok. She and Dani are taking a break now—everyone is getting ready to go over Sturvin's family's social media accounts. I told them to eat first. They're finalizing the autopsy on the aunt first thing in the morning."

"We're two hours out from Washington, Indiana. That's the Daviess county seat. We'll have to double back, though."

"Good. Turn around. You need to go to the Department of Child Services first thing in the morning. Wake them up early. I need you back here by noon."

That was not something she'd expected. "What am I going on here?"

"Paul Sturvin's identical twin brother's son is in the custody of Daviess County. We need to find out his history—and why his aunt and uncle didn't take custody of him after his great-aunt died from cancer and why they didn't take him in six years ago as an infant. I want you to get the file. Persist, if you have to. We need to find out what we can about Sturvin's family. See if we can find where he might go. Or to who."

"Gotcha. I'll let you know what I find."

"I'm sending you a list of questions as well as two additional addresses we need someone to put eyes on. Sturvin could be there. Be careful out there."

"You, too. And keep an eye on our little buddy for me. I know this one is hurting her."

"Always. I'll take care of her."

After he disconnected Miranda just shook her head. "I know you will, Max. But does she?"

"Excuse me?" Taggart asked. "You realize he hung up, right?"

"It's complicated. He's a good friend. In love with Jac. But the two of them are taking the long way around to figuring that out. She... Paul Sturvin's wife was a friend of hers. Jac knows his daughters. And she's terrified for them. I just hope we find them soon. Because I think Jac's struggling more than she'll ever let on."

And that had Miranda worried to her very toes.

There was only so much someone could take, after all.

73

EUGENE LYTEL WAS GOOD ON HIS WORD, BUT THE MAN WAS AN arrogant asshole. High on a power trip.

Paul studied him, there in the Walmart parking lot at nearly two a.m. Lytel hadn't wanted to meet with him, but Paul had persisted. Had threatened to call Max Jones himself and tell him all about the contacts Paul had made within PAVAD. That had been all that had managed to get Lytel there. Paul wasn't stupid after all. "Are they looking for me?"

"Of course they are, you dumbass. You killed your wife and dragged the damned CCU right into the middle of your personal business. You were told to just watch Colonel Jones's daughters. That was it. What in the hell happened? You were told to do a damned job. Get us the information we wanted. Then you'd get paid and could move on."

"Rachel found out what I was doing. And she's good friends with Jaclyn Jones and some of the other mothers at Brynlock."

That was what story Paul was going to stick to. He wasn't telling anyone that he'd lost control. That the instant his wife had questioned him, he'd broken.

Struck out at her.

He'd never hit Rachel before. He'd grabbed her a few times. Shook her once. Scared her far more than he wanted to think about.

But he'd always apologized after.

The last thing he had ever wanted to do was hurt her. She... might have disappointed him through the years, but he had no doubt he had done the same to her. He was larger, stronger, more forceful, more powerful. That had come with responsibility to her. Responsibility he hadn't lived up to.

Relationships were reciprocal, after all. And he had loved her.

For six years, he had loved that woman. Had wanted to *provide* for her. Her and the girls.

From the moment he had met Rachel, he had known she was meant to be his.

All that would have made their lives more perfect through the years had been if they had had a son. And if Rachel hadn't threatened him, hadn't yelled she was going to call Jaclyn that very night and report that Paul was spying on her.

That would have destroyed everything.

He took the money Eugene Lytel held out. Paul counted it quickly. "Where's the other half?"

"Delivery fee. You screwed up. Didn't follow through. Now, I have to get my ass back to St. Louis before my team is needed to search for you. Take it and go—before I bust you myself. I am sure I can find an excuse for why I'm out here. Hell, my mom doesn't live too far from here. Maybe I just stumbled right into you. Wouldn't that make me the hero?"

Paul looked at the son-of-a-bitch's eyes. That was exactly what the man was wanting to do. He had no doubt Lytel had pocketed his money.

His fists balled.

Eugene Lytel was evil through and through.

74

MIRANDA LED THE WAY, HOLDING THE LITTLE BOY IN HER ARMS AS HE slept. *This* was not what she had ever expected to happen. But she had not been about to leave the kid sitting in that...place. It had taken her three extra hours just to track a six-year-old boy down.

He hadn't even been in Indiana.

Someone had hacked the social services database somehow and listed the boy in a completely different state than where he actually was. When she got a chance, she was going to talk to her contacts at the Missouri division of child services. He had been far too young to be housed with teenagers. Teenagers with histories of violent behaviors. What had happened to him definitely shouldn't have.

She didn't have a clue how that could have happened.

Miranda had just been very lucky the state he was in was Missouri. If he hadn't been, he wouldn't be snuggled in her arms right now.

She had a valid license as a foster parent in the state of Missouri. She knew enough people high up the food chain. And she'd be speaking with the legal department at PAVAD about her taking the boy into protective custody as soon as she possibly could.

She had rather just *taken* him, without truly asking permission.

Fortunately, Ed Dennis had told her to do what she had to. That man hadn't liked the photos she'd sent him of the group home, anyway.

Miranda had absolute faith that the director would fix *this.*

That she'd sent him those photos after she'd carried off Bentley Sullivan—well, Miranda would deal with the fallout from that later.

Paul Sturvin could have walked right in with a weapon and taken the boy with very little stopping him. If he'd wanted him. And from the visitor's log at the last group home the boy had been in, Paul Sturvin might have just wanted that very thing.

He'd visited his nephew on a weekly basis.

In her experience, sometimes, it was better to ask for forgiveness than permission. When it was the right thing to do.

"You just walk in and shake up the world all the time? Just do what you want, full speed, damn the torpedoes?" Tag asked.

He'd been relegated to carrying Bentley's single duffel bag of belongings. The little guy had latched on to Miranda and wasn't about to let her go. She'd pulled him from the back seat and he'd immediately drifted right back to sleep.

Stealing her heart while he did it. She shifted him, slightly, to relieve pressure on the cast. He never stirred. It was only two p.m.; yet he slept like he hadn't rested in weeks.

Maybe he hadn't.

"When necessary." She shot the man next to her a significant look. "And admit it—you weren't about to leave him there, either."

"No. I wasn't. But I don't have the director of PAVAD to back me up, though. That was a little nifty."

"Ed does come in handy," a female voice said from a nearby office.

Miranda stopped walking, as the head of forensics stepped out of her office. Marianna smiled tiredly. "Hello, Miranda. Shayna was looking for someone from your team. Who is this?"

"Meet Bentley Sullivan. Paul Sturvin's nephew. He was being

housed in a group home here in St. Louis with thirteen on up. Paperwork had him listed as being sixteen. His social worker had been told he didn't belong there. Yet they left him there for weeks. Said they didn't have another bed. Well, I have a few spares in my condo. So...here he is. The director and Dr. Jones said to take him into custody." So maybe that wasn't exactly how it had happened, but it was close enough.

"How old?"

"Six."

"Oh my. He's very small for six." Marianna put one hand on his back. "And his clothing is far too big."

"And dirty. I don't think he's been bathed in a few days. Maybe longer. That group home needs seriously investigated, Mari. I'm going to send the photos I took on to the proper departments once this case is finished. And I'm going to push, if I have to."

"Just let me know if I can help." Marianna was very obviously inspecting the little man. Marianna was a mother of seven children. Her eyes showed her compassion, immediately. "I'll call home. Ed ran home to take a shower and grab some files not even an hour ago. I have a box of clothing to donate ready for the Brynlock clothing drive in our garage. I know there will be things in there he can wear from my boys, and I think Georgia has some things of Matthew's in there as well. We'll get him taken care of."

"Thanks. I just...couldn't leave him there to be forgotten about. They barely even checked my ID. Sturvin could have walked right in and taken him. Anyone could have. I just had to sign one form and he was free to go with me. Just like that."

"Totally understand. He'll be safe here, while we look for his cousins," Marianna said as Shayna came up behind her.

"What's up, Doc?" Shayna said as her gaze landed on the little boy. And the hot man at Miranda's side. "Well, looks like you've been busy."

"Heard you have, too."

Shayna waved a report in front of her. "Who wants it? Here's the deal. An adult print was found on top of the purple residue on Debbie Miller's rear window. It was purple hard candy, by the way."

"Did it match anyone?" Miranda asked. Shayna had that look in her big brown eyes that said she had found something. "Let me guess? Paul Sturvin."

"Nope. But very, very close," Shayna said. "Want to guess who? It came back to a ten card from Ft. Benning."

"Military? Sturvin was never in the military. Who do we know in the case that has a military record?"

"*Philip James Sullivan,*" Shayna said. "Paul Sturvin's identical twin brother."

"The guy who was killed in an auto accident six years ago?" Miranda just stood there and gawked at the other woman.

"The very one. Interesting twist, isn't it? I'll let you tell Mr. and Mrs. Jones all about it." She turned toward Tag, holding out the report. "Well, you're new. Welcome to Crazyland. Here, Randi looks like she has her hands full."

Miranda looked at Tag, as her mind tried to process what she was hearing. Paul Sturvin had visited Bentley weekly. Not just as the devoted uncle. No, he'd visited just like a parent would. "Just whose child is *this?*"

He smirked at her. "For the moment, lady, it looks like he's going to be yours."

75

Jac, Max, Dani, Whit, and that idiot Barnes were going over the reports they had one more time when Miranda walked in, a small child cuddled in her arms and a tall, gorgeous Black man in a severe suit at her side.

"Randi?" Jac asked. "Who...?"

"Meet Bentley Philip Sullivan. Paul Sturvin's nephew...or son. I'm not entirely certain which. I found him in a group home a few hours from here. But we have a bigger problem. Has anyone spoken to Shayna recently?"

"What?" Max asked, taking the boy from Miranda like the experienced parent that he was. Within a moment, he had the little boy sprawled out on the couch and covered with his own suit jacket that Max had hung on the back of a chair hours ago. The child never woke. "Start talking."

"I spoke with Shayna," Miranda said, taking a sheet of paper from the man next to her. "Everyone, this is Agent Walker Taggart. He's asked to observe this case, and Ed said that was ok. Apparently, Tag is on the short list to transfer to PAVAD. Poor guy is a friend of Knight's, by the way."

"What did Shayna find?" Jac asked.

"There was a fingerprint on top of the candy on the window. It came back to Philip Sullivan's ten card from his time in the army. Whoever is out there, whoever has those girls, it's not *Paul Sturvin*. And probably never has been."

Jac stared at the report as she processed what Miranda was telling her with what Dani was working on as well. "Identical twins do have completely different fingerprints. And it explains the difference between Alabama and Georgia, like Dani thought."

"We have an evil-twin situation going on here?" Dani asked, rolling her chair close to the little boy to look at him, compassion on her face. "So if this is *Paul's* nephew, he's Philip's son. We won't be able to tell via DNA, either."

"We'll probably never know for sure who the father of this child is—or Olivia and Ava Sturvin," Whit said, making notes on his phone. He was an obsessive note taker.

"No, not with Paul and Philip being identical." Jac tried to work things out. She stood, then walked to the board, studying the names and dates written there. She crossed out Paul Sturvin's name beneath his photo and wrote Philip instead. "What if this isn't the first family *this* man has killed?"

"Go on," Max said. She looked back at him, noting how he was showing the stress of the last forty hours or so.

Jac both felt they were making progress—and still no closer to having Ava and Olivia safe. Her gaze landed on all the reports spread before them.

They'd been hitting this nonstop since they'd made it back to the conference room at seven thirty that morning. They'd worked until three a.m. before Max had had to call a halt for people to get some sleep.

"The woman who adopted Philip died fifteen years ago from carbon monoxide poisoning. What if it wasn't accidental?" She shuffled through papers on the table and laid out Susan Sullivan's death certificate. "Paul's adoptive parents were both killed in a fire five years later. Arson investigation was inconclusive. The pair was elderly, and it was thought one of them left something burning on the stove. What if Philip left something on the stove, knowing what would most likely happen?"

"You're reaching a bit," Barnes said. He'd not exactly been helpful, but he'd had a few good insights. Jac hadn't been completely turned off from working with him, at least. "That's a bit simplistic."

"Exactly. Isn't that the point? Three people in their seventies and eighties aren't exactly difficult to kill. And there were UK studies that showed that carbon monoxide poisoning is a common choice for family homicides," Jac said, barely aware of who she was talking to until her eyes met Todd's. "The fire that killed his brother's family would have been more difficult to pull off. But the fact that two families connected to one man die in suspicious fires? There is something going on there."

"Unless it wasn't his brother's family but his own," Whit said.

Max grabbed a nearby file and opened it. "The chief investigator in that case stated that the father was supposed to have been out of town at the time but managed to come home just in time to rush in through a back door. The baby's room was the closest. He was able to grab his son and get him almost to the door before smoke inhalation overcame him. Firefighters pulled him and the baby out of the house just minutes later."

"What if that was a lie? What if he'd driven back earlier? Like it's possible Sturvin/Sullivan drove back early to kill Rachel?" Dani asked. "Started the fire, and just waited? The baby could have been a convenient cover. I mean, if he was the one who started the fire, the older children would have been able to identify him, right? How old were Philip's daughters again? Seven, five, and three?"

Jac nodded. "So...how did he get rid of Paul? Because someone is buried in that grave. And if we go on the evil-twin theory, it's the real Paul Sturvin."

"Report says he had an accident related to the severe weather at the time. Ran off the road, neck snapped on impact. His car was found at the bottom of a ravine three weeks later. There is also a note from the investigator saying he was despondent, and it could have been suicide," Max said, laying out the report next to the one about the fire. "Due to the fact that his wife and three daughters had recently perished."

"What if it was Paul? What if Philip killed him and put him in the car before pushing it over the ravine?" Jac said. It was a wild speculation, but it *felt* right. "He was in the military. He probably knew just how to break his own brother's neck. Then he just assumed his identity. With Rachel and Olivia? Ava might be his, the dates coincide. And except for a similar birthmark, there is nothing that would have made Rachel even know? And how closely does a woman look at a man's birthmark?"

"Debbie's photo albums had absolutely no photos of anyone from Paul's side of the family. In fact, there was a family tree portion in the book—and every member of Paul's family was listed as deceased," Dani said. "What if he never told Rachel he had a twin? Would she have even known to doubt who her husband actually was? How many of us confuse the Lorcan brothers at first glance?"

Jac nodded. "Exactly. We all know how easy that is to do—especially with Sin and Sebastian. Their wives can tell them apart, but if Rachel never knew a twin existed, she wouldn't have ever known the man with her wasn't Paul. Especially if the imposter worked at duplicating his brother's mannerisms. How that ties into finding the girls, I don't know yet. But if it's not Paul who has them…"

"What did the social worker say about the boy?" Max asked, looking at Miranda.

"The file said that after the death of his family, the boy's father didn't feel like he could adequately provide for him, so he asked an aunt to take in the boy. She had him for the next five years before she passed away from cancer at the age of fifty-six."

"So he went back into the system instead of going to his supposed aunt and uncle," Jac said. "When?"

"She passed away July 14 of this year." Whit handed her the next death certificate.

"Maybe Rachel never knew the boy existed? How would you explain a nephew, when you've never mentioned a brother?" Whit asked.

Dani wheeled herself closer to the table and laid out another report. One she'd been working on. "She died one week before the first deposit of unexplained cash—fifteen thousand dollars—went into Paul Sturvin's bank account. I'm still not sure where that money came from."

"If he's anomic, he's financially motivated. But with that type of cash coming in, what would trigger him killing Rachel?" Max asked.

"It's possible that is connected," Jac said. "But I think it's something else. What do we know about the types of family annihilators?"

"Anomic does it for financial reasons, self-righteous blames the wife or mother for ruining the children, disappointed type believe the family has let him down, and there is the paranoid type who believes he's protecting his family from an outside threat," Max listed quickly. "And most show signs of being a mixed type. So it could be anything."

"None of these seem like a paranoid type. They are far too calculated for that." Jac wrote the types on the whiteboard quickly, then marked out paranoid. "We've heard of known financial struggles for the Sturvins. The principal at Brynlock told me that herself. We need to check into the Sullivans' financials as well. Dani?"

"Will do that now, but it'll take some time. And probably warrants. Those are six-year-old records. Not like we can just bring up his checking account out of the blue." Dani was already pulling out her iPad. Jac knew she would be as tenacious as a bulldog getting those warrants now that they were on to something.

"This is all well and good, and the guy has probably done this before. But how is it going to help us find him and those girls *now*?" Barnes. Jac had completely forgotten the man was even there. "Those little girls have been missing for more than a day and a half.

We don't know how much longer this guy is going to keep himself together and not hurt them. We can't just sit here."

"Simple. We've been profiling *Paul* as this being his first event, but it's not. If this is Philip, then he's a serial killer. Which is an entirely different profile than a classic family annihilator," Max answered. "And instead of looking at where Paul would go, we need to find out where Philip would go. Which means…property records. We need to narrow things down. As soon as we possibly can."

"Because…" Jac bit back the bile. "Because if this isn't the first time he's killed his family, then there is even less to keep him from killing the girls the first moment they become inconvenient. He'll kill them and just disappear—possibly to start all over again. It's just a matter of time. We need to learn everything we can about Philip Sullivan."

76

TODD KNEW THEY WERE GETTING CLOSER TO FINDING PAUL Sturvin/Philip Sullivan. The guy had come across as a pansy to Todd, not a damned serial killer. But now they had him on suspicion of killing at least nine people.

That just pissed Todd off and made him feel slightly sick to his stomach. What kind of man targeted innocent kids and old people? The youngest girl killed in that fire had been *three*. Todd had a three-year-old niece of his own. If anyone ever did anything to hurt Esme, Todd would kill them. Without hesitation. He'd face the needle if it meant protecting Esme.

Todd hated when jackasses like Sturvin targeted kids. Kids were completely innocent. Adults were supposed to protect kids.

Not hurt them.

There was a little boy fussing on the couch not fifteen feet from where he stood. Before he realized it, Todd was straightening Jones's coat over him and patting the tiny back until he settled deeper into his nap, just like he'd done Esme a hundred times by now.

He was just an innocent kid with a real bastard for a father.

That the ones who had made Todd that *offer* were also in bed with Sturvin sickened him. That was just wrong.

Todd wanted no part of that.

Combine that with how cold-blooded Lytel was, and Todd suspected he'd done a seriously dumbass thing getting anywhere near this.

He could think of nothing else for the next two hours after he returned to his loaner desk in the CCU bullpen. Todd was doing his damnedest to find people who had known Philip and Holly Sullivan six years ago. But a part of him was contemplating going to Ed Dennis and just confessing it all. Laying it bare.

It could end his career. But the only thing he had done yet had been carrying an envelope from a friend in Texas to a guy in St. Louis.

That it had been the same day Andrew Anderson had been killed could have damned well been coincidence. Something he had only learned since being in St. Louis now.

As far as he knew, the two things weren't connected at all.

But Todd wasn't stupid. In his gut he knew that they most certainly were connected.

That envelope could have been Todd paying Paul Sturvin to commit murder. But if he kept his earlier encounter with Sturvin secret during this case, that could look bad. Real bad.

Todd's gut clenched as he thought about it.

There had to be a way to get himself out of this without destroying his entire life in the process.

Before he could stop himself, he sent a text to the director of PAVAD. As soon as this case was solved and those girls were safe, Todd was going to go to Dennis. Lay it all bare.

Whatever happened, happened.

Hell, if he lost his job—he still had his law degree. He'd go back to Texas, find a small town there in need of a good family attorney, and he'd build a practice. Build a real *life*.

Maybe find a woman who'd love him like Jaclyn loved Jones.

Maybe make a few kids of his own. Finally make his mother happy, with more grandkids to cuddle.

Have an actual *life* outside of the FBI. Yeah, that was exactly what he'd do.

Todd was going to get himself a life.

77

THE GIRLS WERE SICK. AND THEY WEREN'T GOING TO JUST GET BETTER because Paul demanded it. Paul fought the irritation.

Kids got sick all the time, especially kids of this age group. Ava was especially bad about remembering to wash her hands after using the restroom. It was just his bad luck that they had caught whatever cold Debbie and Rachel had had. He rested his hand on Ava's forehead, feeling the fever burning through her tiny body. His gut wrenched in that particular way it did when a parent realized their worst nightmare could happen. That their child could be ill and they just couldn't make them better by wishing illness away.

He had always hated it when she was unwell. She…was his star. His baby. She was the only child born to him since the tragic loss of his other three daughters. He loved Bentley more than he could ever say, but because of what he had done to Bentley's mother and sisters, he had not felt right keeping the son he had loved so much. Bentley had his mother's eyes; every time he'd looked at the little boy, he would see Holly.

The one woman who had ever truly loved him for him. For the

man he'd been before. She'd stuck by him through everything. She had known *him.*

At first, he'd thought she was a poor comparison to Rachel, but now he knew. Rachel had been the poor substitute, because she had never known the real *him.*

That mattered. The one that you loved should know you.

He'd failed her and the children. Failed them all. Until they had almost lost everything they had been working toward. He hadn't been able to face the disappointment in Holly's eyes. The idea of someday seeing that same disappointment in Bentley's eyes had been more than he could bear.

So he'd done what he had to do. But as the house had burned around them all—he'd fully intended he'd die that day, too—his son had cried out.

His son.

A man should have a son, after all. To pass on his legacy. Had Bentley died that day, all that was left of Philip Sullivan would have died, too. He would have been forgotten, invisible forever.

He just hadn't been able to stomach that thought, so he'd carried his son outside.

A month later, *Philip* Sullivan had died, and he'd assumed the identity of the more successful twin. Become a man that he wasn't, but that he had always known he was destined to be. Had *he* gone with the Sturvins when he'd been Ava's age, who were far wealthier, perhaps he wouldn't have become the man he had.

"Daddy, I want Mr. Bird. I want Mommy. Where is Mommy?"

She was what kept him breathing. Ava.

If he hadn't made the choices he had, Ava wouldn't be here today. He could forgive himself his mistakes, because of her. The daughter he and Rachel had created was his most perfect child yet.

Or she would be. After she had been trained.

Paul just tightened his hold on his daughter and rocked until she fell into a fitful sleep. Olivia was already out, cuddled up on the run-down army cot in the corner. She was a far more biddable child in every way than his Ava. Biddable, tidier, easier to handle, far less demanding.

But she would always be a poor second.

This cabin…it had been his and his twin's during the few times a year they were together again. They'd camped and fished and played. Enjoyed the short days they had together.

No one had ever seen into his soul like his brother.

And Paul…he had somehow figured out what Philip had done. Paul had confronted him. Threatened him. Threatened to take Bentley away, too. To take Bentley and give him to Paul's own wife. To Rachel.

While Philip rotted in a cage for what he had done to Holly and their daughters.

He hadn't been able to let that happen.

So he had become Paul.

He'd become *Paul*. For years, he had lived as his brother.

But he'd failed at being Paul, too.

He looked at his ill daughters—even though Olivia had been fathered by his twin, she was still the daughter of his heart—and he knew.

He couldn't keep failing his children. Not like he had before.

It was time.

Paul had to do something.

Before it was too late for all of them.

78

Kalani, one of the PAVAD tip-line supervisors, came into the conference room two hours after Jac had come up with her theory. Max knew with one look at the older woman's face that she had found something. He'd sent all of the team to follow up on various leads. In a few moments, he'd be slipping off to meet with the director about the latest find in the Anderson case. "Kal?"

"Hello, Dr. Jones, I have something that might be relevant to your missing children case." She handed him the standard tip-line report. "It was pretty specific. The clerk recalled seeing him on the news in the breakroom just ten minutes earlier. She's a bit of a crime buff and pays attention. Especially when it's missing kids."

"Did this clerk see the girls?" Max asked, taking the report. They'd already taken hundreds of tips. None had been relevant.

One had even said they'd seen the ghost of Rachel Sturvin in their own dining room. On the table.

In the midst of a séance.

Then they'd claimed they were ancient vampires from Dardanos, Colorado. Rachel's ghost was haunting a castle there, or something.

That had been one of the *better* tips they'd received so far.

"No. But the man she swears was Paul Sturvin, even right down to the birthmark on his neck—that's what made this stand out to me —was buying children's cold medicine and pediatric electrolytes and vapor rub. And two stuffed animals."

"Everything a father would buy when his kids suddenly come down with colds."

"Exactly. I must buy that stuff forty times a year with my kids. Seems like they bring everything possible home from school."

"No kidding. Emery is just now getting over a virus herself."

A virus she might very well have shared with the Sturvin girls. The autopsy reports had indicated that both Debbie Miller and Rachel Sturvin were in the early stages of having cold viruses. It wasn't far out of the possibility that the girls were ill.

The neighbor had said the little one was feeling ill and wanting her mother.

Paul Sturvin/Philip Sullivan was out there now, with two sick little girls. Which could drastically slow him down.

Or send him toppling over the edge.

"We need to get someone out there to get the security camera footage of that pharmacy," he said to the agent next to him. Barnes.

Damn it. Still the man was superfluous now. He should be able to pick up some damned security videos without screwing up. "Barnes, go. Take someone from auxiliary, if you need to. Or Whit. Get the footage, confirm it was him."

"Got it. Jones…"

Max looked at him more fully. Barnes was far more disheveled than he'd been earlier. There was a tightness around the man's eyes, a good deal of the cocky arrogance was somehow gone. Max's phone buzzed. A text from the director, demanding Max get to his office. He didn't have time to figure out why. "What is it?"

"Nothing. Just…thanks for not pushing me aside. I appreciate it. And…I'm sorry about Anderson. I heard about what happened and that he was a friend. I knew him a bit, too. If I don't get a chance to say it, I wanted to now. I'm really sorry."

"Thanks. Andy was a good friend. And we're going to find who killed him. We'll never stop looking."

79

MAX TEXTED HER THE TIP. JAC KNEW HE HAD BEEN SUMMONED TO THE director's office. At the worst possible time.

But that was the way it worked. Sometimes, cases overlapped. Sometimes, you felt split in half, trying to devote everything you could to each.

She had fifteen open cases on her own desk, just waiting for her to have some sort of down time to work on them. Some cases were just more immediate than others.

Miranda had left already. She was taking the little boy to a safe house, along with that guy who'd followed her back from Indiana.

Miranda had a habit of collecting guys, it seemed. Not anything overt that her friend did, they just seemed to be attracted to her vivacious love of life. Most of the time, they ended up friends. Miranda had her own hang-ups where relationships were concerned that she'd have to deal with before she could have anything serious.

Then again, that could be said for just about everybody.

She read Max's text, including the address of a pharmacy just over the Illinois border.

The Illinois border.

Something clicked.

Jac turned and almost jogged back to the conference room. She almost collided with Agent Lytel.

He caught her, wrapping strong hands around her elbows. "Best slow down, Agent Jones. There's plenty of time to get to where you're going."

"Sorry. I just…something's tickling the back of my mind with the Sturvin case."

"Walk; don't run. Keep your hands inside the vehicle. No running in the halls. And anything else I've told my own daughters." He gave her a quick smile, then stepped back to let her pass.

"Thanks, Eugene." She'd worked with him time and time again before. A bit arrogant, but he was good at what he did.

Of course, he was—he was PAVAD.

She found Dani in the conference room, sitting in her chair, in front of the whiteboard just staring at it.

That was a habit Jac had herself. Sometimes, she just had to *see* things in front of her to get the connections. "Dani, that list of properties owned by Philip Sullivan and his adoptive parents? Do you have it?"

"Green file, I think. You're on to something." Dani turned the chair to watch Jac instead; that's when Jac saw the little dog sound asleep on her friend's lap. "Talk it out with me."

"See you've made a friend."

"Sadie's not afraid of the chair. Edith had surgery last year, was wheelchair bound for a while. Sadie took one look at me and hopped right up. Seemed to settle easier. She's been a nervous wreck since Shayna finished with her. She had to be checked out to one of our team. I volunteered." She had a leash tied to the arm of the chair to keep the dog from getting loose. Not that the dog seemed inclined. She was settled on Dani's lap, and now watching Jac unconcernedly.

"They're going to send her to the humane society."

"No, they aren't. Sadie and I understand each other. She's coming home with me."

Jac smiled. At least, there was one happy ending in the works for someone involved in this case. Even if it was just the dog.

"So what are you thinking?" Dani asked.

"I think we can narrow it down. Paul Sturvin was possibly seen at a pharmacy buying cold medicine two hours ago. Considering that most pharmacies are within half an hour of a person's home…"

"Whichever property is the closest to the pharmacy is the one where he's most likely holed up," Dani said, turning toward the digital board next to the whiteboard. With a few clicks of the remote, she had a satellite image on the screen.

"What's the address of the pharmacy?"

Jac relayed that information quickly.

80

"WE'VE CRACKED THE CODE," ED DENNIS SAID. HE SHOT A GRIM LOOK at Max. "Take a seat. This won't take long. Where are you with the Sturvin case?"

"We're getting closer to narrowing down where he went. I just sent Barnes and Whitman to check surveillance tapes at a pharmacy where Paul was most likely spotted. But he's not *Paul*."

With as few words as possible, he brought the director up to speed, ending with "He's both a family annihilator and a serial killer. That changes the profile drastically. But it means we have more to go on."

Maybe. Now, they had to profile both Paul Sturvin—a man who had access to the resources the original Paul had created—and Philip Sullivan. Everything that Sullivan and Sturvin both were connected to would have to be checked. That was going to take time. "But we feel like we have a good handle on *who* we are looking for now. It's just a matter of time before we narrow in on him."

"I have a wrench to throw in, Jones. Take a look at this. It's the print-out of the decrypted files found on Andy's memory cards. Look at the name highlighted."

Max flipped through the fifteen or so sheets of data. "Phone numbers?"

"Yes. From a set of fourteen burner phones. The last page is where you'll find the information that's relevant."

Max turned the page one more time.

There it was. In bright-yellow highlighter.

"Paul Sturvin."

"Andy somehow found these fourteen phone numbers. And he was running everything down that he could. Checking call logs for those numbers. Sturvin's number came up early on the list. Then this number here was activated. Seth didn't know about it. But we have exonerated Andy from being involved with the leak. My thought is that he stumbled on to information somehow and was trying to verify it before he was killed."

Max's gut twisted as memories of that night surfaced. "Which is most likely the reason he was killed in the first place."

"My thoughts exactly."

"Sturvin's listed a few more times."

"Once a month, since July."

Max ran over the dates again. "These calls coincide with some data we found."

He opened his phone and brought up copies of Sturvin's financial recorders. "Here."

He held his phone out for the director to see.

"What is this I'm looking at?" Ed asked, taking the phone.

"These calls coincide with fifteen-thousand-dollar deposits, made once a month, into Paul Sturvin's bank account." Max thought about what they knew about the man so far. "We have profiled him as an anomic family annihilator, motivated by financial failure or success. It's possible that he has been selling PAVAD secrets. That is where these deposits came from."

"So if we find where those deposits come from, we're this much closer to finding the ones responsible for Andy's death," the director said.

Max looked at the data one more time. The final deposit into Sturvins' account was for five times as much as the usual deposits.

And was on the very day that Andy had been killed.

"Is it possible Sturvin was hired to kill Andy? And this was the payout? Just what exactly did he have access to here at PAVAD?"

81

JAC STUDIED THE MAP AS SHE LISTED THE ADDRESSES OF THE
Sullivan/Sturvin properties. There were five to isolate. "Mark the
two to the east off."

"Ok, why?"

"Too far away from the pharmacy. There is no way he would
have left the girls that long, and I don't think he'd have taken them in
the car if they were that sick. The cabin owned by the Sullivans is at
least three hours away by car. A road trip of three hours, with a sick
child or two—that wouldn't be something anyone would ever want
to do. I've done it." When Emery had been six, Max and Jac had
taken her to the Gulf of Mexico. Unfortunately, she'd come down
with strep throat five hours from home on the trip back. Jac had
ended up riding in the backseat with her, just to hold her and take
care of her while Max had handled the driving. "That is not something any sane person ever wants to attempt again."

"The other here would have been about two and a half hours."
Dani removed it from the map. "That still leaves us three properties."

"Isolate the other pharmacies now."

"There is one other pharmacy, but it's the same distance from the cabin here as the other pharmacy," Dani said. "That's not going to rule one property out over another."

"So how are we going to figure out which property he's at?" Jac asked, almost to herself.

"Do a massive sweep. Check them all," Dani said. "It would split manpower, but it might be the only option."

"That's probably exactly what we are needing to do. We just need enough bodies to do it." Jac pulled out her phone. "I'm going to run down Max. Ball is in his court now. But one way or another, we're going to search every cabin until we know where Paul Philip Sullivan Sturvin put his daughters. And then…we're going to make him pay for what he's done. For the people he's hurt."

The dog barked, as if Sadie agreed one hundred percent.

82

Todd liked the pharmacist. She was smart, cute, and definitely no-nonsense. She knew exactly what she was talking about, and she wasn't stupid about it. There weren't any flirtatious games either. She knew they were there on important business. "It's the guy from the television. I asked him how he was doing, if he had any questions about what he was buying. I got close enough to see the birthmark. It's rather distinctive." She pushed her glasses up on her little freckled nose and looked between him and Whitman.

"What did he say? How did he act?" Whitman asked, his phone ever present as he took even more notes. He'd barely even looked at the pharmacist.

The guy had some serious OCD tendencies, but Todd didn't think he was too much of an ass. He half liked the guy.

"He had a few questions about how much Pedialyte to give his kids. Said they were three and eight, weighing between thirty and sixty pounds. I helped him find that, handed him this bottle here." She had a small bottle of pink pediatric electrolytes sitting on the counter next to her. "I put it in the zippered bag to keep any fingerprints on it from getting smudged after he left. I had on nitrile gloves already. So...he was the last one to touch that. He said his youngest was allergic to the food dye in it. He ended up going with the clear version instead."

Well, she couldn't have made it any easier for them. All they had to do was take that bottle back to the forensics lab, along with the surveillance footage, and they'd know for sure if that asshat Sturvin was in this area.

They'd find him soon.

Todd just prayed it was before the man hurt two innocent little girls.

83

By the time Max had three teams ready to hit the three different cabins Jac had isolated as the most likely locations, Whit and Barnes were back.

With fingerprints and video evidence. Whit had watched it on his laptop on the drive back and had confirmed the man on the footage was most likely the man they were looking for.

Max tamped down the excitement. He'd been in this game long enough to know not to rush to the finish line. That was how mistakes were made.

He nodded at Lytel. He would be handling the third team. Max would take the first. Ezra Hahn from REY—Runaway & Endangered Youth—had been recruited to run the second team. He was one of their best at critical response, and Max was glad to have him. Jac could have run the team, but she'd chosen to coordinate at the command post. Eyes on everything.

The rapid processing of details that she would be tasked with doing was where she excelled.

Lytel asked for clarification, then took his team of four men.

They were experienced; half had transferred in from tactical response.

All knew what they were supposed to do.

If those girls were out there at one of those locations, they'd find them.

84

RACHEL HAD ALWAYS HANDLED THINGS WHEN THE GIRLS WERE ILL. Holly as well. But he was going to have to figure it out himself. They had only *him* now. He was going to have to find a safe place for them to start over. After he made it clear to them that they were going to have to change their names, their entire way of life.

He had only forty thousand dollars in cash. That would be a good start. Especially if he found a lower-cost-of-living area. He'd have to pick new names for them all. Build new backgrounds and histories.

And teach the girls to use them. Perhaps he should find an RV or something. Take it west; if anyone asked, he could state that he was taking his girls to learn about the country while he worked over the internet. To distract them from the death of his wife. Perhaps she had died from cancer. Or a car accident.

Something tragic that people wouldn't expect him—or the girls— to discuss easily. He'd need to dye his hair, too. Cover the birthmark on his neck so it wasn't so easily identified. He would have to think of some way to make an income. Two young girls would cost a fortune to raise appropriately. In spite of what had happened to their mother, he owed them a proper future.

Maybe, in a few months, he would search out another mother for them. One with some funds of her own. He could sell insurance, or even real estate. He knew how to get into the right places to build himself an identity. There, he'd find a woman with the right background.

Perhaps he would be fortunate and she would be a redhead this time. One who looked much like Jaclyn.

It would just take time. And planning.

But first, he had to get his daughters well again. And avoid being caught.

He could not go to prison. That would just leave his daughters out there in the world alone. He had seen what that had done to his son.

Bentley would always be his greatest failure. One for which he would never forgive himself. His son was all alone out there now, among wolves larger and stronger and meaner than he could ever hope to be.

He had had no idea how to fix that, to get Bentley out of that place.

Until he'd learned that was the means by which Lytel and the others were planning to control him if he'd failed.

And there was nothing he could do to fix it.

He would not let his daughters suffer the same fate.

85

JAC KNEW THE INSTANT EACH TEAM CHECKED IN THAT THIS WAS GOING to be another wasted endeavor. Max's team was the first to check in. They'd gone to the most likely place.

Nothing.

She looked at Dani next to her. "We need to regroup, reevaluate. What if he *wouldn't* stay close to here? What if he'd cut his losses, take his wads of cash, and run?"

"What about the girls? Would he take them with him?"

Jac thought for a moment. Thought about every movement he'd made in front of her, every word she had heard him say. How controlling he had been with Rachel and his daughters, how he had seemed to want approval from the most popular fathers at Max's house that day. "I think he would. He visited Bentley weekly, according to social services records. He wouldn't have done that if he hadn't felt some connection to his son. He has been a reasonably active father in the girls' lives. Maybe he's taking them and *running*."

"But once again…the magic question is, where would Philip/Paul go?"

"He feels threatened. He has to know people are hunting him.

Maybe Rachel was accidental—though I'm leaning premeditated, considering his past history—and now he has two small girls with him. Children are harder to hide at times than adults. Harder to keep secret. He'll need a vehicle. We have him connected to two SUVs in the Sturvin name and a rental. Miranda and her new buddy confirmed that earlier."

Jac and Dani went over everything again and again, looking for some small key, some small detail to tell them where and how to find Paul. They kept at it until Max and the rest of the teams made it back to the conference room.

Frustration was almost palpable. Max's face was tight, and his shoulders tensed.

And he was the most relaxed of the group.

"No signs of Sturvin or anyone at any of those three places," Max said, coming up behind her. Jac watched him over her shoulder. "We miscalculated."

"We need to get more people going over Sturvin's online searches," Jac said, feeling sick at the idea they had to start back at the beginning. "He's fleeing. He's going to go where he feels comfortable."

"Maybe. Or is he smart enough to know that's exactly how we'll track him?" Max asked. He X-ed off the three cabins that had been searched. He turned to the man who'd entered behind him. "Lytel, we have two more cabins here. Can you send teams to clear each one?"

"Not going yourself?" Barnes asked. "Why?"

"Time. If the other cabins are abandoned as well, we would lose hours."

"Hours we *can't* afford to lose"," Jac added. "We're approaching the forty-eight-hour window now. Once we hit that, our chances are finding the girls safely are cut drastically."

"We'll do. Barnes? Want to ride along? See how it's done by the experts?" Lytel asked.

Barnes actually paled. But he nodded. "Let's go."

86

THE LAST THING TODD WANTED TO BE DOING RIGHT NOW WAS A RIDE-along with Eugene Lytel. The man made his skin crawl.

"Who all is going with us?" Todd asked quietly. There were four men in full tactical gear walking ahead of them. Todd didn't know who they were; he assumed they were just members of Lytel's auxiliary team.

He was damned sure he was walking into enemy territory now.

His only comfort was that Lytel thought Todd was on his side.

"People I can trust." Lytel looked right at him. It felt like he was peering right into Todd's soul, seeing the guilt for the text he'd sent hours ago. Todd forced himself to act cool. To not do anything too stupid. "If we get the opportunity tonight, Sturvin's to be taken out. The man knows just too much."

The men in front of him had heard Lytel. And hadn't reacted. They were probably as dirty as Lytel was.

Todd's stomach clenched. He just nodded. The man was telling him to commit murder. Like they were discussing taking out the trash. Either commit it himself, or sit back and watch it happen. Let it happen.

That it was a child killer who was targeted made little difference. Todd was just supposed to watch it happen.

Then walk away. So that Lytel would have Todd in his pocket, right where he wanted him.

To Lytel that was probably exactly what they were talking about.

Todd used every bit of his training to keep himself from looking like a total asshole. Or a coward.

First chance he got, he was going to go to Dennis, confess his sins. He wasn't about to keep getting deeper and deeper into this.

Not with innocent people dying. He had his own code of honor; murder had no place in it.

Lytel ordered him to stay close. Todd remained in the command post, in the van with Lytel's own computer tech. The guy barely looked at Todd.

It was a wasted trip. He knew it when Lytel radioed back. He didn't let his relief show.

The instant he was getting back to the PAVAD building, he was going to go to Max Jones and confess. See if that guy would run interference for him with the director.

He was going to do the right thing. First chance he got.

87

AVA NEEDED MEDICAL ATTENTION. SHE WASN'T GETTING BETTER, AND he suspected the respiratory virus was triggering her asthma. He didn't know what to do. If he took her to the hospital, it was over for him. He'd be arrested and taken away from the girls in an instant.

They'd become wards of the state.

He couldn't do that again. He couldn't live with losing his children again; not into that horrific system that was destroying Bentley. His beautiful, wonderful, almost *perfect* children. Three of them. He still had three beautiful children living. His legacy for the world was secure.

His mark would be left.

He had to take some solace in that. In knowing that at least he wouldn't be forgotten.

When the time was right, he was returning for Bentley. Going to get his son and raise him with the girls. Raise him properly. It was his duty to his child. To Holly's child.

Bentley was all that was left of Holly, too.

Ava coughed again. She wheezed. It terrified him. None of the cold medicines were working, and her rescue inhaler was almost empty. He used it and prayed. She'd ended up in the hospital more than a dozen times with the wheezing.

Life on the run was no kind of life for her, not with her regular need for medical treatment. Not her, she just wasn't strong enough yet.

He held her until the coughing and wheezing finally stopped and she slept curled up against his chest.

He carried her to the window; it had always soothed her to be carried around when she didn't feel well. Olivia was snoring softly in the bed, congested and feverish but not as ill as Ava, snuggled with the new stuffed animal he had bought her. He'd just wanted to distract the girls from the horrible news he'd given them tonight.

They hadn't known Rachel had died. Thank God Debbie hadn't told them.

That had left him free to tell them exactly what *he* wanted them to hear.

As far as his girls would ever know, the mother who had adored them had died falling down the hallway stairs. Their mother's aunt had died when the car had run off the road—because she had just been too sad to focus on driving safely. He'd told the girls Rachel and Debbie were angels watching over them now.

Now, their father was there, and he would always take care of them. But...the loss of their mother made him too sad to go back home right now.

Ava had believed him. But Olivia...he didn't know if Olivia believed him at all.

Paul stood at the window for the longest time, just holding his daughter, as the fever raged her tiny body.

He had to help her. He just had to.

Paul looked at the little girl still sleeping on the bed. Olivia was waking, but Ava...she was almost comatose. He had to do something. To end this for his daughters.

Paul told Olivia to stay where she was while he gathered everything they'd carried into the cheap motel room. Within ten minutes, he had the car he'd taken from his biological mother's home loaded.

He returned for his daughters.

Paul scooped his youngest into his arms and ordered her older sister to follow him.

It was time he did what he had to do.

His daughters were counting on him.

Paul was going to be the father *his* children deserved.

The sun was just rising, illuminating the damned arch over the city, as he turned the car south.

Toward an address he had memorized weeks ago.

There was only one thing he could think to do now.

88

NAT HAD ALWAYS RISEN BEFORE THE SUN. IT WAS JUST A NATURAL thing for her. Especially after nearly sleepless nights. The idea that two little girls were missing and she was unable to help guaranteed she would have nightmares.

She had too many memories of being left in the woods with only Jac to count on to rest when Olivia and Ava were still out there.

Nat was just finishing her shower when she heard the first sound. She had a house a few miles south of the city. She had wanted enough land for Kudos and Karma to have room to play—where she'd have acreage to train them daily. Jac's new place was closer to PAVAD. Nat had wanted to be closer to the building—chances were good search and rescue was going to be called out again very soon.

She'd checked in with Dan Reynolds, the CCU coordinator, before retiring last night. He'd told her the teams were going out searching cabins. Cabins meant woods. Terrain.

Critical search teams, where time was of the essence. Anything she could do to be ready and get there sooner. Including resting and being ready when the call came.

She'd cleared it with her sister; Jac had given her the spare key the day her sister had taken possession of the house—for this very reason.

Kudos liked to romp around Jac's backyard whenever they stayed over. Karma was more about following Nat at all times. Just watching, with her kind ways.

Nat smiled, stopping on her way to the kitchen to rub over the sweet girl's head. Karma just licked her palm and waited for Nat to speak to her.

Kudos barked from the backyard. Not exactly something that was all that unusual. He was a bit of a loudmouth. Nat usually just ignored it.

Until he just kept barking. Whining.

Nat ran. She didn't have shoes on, but that didn't matter. There were callouses aplenty on her soles. Kudos was in trouble. There wasn't anything Nat wouldn't do to protect him.

Those weren't ordinary sounds out of her boy. Nat knew the difference.

Nat bolted into her sister's backyard, her weapon clutched in her hand.

There was a patio, one her sister had big plans for, and she jumped off the eighteen-inch platform and rounded the side of the house. She could hear him barking.

Loud. Like he'd seen a threat.

He was a search and rescue dog, but he was very protective of her. If something was out there that made him feel unsafe, he would react. He would protect.

He looked vicious doing it, though at heart he was the most sensitive dog she had ever worked with.

She yelled his name. The barking got more excited.

A car door slammed nearby. Loud. An engine revved. Her mind automatically cataloged everything over the barking. The crying.

Crying.

That wasn't her dog making that noise.

A car drove off. Nat stared at the car, burning it into her

memory. There was a man in the driver's seat, but he was too far away for her to see anything other than that.

Nothing identifying, except the first three digits on the license plate number—CH5.

A maroon four-door family sedan, possibly from the early 2000s. With darkened windows on the rear.

Kudos ran back toward her, around the corner of the house. To the side door.

Nat hurried after him. The crying had gotten louder. And louder. There was something behind one of the hedges. Something *moving.* Kudos hunkered down on his front legs, whining. Nat called him back to her side.

He obeyed immediately.

That's when she saw the blanket. Pink and mint green. With yellow-and-cream accents. She looked closer.

It had puppies printed on it, yellow-and-cream puppies.

The blanket was still, for the longest time. Then she saw it—movement. A wiggle.

There was something in that bundle.

Nat switched the gun to safety and tucked it out of sight.

With a careful hand she flipped the blanket back. In a previous case she'd worked, an ex-husband had left poisonous snakes on his wife's stoop—wrapped up in a blanket. Nat wasn't stupid.

Anything could be in that blanket.

Something sobbed. And she *knew.*

She went down on her haunches.

"Hello. My name is Nat, and I'm here to help you."

89

HE'D MANAGED TO CATCH FOUR HOURS OF SLEEP, A SHOWER, something to eat, and a five-minute phone call with Emery before Max rejoined the rest of the team in the conference room. Whit had taken over for him sometime around three a.m.

Jac was sprawled out on the small loveseat pushed against a wall. Max's own suit coat covered her. She'd changed clothes and cleaned up sometime since he'd last seen her. Max hoped she'd grabbed something to eat, too.

He stood over her, just watching her for a quick moment.

Whit looked up at him. "Hey, boss. She's been out for a few hours."

"I don't think she's had more than three hours since..." Max checked his watch. "The night Rachel was killed. And she'd just gotten back from a case before that."

"Jac was about to crash sooner or later, then. Not that it's been a power nap. She's flipped and flopped like crazy. Worse than I've seen her do it before."

"She is a restless sleeper, especially when she's stressed. Worried."

They'd all grabbed catnaps wherever they could when working together before. It was just a nature of the game.

He would have said more, but his phone buzzed. Jac's buzzed nearby, too. Max grabbed his quickly, and tossed Jac's to Whit as Jac sat up with a jerk.

"It's the director," Whit said as he looked at the screen.

"I can take it," Jac said. Whit tossed the phone to her immediately.

Max stepped across the room and took his own call from Dan Reynolds.

When he looked up, his eyes met Jac's green ones. His shock was echoed on her face.

"Let's go," Max said. "I'll drive."

"What in the hell has happened now?" Whit asked.

Max didn't have a clue.

90

THEY CHOSE TO SEND EUGENE LYTEL TO SECURE JAC'S PLACE. JAC HAD one thought as Max drove. "We have Ava. What has he done with Olivia?"

"I don't know."

"Ava might," Jac remembered Nat at four. Jac had been seven. Just like Ava and Olivia. Nat had always been tiny, vulnerable. Jac had been taking care of her Nat's entire life. "We're going to have to question her."

"She'll never make a reliable witness."

"No, but she might be able to give us a direction to go in." Fear for both girls was still uttermost in her mind.

The director had told her that Nat had called for an ambulance, that Ava was definitely in need of medical care. But he hadn't known more than that.

"I'm just thankful Nat was there," Jac said. "She wanted to stay closer to PAVAD, in case we needed to move quickly. She was on call, anyway."

"Yes. If she hadn't been at your place, would a neighbor have found Ava?"

"I don't know. I honestly don't know. But Nat was there, and that's what matters. And now…we'll find Olivia and Paul/Philip. Go from there. But we have Ava. We'll take that as the gift that it is."

"Yes. That's all we can do now."

"He has my address. Why would he take her there?" Jac tried to figure it out. But the idea that he had taken Ava to *her* house didn't fit anything they'd profiled about Paul Sturvin/Philip Sullivan at all. "Why would he have that? I gave it to Rachel. Not him. I wrote that Post-it note myself."

Max hesitated. "I spoke with the director last night. Paul Sturvin has been selling PAVAD information. The director has Sin Lorcan looking into the source of the deposits into the Sturvin account. He's probably copied information on all of us and sold it to the highest bidder."

"That's reassuring." They'd known they were under a threat, and that threat could come against any of them at any time. Jac hadn't forgotten that. She doubted anyone in PAVAD had, not after what had happened to Ezra and Shannon. "This is part of your secret investigation?"

"Sturvin is. I'm not sure if what happened to Rachel has anything to do with it. I was waiting for a secure time to dial you in. Ed…he still wants it kept to as few people as possible. Not even Whit or Miranda know."

Jac just nodded. "He's anomic. He's financially failing? Maybe something with the deposits went wrong, so he snapped and killed Rachel? Took the girls? Or maybe he's not the one who killed her at all? Although that doesn't really work. Since he is the only evidentiary tie to Debbie's crime scene. Kelly is comparing DNA samples from Debbie's nails now. She should have those results within the next few hours."

"There are some questions we won't get the answers to until we get Paul in custody."

91

It took them a few moments to find where Ava was in the pediatric wing. Max could feel the anxiety running through Jac.

Nat met them in the hallway outside the room that Ava had been assigned. Max studied her quickly. He had left it unsaid in the SUV, but Jac would want to see her own sister for herself, too.

Nat looked fine, though her hair was down around her shoulders instead of in the customary ponytail she normally pulled it back in. She looked even younger than her twenty-six years now. And there was a suspicious stain over her left shoulder. From a child.

"Nat? How is she? What did he do to her?" Jac asked.

"Nothing, as far as the doctors can tell. But she does have an upper respiratory infection, bronchitis, and is asthmatic. They are working to get her fever down now."

Jac visibly exhaled. "That's it? He didn't hurt her?"

"Not physically. There's not a mark on her."

"Do you think she can talk with us?" Max asked. "Give us anything to go on?"

"She might. She's...well, she's a bit confused, of course. And she's traumatized. She said her father told them their mother fell down the stairs and went to heaven. Ava seems to think her father is driving Olivia there to see her, but left Ava because she wasn't feeling well. Like the time Olivia got to go to the zoo but Ava had to stay with their great-aunt because she had burning ears. I'm assuming she means an ear infection. And...she's been asking for Jac. Repeatedly. I didn't get a chance to ask any more questions. That's really not my job description. I was more concerned with keeping her safe until you got here."

"Thanks, Nat. Stick around. You'll need to be interviewed and debriefed. I've already notified Hanan."

She nodded. "I'm volunteering to stay with her. She was afraid of me—until I told her I was the little sister, and Jac was the big sister. Just like Olivia."

"I told her about my little sister and her two puppies at Emery's party."

"And that Kudos is big enough for her to ride on. She was fascinated by him. I made her a promise. She gets to see him again as soon as possible. I'm going to keep my word."

Max pushed open the hospital room door, nodding at the local LEO he recognized from previous cases and from Smokey's occasionally. Jac darted around him.

"Dr. Jones, I'm off the clock. Happy to do a security detail if you need it," the officer said, shooting a look at Nat, who was now speaking with a nurse. A look that told Max why the man had offered—it wasn't to snag some overtime.

"Thanks. We'll have a PAVAD guard here shortly, but we appreciate you staying until they arrive."

He followed Jac into the room.

Ava watched every move he made.

92

J<small>AC TOOK IN THE FRESHLY BRUSHED HAIR AND THE HOSPITAL GOWN</small> printed with dogs and cats. There was a stuffed animal tucked against Ava's side. It matched the one on the receipt from the pharmacy. It was a dog.

Paul had given his daughter a stuffed puppy because she loved dogs.

"Hi, sweetheart." Jac started, softly. "How are you feeling?"

"*Aunt Jac!*" Ava almost screeched it, reaching.

Jac stepped closer to her immediately. She sent a look to her sister, as she stepped further inside the small room behind Max. "Has she been...processed?"

"Yes. The staff in the ER here is quick," Nat said. "Nothing that shouldn't have been there, Jackie. Initial exam showed no signs of trauma. There are no unexpected bruises, just a small contusion from the seatbelt. Most likely from when she was in the aunt's car. Mostly, she has a respiratory infection, with asthma. That's it."

Jac reached out and put one hand on Ava's head. "Hi, baby. How are you feeling?"

"My throat hurts, Aunt Jac," Ava sent a sad look at Jac that went right through her. She gave a pitiful little cough. Ava had an oxygen tube around her head. Jac settled into the chair next to her.

To her surprise, Ava whimpered and tried to climb out of the bed. "Hold me."

"Hang on. We need to adjust the cord." Jac made short work of that, then pulled Ava into her arms, much like she had Emery when she'd had her appendix out. "Nat, hand me that blanket."

Her sister helped her get Ava settled. The chair was a rocker, put there for parents to rock an ill child. Soon she had a steady rhythm going, and Ava slumping against her. "Can you tell me what your daddy said before he took you to my house today? Emery's daddy is trying to find him. He has some questions for your daddy about important work things."

Ava's little hand went to her mouth, and she chewed on her fingers. Like she had before, at the party, when she had started to fall asleep in Jac's arms. "He said you'd be my new mommy. Like Aunt Debbie was my old mommy's new mommy, too. Until he could come back for us. He said you'd make me feel better."

"Daddy was right. I will take good care of you. How is Livy? Is she not feeling good either?"

Ava whimpered. Jac brushed her hair off her forehead. Ava was still hot to the touch. An ill four-year-old as a witness would never hold up in court. But Ava was now all they had.

"Ava? Where was Daddy taking Livy?" As much as Ava needed the rest, they needed the information from her. Olivia's very life could depend on it.

"Daddy and Livy were going to move away. Until they came back to get me and you when I feel better. Daddy said you'd be my mommy, and I wouldn't have to be alone. That he would come back for both of us."

"Where were Daddy and Livy going to move to? I should probably call Daddy and let him know that you're ok. That Nat and Kudos found you."

The little girl smiled, a dead ringer for her own mother's smile. That jabbed straight into Jac's gut. Except for the darker hair, Ava would grow up to look very much like Rachel someday. "Kudos is big. And he licked my face lots. Aunt Nat says I can see him again. When I feel better."

She was wheezing as she spoke. Jac knew enough to read the oxygen stats on the monitor. Emery had asthma, too, but it was reasonably well controlled.

"Kudos is one of the two best dogs in the world," Jac said, rocking her in the chair as Nat waited by the door.

Max just stood next to the window and listened.

"So where was Daddy going? Was he in his car? Or did he get a car somewhere else?" Max finally asked.

"Somewhere else, Emery's Daddy." Ava peeked at him. "There was a old barn. Daddy had to open the doors. He said the bad words. Livy said sssh and made me be quiet."

"When was this?"

"Yesterday."

That confirmed that Olivia was alive as of yesterday. As much as Ava could count as *confirming* anything. "Where was Livy when Daddy put you on my porch? Did Livy get to see Kudos?"

Ava nodded. "Kinda. She wanted to get out of the car, too, but Daddy yelled at her. He said she had to stay with him. But I had to stay with Aunt Jac."

"Did he call me Aunt Jac?" She had been Miss Jac before. Because Rachel had introduced her that way.

Ava nodded. "He said. Just like Aunt Debbie took care of my mommy when she was little. He said, he promised, you would take care of *me*. That he knew you would. He promised. Where's Emery? Can she come play with me here?"

"Emery is at school right now."

"Livy is supposed to be at school, too. But Daddy said we have to do homeschool now. Livy is mad. She wants to go back to school with Ruthie and Lucy. And Daddy is going to make my hair yellow like Livy's. And his. Daddy's hair is yellow."

Paul Sturvin had died his hair. She'd send that information along as quickly as she could.

Ava drifted off in Jac's arms, giving them nothing more. Jac brushed a kiss over her forehead, then looked at her sister. Nat hadn't left the room. She'd just been quiet the entire time.

Jac kept holding Ava. Jac tightened her arms around the little girl, then turned to her own little sister. "Tell us exactly what happened."

"I got a partial plate and a description of the car. I've already called it in to your Agent Whitman, Jac. Kudos was barking. I ran out to find out why. He led me around the house. I heard the car, visually confirmed it was a white male of around forty years. Matched the description of Paul Sturvin. He was already at the vehicle, and then I noticed the blanket. It was moving. Kudos beat me to her. The car drove away. I could have chased him, but—"

"First priority was Ava—and your safety. You couldn't chase after a serial killer," Jac said, probably more sharply than she should have. The idea of her sister anywhere near Paul Sturvin made her sick. "What did she come with? Every detail."

"The blanket. Obviously a child's twin-sized comforter. Pink, with puppies and kittens. I had everything sealed and bagged for PAVAD. But the stuffed animal had to stay with her. She was inconsolable without it. She was wearing footed pajamas, but they were fresh. Clean. Still had the factory inspection tag stuck in the left leg. He most likely bought them for her recently."

"So he has some money. Which fits with the withdrawals found by Dani. She estimates he probably has more than thirty thousand dollars on him," Max said. He moved to Jac's side, then leaned down and scooped the now sleeping little girl into his arms. He settled her in the bed while Jac watched.

Max was a natural father. It was so easy for him, even though she had seen the struggles he'd had through the years to make certain

Emery had what she needed. Nothing mattered more to him than his daughter.

Maybe some small part of Paul/Philip felt the same.

If Olivia even *was* his daughter. No one would ever know for sure.

93

Paul wept as he drove. Olivia had cried herself to sleep in the rear seat. She hadn't wanted to leave her sister; Olivia always mothered Ava when she wasn't feeling well.

He hadn't wanted to leave her. Ava was the best of him. Olivia would forever always be a pale second.

Like Philip had always been to Paul.

She was not the child of his body. He had always felt like second best with Olivia. And like he had not deserved her. Not after what he had done to his three elder daughters. And Bentley.

But he had always treasured her, from the moment he had first held her when she had been all of fourteen months old.

Bentley had been almost as much a star as Ava. Now, he was being ruined. No matter what he had done to try to save him, he couldn't save Bentley.

Philip hadn't been a good enough father for him.

For any of them.

He had seen the woman come out of Jaclyn's home, and had recognized her as the sister. He had still had to leave his daughter.

He hadn't known what else to do. Not without getting caught and separated from Olivia, too.

He'd made a vow to his brother as he'd stood over Paul's—the old Paul, not the new one—broken body that day. A vow to always take care of the child his brother had loved so much.

Every day had been devoted to finding ways to make that happen.

Night after night he'd laid awake next to Rachel, worrying about how he would provide for her and the girls and still find a few dollars to give to his biological mother for Bentley's care. Bentley had been her second chance to have a child to raise again. Bentley had meant the world to her. When she had died, it had been some of the darkest days of Paul's life.

Losing her had hurt far more than even losing Holly and the three girls.

She was his *mother*. Everything that had ever mattered to him.

After he and his brother had been taken from her, he had grieved her every single day. He'd just wanted to make *one thing* right after what he had done to his brother.

He'd killed his brother, then gone home to his brother's wife. To her bed. The first time he had ever touched Rachel, he had hidden in the bathroom after and wept from the beauty of her.

From the guilt of him.

He had assumed his brother's very *life*. He had become Paul then. Left Philip Sullivan behind forever that day. He was *Paul*.

There would be a cost for that.

But Paul knew he had already paid it today.

Ava. It had cost him Ava.

He had known that, always known that. He hadn't deserved her. Not truly.

Olivia fussed in her sleep. Her fever had broken an hour after they'd left her sister on Jaclyn's doorstep. But she still wasn't up to full speed.

She was bigger, stronger, healthier than Ava. He had always hated that fact. His brother's only child was stronger than his.

But now as he looked at her, he was glad of it. Olivia would have to be strong for what he would have to do.

And he would do it, too.

For Rachel. For Ava. And for all the ones he'd loved who had gone before.

THEY'D WAIT OUT THE STORM AT HIS MOTHER'S PLACE, HE'D LET HER sleep in Bentley's room, then they'd take off first thing in the morning. He'd love the opportunity to take a shower, too. Paul had never enjoyed being grubby like this.

Olivia needed a bath and clean clothing as well. He would see to cutting off her hair and dressing her in the boy's clothing he had purchased at the store at their next stop. How he was going to make her cooperate with being a boy for a few weeks still wasn't clear to him.

Unless he just ordered her to do it, and he kept her as isolated as possible. Until she was more comfortable with their new life.

It would confuse her, but she would have him to help her adjust. She was a smart girl, after all. She would adjust.

But first, he had to check on Ava.

Paul had one number he could call. He did that quickly.

And he listened.

When he disconnected, he rushed to the nearby bathroom and lost what breakfast he had eaten that morning.

Eugene Lytel was a cold-blooded killer.

There was no way he was going to let that sonofabitch near his daughter.

"Daddy, I don't feel good."

Olivia came to him, where he sat at his mother's dining room table. Paul snuggled her close. She was getting fever again. All of this driving around in the rain was keeping her from resting, from healing.

He wasn't being much of a father now. Wasn't keeping his promise.

Paul carried her to the couch and tucked her beneath a planet-covered blanket from Bentley's room.

He was going to have to do what he had to do.

Paul found what he needed in the medicine cabinet. They hadn't expired yet. That was good. He hadn't gotten around to cleaning out her home. It would have been too difficult to explain her to Rachel, and he hadn't been able to take time off from work.

The business his brother had started before Philip had become him had been *hard* for him to keep going. To learn. He had been a contractor before. Had built himself a reasonably successful business —with his hands. Not his head. He liked to think he had used those skills with his new consulting business.

He had managed.

Had gotten this far. He would get through this, too.

But the last thing he wanted was Olivia getting in the way.

He gave her fruit punch. She had always loved red drinks. Ava… Ava had preferred purple.

Paul held his daughter until she was limp in his arms.

He carried her to the back of the house—to the bed of the cousin she didn't know she had.

And he left her there.

He had done what he needed to do.

Now, he had to do what he had to do—it was time to end this, for all of them.

94

"Take care of the house," Lytel ordered the men who had accompanied them out to this run-down ranch house near New London. Todd tried not to puke. They were a mile from the house where Paul Sturvin/Philip Sullivan had holed up in.

The man had stupidly called Lytel, wanting to meet. Gave a damned address. Idiot.

He should have taken his daughters and headed for Canada hours ago.

Lytel had ordered Todd to accompany him here. Now, Todd stood back as the two men argued.

Sturvin wanted money—and a guaranteed way out of the country.

Or he was going to call Jaclyn Jones and spill everything.

Todd flinched inwardly at what that meant. Jaclyn would have to be told, have to be warned.

The last thing she needed was Lytel.

With one shot, Lytel ended the search for Paul Sturvin forever. Todd dropped his hand to his own weapon. It would be stupid to think Lytel wasn't thinking of doing the exact same thing right now.

The older man looked up at Todd. There was a light of madness, of sheer *enjoyment,* in the man's blue eyes. "You'll need to change your shirt before getting back with Mr. and Mrs. Jones, Barnes. You have high-velocity spatter on your collar. One of them is likely to notice."

Todd just nodded, biting back the bile.

Paul Sturvin's fake blond hair was now blood red. Todd held in the puke with everything he had.

"Barnes?" Lytel asked quietly. "Is this going to be a problem for you? Better pick your team now before you ride the pine bench from here on out."

Todd shook his head, immediately. He just had to play it cool with Lytel.

Or he'd be lying there right next to Paul Sturvin, bleeding into the muddy Missouri ground.

And his mother and sisters would be fed a full pack of lies about him, destroying their perception of him forever.

He didn't want that.

Todd wanted a chance to have a damned family of his own.

"So what do we do now?"

"We leave him and hightail our asses back to St. Louis. We'll have to check in with the Mr. and Mrs. in a few hours. We should just be able to manage it."

"What about him?" Todd asked as dismissively as he could. Sturvin's lifeless eyes were staring right at him.

"We leave him. Jones and Jones are on the right trail. They'll find their way to him, as soon as I give them the message about the partial license plate I intercepted. If not, an anonymous tip might be in our future. Let's go. You follow me, but not too close. Don't want any of the locals to see our vehicles on the road together. Haven't you ever played undercover, Barnes? This is just one big game we're playing, you know."

Todd just looked at him.

"See you in a few hours, pal. And watch out. Fire response will be on their way soon."

Todd waited until the other man and his buddies drove off. He dutifully turned the SUV he'd rented over a week ago around and made it look like he was following Lytel and his dirty team.

They disgusted him. Those bastards had betrayed everything the bureau stood for.

They had taken the same damned oath to protect that Todd had.

That mattered.

He'd made it three miles down the highway before he remembered. *The girl.*

Paul Sturvin's daughter would have been in that house. Somewhere.

And Todd could smell the rising smoke in the distance.

95

JAC KNEW THEY WERE CLOSE. SHE COULD JUST FEEL IT. MAX HAD called the entire team back. Miranda was there. Jac looked at her friend quickly. "Bentley?"

"Agent Taggart has been reassigned to protective duty for Bentley. Dan Reynolds cleared it with his supervisor in Indianapolis."

Jac nodded. "Nat and two agents are going to stay with Ava until she's released. She'll be brought back here when the physicians release her."

She studied the people around the digital conference table, where all the evidence they had so far was now displayed. Whit, Miranda, Dani, Max. Barnes slipped in, and took the far seat. She studied him for a moment.

The toll the case was taking on them was most noticeable on Barnes. He looked horrible. Pale. Disheveled, though she thought the shirt was clean, at least. The man looked almost sick.

He wasn't holding up for this. She hoped he realized that and would leave PAVAD and never look back. Not that he'd been horrible, actually. He'd been adequate as an investigator, at least. Not great, but she'd seen worse. He had a file in his hand.

The file she needed. Things clicked into place. "Adoption records."

"What?" Max asked. Everyone turned toward her.

Jac went to the old-school whiteboard. She grabbed a marker. "Philip and Paul were adopted when they were four. They found new families then. But a four-year-old, they are capable of retaining some memories. And these were open adoptions. How could they not be? Paul and Philip were identical, and they went to two relatives, one maternal set, one paternal. People knew the story. But... why? Why would two boys be split up and adopted to separate, but connected families? It had to be a traumatic event. Had to have shaped them."

"Bentley went to a maternal relative," Miranda said. "She was the sister of the woman who adopted Philip."

"What relatives does she have remaining?"

"I'm already on it. She passed away six months ago. Ronalda Sullivan Carionni. Cervical cancer. No listed next of kin."

"Where did she live?" Max asked.

"A few miles south of New London, Missouri," Dani said. "It's sat vacant ever since. But...there's a trust attached to it. It's been left to...Bentley Sullivan. Which makes sense; she was raising him, after all."

Jac was flipping through the adoption records. "Paul and Philip were born Paul and Philip Koehler in Columbia. To...Ronalda Sullivan. She was sixteen at the time. Four years later...we have court records. Prostitution in St. Louis, drug charges in Kansas City a few years later. Looks like she signed the boys over for adoption a few weeks after the first arrest."

"She obviously still had contact with Philip. She took in his son."

"He's been visiting Bentley weekly. There is no indication he wasn't visiting Bentley before Ronalda's death as well," Miranda pointed out. "Bentley said his dad was teaching him all about the stars before his grandmother's death. I asked; he said Grandma liked telescopes. That his father had bought her one for her birthday and bought Bentley a toy one for his. I tried to get him to talk about his father as much as I could. He very clearly identifies the man visiting him as his father." She stood and pointed to the address on the digital map. "There are a lot of fields around Ronalda's place. Plenty of places to put a telescope."

"He still has a child with him, one who isn't feeling well. The weather is about to turn bad. He's going to drive someplace he feels safe, at home. He's going there." Jac was almost sure of it. "Ava said... he was taking Olivia where she could see the other stars."

Max jerked a bit. "He called them that. Said Olivia and Ava were his *stars*. At Emery's party."

"Just an off comment?" Barnes asked.

"I don't think so. He said it a few times," Max said. "To me, and to Chalmers."

"Rachel said he wanted to be with the stars of the show at all times. He had astronomy books in his home. And his office. It was a lifelong passion," Jac said. "He was going to take the girls to a planetarium while she helped me with landscaping. She'd told me she had to wait until Paul was busy with the girls before she could come over."

"He kept in touch with Ronalda, as Philip," Dani said quietly. She was clicking away at her laptop, doing a preliminary database search on the biological mother. Her screen was visible on the digital screen behind her. "Phone calls, emails. I'd say he had an active relationship with his biological mother. Not so for Paul Sturvin. The *real* Paul Sturvin, anyway. There are a few emails from Paul to Ronalda, about once a year. Stilted. Until *after* Philip Sullivan #1's supposed death. Then the tone warms considerably."

"Is it possible she knew which twin was which?" Jac asked, looking up at Max. "I mean...the saying is *a mother knows*, right? Marianna Dennis certainly knows how to tell her twins apart. Maybe Ronalda confronted him about what he'd done to his brother and he gave her Bentley in exchange for her silence?"

"*I know what you did, P. A mother always knows.* That is the first email she sent Paul after his brother's death. I can only imagine where it went from there," Dani said. "I'm cross-referencing everything I can find on her now. I'll have addresses and license—whoot!"

Jac stepped closer, to see the screen for herself. There it was: the license plate number of a maroon family sedan. It matched the partial Nat had gotten.

"Is it possible he took Olivia back to his mother's? To his actual birthplace?"

"It might be the only place he ever truly felt safe," Max said quietly. "Bring up the satellite images."

Dani worked quickly.

"That place is within twenty minutes of the pharmacy," Jac said. "And Ava said there was a barn. That could be it right there."

It felt right. Jac knew it.

"We need to get up there," Max said. "Meet up in fifteen. I'm calling in Lytel's team. They can meet us there."

96

LYTEL'S TEAM SOMEHOW ENDED UP ON THE ROAD AHEAD OF THEM. Max followed. "This could be another dead end."

"Or a stepping stone to the finish line." Jac rubbed one hand over her eyes. Any lethargy from only sleeping three hours since the case began was gone. All that was left was a sense of urgency she couldn't explain, but was experienced enough to know not to resist. "Paul/Philip is going to run out of places to go soon. At least staying in this area. He has to realize this. And he's not stupid. He'll know exactly how hard it is to go on the run. He might just decide to cut his losses, kill Livy, and start all over again with a new family somewhere else."

"We've heard of a lot of strange things, but killing your twin and assuming his life is probably at the top of the list," Max said. "Maybe."

Jac checked over her shoulder, at the convoy of vehicles behind them, then looked at the one in the front. Lytel and his team were in one vehicle, Whit and a few other agents they'd recruited took the other.

If Paul/Philip was at the house where he'd spent the first four years of his life, they would find him soon.

She just hoped they found Olivia with him.

The longer she was out there, the further away Olivia would slip. Jac wouldn't give up hope. Not yet.

Not yet.

She wouldn't stop looking until she found Rachel's older daughter.

Jac saw the flashing lights when they were approximately a quarter of a mile away from the property. "Max...the only house out this far on the satellite was Ronalda's."

He pressed on the gas. "I know."

"No, no, no. Damn it!" Jac leaned forward in the passenger seat, trying to get a better look through the storm. "The house is on fire!"

"I'm going as fast as I can. I'm not about run us off the road," Max said. Jac grabbed her radio and relayed the information to the two SUVS behind them.

Not that that was necessary.

Max pulled in. There were six fire-response vehicles and a dozen firefighters combatting the fire consuming the house.

The house was a total loss.

Jac waited until he threw it into park then hopped out. She pulled her credentials out and flashed them at the local sheriff who had jogged up to meet them. "PAVAD, Jaclyn Jones. Can you tell me, was anyone inside?"

"Not sure at this point," he said. "Deke Colton. This is my scene for now. Give me one good reason I should turn it and the DB over to you, and it's yours. I'm rather busy tonight."

"You said you didn't know if someone was inside," Max said, coming up behind Jac. "Hello, Colton, how have you been?"

The man's expression cleared. Jac gave thanks—Max having a connection to the sheriff would just speed things up. "Not bad, Jones. I take it this is related to something of yours?"

"We're looking for a man named Paul Sturvin, and his seven-old-daughter. He's a fugitive, wanted for the deaths of at least ten that we know of, including three children under the age of eight."

"DB's this way—"

Jac saw her then. Saw the ambulance and the familiar blond head. *"Olivia!"*

She didn't wait, didn't ask questions. Jac just ran. A deputy stepped into her path. She held up her credentials. "I'm here for Olivia."

———

It took a few minutes for him to sort everything out with Colton and the responders. Max knew where Jac's full focus was going to be.

Olivia.

He looked at the sheriff, ignoring the yells and the sounds of an active fire scene. "Where's the DB?"

"Here. Dumped in the front yard. We almost ran over him with a damned fire truck. Missed him at the last minute. Thought smoke inhalation got him, but he's clean. Except for the forty-caliber round between his eyes."

Max swore as he looked down at the remains of Paul Sturvin/Philip Sullivan. The man was sprawled out like trash.

The storm was going to wash away evidence tonight, and it would be a few hours before forensics could get there.

Damn it.

They'd been after Sturvin, but now…who the hell had shot him?

Another player in the game changed everything.

"Yeah, that's what I thought. What in the hell is going on here, Jones?"

"I'll have to fill you in later. Because I don't have a damned clue what's going on here."

"Found the girl over here. Wrapped in a blanket, propped up against that monstrosity." There was a concrete birdbath with a three-foot stone dolphin weathering in the center of the front yard. "Thought *she* was under because of the smoke, but EMTs say she looks like she's been sedated. Has a fever as well."

"How long has this been burning?"

"A few hours at the most, as far as I know now. You want to tell me about this? This the guy on the news?"

"Yes. Paul Sturvin. Killed his wife, abducted his two daughters."

"We got another kid in there?" Panic immediately hit the other man's tone, and he stepped toward the flames.

Max held up a hand. "No. We recovered the younger girl. She's safe now. We are damned glad to find the older girl."

"Glad I could help, such that it is. And now…I've got a drug bust going on forty miles from here. And I don't have time to fight for jurisdiction on this. Case and the DB is all yours."

"Anything to go on?" Max asked as the detective he'd known for years started toward his squad car.

"Not a damned thing. Good luck, Jones. See you later."

"Thanks, Colton, I owe you one."

"Damned straight. I'll collect on it someday."

97

Todd had to get out of there. He'd seen the anger in Lytel's eyes. It was only a matter of time before he figured out that it wasn't Young or Harris who had carried Sturvin's little girl out of the house.

There would be only one man who could have done it, and Lytel would know that.

Those three fuckers had left a drugged little girl to burn alive in that shack. She couldn't identify them. She posed no threat to them. They could have done exactly what Todd had—he'd wrapped her up in her blanket and carried her outside, where she'd be safe. He'd been careful, there would be no way to tie him to her.

They didn't have to just leave her. They'd taken oaths to serve and protect.

And they had just left her there.

Todd wasn't going to be a part of it any longer.

He didn't trust Lytel not to come after him next. Sturvin had become a liability. Anyone could see that.

Todd wasn't interested in playing that game any longer.

He had to be able to look at himself in the mirror each day.

Throwing his lot in with baby killers, especially baby killers wearing the same damned badge Todd wore every day, was never something he would be cool with.

Todd opened his laptop. He had a confession to write, an email to send. Then he was getting his ass out of here. He had relatives in Canada. By the time he sent the email, his plane would have landed north of the border, and he'd disappear up there. He had some savings, and he was a hell of a lot smarter than Paul Sturvin ever could be.

But he wanted the email to Ed Dennis written first. Then he'd hide his ass until Dennis told him it was safe for him to return. Just how that was going to happen, he didn't know yet.

It took him two hours to get the words just right. He was supposed to be sleeping.

Max Jones had put everyone on stand down for the next ten hours, considering most had been up almost around the clock since Rachel Sturvin's body had been found.

The girls had been found, were safe. They had time for people to get some damned sleep.

Todd wasn't going to be able to sleep until he got this shit off his conscience somehow.

He signed his name and scheduled the identical emails for first thing in the morning. He duplicated one, then added a few more things, things of a more personal nature.

Todd was going to tell Miranda even more. He didn't know why, but he just…didn't want her thinking he was seriously involved with the kind of men who would leave a seven-year-old to burn. Maybe he'd never see her again, but he wanted her to think he was a better man than that.

He had just packed his belongings, emptying the hotel drawers quickly. He had forty-five minutes until his plane departed. And he left everything he'd ever cared about behind.

98

ALL THEY KNEW FOR CERTAIN WAS THAT PAUL STURVIN HAD KILLED Debbie Miller.

They didn't have anything definitive—such as DNA or a murder weapon with his prints on it—that said he had been the one to bludgeon Rachel to death.

Dani and Whit were going to handle the wrap-up and wait for the final forensics reports.

They had a lot of speculation on him killing every victim involved. They would have to tie him to the rest of the deaths over the next few weeks or so. Things took time. They still had to find the actual murder weapon.

And whoever had killed the man masquerading as Paul Sturvin.

Max's mind was running over everything as he and Jac walked back into the PAVAD building five minutes before midnight. It had taken hours to sort everything out and make it back. Then she'd wanted to stay with Olivia at the hospital.

Eventually, Olivia had ended up in the same room as her sister. Nat had taken a few hours to sleep and shower that afternoon; she was now back at the hospital and would stay in the room with the girls for the night—with a two-agent PAVAD detail, consisting of Maria Angel and Lucas Armitage, agents that Max and Jac trusted. The two had volunteered when they'd learned it was two young girls needing protected.

There were a few reports Max needed to go over, and then he was putting his foot down. Jac was going home with him tonight, and they were going to sleep. Period. They'd connect the dots between Paul Sturvin and Andy's murder first thing in the morning.

There was a connection there—Max was almost certain of it.

He was beyond exhausted, and Jac wasn't doing any better.

Max was taking her home.

They could deal with everything else in the morning.

She didn't even protest when he led her to his SUV. "You're camping at my place tonight. I arranged with Julie Cooper to take Emery home with her after basketball practice. She's going to spend the night with Kacey."

"Am I? Taking charge, Max?" she asked around a yawn.

"You'd better believe it. If nothing else this case has taught me one thing."

"And what is that?"

"Time is short. I'm not going to waste it again. Especially with you."

She didn't say anything as he drove, as they got out of the car, as he unlocked the front door.

"Come on, inside." He practically guided her into his living room. Jac just docilely did what he wanted.

"They have no one," Jac said in a quiet tone. "Paul, Philip, whoever he actually was, had no living family, Rachel only had Debbie. The girls...social services is going to take them and Bentley, and they'll be put into foster care. Their entire lives are going to be destroyed. *Were* destroyed."

"I know."

"I can't let that happen, Max. I just can't."

He'd never forget the look in those green eyes he loved so much in that moment.

Then his arms were open. Jac threw herself into his arms, and he just held her.

While she cried.

They'd found Rachel's daughters.

Now, they had to figure out what happened next.

99

SHE FELL ASLEEP. RIGHT THERE, CURLED UP ON MAX'S CHEST LIKE A damned cat, Jac fell asleep on him. When she woke, it was at least a few hours later, and he was sleeping beneath her.

Jac could feel his heartbeat beneath her cheek. Strong, sure, steady. Real.

She stared at him for the longest time. Sleeping in a chair on top of a man's lap was *not* something she had ever done before. It wasn't as uncomfortable as she'd always imagined it would be.

For one thing, Max's chair was oversized and he'd kicked out the foot. She'd been snuggled up against his side as if she'd slept there a million times before. Her head had been pillowed on his hard chest and his arm had been holding her tightly to him.

As if he wanted her right there.

Jac sat up and ran a hand over her eyes. She was sitting on his lap. And he was moving beneath her.

Her gaze flew to his face.

To meet heat-filled eyes. His hand tightened on her hip. Holding her in place. "Don't move. I am not ready for you to move yet. I need to hold you for a while. Do you know how many nights I have dreamed of having you right here? I can tell you. Every damned night since we kissed."

"I...shouldn't be on your lap." But she made no further move to get away. Somehow while she'd slept his hand had slipped under her FBI polo. His fingers spread, right on her skin. Over the ridges of scars she'd always wanted to hide.

But instead of immediately stiffening like she normally did whenever a man had touched her there, she didn't.

Because she trusted him? Max wouldn't look at her with pity in his eyes once he learned of just how the colonel had liked to punish his willful daughters. Far from it.

He'd be angry for her. And proud of how far she had come.

Because he was Max. Max loved her. For exactly who and how she was.

That punched her gut like a fist.

Max loved *her.* Exactly how she was.

Jac relaxed against him, her head fitting on his shoulder as if he was made for her.

Her hair was loose, and he was actually almost playing with it. As if he couldn't get enough of touching her.

Jac wasn't ready to ruin the moment.

She probably never would be.

THE LAST THING MAX WANTED WAS FOR JAC TO MOVE OFF OF HIM. He'd been awake for the last hour, just enjoying having her pressed against him. Tangling his fingers in her braid, running his fingers up her spine. Just holding her, touching her, being so damned thankful that he finally could.

He'd listened to the sounds she made in her sleep. They had driven him crazy, tempting him.

He'd wanted to kiss her awake. He'd wanted to somehow get out of the chair and carry her to his bed.

Where she belonged.

This was nothing like what it had been with his ex. This felt like it had far more depth and meaning. Like he was an entirely different person than he was then, messing around with Pamela.

He and his ex had started off as casual lovers. There had been no love between them at the start. He wasn't certain there ever had been *love* on Pamela's part. Not deep down.

But the desire he felt now went deeper than anything he'd ever felt for a woman before. And he hadn't even truly touched Jac yet.

This was what he'd been afraid of. That, once they were together, he'd never be able to stop wanting her.

Hell. They weren't even together yet, and he couldn't stop wanting her.

She was already *his life.* Her and Emery. He could give up anything else in the world—his house, his career, anything.

But to lose Jac and Emery...would be to lose his everything. Max wasn't going to be stupid anymore. He pulled her closer. His fingers cupped the back of her head. She gasped. He caught the sound with his mouth.

Then he was kissing her. The way he had wanted to for a long, long time.

100

THIS FELT DIFFERENT THAN IT HAD THAT NIGHT. THIS...THERE WAS NO hesitation in his embrace. Not now. Now, it was hungry man with the woman he wanted. Jac knew more than enough about human nature to sense that.

Her fingers tightened on his shirt. Her other hand was trapped between them. She shifted, just enough so she could work her hand to the buttons on his chest.

Come to think of it, she wanted his clothes out of the way too. And her own.

She wanted to feel *alive* with him.

Even if just for tonight. She made a sound in her throat when he pulled back. One of frustration and demand—on some level she was aware the sound was one that would have embarrassed her if she'd been with anyone else. But she wasn't. Jac was far too focused on Max to care.

She was with Max now. Was going to be with him in every way that really mattered.

His hand slipped around her side, his fingers spread out over her stomach. "I want to take these off of you, Jaclyn Jones."

She almost thought he emphasized her last name, but she didn't stop to wonder why. "I think I would like that very much."

It didn't matter about the scars he would no doubt see. What mattered was that she wanted to feel that connection to him.

To him.

Because with Max, that mattered.

No man had ever mattered to her more than the one she was with now.

No man ever would.

Jac stopped hesitating. Her fingers went to the buttons of his shirt.

She popped the first one through the opening.

Then the next. And the next. To reveal the plain white T-shirt beneath. Because Max was a creature of order. Nice and neat and well put together in everything.

That was oddly comforting.

She'd have to figure out why later, but tonight was for *this*. Not analyzing or anything else. Tonight was about connecting and feeling alive.

Because tomorrow would come soon enough for them both.

101

Ed stared at the paperwork in front of him, trying to make sense of it. There was no real explanation for the pattern he was seeing. Burner phones.

Andy Anderson had died because of a connection between fourteen burner phones.

The next step was to locate those phones. Try to figure out who had purchased them and how they connected to PAVAD.

Paul Sturvin had had one of those burner phones. He had been that close to Ed's family. Ed hadn't even seen the snake in their midst. Fury from that had his hands almost shaking.

He couldn't continue to live like this. He was five years past mandatory retirement age. He wouldn't be working another five.

Ed stepped out of his office and walked the halls of the very building he had been instrumental in designing. His heart was in this building. His soul.

But his world—his world was a beautiful blue-eyed woman currently in the basement lab, their seven children, his daughter, her two children. Ana McLaughlin and the child who was his granddaughter by choice. Jasmine, his assistant who had worked just as hard as he had over the last five years to make PAVAD happen. She was another daughter of his heart, and he'd freely admit it.

Julia, down in the morgue, he'd loved her for almost a decade now. Yet another child of his heart.

Ed Dennis was a very rich man. And he knew that. He didn't mean the fortune he had amassed from investments. Investments made from the money he had inherited from his parents so long ago. That money mattered very little.

It wasn't how much gold or silver a man had that mattered.

Wealth was measured in love. In family.

The friends he'd made over the last ten years were in this building. The agents he had taught, and trained. Guided.

Ed walked down every hallway, on every floor. Just making note of the people who were there because of *him*.

He had a destination in mind. Marianna. She would always be his direction. He loved that woman more than words could ever say.

His daughter's department was his next-to-last stop. He just wanted to look at her for a moment. She had been through so much —much of it because of *him*. No parent could ever accept that easily.

Ed leaned over the rail next to the open stairs and looked down into the bullpen, right there outside his son-in-law's office. Hell was inside, his desk phone to his ear, in an intense conversation by the looks of it.

They had had a rocky relationship for fifteen years. Until Hell had fallen for Ed's only daughter.

Now…Ed would kill to protect that man. For his daughter, for his grandchildren. For the baby they would have in a few months.

Ed turned back toward the CCU bullpen. Someone below him laughed.

One of the Lorcan brothers, though he was too far away to see if it was Seth or Sebastian. It wasn't Sin. Sin was busy at the moment, digging into Sturvin's connections and contracts and those damned burner phones.

Sin...Sin could run PAVAD someday. So could Georgia, though he knew she didn't want that. Not with the children so young.

There were many in PAVAD who could run it someday. It would be in good hands when Ed stepped down.

He could rest assured with that.

His legacy for the bureau would live on.

There. He saw her. Georgia was coming out of her office—waddling out of her office. Ed smiled, not surprised one bit at the love that immediately rushed him. His baby girl. He hadn't done too bad of a job raising her by himself.

He just watched her as she met up with Carrie Lorcan. They had a discussion about something, as Paige Brockman joined them. He studied the people present beneath him. Georgia, Carrie, Paige.

Josh Compton and his wife were discussing something heatedly near a back desk, a file flapping in her hands, heatedly.

Dan Reynolds, Ed's closest friend and Compton's father-in-law, was heading in their direction.

Dan would be retiring in one week. He'd wanted to be completely retired before the beginning of the year.

Dan's biggest plans were to join the Brynlock PTA. His young twins would be old enough for preschool in a year or so. Ed smiled, thrilled that his friend had the second chance he'd so deserved. Dan's wife Allison was in the basement lab, most likely. The elevators dinged—Cody Lorcan, Sin's wife, stepped out.

People. PAVAD wasn't just agents; it was *people*.

And someone was threatening those people. People Ed loved.

He would never rest easily while that was happening.

Max Jones walked through the bullpen, stopping to talk to Agent Whitman. Ed smiled, remembering what the man had told him about the beautiful Agent Jones. Finally. He had been expecting those two to tie the knot for *years*. They belonged together—everyone had been able to see that. Except perhaps the two of them.

Someone came up behind him. Put a hand on his shoulder. Ed

knew who it was immediately. He would always know. She must have taken the back elevator. "Mari."

"You are up here, looking very serious. Anything I can help with?"

"I'm ready to retire." Four words he had never said to her. But four words that held power.

Blue eyes widened. "Ed? What happened?"

He took her into his arms, not caring who was watching them from below. "Nothing. I'm just...I've almost accomplished what I wanted here."

He had one more department to get off the ground. The one dearest to his heart. Cold cases. The forgotten.

Then... "I'm ready for more. To let someone else take PAVAD to where it is meant to go. I...want to concentrate on being husband, father, and grandfather and friend now. This stage of my life is coming to an end. I want more."

He had three cases he needed to finish first. Andy Anderson, Darrin Hull, and one more. Hers. The one woman other than Marianna that he had once loved, truly loved. He owed it to *her* to answer the questions about her death.

More. He owed it to her two daughters.

And he had to find the people responsible for the leak in PAVAD.

Ed was making that his final mission.

He'd make certain PAVAD was safe for the ones who came after.

102

THERE WAS NO WAY TO FIX THIS. EUGENE BIT BACK A CURSE.

He still had that bastard Barnes's blood on him. He'd have to find a place to change clothes. Burn the evidence.

He knew enough about forensics to know what he needed to do. He hadn't enjoyed that. The rush just hadn't been the same.

Maybe he was getting tired of it. The death and killing. He saw so much of it; it had been bound to twist his soul eventually. Or flat-out bore him to his teeth.

How could it not? Nothing lasted forever, after all.

Barnes had completely screwed everything up. Eugene had told the others that he was a bad choice. Barnes shouldn't have been brought into this at all.

Barnes was too stupid to have followed through.

Two mistakes such as Sturvin and Barnes were something they couldn't afford. Not on Eugene's watch. He'd already been cussed at one time too many over Sturvin now.

Fallow and Young and the others were watching him now. Mistrusting him.

Once again, he had been ignored. And now Barnes had spilled his guts.

He might have even named fucking names.

Lower man on the hierarchy—Eugene's words hadn't mattered. Exactly like every time before.

No matter where he turned, whichever way he looked at it, Eugene would always be the guy who did all the grunt work. Both inside PAVAD and out of it.

Well, fuck that.

He was finished. It was time to take all of his damned money and find a beach somewhere.

As soon as he cleaned up a few things first, he was going to put in his papers. Claim he was having a mental breakdown or something, like Stephenson had years ago. He was just done.

He'd seen that before.

The PAVAD shrinks were all about mental wellness now, and taking time off if the ugliness of PAVAD got to be too difficult to handle.

He'd put in for some extended comp time, find an island south of the equator, then fake his own death. Erase Eugene Lytel as if he'd never existed.

Get out from under everything—everyone—who had ever dragged him down. Including the wife and kids.

He would miss the grandkids, though. He liked most of them.

But they were getting old enough now to be on the internet. Maybe he'd friend them under a fake name or something. Keep an eye on them that way.

The more he thought about it the more he liked the idea.

That was exactly what he was going to do.

But first…he had a personal score to settle with Colonel Boyd Jones.

He had always hated that sick son-of-a-bitch.

And there were only two beings that bastard truly cared

about. Two people, if the colonel was capable of caring about anyone.

It was time to take one of those away from him.

Eugene had been looking forward to it, for weeks.

Ever since the girl had transferred to PAVAD.

He'd discounted Jones's older daughter—she wasn't Jones's by blood. Eugene snickered at that.

The younger one wasn't either, for that matter.

But old Boyd didn't acknowledge that.

He'd discovered that for himself when he'd casually asked Jaclyn about her relation to the bastard from Washington, several years ago.

She had made it very clear she despised her stepfather. And wanted no part of him. Her hatred had almost been tangible. Eugene had done some digging, checked some old dates in some old records and done a small bit of *math*.

The colonel's wife had stepped out on him—just in time to make the younger daughter.

He'd watched the elder the years she was in St. Louis, to see if the colonel ever had influence over her life.

The bastard hadn't visited Jaclyn even once.

Jaclyn—she was very much like her mother had been twenty something years ago.

It had led Eugene to seeing her in a different light, made him feel almost paternal toward her at times. She'd been very young to have no family.

He'd hate to see something happen to her.

But the younger girl…

Boyd had told everyone she was his; that she was his *blood*.

Blood was what mattered to that sick son-of-a-bitch. Even if Boyd had deluded himself. Girl didn't look a thing like him.

But that dark-brown hair—it sure looked like the other sister's she didn't know she had.

Eugene knew that woman, too, after all.

As the girl loaded those damned dogs of hers into her four-door Wrangler, Eugene just watched her and waited.

When she left the driveway of the home that was far too large for one lone woman, he pulled out...and followed.

103

She hadn't wanted to leave him. But Miranda had to file her reports and help wrap up the case against Philip Sullivan/Paul Sturvin. She couldn't stay with Bentley forever.

No matter how much she had wanted just that.

Bentley had cried, terrified she'd not come back for him, no matter how much she had promised. She hadn't wanted to leave him with strangers, but she hadn't known what else to do.

Marilyn Brockman was the only choice she had. A retired child psychologist who had three children, two daughters-in-law, and a son-in-law working at PAVAD, she had volunteered to babysit the foster children Miranda had had before.

Leaving those children had not felt like *this*.

But Marilyn would take care of Bentley. Miranda knew that. The woman had written most of the textbooks out there on dealing with traumatized children. She would be able to help him, Miranda had to keep telling herself that. Marilyn's daughter had been there as well. Spending the day with Marilyn and all the children Marilyn watched.

Bentley would be just fine. He was safe. He was with children his own age. Marilyn and her husband were experienced in dealing with traumatized children.

Bentley would be ok.

That didn't help Miranda fight the urge to cry herself.

That little boy had stolen her heart from that first moment she had seen him in that group home. That wasn't something she was ever going to deny.

When he had lifted his arms to her and asked her if she would just hold him for a minute, *please*, because he missed being held he had wormed right into her soul.

He'd spent six months in that place of hell, after losing the woman who had been raising him. His security and safety. She would probably never fully know what had happened to him there.

Miranda knew what it was like to lose your mother. Even though she'd had her sisters, and her father, and her cousins, and her grandmother and aunt, she would never forget that pain.

Bentley didn't have anyone. Except for a four-year-old half sister he had never met.

And her. Someone had to advocate for him.

As she pulled into the PAVAD parking garage, Miranda tried to figure out exactly what it was she wanted to do.

She couldn't just let him go, disappear into the foster system to be forgotten. She just couldn't. He needed someone to stand up and say "Hey, he matters."

She was the only one in line to do that. What that meant for her future, she didn't have a clue.

When she stepped inside, the first person she saw was none other than Knight. Her stomach clenched; the last thing she needed right now was to deal with him.

Not when she already felt so shaken.

Miranda just kept walking. Even though she could feel him watching her.

She'd find Max and Jac, find out what was happening with the two little girls. Then she was going to put in for some more comp time. Spend it with Bentley.

She had a lot of soul-searching to do.

Because one thing was clear—she'd made a promise to that little boy. One she fully intended to keep.

Jac was nowhere to be seen. Miranda had been hoping to find her, to spill how she was feeling to Jac. See if her friend could help her figure out an answer.

But Max was right there, big, strong, and beautiful.

With a smile twitching at his lips.

Well. Something good had happened to him.

She would bet it had entirely everything to do with her best friend.

MAX MET THE DIRECTOR AND SIN LORCAN IN THE DIRECTOR'S OFFICE less than five minutes after he signed off on his final report regarding the Sturvin girls' case.

They had opened an additional case into the murder of Philip Sullivan—but that case was being redirected to team two, under Sebastian Lorcan—and Jac.

To free Max up to devote his time to finding the ones responsible for Andy's death.

With Andy's code broken, they finally had something to go on.

"The leak is originating in the auxiliary department," the other man in the room said.

Sin Lorcan looked as somber as the soberest of judges. Immaculately put together, there was a hardness in his eyes that would terrify those who didn't know him well.

Max just saw it as the determination that it was.

The woman Sin adored had nearly died because of this leak. Max wouldn't have been any less determined if had been Jac. Or less pissed.

"Do we have a name yet?"

"That's what I want you to find. You finished the wrap-up on the Sturvin case?"

"Yes. I have Dani and Whit finishing indexing the forensics and confirming the loose ends. We'll have one of the support teams for the CCU investigate the other deaths associated with Philip Sullivan. But the man is dead—we'll never be able to charge him."

"No. But we'll have the answers. It's a wonder no one knew the difference between the two men," Ed said. "That's just insane."

"No kidding," Sin said. "Cody has never confused me with one of my brothers. Neither have my sisters-in-law, that I know of."

"I think their mother did know. He kept in touch with her, when the real Paul Sturvin wasn't close to her."

"Now, it's time for things to move on," Ed said.

"Sam from ballistics got back to me ten minutes ago. The bullet that killed Paul Sturvin, or whatever name he actually went by, matches the gun that killed Andy. A forty-cal. Same striations."

"Have we tied the fourteen burner phones to anyone specifically?" the director asked.

"Paul Sturvin. That's it. One of the phones, the one ending in -5758, dialed Sturvin's number on a regular basis," Sin said. "We're still tracking down the others."

"And the deposits coincide with the dates of the calls exactly?" Max asked.

Sin nodded. "That's been confirmed. Carrie has finally been able to get into the hard drive on Anderson's laptop—with some tweaking. I don't know if what she found will hold up forensically in court, considering what she had to do to reconstruct, but it gives us a direction. We found scanned copies of his notes. He was trying to tie the phones to five men—from auxiliary."

Max swore.

The auxiliary team was the backbone of PAVAD. Without those agents there to support the various divisions, and the teams, the job for frontline PAVAD agents would be even more dangerous than what it was.

The idea that agents in that department were dirty—that jeopardized every live investigation they had.

105

He was going to have to change his plans a bit. He hadn't planned on harming Jaclyn. The redhead was a nice woman and a decent agent. Eugene had never had a problem with her, and she had always treated him with respect.

She wasn't connected to either of the two men he wanted to stick it to. Well, no more than her mother had been involved with both of those men at one time or another.

Jaclyn most certainly didn't even know that. He couldn't see the colonel sharing that his wife had fallen for another man. Not with Boyd's ego.

He didn't know much about the other daughter. She wasn't that remarkable. Small. Hell, she was barely bigger than his ten-year-old grandson. To be honest, Kayden probably outweighed her by a good fifteen pounds.

Not that that gave him pause. Eugene had killed kids before.

When it was necessary.

He had been trained in the army more than thirty years ago to do what was necessary when it was necessary. Those skills were some of the very reason he'd made it this far in the bureau in the first place. That and his previous connection to Edward Dennis.

He snorted at that.

He was the monster they had made him. Good old Ed had had a hand in shaping him just the way he was.

He had always found that ironic.

Natalie Jones turned the dogs loose in the backyard, then stepped up to her sister's front porch.

Walked right in.

Eugene just sat back and waited.

The women would have to come out sometime.

Then he would have her.

A bullet between the eyes. That would be it.

A clear message to that son-of-a-bitch Boyd Jones that he never should have pissed off the wrong people in Washington. Another message to Ed Dennis, too.

No one was safe, after all.

Then Eugene was retiring.

It was about damned time.

106

"You've slept with Max!" Her sister squealed. "It's about time. I thought you were going to be stupid about him forever."

Well. Leave it to a baby sister to put it in those terms. "I am not the one who ran for the hills. Max was."

"Uh-huh. I think you are just telling yourself that. You should have jumped that man and gotten him naked five years ago. The first time he looked at you like you were everything he ever wanted. Miranda and I have been taking bets about when you'd finally figure things out."

"Nice to know you have my back."

"Always." Nat sent her a smile that was identical to their own mother's. "So what's next?"

"Not sure yet. We're going to take it slow, figure things out between us. We need to make certain Emery's ok with such a radical change. This will be a huge shock to her."

"Oh, like you being at their house seven nights a week instead of four or five? I think that kid has been asking Santa Claus for a Jac-as-Mommy for years. You'll make her biggest wish come true. You'll be a beautiful mother. You already are. I've seen that every time I've been with Emery. Any children you and Max have are going to be the luckiest kids in the world. No matter how you get them."

Jac hugged her sister again. "I need to get going. I'm swinging by the hospital to check on the girls. And…return Mr. Bird." She'd spoken with the head of forensics herself. The stuffed emu hadn't been processed—it hadn't been needed. And would be returned to his owner immediately.

Jac had him all ready to go, along with a stuffed horse she'd picked up specially for Livy.

"I may stop by and check on them myself this afternoon. When are you on the clock?"

"I have to be there by noon today, for half a day. I've cleared it with Carrie. We're taking Emery to her favorite restaurant tonight to talk to her about what has happened and what changes there will be. We're going to go only as fast as she can handle."

"You're thinking to move straight in with Max, aren't you?"

"Yes. We've wasted enough time as it is."

"No kidding. Grab ahold of him, Jacs. And hold on as tight as you can. Time…it's too fleeting not to."

Jac wrapped her arms around her little sister one more time, wishing she could erase the grief.

But she would never be able to.

The grief was a part of Nat now. And always would be.

Maybe with time, it wouldn't sting her sister quite so much.

107

MAX FINISHED WITH THE DIRECTOR AND HEADED BACK TO HIS OFFICE. There were a few things he wanted to check into—things the director and Sin had brought up that were tickling the back of his mind.

Max also wanted to text Jac, to see how the Sturvin girls were doing. He knew she was on her way there today.

He wanted her to check in with him, give him an update on the girls. Talk to him. He needed to make certain she was ok with what had happened between them last night.

He had a ring in his pocket. His grandmother's. Pamela had never been offered it, but Jac—it would be perfect for her.

As soon as he figured out the best way to ask her.

They had waited long enough.

Hell, Max knew it—he was just wanting to see her.

Confirm that things that had changed between them were real. Corny, but until he had her in his house, married to him, and at his side where the woman belonged—a part of him would be afraid it wouldn't happen.

Not until it did.

He wasn't willing to take any chances she'd escape him.

He opened his email account. He had work to do. As soon as every loose end with the Sturvin case was tied up, he would clear his schedule.

It was time to hit Andy's case as hard as he possibly could again. To find the traitors threatening them all.

PAVAD was still being hunted. It was time they doubled the guards, armed the sentries and prepared for attack.

He was going to be a part of that.

There were still answers out there. Max just had to find them.

He read what was there in the first email and swore.

Max jumped to his feet, and grabbed his phone.

All thoughts of finding Jac were gone. The attackers were closer than any of them had realized.

He dialed Sin Lorcan's number quickly. When the other man answered, Max just had one thing to say.

"We need to find Todd Barnes now. He has all the answers we've been looking for."

"I'm on my way."

"I'm heading to the director's office now. Meet me there in two minutes."

108

EUGENE WAITED. HE'D BEEN GOOD AT WAITING FOR YEARS. ONE OF HIS skills. Waiting, and following orders.

That was apparently what he was known for—waiting and doing what he was told.

He'd done what he was told twenty-three years ago.

It had gotten a woman he actually had cared about killed. Hard to forget that.

He was just a damned grunt. A year away from mandatory retirement—unless he was given special dispensation by a director—he had spent thirty-two years doing what he was told.

The quintessential yes-man of the FBI.

He didn't have much to show for it. The investments that were paying off so well were investments he'd made himself. Not like he'd gotten rich working for the bureau.

He had just enough for one man to retire to a Caribbean island and live the good life. Without any worries.

He'd joined the bureau because it had seemed like a good idea at the time. Because Ed Dennis had given him a recommendation and had promised the bureau would serve him well.

In a way, Eugene had followed orders back then, too.

He'd had three kids to support, after all. Then the job had just become habit.

His damned security blanket. A way for him to have some fucking *excitement* in his life. Something beyond diapers and school plays and kids who whined all the damned time—then only came around once every few months when they were adults.

Eugene was done with all of that.

If it hadn't been for that bastard Boyd Jones and what had happened fifteen years ago, he wouldn't be just a lowly grunt. He'd have moved up years ago. Would have had a higher position in the bureau than PAVAD auxiliary supervisor. That everyone in the auxiliary department reported to him mattered little.

Boyd had been dogging Eugene since the day they'd buried Boyd's wife all those years ago.

Felicia Jones's funeral was the last funeral Eugene had ever attended where he'd actually *felt* something more than boredom.

Boyd had been insinuating himself in Eugene's career from a distance.

Screwing him over.

When he'd been offered a chance to get back at Colonel Boyd Jones for all the man's sins, of course Eugene had jumped at it.

He had four men that he trusted fully to do what he was telling them to do. And he wasn't even the one paying him for their loyalty.

Eugene wasn't stupid; Young, Harris, Garbison, and Fallow would sell him out in a heartbeat to save their own skins.

He'd finish this one thing, mostly because he despised that son-of-a-bitch Boyd Jones. Then he was out of there.

He had enough blood on his hands. It was time to retire.

109

THEY WEREN'T GOING TO GET ANY ANSWERS FROM TODD BARNES. Within half an hour of receiving Barnes's email, Max had mobilized whomever he could find and tracked Barnes down at a hotel.

He'd been too late.

Max looked down at the man as the paramedics tried to get him stabilized and bit back a curse. He should have looked closer. Should have watched what Barnes was doing a bit more.

There had been a reason Barnes was brought in right now. They should have realized that.

That they hadn't was on Max's conscience.

Barnes wasn't conscious. And from the looks of what had happened to his head, he might not ever be again.

Max looked at the other men surrounding where Barnes had been found. "What do we know so far?"

"We found him like this," Ken Chalmers said. He had blood on his hands and his shirt. "Thought he was gone, until his hand moved. Looked like he was dialing a phone. Or had one clenched in his hand when he was shot."

Max swore.

He didn't personally care for Barnes, but that he'd been shot in his hotel room like this sickened him. "We need to find what he's involved in."

"Someone took his laptop," Knight said from behind Chalmers. Max wasn't certain why the man was even there. He bit back a curse.

Knight hadn't looked all that different the day he'd been shot in the head in his own apartment a few years ago. Max had seen the other man for himself that day.

Not an image he was going to forget. No doubt, this was bringing that back to the surface for the other man, too.

"Knight and I were consulting a local detective about a case when the call went out that the director was looking for Barnes," Ken said. "We were close enough to the hotel to get here quickly. Found him like this."

"How long do you think he's been like this?" Max asked.

Kelly Compton looked up at him, from where she was starting on the blood that had been beneath Barnes's body.

Blood and…bone fragments. Hair.

Max bit back the bile.

He couldn't stand Barnes, but seeing this…

"From the looks of the bloodstains, Max, he's been bleeding slowly for a few hours at least. But…nothing definitive yet."

They had Barnes on the gurney.

To Max's shock, the man's eyes opened.

Stared right at him.

Kelly stood.

She took a jerky step back when Barnes's hand shot up and wrapped around her bony forearm.

Barnes didn't let her go. Max freed her quickly, as gently as he could.

Max stepped closer to the wounded man. "Todd? Todd, can you hear me? Do you recognize me?"

"Max—"

He did. Barnes was aware of what was happening around him.

"You're going to be ok, Todd." Max told him, leaning close enough to fill Barnes's vision. "We'll get you to the hospital and fixed right up."

"He...going after... others...PAVAD..."

Max's heart stopped beating for a moment. "Who, Todd?"

"Didn't...know. Lytel...it's Lytel. Dirty."

"We know that, too. Did he shoot you, Todd? Was Eugene Lytel the man who shot you?"

"Yes...killed Anderson...whole team. Dirty. Young...Fallow... dirty. All of them. Didn't know...till...got...Saint..."

The man's eyes closed. The paramedic jerked his hand, for Max to get out of the way. "We need to get him to the trauma center. Every moment counts."

Max nodded, stepping back. "Thanks, Barnes. I'm going to get him. I'll see he pays for this."

Barnes never said another word.

Max looked at the agents surrounding him. "Eugene Lytel. What do we have to do to find him?"

"And are the men on his team as dirty as Todd Barnes—an agent no one really likes or trusts—said?" Knight asked.

"We need to see what he sent in that email again." Max had read them. And knew in his gut there was at least some truth to them. Information Todd had written in that email had lined up with information that only the director and Max and Sin had had.

"One thing to consider—if whoever has his computer tracks his email, they're going to see whoever those emails were sent to," Knight said. "Making them potential targets."

There had been others cc'd on those emails.

"The director, me, Jaclyn—and Miranda Talley. Barnes has a thing for Miranda this time. He sent her *everything*. Said it in the email to me itself."

Knight swore. "Someone better find that woman, then. Fast. Because if your pal Lytel has a team of his own, and they're in the PAVAD building, there are plenty of people to go after all of you.

And it's not going to matter one damned bit if it's in the PAVAD building or not. If they want to get to someone inside, they will."

Max swore. The other man was right. They didn't know how many in Lytel's division were dirty. And they were right there with Miranda, Nat, and Jac.

To a man as skilled, as trained, as familiar with PAVAD as Lytel, that meant one thing.

Jac and the other two women he cared about were as good as sitting ducks.

110

MORE WAITING. HE COULDN'T GET THE SHOT. HE WATCHED AS THE elder Jones girl headed out. She was such a classy woman. Cool and sophisticated, just like her mother had always been.

He'd felt good when he was with her. Less invisible, though he'd never laid hands on her. He wouldn't have dared.

Strange that Jaclyn and her sister would have chosen law enforcement. Something as common as law enforcement wasn't good enough for one of Colonel Jones's daughters.

Not them.

Even when they'd been fucking teenagers, the good old colonel had gone on and on about how perfect they were, especially the younger one. How they were destined for the top.

Poised and graceful, and perfect.

Hell, the colonel had been prepping them to be married off to the highest bidders when they were barely old enough to drive.

Strange that they'd end up working PAVAD.

Then again, considering Boyd's *connections* to Ed Dennis, maybe it wasn't.

He wondered if Ed Dennis even *knew.*

Beautiful girls, though the redhead was more classically beautiful. The younger woman looked like a lost waif.

He sighted the rifle on first one sister, then the other.

Eugene had hated Boyd since the moment he had learned about Felicia's death.

Her murder.

His grip tightened on the weapon. He would give anything to get back at that smug bastard.

Jaclyn stopped to say hello to one of her neighbors. Eugene watched her, struck again by just how graceful she was. By how much she favored Felicia.

No wonder Max Jones had it so bad for her.

When he turned back, the younger sister had already loaded those dogs of hers into her Wrangler.

He studied her through binoculars instead, thinking that just around the eyes, around the hairline, she looked like the father she had never known.

He wondered if Boyd had ever noticed that little fact.

At the angle she was now, there was no way he could take the shot clearly. He would have to wait.

111

THERE WAS A SIX FOOT FIVE, BROAD-SHOULDERED, DARK-HAIRED PAIN in the ass staring at Miranda from behind mirrored glasses.

Knight had shown up two minutes ago, covered in blood, with a hard look on his face. He'd come right to her side and just…sat there.

Miranda didn't say a word. The last thing she needed now was Allan Knight just staring at her. Especially a bloodstained Allan Knight.

The man gave her the shivers. Sometimes not in a good way. "What are you doing here? Shouldn't you be across the street, digging into the past?"

He shook his head slowly.

"Knight…whose blood?" He didn't look hurt. She hadn't heard a call about an agent in trouble.

"Todd Barnes was shot in the head in his hotel room not even two hours ago. Chalmers and I found him. It's Barnes's blood."

Miranda flinched. "Is he going to make it?"

She barely kept from staring at Knight's scar.

Knight shook his head. "I'm not sure. He was talking when we left. Able to identify his shooter. Recognized Jones, too."

"So why are you *here* instead of doing your knightly duties elsewhere?"

"Simple. Whatever Barnes sent you in that email today—apparently, it's enough to get you killed. So…just consider me another guy for your collection. Seems you have a few new ones lately. So…tell me…you and Barnes?"

Miranda just sank into her chair and stared.

The man was serious.

"What is going on around here?" Then something he said clicked. "I…haven't checked my email yet today. I had…something *else* going on."

"Maybe you'd better do that now." He sent her a gorgeous smile. "Before something else happens around here. It's just a barrel of fun around PAVAD lately, isn't it?"

112

EUGENE HAD TAKEN THE TIME WORKING THE SCENE AT JACLYN JONES'S home earlier to study every entry point and exit. She had an alarm system in place. It was new, the sister had said, when Eugene had interviewed her at the hospital yesterday. A prototype for Lucas Tech or something that Jaclyn Jones had been asked to test out for the head of computer forensics.

Natalie hadn't even realized he was grilling her for information, as she'd stared at him from Felicia's eyes. Silly girl had trusted him.

He'd wanted to be the one to talk to Natalie Jones himself. To see just how much killing her would hurt Boyd.

The girl looked nothing like him. Up close, though, she looked a good deal like her father, and like the other sister she didn't even know about.

He'd found that amusing.

He'd found the code to the security system written down in Jaclyn's kitchen drawer.

She should know better than that. He'd tested the alarm when it was just him and his team on scene, after the forensics van had left. Just a few minutes of their time, and he had all he needed.

He followed the younger girl to the park. Watched as she worked with her dogs. Intensively. She put them through their paces, and it was obvious the girl knew her stuff. Bright, talented, capable—just like her father.

Her *real* father, anyway.

Colonel Boyd Jones was just a screw up who'd networked his way into his position.

For a moment, he toyed with the idea of just letting things go with Boyd. Just taking off for Mexico before anyone even realized he hadn't clocked in for the next shift.

Maybe even coming back and finishing with the girl later. Planned better, anticipated more.

Or leaving Felicia's daughters alone.

Let them have their perfect PAVAD lives. It was only a matter of time before the elder ended up in Dr. Jones's bed. Until the younger found some PAVAD superhero of her own to shag and snag.

Felicia's daughters hadn't done a damned thing to him, after all. She'd even bought him a cup of coffee there in the hospital cafeteria yesterday, very sweet in a quiet way. Graceful.

Once again just like her mother.

He really was a rank bastard anymore.

But no.

He hated Colonel Boyd Jones, after all. Had told himself that so many times over the years that he almost believed he could feel that hatred. He wanted to get one more blow in against that bastard while he still could.

That was why he'd signed up on this special little team in the first place.

He followed Natalie Jones back to her sister's place.

Watched as she released her dogs into the fenced backyard.

And waited.

113

JAC HAD A PIANO IN HER DEN. IT HAD BEEN THEIR MOTHER'S PRIZE possession. Nat always loved to sit at it and immerse herself in the old memories.

She had been three and a half when their mother had died. She had no real memories of the woman; not like Jac had. But she remembered her mother at the piano.

Her fingers touched the ivory keys. Jac had had it tuned recently, she'd said, though Nat doubted her sister had much time to play now.

Jac had once been a very talented pianist.

Nat, too.

Until life had taken the time for such pursuits from them.

Nat made herself a vow; she was going to build herself a real life again.

It was what James would have wanted.

He had been larger than life, so full of humor and fun.

He'd made her forget the darkness they saw every day on the job. The way people hurt each other.

The way her father had hurt her, hurt Jac.

Damn him. Her father would always be her nightmare.

He had called again that morning.

The colonel would be in St. Louis in two days. The colonel had demanded she meet with him. Said he had something important he wanted to discuss.

She was going to be a coward—she was going to take Jac with her.

Maybe even see if Max could go with them.

The one time they'd introduced Max to the colonel the colonel had actually behaved himself.

Max had growled at him after the one nasty comment directed at Jac that the colonel had made. Max was rather protective of her sister. It was beautiful to see—Jac had spent so long being the protector, she deserved people to protect *her* now.

Nat ran through the warm-up scales absently, lost in the memories of her childhood.

The nightmares.

It hadn't been all bad. She'd been granted opportunities most people weren't. All the top schools, the best connections, that only an upper-class childhood could bring. Barriers hadn't existed between her and what she had needed or wanted in life.

Just the Colonel and his fists.

She'd have traded every single advantage if she and Jac had just been *safe*. With people who didn't hurt them for the slightest wrong move.

She was still dealing with the trauma of her father. She probably always would be.

Losing James had set her back years. She finally felt like she was starting to come out of the fog. He would not have wanted her to just turn into a ghost like this.

She had to remember that.

If nothing else, she would build a life again—for him. They should have decades together.

He'd given her the ring a week before he'd been murdered.

A week. That had been the happiest week of her life.

She'd thought about burying that ring with him. But she couldn't do it.

It was all she had had left of him.

He hadn't even told his parents and brother about her at that point. They hadn't known.

Had fought her on what should happen to him after his death.

They had blamed her for not stopping what had happened that day. It had taken her a while to accept that she *couldn't* have done anything different. Nothing would have changed what happened to James. Nothing.

She'd had his will, had his instructions, and his power of attorney. That was all she had had left of him.

His final wishes. Details.

Today…would have been his thirty-third birthday.

She should go home. Or take Kudos and Karma on a hike somewhere. Anything but sitting there with the memories.

Nat couldn't go home. Not yet. She'd go crazy there, pull out the lone album of photos she had of him.

Nat stopped playing, dropped her head to the keys and wept.

Until a hard hand wrapped around her neck and jerked her to her feet.

Around.

Nat stared down the barrel of a gun and froze.

114

AVA AND LIVY HAD BEEN FEELING A BIT BETTER. LIVY WAS clearheaded enough to understand that her parents and aunt were all gone. That she and her sister were alone. Unlike Ava, who truly didn't understand that death was permanent—Livy did.

Jac had spent most of the ninety-minute visit holding the girls and reassuring them. They wouldn't be alone.

She was going to take care of them. She'd promised.

There had been a social worker in the room now.

One Jac had known well. She'd been the same social worker who had handled the case for Miranda when she'd kept a three-year-old girl whose mother had been a victim in a previous case. It had been a temporary placement. The social worker was a good one—was one that cared a great deal about the kids she had on her docket.

After Ava and Livy finally fell asleep again, Jac and the social worker had had an honest talk. About what would most likely happen to the girls—and Bentley—if someone didn't step up and offer to take them in, as fictive kin.

As it was, Olivia would have to transfer out of the private school, their parents' house would have to be sold, with the proceeds going to debts and funeral expenses, and they were all three now wards of the state.

If someone didn't have enough beds, or if someone decided they were better off apart, they would be separated. Their world had been completely destroyed.

And now they were literally waiting for someone to step up and fix things for them.

Jac had come to a decision. One she hoped Max would fully support.

She had promised Rachel she would take care of them. She had promised the girls she would take care of them, too.

They reminded her so much of her and Nat when they were younger. Alone and facing the world of monsters with just each other.

No child should ever have to face that.

Jac intended to keep her promise.

But first...she had to stop by her house again. Ava had spilled grape juice down the front of Jac's blouse.

She had just enough time for a quick change of clothes and get back to PAVAD.

She wanted to grab Max, have a heart-to-heart about the Sturvin girls.

See if what she wanted now would change things between the two of them again.

She didn't want to admit it, but a small part of her expected him to run. To want no part of it. It would be a massive life change neither one of them could ever have predicted, after all.

He'd run from her before. With far less provocation.

Another, larger, part of her knew that was stupid.

Max had explained why he'd run. And she'd understood.

This was just the first bump in the road they'd have if they were going to make a relationship between them work.

She suspected that was exactly what they were going to try to do. She was willing. He said he was, too.

It would just take time. Like everything else in life worth having.

She pulled into her driveway, behind Nat's Jeep. She was glad her little sister was still there.

Nat would be a good practice conversation for the one she'd be having with Max today.

Jac had just made it to the front porch when movement from the side yard caught her attention.

Karma. Whimpering and hunkering down. Afraid.

That wasn't right.

Her sister's dog shouldn't be out of the fenced backyard. Her sister's dogs didn't do what they weren't supposed to do. They hadn't acted out in years, since puppyhood. Especially the extremely timid Karma, who rarely wandered that far from Nat's side.

Fierce growling came from the backyard. Barking. Snarling. Angry.

He wasn't stopping.

Kudos.

The dogs wouldn't be doing this—not without something being wrong. Not to mention, Nat would have calmed, comforted them—if she was able. Nat was exceptionally attuned to the dogs' needs.

Someone, some *thing* must be stopping her sister from doing just that.

Jac grabbed her phone and brought up the security app. She'd had cameras installed just two days before Rachel had been killed. It was a system Carrie Lorcan had designed for her own brother-in-law's company.

She'd asked Jac and several others in computer forensics if they'd like to test it. Jac had agreed—this system hadn't even been released to the public. She hadn't been taking chances with her safety—not with PAVAD being targeted.

Her sister's dogs wouldn't be doing this without a problem.

PAVAD agents were all at risk right now.

Including Jac; including Nat.

The camera for the living room buffered.

Where Nat stood.

Nat wasn't alone.

There was a man in Jac's house. In full PAVAD tactical gear.

With a semiautomatic.

Aimed right at her sister's head.

115

HER GREEN EYES WERE RED-RIMMED. EUGENE HAD STOOD IN THE corner of the living room, right there by the back door—he'd slipped inside using the key he'd found earlier, after letting that big brute of a dog out of the fence.

Eugene could have killed her so easily, just put a bullet in the back of her head and walked away. No one would have ever connected him to her.

Not now that that son-of-a-bitch Barnes was taken care of.

Just one shot and it would be done.

He'd wait until he was in a safe place and go through that asshole's computer and emails later. See if anyone else out there needed to be taken care of; then he was finished with this shit.

Mexico was waiting.

But the girl had been weeping as if her heart had been breaking. The sheer amount of emotion coming from a woman so small had had him pausing. Watching.

She had been playing a classical piece on the piano that was far too big for the room. It hadn't seemed as if she was even aware of what she was doing, as if the ranch house was in actuality a grand concert hall.

How could a woman so young have experienced enough *life* to play like that, to grieve like that?

Eugene didn't know.

But he had listened. Had watched. Had remembered the emotions he had felt when he had listened to her mother play all those years ago.

If he had ever had a *friend* in his life, it had been Felicia Jones.

Eugene wanted to see Felicia in her daughter's eyes when she died. Wanted to imagine that was what Felicia had looked like when she'd been murdered.

He'd needed to see that.

Had wanted to see if he could find the grief he'd felt for Felicia once more.

Could understand it.

Emotions—he'd admit it, he wasn't one who understood every nuance of emotion like so many of those damned shrinks in the CCU and elsewhere in PAVAD. No. He was the kind of man who did his job—without messy emotions screwing everything up.

But he had always been fascinated by those who did feel like that.

Felicia had felt so damned much. Love, for her friends, for her daughters. For Eugene and Ed and everyone else who had been assigned to guard her all those years ago.

And for that bastard who hadn't deserved even a moment of her love.

Now, Felicia's daughter was hurting. Feeling.

Eugene only felt emotions of that depth when he watched others die. Then and only then could he get an inkling of what they felt.

He wasn't stupid, he knew the technical term for what he was: sociopath.

Eugene was a confirmed sociopath.

He was incapable of feeling much at all.

Oh, he'd wanted to. Wanted to understand what everyone else seemed to take for granted.

But Eugene just didn't care about other people.

Maybe his wife, to some extent. He was supposed to, after all.

Or he once had.

Mostly, he'd married her because she was convenient sex and someone to listen to him talk. She'd taken care of his mundane needs like laundry and food while he was busy building his career.

He'd stuck with her because it was easier than leaving.

But now…he wanted to try a few other things before he died, first.

He had to finish with the past first, too.

With Felicia's daughter.

Eugene tightened his grip around her neck. Silky hair fell over his hand. Soft.

Pretty girl; not beautiful like her older sister, who was the spitting image of her mother, but she'd do.

Well, she would have.

If she'd lived.

He pointed his spare weapon, one taken off a street punk a long, long time ago, right between those unusual green eyes of hers.

Waiting for the terror.

It didn't come.

That gave him pause. Felicia would have been shaking like a leaf, passing out from the fear. But her daughter just stared at him from eyes shaped like her biological father's.

He'd always hated *that* man's eyes. They were brown, not the green of this girl's, and capable of stabbing a man in the gut. But it didn't matter; he looked at her, and he saw the truth.

"Don't move. Or this will be over in a blink."

116

For a moment Jac just stared, unable to process what she was seeing. For just a nanosecond. Then training kicked in. Training that went well back before she'd ever stepped foot in the FBI academy seven years ago.

Before she could even think about what she was doing she had the door open and was calling out her sister's name. "Nat! I'm back! I need to change shirts, then we can go to Smokey's for lunch. You won't believe what happened."

She hoped she was distraction enough for the man holding a gun on her sister.

Jac had hit speed dial and video on her phone before she'd unlocked the front door. She sat it deliberately on the counter in her kitchen, keeping her back to the living room, as if she hadn't even realized someone else was there with Nat.

She pointed the phone right at the center of her living room, hoping it would grab what she needed it to.

It would be PAVAD.

Be help.

There was no way she was losing her little sister.

"Nat? You almost ready?" Jac was a damned good actress—she'd learned at the colonel's knee how to portray exactly what he had wanted. Those skills had just grown over the last decade. "Do we need to walk Kudos and Karma first? I saw her in the front yard, and he's in the back, acting like a total idiot again. I know she's ready to just take off on an adventure, like always."

Karma had never taken off on an adventure in the five years she'd been a certified rescue dog. Jac and Nat were both well aware of that.

She just had to communicate with her sister—let Nat know that Jac was planning something.

That Nat wasn't facing Eugene Lytel alone.

117

Eugene Lytel. His entire team. Five men Max had trusted at his back for years. That they were involved in targeting PAVAD pissed him off and made him want to rip them to shreds.

Jac had depended on them, too. Jac, Miranda, Whit, Alessandra, Carrie, Evan, Jazz, Josh, and J.T.—agents Max had worked with hundreds of times.

None of them had ever forgotten how dependent they were on the auxiliary PAVAD teams for backup and security. Auxiliary were an integral part of the success of PAVAD.

Needed and necessary.

The betrayal cut deep.

Barnes had outlined everything he knew and everything that had happened in front of him since he had been asked to deliver an envelope containing ten thousand dollars cash from an agent in Dallas. One Barnes had named as the woman who had recruited him to this special, secret task force designed to put PAVAD in check.

Sponsored through another organization Barnes hadn't fully identified. Barnes had given what he could—but he'd been kept in the dark, the email had said. Because he hadn't earned his place yet.

Barnes had made certain to say several times he hadn't known what he was getting in to.

Ed Dennis had sent Sin Lorcan and Mick Brockman to Texas to grab that team leader as soon as possible.

Barnes had sworn in his statement that he'd just thought he'd been doing a favor for his team leader: she'd told him she'd purchased a piece of land in south Texas from the man and was paying for it with cash. Barnes had called himself an idiot for believing her.

Supposedly, Barnes hadn't known it was Paul Sturvin he had delivered the money to until the night Eugene Lytel had taken him to meet Sturvin and had killed Sturvin right in front of him.

Barnes had carried Olivia out of a burning building, after Lytel and the others had left.

He said he'd known that would bring Lytel's ire his way, but he wasn't about to leave a child to die like that. That Barnes took his oath to the bureau seriously.

Barnes hadn't given a damn about angering Lytel—his email to Miranda had been far more personal, and had showed a side of Barnes that he doubted the other man realized he'd revealed.

Security cameras had put Lytel in the hotel just minutes before Barnes had been shot. Another had put his bureau-issued vehicle within two blocks.

Lytel hadn't been careless—but PAVAD was good. Sin Lorcan and his private team was even better.

The director had Carrie Lorcan and Shannon Toliver and J.T. Thompkins going over everything Lytel had touched for the last three years. It was going to take a while.

Max wanted Lytel. Wanted him bad.

He battled back the rage.

The man was scheduled to be back at PAVAD first thing in the morning. The easiest way to catch him was to let Lytel come to them.

It was best not to tip their hand. Yet.

Every possible agent from the CCU was out there looking for him now.

They were rounding up Lytel's team now. They just had to do it without alerting the other agents on Lytel's team what they were doing.

The director was on the warpath. Max was right there with him.

His phone beeped.

A familiar ringtone.

Jac.

She had turned her phone off at the hospital. He hadn't been able to reach her yet, to update her what had happened to Barnes.

To tell her about Lytel.

He paused outside his office and hit *accept* on his phone.

A video chat immediately popped up.

Max almost said her name...until he saw.

Eugene Lytel was right there in front of him—in Jac's living room.

118

This was not what Eugene had planned. "Well, look who came home early."

"Yes, had a problem with some grape juice and a four-year-old," Jaclyn said, her Glock pointed at him. "Agent Lytel. I'm not going to say hello. I will say that I have questions."

He had on his vest—it was a part of his daily uniform now, and it was of the newer Lucas Tech material. Nice and lightweight.

But Jaclyn Jones had some of the best marksmanship ratings of PAVAD. He'd seen her on the gun range himself and been very, very impressed. She was even better than the men on his own team.

She wouldn't need to aim at his chest to kill him. "Put down your gun, Jaclyn. All I have to do is pull the trigger."

Hell, no, she shouldn't put down her weapon. He knew the statistics.

Her best chance for survival rested in that Glock she held so steady.

His evaluation of her went up—she had to know just how precarious of a position both she and her younger sister were in now. He certainly was.

He was going to have to kill them both in order to get out of this now. With her armed, that was going to be harder than he anticipated.

Unless he killed the sister now.

But as soon as he pulled the trigger, Jaclyn would do the exact same thing.

He might not have *time* to kill them both. And if that behemoth of a dog got through the glass door anytime soon, he could have more of a problem than he wanted.

Especially with Jaclyn armed.

He stared at her for a good four full minutes while he contemplated his options.

She never said a word. She had the training; training Eugene had helped design—in a negotiation scenario, whoever talked most lost.

Her eyes never wavered.

"Well, I suppose we should chat, shouldn't we? Isn't that how this is done?"

"Lytel, what's going on here? Why are you doing this?"

The younger girl never moved, just stared at her sister.

Almost...calmly.

Trustingly.

Hell, maybe she didn't *feel* anything either—but whatever grief had had her weeping her heart out.

"Jac, I love you."

"I know, Nats. I love you, too."

"Good. I think we needed to get it out there."

They sounded like their mother. Their voices were similar to one another's, of course, but mostly they sounded like Felicia. It was like stepping back into the past for a moment.

Did they even realize Eugene was *there*?

Jaclyn's eyes met his. Eugene pulled the sister against his chest. Between her ridiculously small body and the vest he wore, he was about as protected as he was going to get.

He wished she was six inches taller and fifty pounds heavier.

His heart was pounding in his ears. From actual excitement. He ran the barrel of the Hi-Point through the silky dark hair the younger sister had left down. She smelled like honey and flowers. His other hand dropped to the front of her narrow chest to pull her closer.

There wasn't much there.

Hell, he was a man. Grabbing a woman there was fun. "Hold still, little Natalie. We don't want to make big sister nervous."

"She's not nervous, Agent Lytel. Jac is angry. Very, very angry you're doing this. And you're going to pay."

"No, Colonel Jones is the only one who is going to pay now."

119

MIRANDA HAD BEEN ORDERED BY THE DIRECTOR TO STAY BEHIND, after Max had run from the bullpen, yelling for someone to get agents to Jac's place.

The director had ordered her to coordinate the teams from the PAVAD tactical op room. Then the director had run, on Max's heels.

Max was already on his way to her.

To get Agent Lytel. But Jac lived fifteen minutes from the building.

Fifteen minutes was long enough to die. Miranda bit back the panic.

Now, Jac's phone was on the big screen in front of them, audio playing around them. Carrie Lorcan had remotely accessed Jac's bureau-issued phone as if it was right there beneath her fingers. Had done what she could to keep the call open.

Max had given Miranda his phone. So that PAVAD could see what was happening.

It was the only connection to what was happening that they now had. All the resources PAVAD had, and Miranda knew they were useless to stop what was happening.

It was all up to Jac and Nat now.

Dani was there; Dani and Agent Ward and Carrie Lorcan and Shannon. People who had already been in there when Miranda had run in and demanded someone get Jac's phone on the big screen.

Four minutes. It had taken four minutes to make that happen.

Four minutes, Jac had stood there, staring at Eugene Lytel as he held Nat in front of him.

Jac's *sister*. Her baby sister. If it had been one of Miranda's sisters, she didn't know if she could have been as calm as Jac appeared right there on the grainy screen.

Not her sisters.

It was Miranda's job to protect them. Jac felt exactly the same for Nat.

They were all just waiting. There was nothing else they could do.

Miranda just stood in the center of the room and listened.

Someone put a hot hand on her shoulder.

Miranda turned. Knight was standing there next to her. Big and strong and a little frightening, in a perfectly pressed suit.

He had the glasses off now. Gray eyes the same color as that suit showed his concern.

He wrapped his other hand around her arm, just above the damned cast. "Jones is on his way to her now. You won't do any good standing here worrying about her."

She knew he was right, but that didn't help. She was too far away to do anything else. "She lives fifteen minutes away, Knight. He won't get to her in time."

Everyone was watching her. She hadn't realized that. Miranda turned back to the screen. Just as Nat spoke again.

120

"What does the colonel have to do with this?" Nat asked. "He has no bearing on our lives."

"Well, he has bearing on mine, sweetheart," Lytel said. "Constantly doing what he can just to keep me down. Colonel Jones is a real piece of work, you know."

"We know," Nat said.

Jac kept her weapon steady. Nat was staying calm. She wasn't stupid.

This was a scenario their bastard of a father had made them roleplay time and time again, when his paranoia that someone was after them in the dozen foreign countries he'd dragged them to would rise up and take over *him* too.

Over and over and over, he would put them in similar situations with differing men every time. So they could practice. Prepare.

Time and time again, he would yell at Jac that it was *always* her responsibility to protect her little sister. That failure was never an option.

Jac had learned that lesson long ago.

"We know he's a bastard, Eugene. How well do you know him?"

"Pretty well. Well enough to know he's not the only bastard in the Jones family. Bet you don't know that, do you, honey? Your sister isn't even his. I've always wondered if he knew that. We were overseas together, too. I watched that arrogant son-of-a-bitch get four young men killed, with barely a blink. Like he didn't care. Then he went home to your sister's birthday here. How old was she? Nine, maybe? Same age as Max's girl is now."

Jac didn't waver. He was trying to get her off her stride, bringing up Emery.

"Maybe after I leave here, I'll go find Emery. Have her give her father a message for me. Or from you. I bet you would like that, wouldn't you? I know you love her. A good little mommy you are."

"I remember that day. He was angry with me for not wearing the right dress. After the party, he beat me with a belt for forty-three minutes," Jac said as levelly as she possibly could. "I could see the clock. Could hear Nat screaming at him to stop. I counted the minutes that day. I was twelve."

"Seems like we all have bad memories of that day," Nat said.

"What are you hoping to accomplish here? Killing either one of us, or both of us, won't even be a bleep on the colonel's radar. If anything, he'll just benefit from the outrage and sympathy to have both his daughters murdered by a rogue FBI agent, after losing his wife so tragically. Just make him even more popular. None of us wants that."

"Well, no," Lytel said, shooting her a small smile. His hand tightened on Nat, pulling her even closer. "No one wants to make Boyd's life better, stupid son-of-a-bitch."

He was six four or so. Broad.

Nat was a full fourteen inches shorter, and one hundred sixty pounds lighter. She looked no bigger than a twelve-year-old right now.

There was plenty of target space. Even with the bullet-resistant vest.

But he was an experienced federal agent, with years in the special tactical forces. He'd faced down weapons before.

Jac would have to be careful.

She would have only one chance to do this right.

He was studying her every move. Just as she was studying his.

He knew they were at a stalemate.

What he most likely didn't know was that her phone was still on. Right there pointed straight at them. She had no doubt help was coming.

Max had been on the other end of the line. She had just seen that before she'd sat the phone down.

Max was coming for her.

And all PAVAD had to do was bring up the security system she had discussed with fellow agents from the computer forensics analysis department. She and Carrie and Shannon and the rest—they knew every aspect of this system. Inside and out.

Carrie had her security information. She'd designed the system; Carrie could log into it at any time.

Most likely, the other woman already had.

Cameras were probably pointed right at Eugene now. With audio.

No matter what happened, he wasn't getting away today. Every word they spoke would be immortalized forever.

Jac knew what he would expect to see from her. With him having her only family at gunpoint. With her being younger and female and not as strong. As experienced.

Weakness.

He'd expect her to waver, to be weak. Unsure. Nervous and afraid.

"N-nat, you j-just stay real still, ok?" She infused her tone with just that. Fear.

It wasn't hard to do—she was feeling all of those things.

Her sister's eyes were burning into her now.

But years of training kept Jac from showing it. Until she wanted to.

She deliberately let her hand on the gun shake. She lowered her left hand and wiped sweat off her palm.

Lytel's gaze followed the movement.

He smirked.

Jac pulled in a deep breath, so he could see.

"Just let her go. You can leave, Eugene. I won't stop you."

"Like that would happen. Don't try to negotiate with me, Jaclyn. I've been rewriting the hostage negation manuals since you were preparing for the prom."

"I didn't go to the prom. I couldn't. I'd already left home by then. I graduated school early; easy to do when we'd grown up with tutors. The colonel kicked me out two days after my sixteenth birthday party when we hit stateside. Gave me a thousand dollars and told me to go—he didn't know at the time that my mother had set up trust funds for me that provided interest starting on my sixteenth birthday. Clever of her, wasn't it? He feared I was having too much of a rebellious influence on Nat. I was teaching her to think for herself, you see. So that he couldn't own either of us."

Jac kept her eyes on his hand. His hand would be where the betrayal would be. It would show her exactly what was going on in his head.

Maybe he thought he'd been rewriting those so-called manuals, but she had been *living* them, with a monster.

And there was one lesson he had beaten into her and her sister both. Time and time again—until they had learned it.

She and Nat had been good students back then.

"Why did you betray PAVAD? Your friends?"

"I have no friends, not any longer. Not in twenty-three years. I have colleagues. I have moderate success. And in a year, honey, I'm going to be shoved out the door into mandatory retirement."

"That's the way it works with the bureau. We know that when we sign on. And what other job lets us retire early, except for the military and local law enforcement? I thought it sounded like a pretty decent deal. Plenty of time after fifty-seven to do things."

"I, like so many others, am tired of being invisible," the man said. "Third tier under the great Ed Dennis, and under Nutless Wonder, Boyd Jones. I have always hated him. There are plenty who feel the same. And they are working together to bring that bastard down where he belongs."

Jac didn't believe him.

There were other reasons motivating Lytel.

"You hate the colonel," she said flatly. She needed to keep him focused entirely on her. Even with all the possible distractions. "Tell me why."

Kudos was barking viciously, throwing himself bodily against the patio door, desperate to reach Nat.

That dog would die for her, die to protect her in an instant.

Jac wasn't about to let that be today.

She looked into Lytel's eyes. There was nothing there.

Nothing. Except excitement.

He was enjoying this. He could die at any moment, or kill at any moment. And the sick bastard was getting off on it. She'd come up against sociopaths before. This man was no different. Her gaze dropped to his weapon hand.

"PAVAD is a family. My family. I have people there who care about me—and Nat. I'd do anything for my sister. And for my family. My friends. Especially those friends at PAVAD."

"Likewise," Nat said. "Anything at all."

"How sweet," Lytel said. "I know you are stalling. Who did you contact?"

"Who do you think?" Jac wasn't going to lie to him, unless necessary. He was trained to see right through that. But…she let her hand wobble again.

She wanted him thinking he had her off guard. That she wasn't fully in control.

"The great Dr. Jones."

"I contacted PAVAD."

"Your family," he said, smirking. "That jackass Anderson begged me not to kill him—he wanted to stay with his family. Those girls of his. Pathetic."

"You killed Andy." She wanted that confession on video. Angie and the girls deserved to know one hundred percent who had killed the man they had all loved.

"Yes. Dumb schmuck actually called me, can you believe that? Invited me to his place to talk. Thought there was a dirty agent in my department and I could help him flush the rogue out. Well, I took care of that problem."

Jac bit back the bile. Max had said the killer was someone Andy had known. Had trusted. Eugene fit the bill.

"There is one lesson the colonel beat into me that I have never forgotten, Eugene," Jac said softly. Very softly. It was time.

"And what is that?"

"The most important rule of *family*." Her next words were for her sister, only. There was one more sentence her father had made them both repeat over and over again. The signal. "You always *protect* your sister."

The word *protect* was the signal for her sister to drop to the floor. Like it always had been.

They'd rehearsed that scenario more than they'd ever rehearsed the piano.

Jac pulled the trigger, knowing her sister would drop as best as she could—giving Jac an even bigger target.

It didn't matter.

Lytel was just so much bigger than Nat, the target was right there. Easy to see.

Jac's bullet hit the mark. Just like she'd learned to do as a young girl no more than thirteen. Only they weren't using paintball bullets now.

Eugene Lytel took the shot—right between his eyes.

Just like Andy had.

Lytel dropped, straight back. His hand tightened reflexively on his own weapon.

Lytel's shot went wide, shattering the patio door. Glass rained down around the dog snarling so viciously right there.

Kudos whimpered and ran, disappearing into the yard.

Nat was on the ground beneath the bastard's body. Jac kicked the man's gun across the floor, calling her sister's name.

It took Nat a moment to answer. "I'm ok. But he's crushing me. The man weighs a ton. Especially now. Dead weight. Literally here."

There was a slightly hysterical undertone to her sister's words.

Jac grabbed Lytel's arm and heaved, not caring about respecting the dead.

Not now.

She rolled him off her little sister and yanked Nat into her arms. "Thank God. You're ok."

"I'm good. But...I told you pink carpet was just going to stain someday. You should have gone with the hard wood."

121

Max and the three agents he'd commandeered, plus the director, arrived just in time to see Jac's neighbors rushing out of their house.

To see a blood covered Kudos streak across the front of Jaclyn's yard.

He yelled to Stephenson to grab the dogs. Then he was moving, weapon drawn.

He jumped over the small hedges and ran toward the front door.

Just as it opened.

And there she was.

His heart.

There was blood on her. She had her Glock in her hand. Had her younger sister by her side.

Nat was covered in blood.

Already calling for her dogs.

"Glad you're here. We handled things. He's inside," Nat said. "Ruining that hideous pink carpet."

That was it.

Made of steel. Jaclyn and Natalie Jones were made of steel.

Max opened his arms, not caring about evidence or the blood covering the woman he loved.

"I love you, Jaclyn Jones. It's about time I said that loud enough for the world to hear."

She sent him a shaky smile. She came close enough to lean her head against his chest. "I don't want to ruin that shirt. I bought it for you, and have always loved it on you, remember."

His fingers sank into her hair. Told her again.

Just as Malachi Brockman came up on the porch behind them. "Hate to tell you this, but the whole world already knows how you feel about her. Have for years. Get her back to PAVAD; get her and her sister processed. Then take a vacation. I think the two of you have earned it."

That sounded like a good idea to Max.

Nat returned, two woven leashes in her hand. "I need to get him to the vet. He's got some cuts from the glass. And I think he was grazed by that forty-cal."

"We'll take him back to PAVAD, Nat. Shayna can take a look at him. She has her veterinary license. We'll take care of him there," Max said. She would be concerned for her dogs now.

And would break down later.

Just like her older sister.

Max wanted both of them were he could see them, protect them. Until they knew for certain that this was over.

122

SHE WAS STILL SHAKING. JAC PROBABLY WOULD BE FOR A WHILE. BUT Nat was safe, Jac was safe—and the man who had killed Andy Anderson would never hurt anyone again. "Lytel confessed to shooting Andy."

"We'll talk about it back at PAVAD. Right now...I want to get you and Nat out of those bloodstained clothes and have Jules or Mia take a look at you."

Nat was at her side. Karma pressed close to Jac's leg. She couldn't let the dog get too close—her clothes would be evidence, though she hadn't gotten close to Lytel until after he was dead.

When she'd pulled the man's corpse off her baby sister.

Jac checked Nat one more time. There were nightmares in her sister's green eyes. "You ok?"

"Yes. Shaken, but I'll live. Do you think what he said about the colonel was true?"

"Which part?" Jac asked. She hadn't focused on his words, just on his gun and getting him where she needed.

"All of it? Any of it? The part about me not being the colonel's?"

"I'm not sure. We'll have to figure out the answer to that later."

She wanted to hug her sister, but didn't. They were both evidence at the moment. Even though it was most likely on video, PAVAD would want the physical evidence to support what had happened here today.

Jac was never going to live in this house again.

She just couldn't.

Max had her hand in his. "Come on. Let's go. PAVAD's waiting."

Jac just looked at him. Emotion shot straight through her. "I knew you'd come for us, for me, by the way."

"I always will. No matter what."

"I know." Jac tightened her fingers around his. "I love you, too, you know. We'll figure out what happens next later."

"I'm going to hold you to that."

123

Miranda was waiting at the front of the CCU bullpen, Knight hovering behind her. She wasn't moving until her best friend was back where she belonged. Safe.

Word had gone out that Lytel was pronounced dead at the scene. A part of Miranda knew she should have some regret for that—she'd known and worked with the man for years—but word had also spread that he had been responsible for the death of Andy Anderson.

Miranda had heard that on the audio from Jac's phone as well.

Lytel was a cold-blooded killer. She was glad he wasn't in the world any longer.

Loud cheers went up when a small crowd of people, including the director finally entered the bullpen.

Jac and Nat were behind them. Wearing PAVAD coveralls and their hair in matching pony-tails.

Processing was finished, then.

Miranda bit back a gaspy sob. She was a professional. She couldn't fall apart just because something had happened to Jac.

"You two are ridiculously close, aren't you?"

"She's my best friend, Knight. Haven't you ever had one of

those?" She shot him an annoyed look. It was easier to be annoyed at Knight than weepy over Jac and Nat.

"I used to. Your new friend Tag was one of them."

"You should build that relationship back up. Don't lose it because you're a stubborn cranky-pants. Or because he's as serious as a rock."

"I think you'd be the last one pushing friendships considering what happened in Masterson."

Miranda thought to the best friends she had lost. One in particular. "Not all besties are bad. And don't be an ass, Knight. Unless you just can't help it. We might want to work on that going forward."

All thoughts of needling Knight went out of her head when Jac finally got near. Miranda pushed through the crowd.

She had a bestie to check on now.

EPILOGUE

ED WATCHED HIS PEOPLE AS THEY SURROUNDED THE JONES SISTERS. Miranda Talley practically had the older sister in a neck lock, she was hugging the shorter woman so tightly. As he watched, she reached out and snagged the younger sister as well.

Hugging her, too.

While the two young women had been getting processed by Marianna and her people in the lab, he had reviewed the eight-minute audio of what had happened.

He'd listened to every word. Repeatedly.

One thing Lytel had said had seared itself into Ed's brain.

He'd rewound and listened to it multiple times.

His hands shook at what it meant.

Unless there had been someone else all those years ago, Ed had been lied to.

About something he couldn't bear to contemplate.

He had listened to Jaclyn's words about Colonel Boyd Jones as well. About how he had beat his stepdaughter. That abuse had been dealt out to the younger girl as well, most likely.

They had lived in hell. He hadn't known that. If he had, he would have done his best to stop it all those years ago. He would have protected them.

For Felicia.

He had loved her, too.

Ed spoke with a few more people, including Georgia, as he kept one eye on the Jones sisters. Especially the younger.

Finally, he slipped away to the top of the stairs, where he could look down at the open bullpen below him.

Marianna found him there. "Eddie? You ok?"

He was still watching Georgia. Still watching the Jones sisters. Right there, in the midst of the CCU, Max Jones hit one knee.

Ed nodded in that direction. "Look. It's about time."

Marianna's romantic heart had her sighing. Had her fingers wrapping around his. "That's beautiful."

The redheaded sister flung herself into the man's arms as wild cheering went through the crowd.

"I think she said yes," Marianna said. "I remember how that felt."

"Best moment of my life; tied up there with the day Georgia was born, and the day the adoptions were final."

Jaclyn was hugging her sister. Georgia was behind Natalie now. She wasn't much taller.

The hair color was the same. Georgia and Natalie Jones—that rich dark brown. Ed's had been that color, once.

"Marianna, there is something I have to tell you. About Felicia."

She knew all about the murder of Felicia Jones and the case that still haunted him. Very few people even knew Ed suspected the woman had been a victim of homicide. But Marianna had seen the case files, had offered to help him find the answers.

She knew he had once loved Felicia. And she understood.

He just hoped she would understand what he had to tell her now. Ed hoped they all would.

As his gaze once more landed on the darker-haired Jones sister, he wondered just how he was going to tell Natalie the truth about her mother.

How he was going to tell her the truth about *him*...

CURIOUS ABOUT MIRANDA AND KNIGHT?

Miranda and Knight will be getting *several* books in the next few years...if you're curious about the two of them and *missed* the PAVAD/Masterson/Finley Creek cross-over featuring the two of them, check them out in

Buried Secrets!

VAMPIRES?

If you've ever wondered just what goes bump in the night, check out Calle's paranormal romances, written under the pen name
C.J. Brookes!

If you don't know if you'll enjoy vampires falling in love, check out Calle's sister site: www.callejayebrookes.com.

You'll find some free reads there!

ALSO BY CALLE J BROOKES

TRILOGY TWO (FINLEY CREEK GENERAL)

If the Dark Wins

Wounds That Won't Heal

Hope for Finley Creek (bonus novella)

As the Night Ends

QUADRILOGY THREE (FINLEY CREEK DISASTER)

Before the Rain Breaks

Lost in the Wind

Walk Through the Fire

We All Sleep Alone

MASTERSON COUNTY NOVELLA SERIES

Seeking the Sheriff

Discovering the Doctor

Ruining the Rancher

Denying the Devil

SMALL-TOWN SHERIFFS

Holding the Truth

SUSPENSE/THRILLER

PAVAD: FBI CASE FILES

PAVAD: FBI Case Files #0001

"Knocked Out"

PAVAD: FBI Case Files #0002

"Knocked Down"

PAVAD: FBI Case Files #0003

"Knocked Around"

PAVAD: FBI Case Files #0004

"White Out"

PAVAD: FBI Case Files #0005

"Buried Secrets"

Calle has several free reads available at

www.CalleJBrookesReads.com

For my grandfather, the best man I have ever known.

You will be missed.

Oct. 2015

For my grandmother, who gave me the courage to try. Without you and your love of romance, I never would have made it this far.

Feb. 2016

For my papaw, whose children loved him deeply, and will always miss him.

Oct. 2017

Calle J. Brookes enjoys crafting paranormal romance and romantic suspense. She reads almost every genre except horror. She spends most of her time juggling family life and writing while reminding herself that she can't spend all of her time in the worlds found within books. CJ loves to be contacted by her readers via email and at **www.CalleJBrookes.com**. When not at home writing stories of adventure and wrangling with two border collies and a beagle puppy, CJ is off in her RV somewhere exploring the beautiful world we live in, along with her husband of she can't remember how many years and their child.

PAV05052021

Printed in Great Britain
by Amazon

70491537R00260